James Phe... ...or of twenty-nin... ...teens he wanted to b... ...at a real job, studying and working in architecture before ... English literature, spending five years at a newsp... ...ing an MA and PhD in literature...

The ex-CIA character of Jed Walker was first introduced in *The Spy*, which was followed by *The Hunted*, *Kill Switch*, *Dark Heart* and *The Agency*.

James has also written five titles in the Lachlan Fox thriller series, and the Alone trilogy of young adult post-apocalyptic novels. A full-time novelist since the age of twenty-five, he spends his time writing thrilling stories and travelling the world to talk about them.

To find out more about James and his books,
visit www.jamesphelan.com

Follow and interact with James

www.facebook.com/realjamesphelan
www.twitter.com/realjamesphelan
www.instagram.com/realjamesphelan

BY JAMES PHELAN

The Lachlan Fox books
Fox Hunt
Patriot Act
Blood Oil
Liquid Gold
Red Ice

The Jed Walker books
The Spy
The Hunted
Kill Switch
Dark Heart
The Agency

The Alone series
Chasers
Survivor
Quarantine

James
Phelan

Red
Ice

CONSTABLE

CONSTABLE

First published in Australia and New Zealand in 2010 by Hachette Australia,
an imprint of Hachette Australia Pty Limited.

First published in eBook in Great Britain in 2018 by Constable

This paperback edition published in Great Britain in 2019 by Constable

1 3 5 7 9 10 8 6 4 2

Copyright © James Phelan, 2010

The moral right of the author has been asserted.

A CIP catalogue record for this book
is available from the British Library.

ISBN: 978-1-47212-934-5

Typeset in Simoncini Garamond by Bookhouse, Sydney
Printed and bound in Great Britain by CPI Group (UK), Croydon CRO 4YY

Papers used by Constable are from well-managed forests
and other responsible sources.

For Tas Phelan

AUTHOR'S NOTE

In 1867 the United States and Russia signed a treaty. The signatories were William H Seward, US Secretary of State, and Eduard de Stoeckl, Russian Ambassador to the United States. The document contained the phrase: *'His Majesty the Emperor of all the Russias agrees to cede to the United States, by this convention, immediately upon the exchange of the ratifications thereof, all the territory and dominion now possessed by his said Majesty on the continent of America and in the adjacent islands.'* The US copy is available for viewing at the Library of Congress.

Many international treaties have amendments, some of them secret. A famous example of this is the 1939 Treaty of Non-Aggression between Germany and the Soviet Union, also known as the Molotov–Ribbentrop Pact, which had a secret amendment attached about how the two countries would divide up postwar Europe. In 1992, the document itself was declassified only after the dissolution of the Soviet Union. These treaty amendments are known as *Secret Protocols*.

PROLOGUE

PARIS

FRANCE

It was his silence she could not stand. She heard him enter the house, pause for a moment in the adjoining dining room and then head straight for the drinks cabinet. When she'd first met him he'd gone through a bottle a day, sometimes more. After they were married, she'd got him down to just two or three measures and in ten years he'd gone from a mid-level foreign policy adviser in the Kremlin to ambassadorial postings in Portugal, Denmark and now France. If only he could understand the sound of her silent fury.

Katya was used to him not speaking, but today his silence made her angry. He was late, again. *Important business.* Important *slut* more like it. Silence. The bottle of Alsace riesling next to her was empty. She drained the last of her glass and wiped away a tear. It had taken this final straw in their relationship for her to understand how he must have felt to be stressed into drinking, lost to the numbing sensation that came with wanting to shut reality away.

He'd changed so much since they'd moved to this posting in Paris – she wondered if his mistress had noticed it, too. She thought she'd even seen her once, a lithe North African woman no more than twenty-five, as slim as she had been when they'd first met. That was years ago, when she'd had dreams and ambition and hunger, when she'd had the strength and belief to right this man. She'd dropped everything for him – and now this? Well, she had found someone else, too. It was the French way, *oui*, darling? And soon she would . . .

She heard the clink of bottles as he refilled his glass. *Pig*.

Even before the end of their first year here she'd been desperate to leave, but he'd always make her some promise so she'd stay. Then last month he'd started talking about going home, that there was big news he would soon share. News that would *set him up* in the party. They'd be *made for life*, he'd said. She suspected she knew this 'news' – *she'd* taken that old diplomatic diary to him in the first place; the diary that had started what would be the search for . . . *What?* She rubbed her temples, trying not to think so much about how he turned everything around to make himself the hero. He was such a clichéd part of the modern Kremlin machine in that way, spinning every lie into a convenient truth.

She heard him place the glass on the antique dining table. She figured he'd reek of that slut. It was everything she could do not to get up off the couch and slap him across the face – that was the French way too, *non*, darling?

He was going to Shanghai this weekend to meet with the Russian leadership. That was new. His tickets were on his study desk upstairs, first class on Swiss Airlines, paid for out of their personal account – strange, because it was the first flight not covered by the state and they'd never flown first class, either on the state or out of their own pocket.

He didn't tell her when he'd be back, just said, *When Putin is ready to send me back*. He'd stopped telling her all the details, stopped talking about the great new life they'd have. She knew why. He was going to offer it to his mistress instead. The life that he'd always promised *her*. No. It was not going to happen this way, not if she could help it. She'd seen a lawyer, taken steps to ensure she'd win. Her payday would come; she deserved it. Her hands wrung into tight fists and it was all she could do not to get up off the sofa and scream at him. She thought of a happier time.

This morning.

She'd met with her lover this morning, spoken to him again about leaving his wife. He was close to doing it . . . But maybe she'd appeared too desperate. She'd told him about the diary, and how it might help set them free. She looked at her Nokia on the table in front of her – she wanted to hear from him now, his deep French accent telling her everything would be all right. His calming voice reassuring her he'd be there for her no matter what happened when her husband went to the safe and discovered the diary was gone.

She could feel him now, moving towards her, but she didn't care. No matter what her drunk husband said or did, there was a man a few neighbourhoods away in this very city who loved her, truly loved her.

Today, she'd sent him that old diary from the safe, and he had promised to follow her instructions about giving it to a third party, someone her husband could not possibly know about, a safekeeper to buy them the time to follow their love.

Her eyes flicked to the American cop drama on the television, its story so violent yet so prudish. In the reflection of the display cabinet she could see his shape, sensed him staring at her.

Did he know? About her rendezvous today? She'd often wondered if he had someone from his staff follow her, but she was always careful, changing trains and taxis and routes. She had a pre-paid SIM-card she used in her phone to call her lover and – and it was still in her mobile now! She looked at it sitting on the table, realising she'd been willing it to ring all day and night and now it was still there and *he* was home and it would probably ring. She felt a drop of sweat roll down her temple to her neck, a tear of panic. How to do this?

The television show cut to a commercial break. She leaned forwards, put her wine glass on the table and picked up the phone, knocking her glasses to the floor.

She unlocked the keypad and held down the off button.

The television flicked to a scene with emergency lights flashing in a rainy street and she almost thought it was the cop show again, but when she squinted she could make out that the news tickertape was in French and bodies were being taken out to waiting ambulances . . .

It was a familiar street-scape; the footage was coming from outside the Russian Embassy. She picked her glasses up off the floor and put them on.

Her mouth opened to speak – she was about to turn her head to her husband – when she saw him on the television screen. He was being wheeled out to an ambulance – the blanket covering him had come loose from his face and the reporter on the scene said:

'It's confirmed: the Russian Ambassador has been killed in an explosion at the embassy, two others are missing in the blast . . . '

The screen went blank. She felt the bile well up in the back of her throat. Her back and face were sweating.

The man in the house – the man standing behind her now with the remote in his hand, the man who she could see in the reflection of the television cabinet – was not her husband.

PART ONE

1

PARIS

Tyres screeched as the car swerved around him with a double blast of the horn and some familiar French swear words thrown from the open window for good measure.

'Welcome to Paris . . .' Fox said to himself, waiting for another car to zap by before crossing the cobbled street.

Lachlan Fox felt like a marked man, having already escaped death at the hands of lunatic drivers three, maybe four, times before the sun had come up today. If the Parisians had such weapons as the hatchback automobile when the Nazis were invading, they never would have needed bailing out by the Allies.

Early morning in Paris, a city that thrived on visitors' enjoyment of its splendour, was proving more work than he'd imagined. It'd be easy to lay all blame on the maniac French drivers, but Fox knew that his rubbernecking at the scenery hadn't helped. He'd let his guard down; having served as a special forces soldier in Iraq and Afghanistan and a frontline reporter on the War on Terror, he'd thought being a tourist should be easy.

At the next intersection he was stopped by a couple of uniformed cops who asked for his ID. He handed over his passport.

'Ah, Australian,' the shorter of the cops said, checking Fox's passport was in order. 'You ride kangaroos?'

'Funny,' Fox said. 'You play with frogs?'

The cop looked to his partner, neither of them much appreciating the comeback.

Fox wasn't surprised by the visible police presence since he'd arrived in the country. There had been an explosion at the Russian Embassy just a few days before, perhaps an accident in the gas main, but possibly terrorists – *definitely terrorists*, if you read the right-leaning news commentators who were calling for a crackdown on immigrants. Perhaps these cops took Fox's unkempt dark hair, deep tan and three-day stubble for something more sinister than an Australian tourist wandering alone in the breaking dawn. Fox was used to arousing the interest of security types – he couldn't remember the last time he *hadn't* been stopped and screened for explosives at a commercial airport. He knew he had that 'don't fuck with me' air, that gait of military training, eyes that reflected all too well some of what he'd seen and done in his thirty-three years, and a physique and stance that showed he could handle himself. Why hide it?

'What is your business in France?' the cop asked him.

'Holiday,' Fox said.

'Alone?'

'Are you asking me out?'

The cop wasn't amused. He gave Fox's passport to the younger, taller cop.

'What are you doing out so early?'

'Walking.'

'Where are you staying?'

'A friend's house, out of town,' Fox said. 'Giverny.'

'Long way from here.'

'My friend drove me in,' Fox said.

'Where is this friend?'

'Work.'

'Where is this work?'

'He's a reporter at *Le Figaro*.'

'His name?' the cop asked.

Fox told him. Told him how he'd walked from Renard's office on Boulevard Haussmann, down the Avenue de l'Opéra with its romantic nineteenth-century streetlamps. How a beautiful woman had jogged past, smiled at him, how he'd waved in reply – and a garbage truck rushed by in front of him. Look *left*, he'd reminded himself again as he crossed another street. Despite a couple of years living in New York as an investigative reporter specialising in covering the world's flashpoints – rarely home, always somewhere overseas and dangerous – he was still used to a lifetime of vehicles driving on the left-hand side of the road. He gave the cop details and remained friendly.

The young French officer listened to him and watched, his right hand rested on his hip close to a holstered SIG Pro 2022, while his partner radioed in to check Fox's details were bona fide.

'Okay, we'll see,' the young cop said.

'Welcome to Paris,' Fox said again, this time under his breath.

'Sorry?' The policeman looked at Fox, hand still resting on the holstered pistol.

'I said: *I sure love Paris*,' Fox replied. Fucking French. When did they get guns?

A couple of minutes later Fox was handed back his passport.

'You are Lachlan Fox!' the short cop said. His previous sour expression had vanished, a cherubic grin in its place. He passed his mobile phone to his partner and pulled Fox in to have their photo taken. The younger cop was staring at them curiously and Fox looked down at the smiling Frenchman with his arm around his shoulder; a man who stank of stale coffee and garlic and cheap deodorant beamed up at him.

'This man, hero!' he said to his young partner, still in English for Fox's sake. 'Reporter – arrested Russian gangster Babich, yes? I read your stories!'

Fox nodded, and the other cop shrugged, motioned them to stand a little to the left for a better framed shot and snapped the picture.

'Thank you!' Fox's new fan said, shaking his hand and then saluting.

Fox watched them walk off – the fan cop talking animatedly, trying to explain the situation to his buddy. They looked back, and waved. A bit further down the street he saw them stop a young Maghreb guy making him sit on the ground and empty his bag while they checked his papers.

Fox shook his head and continued on. *Paris.*

An inordinate number of buildings in this neighbourhood were masked by scaffolding. His journalist friend Renard had explained on the drive into town that morning the Parisian law requiring buildings to be cleaned every ten years. Tourism, Fox surmised, walking through the world's most visited city, had made Paris into a romantic museum. He watched a sandblasting unit set up their crane, shifting their canvas canopy to protect passers-by from falling debris; the buildings to one side were a grimy brown with soot-coloured streaks, to the other side, creamy façades with glints of mica. They certainly looked after what they had around here. There was something soothing about watching a job being done that showed tangible results and it reminded him of his naively placed idealism when joining the military at eighteen.

Most Parisians were still asleep as he reached the Seine, stood on the Pont Royal and watched the sun rise over the roof of the Louvre. This was a place that never ended, it seemed, the city of light as eternal as the river flowing beneath him. He followed the Right Bank crossing at the Pont de la Concorde, and was almost run over as a double-decker tourist bus flashed past, a giant La Perla advert on the back with a woman in lingerie blowing him a kiss over her shoulder. *Ah, Paris . . .*

•

Ten minutes later Fox sat behind the wheel of a dark silver VW Golf. He had the window down and the summer breeze rolling in – but since he'd exited the rental agency at Invalides Metro station he'd felt uneasy driving. Small cars hurtled by as if at the hands of stunt drivers and his eyes were constantly shifting from the road to his mirrors, scanning for street signs as he weaved his way from the Seine.

He reached across for his iPhone as it bleeped. The screen showed a cheesy picture of his mate, Al Gammaldi. They'd been friends since high school, through the Defence Academy, and to this day Gammaldi continued tagging along on Fox's adventures without ever really being asked. Well, maybe he'd had to twist his arm once or twice.

'Where are you?' Gammaldi asked, his voice gravelly from their late night together.

'Paris,' Fox said, using the speakerphone. 'Just picked up a hire car. You just wake up, lazy arse?'

'I don't even know if I've slept yet,' Gammaldi replied. 'When did you guys leave?'

'Early,' Fox said. It was dark when he'd left his friends behind at Renard's farmhouse in Giverny. Renard had dropped him off in town before heading down to Dijon to chase a lead. He would be back in a few days, but he'd been good enough to let Fox have the run of the farmhouse for as long as he wanted. He'd stay at least until they wrapped their story together.

'God, that Renard can drink,' Gammaldi said. 'I'm amazed he could drive this morning – he wouldn't want to be pulled over and breathalysed.'

'Yeah, well,' Fox said, 'I'm thinking that maybe they don't have road rules in France.'

'I think Renard would break them for you if they did; you're like his idol or something.'

'Yeah, right,' Fox said. He hadn't told Gammaldi about the investigative reporting piece he was working on here with their friend. Really, he should have accompanied Renard to Dijon, but circumstances had changed; he had to play tourist.

'Where you headed?' Gammaldi asked.

'Grabbing us some supplies then coming back,' Fox said. The streetlamps blinked out as the sun hit the road. One thing in his favour was that he knew exactly where he was going and his military-trained memory for maps was excellent. Resembling a snail's shell, the city's twenty *arrondissements* arranged in the form of a clockwise spiral made navigating easy. Relatively easy. It was the one-way nature of the streets that bugged him. The Rue Cler market was only a couple of minutes away – if he could zigzag his way through the one-way mess. 'Kate up yet?'

'I thought she was with you.'

'No,' Fox said as he zipped along the near-empty Quai d'Orsay, too busy taking in the view across to the Right Bank and trying to get the radio off what sounded like the worst of the Eurovision Song Contest to notice a driver in front had slammed on their brakes. Fox halted suddenly and the truck behind nudged into his bumper.

'What was that?'

'Nothing,' Fox said. No damage done, but a few choice French words flew his way from both drivers. He wondered why he'd been the cause of both their anger: Oh yeah, they were French, he wasn't. A few departing toots of the horn later and the traffic resumed its flow.

'I haven't seen Kate,' said Gammaldi

'She must be asleep still,' Fox said, changing up through the gears. He and Kate had both been sleeping better since coming back together, the comfortable rhythm of having someone you love sleep next to you at night.

'Well, don't be stingy on the food shopping.'

'Al, I could bring you back a shipping container of food and you'd still want more,' Fox replied, overtaking a heavily laden truck. The Golf's twin-charged 1.4-litre petrol motor didn't sound like much on paper, but it had plenty of pick-up through the streets of Paris, plus quick reactions to his foot on the gas and good brakes, thank God. It was the *other* drivers out there who worried him. Cars, trucks, motorcycles, all hell-bent on dominating the road, all driven with fervour and with one purpose: getting *moi* to destination *rapide*.

Gammaldi started rattling off a list of items he wanted.

The traffic was not yet heavy but it reminded Fox of London, where tiny streets not designed for the car caused chaos. He waited his turn and took off up a cobbled street, catching sight of some little dogs getting at it while their owners kissed in greeting.

A Smart car flashed past at warp speed, lights off, barely noticeable were it not for its blaring horn and some French cursing directed at Fox for missing his stop sign.

'Al, just text me what you want, I'm getting off the phone to concentrate.'

He ended the call. Turned up the news on the radio: the G20 summit was underway in Shanghai. Listening to the politicians' smug tones reminded Fox why he'd bugged out of the Navy job. Well, he hadn't had much choice in leaving what had been a promising but short-lived career, but the choices that had led to his discharge were all his, and he had learned to sleep soundly at night because of them.

'Not that soundly,' Fox said out loud, catching his tired eyes in the reflection of his rear-view mirror. *More soundly* than he would have if he'd not taken action when he'd felt he had to. A sense of knowing more than the bureaucrats, a belief that politics and power were too self-serving to do what was right, had always been with him and he was amazed he'd ever been accepted by the military in the first place. Maybe they'd wanted to diversify. Probably they'd just been desperate to fill recruitment quotas. Still, following a big turn-around in second year thanks to a decent officer telling Fox and Gammaldi to pull their socks up, he'd managed to finish second in his academic class and fifth overall in his graduating year.

He turned onto Rue de Grenelle and pulled into a parking space near the closed street market. The car parked itself, parallel, not something he'd let it do again.

Since he'd left the Navy, Fox had been recruited into the dream job of an investigative reporter with the Global Syndicate of Reporters (GSR). He had his pick of assignments, headed the military bureau, made a nice salary, had bought a good apartment in SoHo in Lower Manhattan . . . What was not to like? Why did he feel so uneasy? He felt he knew: it wasn't really his calling. To seek out the truth? Maybe, or some variation thereof. But to disseminate that to an increasingly uninterested public via syndicated news items? What was next?

He knew what was bringing all this uncertainty to a head: Kate re-entering his life. He was at the tail end of a six-month enforced sabbatical that had been driving him nuts, and hanging out with her was becoming more and more desirable.

Women . . .

He reached down for his iPhone as it bleeped, and clicked on the text message: it looked like a shopping list for a month's supplies.

He typed a reply: *Jesus Al, that's like two of every animal . . . You building an ark?*

Locking the car, he walked towards the busy market, where Saturday shoppers were already snapping up the best produce. He waited at a café window that faced the intersection, the smell of good coffee making his stomach groan. There was the rumble of an aircraft overhead, louder and louder. He looked up as he neared the front of the queue, ordered his triple-shot café au lait, looked back up to the sky; a massive A380 was banking overhead.

Al's reply blinked through: *Making cassoulet. Don't forget the confit duck. CONFIT!*

OK MOFO! he replied and put the iPhone in his back pocket. He looked back at the café window as he crossed the street and entered the market, checking the reflection behind him.

There were a few tourists among the locals buzzing about, and plenty of vans dropping off fresh produce with FedEx-like speed and precision. Hard to make out on the busy side of the street, but at least two figures sat in a blacked-out Peugeot sedan, parked a few spaces down the road from where he'd left the Golf. They were watching him. He'd seen them earlier making the same turns, driving after him.

Following him.

He bought a newspaper from an old man on the corner. A familiar face looked back at him from the front cover of *The International Herald Tribune* – Roman Babich, headed for trial at last. A quick skim of the article revealed that the corrupt Russian oligarch was being transferred soon, that his first trial was expected to take place in Rome in the coming month, and that the Russian judiciary were cooperating with the FBI and Interpol in providing damning evidence against the man who, until recently, was one of their vaunted business kings.

As Fox turned to the market he glanced back across the intersection, at that black Peugeot 607 – still with the outlines of two figures just visible behind a half-open tinted window. Watching him, waiting.

Fox went on his way, the back of his neck prickling with sweat. He was beginning to feel it was the start of a very long day.

2

HIGH OVER EUROPE

'Entering some turbulence in a couple of minutes, better buckle up,' the flight captain announced.

FBI Special Agent in Charge Andrew Hutchinson looked across the aisle at his prisoner, Roman Babich: he was buckled in well, and seemed to be asleep. The two FBI agents sitting opposite were locked into their reading: the young one slowly turning the pages of *Esquire*, the other engrossed in the latest Vince Flynn.

'Capel,' Hutchinson said as he stood and braced against the headrest. 'Don't go letting any of that Mitch Rapp head-cracking interrogation seep in.'

'Rapp knows what he's doing,' Capel said. 'I think you're thinking about Jack Bauer.'

'Don't get me started on him,' said Hutchinson. He headed towards the cockpit, holding onto the backs of the chairs as the Gulfstream aircraft bucked and sucked its way over the Med. Designated C-37A in US Air Force service, the Gulfstream V twin-engined business jet fulfilled missions for government and Defense Department officials, everything from senior officer and VIP transport, to rendition flights such as this.

'What have we got?' Hutchinson asked the USAF pilots.

'Summer storm, sir, big one at that,' the co-pilot said over his shoulder, his hands busy at the flight controls. 'Will probably last about twenty minutes or so; we're climbing a little higher to try to get out of it quicker.'

Hutchinson looked out the cockpit windows. Dark clouds had appeared out of nowhere, and shafts of brilliant orange sunlight were piercing through, giving everything to the east a golden lining.

'This normal?'

'Define normal,' the pilot replied. 'Seriously, weather's never normal, especially these days.'

'Climate change?'

'It's certainly changing. The Med's getting more and more hurricanes each year, big ones at that.'

'We're flying into a hurricane?' Hutchinson asked, his fingers tightening on the seat back in front of him.

The pilot shook his head, a hand to his earphone listening to the air-traffic controller.

'He likes to spook people,' the co-pilot said in his East-Coast tone, hands jinking on the controls as the aircraft shook and vibrated its way up through a turbulence layer. Both pilots were Air Force flight officers out of Andrews, both were among the best trained in the world; neither did much to put Hutchinson at ease with what was already a nerve-racking prisoner transfer without the weather's interference.

'The mistral's blowing through France and Spain and the cool air is colliding with the hotter air coming in off the Med and the African continent,' the pilot said. 'It's going to get dark and bumpy for a bit, that's all.'

'Bumpier than this?' Hutchinson asked.

'This ain't that bumpy.'

'Bumpy enough to knock our radar out.' The pilot looked across, frowned, toggled some controls. 'Damn.'

The co-pilot tapped the LCD screen and flicked a couple of switches.

'Damn,' he concurred. 'It's out good.'

'Damn? What's damn?' Hutchinson asked. The pilot looked to the co-pilot, pointed at another section of switches and shook his head. 'We need a radar, right?' Hutchinson continued, 'I mean, it's a handy tool flying into a dark storm, right?'

'It is pretty handy for mapping the weather, no doubt,' the pilot replied and gave Hutchinson a reassuring look, but the co-pilot flicking through the aircraft's instrument manual wasn't providing the reassurance he was after.

'Don't worry, Agent Hutchinson,' the pilot said. 'We're thirty-five thousand feet and climbing, with nothing but the Med down below. We're not gonna crash into a mountain, and our GPS and all flight management navigation systems are working fine.'

'And, we know where we're going, right?' the co-pilot chimed in, looking up from the manual and peering out the window, pointing towards the faint glow of the sunrise backlighting the dense clouds. 'East, I think. We're headed eastwards, right?'

The airmen laughed, big joke.

'Great,' Hutchinson said. 'Just get us there and back home in one piece, if that's not too much trouble?'

The aircraft pitched up and down violently. Hutchinson banged the top of his head on the cabin's ceiling. The co-pilot started calling in to the control tower whose airspace they were in, his voice matter-of-fact and clear.

'Agent Hutchinson, you might want to take a seat, sir,' the pilot said, serious, his arms steady at the flight controls. 'This will get rougher before it gets any better.'

'Right . . .' Hutchinson said, before finding his way back into the cabin. What he wouldn't give to be some place else right now – on the ground, carefree, far away from this chaos.

3

PARIS

This would be a lot easier if it weren't for the pandemonium of the crowd. Newspaper tucked under his arm, into his second coffee, Fox's basket was half-full of produce as he walked back along the market street, Rue Cler. He took time to check behind him, pausing at stalls and storefronts and changing direction at random to try to catch out anyone following him. No one stood out, but if he was being tailed it would be by professionals better trained and practised than he.

Rue Cler was a quaint cobbled pedestrian street lined with shops and aproned fruit-stall attendants coaxing passers-by into trying their ripe berries and stone fruits. He bought some nectarines and cherries, the supplies Gammaldi needed from the butcher and *poissonnerie*, and headed back up the street on the opposite side, towards his car on Rue de Grenelle. He'd deal with the Peugeot then, if it was still there. He couldn't shake the conviction that it had been sent by Babich's people to settle the score, maybe even . . . No. If they knew he was here chasing up a story to ensure their boss was finished, he'd be dead by now.

As he walked and shopped, he worked through alternative routes back to the farmhouse, eliminating options that were too direct in getting out of Paris. He took his time heading back to the car, not wanting to start the Golf until he had a couple of good options mapped out in his mind's eye. He considered abandoning the car altogether, but discounted the idea – there could well be someone watching him now, and he preferred his chances behind the wheel rather than on foot.

Whenever he stopped at shops, he casually glanced around, creating new sightlines and checking his blindspots as he squeezed fruit and perused breads and pastries. Every Parisian here seemed to love shopping – parents with children, friends with smiles, lovers with linked arms, old couples with wheeled baskets – whole neighbourhoods seemed to be here making a morning of it. He couldn't pick out anyone following him. Maybe he was overreacting – it had been a while since he'd been out like this without the protection of the FBI. Perhaps the occupants of the Peugeot were innocently shopping here, too? Maybe it was just a coincidence that they'd followed his roundabout route from near the car-hire place to the market. Maybe. He felt a little disarmed by the gaiety around him; it seemed all too easy to blow off the danger and get lost in the atmosphere of the Left Bank . . .

But Fox's alertness was unshakable, and he had the same physical feeling and reactions now he'd had when he'd been on patrol in Iraq and Afghanistan. Here he was ambling and shopping, leading the closest thing to what he could imagine was a normal life, yet he felt in the middle of his own war zone. Anyone in the masses around him could be hostile and he knew if he had to he'd use the crowd in his favour.

Fox had spotted plenty of the young bourgeois who'd moved into the Left Bank, just as Renard had mentioned over drinks earlier in the week. They were easy to spot with their Lacoste polo shirts and loafers, shopping for produce by sight rather than that Parisian way of touch and smell; they were busy gentrifying the area, as similar classes had done to other places he'd lived in within Manhattan and Brooklyn. The shopkeepers helped them efficiently and cordially, and then warmly greeted the next customer, someone they'd been serving for two decades. Both parties knew there was nothing to be done about the change that was coming but to shelter under the scaffolding and wait for the sandblasting to be over.

Fox noticed a squad of happy young men in military uniform, probably from the nearby École Militaire, Napoleon's alma mater, walking the street and watching girls. Fox had always been an atmosphere kind of guy; being in the exact space, walking the same ground, breathing the air where momentous events had occurred was exciting to him. Part of the reason he'd joined the military was to see the world, and he'd done plenty of that. The reporting gig was better, supposedly safer – in theory – but in practice he'd been the right guy in the wrong place more than enough times. Yet there was no denying the drive in him that made him want to shape a story rather than just report it, a feeling that – despite the passing of time – he found impossible to shake. His current enforced sabbatical was making him question where a guy like him truly belonged: in the arena or the press box? Certainly not here, getting elbowed by the tourists who had started to arrive en masse.

Last on his list were the cheese, wine and a few things from the supermarket. Outside the *fromagerie* was a long, narrow, canopied table displaying an array of coloured packages. The shopkeeper explained that the shapes of cheeses signalled their place of origin, which was as important with cheese as it was with wine; something that heralded their *terroir*, a concept Fox was still trying to fathom.

He left the wine store with a mixed half-dozen, grabbed a few things at the supermarket, crossed onto Rue de Grenelle and headed towards his car. The Peugeot was still there. He played through his escape and evasion plan, revised it, took in the vehicles coming up the street and revised it again.

Fox smiled as he thought about what brought him to Paris this week: a story. Information that would perhaps help seal the fate of Roman Babich, the man who was making his and others' lives a living hell. His two companions back at Renard's farmhouse were unaware of the real reason he was here, but then they didn't need to know, right? He was here to do this for all of them, to make life simpler, safer. Sure, this trip was a respite from New York, where they were constantly being minded by the FBI while Babich was headed for court – and Renard's off-the-beaten-track farmhouse was as good a hiding spot as any.

Back at his car, parked in front of about a hundred bikes and scooters, Fox stowed the shopping, checking the traffic coming up the street. As he got in he checked his rear-view mirror – the eyes that looked back at him were unfamiliar; his own, but with that edge of unease he'd carried for too long now. He adjusted the mirror and saw the blacked-out Peugeot had its running lights on. He knew that no matter where he went in the world, as long as he kept looking under rocks there were those willing to kill for the information he obtained.

Fox revved the Golf's little engine. He had a couple of routes mapped out in his mind, none of them direct to the Normandy highway, let alone the farmhouse – he'd shake this vehicle in the tight one-way maze of Parisian backstreets.

He gunned the accelerator, handbrake off, waited for a truck to block the Peugeot, then slammed into drive and took off.

4

PARIS

Boris Malevich sat behind the wheel of his nondescript sedan, tense. The reporter wasn't an easy target to follow – clearly the guy was wary, perhaps had suspicions that he'd be targeted, knew the stakes of this game. He'd rather not take him in public, but if an opportunity arose he would. Better to follow him, follow him and wait for the chance that would undoubtedly soon present itself. He fantasised that he had the luxury of time to simply do this, let the reporter complete his work, and *then* move in, relieving him of what they all sought. That would be ideal, but his deadline was today – today or never – and his own life trumped that of any life he may be forced to take.

Malevich's hands shook, they had been doing this since that night at the ambassador's residence. Everywhere he looked he imagined her blood. He saw it on his hands, he saw it when his eyes were closed; it was everywhere. He'd never wanted to kill, especially not a woman. He remembered every little detail in vivid colour. After the deed, walking briskly away, he'd had to stop in the street to vomit until he was dry. He remembered the breeze, and he would never lose the guilt, everlasting, of taking a life. Killing came so easily for those thick-necked operations men Moscow had sent to blow up their own embassy. Whatever it was those men had, he'd missed out on it. Nothing about killing had come easily or naturally to him, but he'd known before he'd even touched down in Paris that the day could well come when it would be asked of him.

The state had trained him to kill. It was all abstract and arbitrary then, a kind of macabre lottery in which he hoped his number would never be called, that he'd never be activated. He remembered the exact time – fifteen minutes to midnight – when he'd walked into the ambassador's compound, the smell of jasmine on the rain, the copper of blood. He owed it to the state to kill again and it was the kind of obligation they made sure you never forgot. When all this was over? He'd run, run away from all this, away from everything.

He breathed deep and pressed on, focused on the task at hand.

Tailing someone was no longer a fine art; the old KGB had been very good at teaching and employing such fieldcraft. One of the keys to their Cold War successes, of course, had been their sheer number – the KGB were once a mighty force, when the ideology and political influence of their nation ensured that there was a swarm of officers running their agents around the globe. Sure, Putin had gone some way towards making up for that shortfall, but the post-Soviet breed was nothing on the old-school intelligence officers. Malevich was one of a dying breed, a state-trained sleeper who was so entrenched in his cover life that he'd almost forgotten his obligation, his duty, to the Rodina, his motherland.

He'd liked his teaching job here in Paris, liked this homeland, his colleagues and students, but now he was an activated agent for his country. He'd been an agent all this time, but it had never felt real. Had he ever thought it would? No, not like this. Stealing some secrets, following someone and reporting their activities, posing as someone he was not; that was the work he was expecting. Not murder. Not like that. And all for – what – a goddamned diary written by a Russian statesman who'd been dead for over a hundred years?

He wouldn't be able to stay in Paris now, that much was clear. Not after what he'd done . . . Oh, what he'd done. His hands clenched the steering wheel, his knuckles white. He was a disposable asset, there to be used on a rainy day, when there was something about him that would suit the job. He had no way of questioning the order given to him, and no place to do so. They owned him.

He thought of his sister – and the thought gave him the strength to keep going. She was a constant glimmer of hope on his horizon, ever present, his northern star. A future.

Malevich reached for his mobile, tried calling her again. Her phone was off – perhaps she had gone to the airport early, perhaps she was already on the plane to her new life. His orders came with money, which meant a new life for her, too. He didn't want to leave Paris and start again, but he was duty-bound to serve his country. It was more than repaying their investment in him – in setting up this life he so enjoyed – it was what his father and grandfather had done and their fathers before them.

He'd almost been sent to Afghanistan but had been spared that horror, and he'd left military service before his unit was sent into Chechnya. So, finally, he had served his country on a frontline. *Was* serving his country. There was still work to be done, all of it by tonight. He changed the radio station and shifted in his seat. Soon, with his next target now acquired, all this would be behind him.

5

PARIS

Shaking a tail was a skill Fox had learned the hard way. He hammered the Golf along Rue de Grenelle, weaving in and out of the growing number of vans and cars on the road in the early morning. The black Peugeot was mirroring his moves a couple of hundred metres back, albeit a little less recklessly. There was something in its controlled and patient presence that was far more unsettling than if it were right at his rear bumper trying to run him off the road.

He raced through an intersection, geared down and hit the brakes hard, turned sharp right onto Avenue Bosquet – hitting over a hundred kilometres per hour as he crossed the wide expanse of lanes and shifted up through third and fourth gears – then saw an opportunity coming up to his left and veered across the road, taking a side street, gunning the accelerator.

In the rear-view mirror Fox saw the Peugeot make the turn, its rear sliding out as the heavy sedan fishtailed before the engine power corrected its course and the car surged after him in a cloud of tyre smoke. On the open road his vehicle would be no match for theirs, and he had no chance if they tried to ram him into submission – let alone if they had weapons; best he had was a few baguettes on the back seat. He played leap-frog with a few vans, moving in and out as he overtook them, and again saw the Peugeot mirroring his moves. There was no way he could risk leading them back to his friends – he had to lose them here in Paris, and he had to do it fast. Up ahead, a possibility: the Eiffel Tower. She stood tall and graceful, seemingly lighter than air, a delicate-looking latticework of metal illuminated in the morning light.

Fox checked over his shoulder, the Peugeot was still there. He looked ahead, missed the stop sign and yanked at the wheel, skirting around a group of racing bicycles, the Golf drifting sideways on its low-profile tyres as he geared down, turned the wheel into the slide and powered out.

Flashing blue lights appeared in his rear-view mirror, weaving through the other vehicles, to the piercing sound of the two-tone French police siren. The cop car – a little white Renault hatch – joined the chase, riding hard next to the Peugeot, which seemed to let the cops overtake.

Two options. Keep going and hope to lose them, or pull over and take whatever was coming – from the police and from Babich's men. No doubt Babich's Umbra corporation had help via sources in the French police or intelligence; how else had they known he was here in Paris? Fox and his friends had flown in on a private GSR aircraft and used a backdoor customs entry, courtesy of the FBI. How could Babich's men know he was in France, let alone in Paris, this morning, without inside help? *Fuck it!* But what – did he really think he could lose the French cops in their own city? Was he mad? He knew he was damned if he stopped, damned if he didn't.

He slammed on the brakes, did a tight handbrake turn so the back slid out, made a sharp left and jammed the accelerator to the floor. The flashing lights were still there behind him, but Fox was gaining distance since the take-off; still in the background was the Peugeot, black and squat, biding its time.

Fox made a high-speed right turn, merged with the traffic, weaved through it, glanced in the rear-view mirror: *Slam!*

A taxi clipped the rear of the cop car and it spun across the lanes of oncoming traffic, smashing hard against some parked cars. The Peugeot was still there, a way back now, hunting him as it surged ahead.

Fox slammed on the brakes again, the anti-lock braking system shaking the pedal underfoot as he just managed to avoid a nose-to-tail with the car in front that had slowed to rubberneck the accident behind them. He overtook on the inside lane, made the next left turn and took the avenue alongside the base of the Eiffel Tower. He leaned on the horn, scattering a few jaywalking tourists as he sped by, turned right, and headed for the bridge around the other side of the tower.

He powered the Golf eastwards along the bank of the Seine, doubling back.

Ahead to the right, he could see blue lights racing along the other side of the river – they'd cut the chase off from there.

And now dead ahead – strobing through the other vehicles in the oncoming lane – the beaten-up cop car from before, its back bumper dragging in its wake.

Fucking great . . .

Fox checked his rear-view mirror, the Peugeot sedan was lurching in and out, right on him and closing the gap, no chance to evade right now . . . He couldn't stop and hide either, however tempting that would be. Even if just the cops got him now . . . That'd leave Kate and Gammaldi alone out at the farmhouse; alone long enough for Babich's guys to track them down.

Across the river the cop cars were rushing towards him – two of them, racing along the *quai*.

The bridge was coming up; he needed to cross it and take a route through La Défense, lose them before the highway. That meant splitting his way through those cops.

Two-tone sirens howled as they bore down, closer, faster.

The damaged cop car veered across lanes to cut him off – Fox planted his foot flat on the floor, tweaked the steering wheel and winced as the Renault scraped past, then slammed on the brakes, pulled hard right, the Golf on two wheels for a moment as he steered it onto the bridge.

In the rear-view mirror, speeding like he was, he only glimpsed the base of the Eiffel Tower and the black Peugeot, the beaten-up cop car mounting the kerb as it turned to follow him; up ahead, two police cars turned onto the bridge and headed straight for him.

He tightened his grip on the steering wheel, kept the accelerator flat to the floor and braced for impact.

6

HIGH OVER THE MED

Hutchinson had never felt so nauseous. The aircraft jinking and pitching up and down and rolling side to side like a rollercoaster from hell.

He filled his sick bag again, his eyes watering from the effort.

Across the aisle, Capel had gone green, his book in his lap and eyes closed as he clutched the armrests. The other agent, a beefy former Hostage Rescue Team member nicknamed Brick, was still reading his magazine as if oblivious to the motion, and Babich – Babich still appeared to be asleep with his head turned away, facing his window. Maybe he was just good at hiding it, maybe he was as sick as him.

Hutchinson couldn't take it anymore. He sucked in some deep breaths, settled himself, and when there seemed a slight lull, unclipped his belt, got up and headed forwards to see if there was anything the pilots could do to get them out of this mess.

They'd taken no chances in this prisoner transfer. Babich had been moved to an Air Force hangar in DC that housed three identical Defense Department C-37As, from where they had taken off in tandem the previous night, followed three different flight paths to land at three different Italian Air Force bases. Trust his flight plan to be the one going through this commotion.

'Where're we at?' Hutchinson asked, gripping the back of the pilot's chair as they dropped altitude.

'Radar's still out, but I can see clearer skies coming up in a few minutes,' the pilot said over his shoulder. 'Hang tight back there, won't be long.'

Hutchinson grumbled a reply, returned to his seat, buckled in, knuckles white on his armrest.

Brick just kept on reading. Babich had woken up, and was sitting forwards, staring down at his toes. Didn't look so fucking cool and collected now, Hutchinson was glad to see.

No doubt Babich was used to travelling in a more luxurious style; he'd been vastly wealthy and untouchable . . . Until now. Even the Russian government was thankful the US had finally done what they didn't have the stones to do themselves. Many influential Russians would be afraid of the information he might spill – politicians, judiciary, you name it. A guy like Babich hadn't got this far and amassed so much without a lot of illegal back-scratching, and once all the dust had settled, a decade from now maybe, Russia's corruption index might just drop out of . . . Ah, who was he kidding? This case would make a decent dent, but such corruption was here to stay, forever, everywhere.

Hutchinson closed his eyes, waited for the bucking and rocking to relent. Why couldn't he have outsourced this one? Could have sent his second in command, Valerie, while he spent a few days' R and R somewhere as reward for a job well done in getting this guy to trial. He tried to imagine himself lying on a beach in Mexico, beautiful girls strolling by, a drink in hand . . . The plane rolled to the left and he reached for another sick bag.

7

PARIS

Fox picked up the pace, leaving the two police cars spinning in his wake. He flicked the gears into second and took a tight left turn onto a cobbled street wet from the street cleaners up ahead. The Golf's tyres skidded as he kept the accelerator to the floor – the engine red-lined, upshifted gears – mounted the kerb to get around the cleaner's truck and lost a side-mirror in the process of getting back on the road.

Two more police cars pulled out of a side street, headed straight for him; the Peugeot still behind him, just rounding the corner, closing fast.

Fox pulled the handbrake, executing a tight turn to the left and the cop cars flashed by where he'd been, one skidding into the Peugeot as it made the same turn. Fox shot down the side road, a motorcycle swerving hard to avoid him.

Behind – no cops, no lights, just the Peugeot, still there, in hard pursuit. Fox kept the Golf revving high as he wound through a couple more cobbled lanes, took a sharp right, hauled arse down a narrow passageway and – hit the brakes, just managing to stop before a street sweeper, a young African guy plugged into an iPod, who gave Fox the bird and slowly pushed his motorised cart across to the opposite pavement.

A siren growing louder, closing in somewhere to his left. The second the street sweeper was clear, Fox floored the accelerator and took off again. He rounded a curve and was back on a main street, packed with traffic leaving town, the way he wanted to go, directly towards the highway to Normandy.

The rear-view mirror was clear – then an old Beetle came up fast behind him, tooting its horn hard . . .

His eyes roamed the traffic, trying to find an answer.

He backed the Golf the way it had come – hand hard on the horn to urge the Beetle back, jumping his car with the brakes a couple of times to get the point across: *Move it, buddy, or I'll ram you.* The Beetle driver was yelling at him and the scattered pedestrians near the pavement café joined in. He was nearly clear when a delivery van pulled in and blocked him from behind.

Just beyond the van, slowing as it closed in on Fox: the black Peugeot. It moved smoothly, as if its driver was well practised in tactical patience. The siren sounded like it was right next to him. He looked ahead; the Beetle had long gone, merged with the traffic. Fox checked his rear-view mirror, the cops' little hatchback took the place of the retreating van and tried to box the Golf in. The Peugeot waited.

Fox headed straight for the police in reverse, hard and fast. He braced for impact and just managed to punch his car into the right front corner of their car. His own car spun – flashing right past the Peugeot – and ended up pointing down another side street. He slipped it into drive and raced to the avenue ahead, the Peugeot and the slightly damaged cop car in pursuit.

Just ahead of Fox, two more police hatchbacks slid into the intersection and completely blocked his path. *Fucking great, game over*, but he was still driving flat-out in third gear . . .

He slammed on the brakes and hung hard on the wheel, the car spinning 180 degrees and continuing on, barrelling backwards into the cop cars. Parked nose-to-tail with not a metre in between, he split the gap hard.

Whipping the wheel again, he whirled back through a reverse 180 as the Peugeot and the pursuing cop car raced through the wreckage in Fox's wake.

He was on the Right Bank's main road now, headed towards the La Defense tunnels, travelling against the traffic, and the double lanes were mostly clear.

The Peugeot and the remaining cop car were gaining on him as he slid into a right-hand turn.

Two more police cars rushed towards the intersection up ahead. Two ahead, one behind, and the Peugeot. It was all about the timing.

Fox slowed, then sped up quickly.

The cop car behind hit his bumper, so Fox accelerated through the upcoming intersection, his pursuer lagging just enough –

A Yop delivery truck slammed into the police Renault, an explosion of crushed metal and glass under a fountain of white yoghurt drinks.

8

HIGH OVER THE MED

Thank Christ for calmer skies, Hutchinson thought.

He glanced over at Babich. The man went back to looking unperturbed out his window.

Hutchinson closed his eyes and thought back to the conversation he'd had with Bill McCorkell before he'd left DC. Bill was a good guy – by far the smartest and most level-headed of any government security expert he'd ever come across – and having him as liaison with the White House on this Umbra case had made the difference in this becoming a model for future transcontinental corruption cases. Bill and he both worried about whether the Italian legal system would put Babich away long enough for the US litigators to line him up, but that kind of multinational cooperation had proved effective when it led the Russians to come into the fold and instigate legal proceedings of their own.

McCorkell had been instrumental in negotiating Babich's arrest with Moscow – and some six months later, they were getting somewhere, albeit slowly. Nevertheless, it was the end of the line for Babich and his network, one way or another.

Hutchinson looked back over at his prisoner. Even after his conversation with Bill McCorkell, it still puzzled him why the Russians had let a man like Babich acquire such power from the ruins of their Soviet system.

•

McCorkell had been keen to explain. 'He used his money and power to interfere in a lot of other states' affairs – Georgia, Nigeria, Chechnya – where his influence and activities ranged from political campaign donations to attempted coups and orchestrated election results. In Chechnya's elections a few years back, he shipped in busloads of illegal voters from across the borders, and we know how that worked out: You seen Grozny? Looks like Berlin circa 1945. United Nations still call Grozny "the most destroyed city on Earth". And then there was Nigeria; well, you know all about that . . . But you know what? He always stayed out of Moscow's politics.'

'And that's it? That was his saving grace, that he stayed out of politics at home?' Hutchinson had shaken his head. 'There has to be more to it.'

McCorkell continued, 'He helped them out economically – and not just through his corporations and taxes. Take Georgia. Remember when he put those Umbra security forces in? Partly to aid the passage of his oil and gas pipelines –'

'And curry favour with the Russian government.' Hutchinson nodded his head. It still wasn't enough. McCorkell could see that too, couldn't he?

'Stirring the pot like that sure helped the Russians out.'

Hutchinson had paced McCorkell's Eisenhower Executive Office Building (EEOB) office next door to the White House.

Their celebratory drinks remained largely untouched atop McCorkell's desk, so he took the single malt and sipped at it. There was something they were missing. Babich had an ace in the hole, and despite being incarcerated for all this time, Hutchinson had no doubt it was one of those get-out-of-jail-free kind of gigs. He'd gone all this time without his government stopping him, as they'd done for so many other oligarchs who'd outgrown what the Kremlin considered acceptable, yet they hadn't moved on him until the writing was well and truly on the wall in international jurisdictions.

'I don't buy it either,' McCorkell had said eventually, and as if reading Hutchinson's mind: 'Why have they let him get so big for so long? He must have a few tricks up his sleeve. He has to.'

'Like?'

'He was one of their top security advisers before the fall, a rising star in their intel community, better regarded than his colleague Putin, but he'd made the wrong alliances in the last days of Yeltsin. The answer's gotta be wrapped up in there somewhere.'

'He knows . . . what? What's he know?'

'Information is power . . .'

McCorkell was grinning, enjoying watching the younger man think it through. Hutchinson snapped his fingers. 'He knows every little secret the current Russian leaders have? All the details of how they ascended to power?'

'And how they keep power.'

'That's what it's gotta be. Right?'

'It's information we kinda know their regime has killed for, many times,' McCorkell had said, draining his drink and looking out at the sun setting over the Capitol. 'But then, why would they wait around if there's a fear he'd spill the beans one day?'

'They thought he'd never need to, as long as he was left to do his thing. He's never used it, all this time . . .'

'Never had to.'

'Until now.'

'*Until now.*'

Hutchinson couldn't rest, couldn't quiet his mind. *But now they're turning against him . . .* Thing was, with this kind of power, why would Moscow risk this guy not rolling over in some kind of bargain? Babich was undoubtedly smart, as good an intelligence operator as any, so he'd protect his life with some kind of fail-safe back-up plan should the day come when the authorities came gunning for him. Well, that day was here. Did he know that? Hutchinson looked over to Babich, sitting, eyes closed, easy smile, as if he hadn't a care in the world. Didn't he realise the gravity of his situation? What could make such a man so calm?

9

PARIS

Fox couldn't really see the police Renault amid the debris of the Yop truck, but he caught glimpses of it behind the traffic.

Gotta warn Renard – he reached awkwardly for his iPhone, still in his back pocket, swerved to avoid an oncoming car, and the mobile fell to the floor.

One of the two inbound cop cars drove up on the pavement, scattering a tour group, and launched off the gutter to cut in front of him. But Fox was too fast. He was already past them, just a flash of metal grinding along their front bumper. One of the cops jumped out, pistol drawn, and Fox swerved quickly to avoid the shot.

The other cop car was trapped by the oncoming tunnel traffic, but the Peugeot had gained on him; a black panther hunched low to the ground, it chewed up the distance on the flat run.

Fox flashed his lights on and off and raced northeast, weaving through the other cars on the road, but he was followed closely by the unshakable black sedan. He scanned the split roads before him and took the tunnel that led into the business district of La Defense. Blue lights followed him in – the cop car was back.

Inside the tunnel, cars yielded to Fox's high-beam and urgent speed. A taxi tried to jump into Fox's wake but was pushed back by the cop car, the taxi then ricocheting off a concrete barrier and into the path of a jack-knifing truck.

The Peugeot had gained on Fox and was hitting his bumper, trying to spin the Golf out. Fox floored it, struggling to keep ahead. The speed, the bumping, the neon overhead lights strobing like a flickering reel-to-reel projector movie . . . The light of the tunnel's end loomed up ahead, his foot was flat to the floor, the sedan bumped him again.

The two cars shot out of the tunnel, the road ahead mostly clear.

Fox glanced across at the merging traffic on a ramp to his right – looked back – and jerked on the steering wheel quickly to avoid an almost-stopped Citroën. The cop car flanking the Golf slammed into the Citroën's rear, spinning it into the path of the Peugeot, which finally screeched to a stop. The cop car, the Peugeot and the Citroën were locked into a mess of bumpers as Fox drove on.

He looked behind – the Peugeot's passenger window slid down and a swarthy guy in dark glasses watched the Golf disappearing. The cops were getting out of their car and approaching the Peugeot cautiously, hands on their holstered side-arms.

Fox turned off the highway, leaving the carnage behind him. Several blocks, side streets and turns later, when everything seemed quiet around him, he found a turn back onto his chosen path.

Minutes later, he had settled into a more sedate pace, happy to see other Golfs on the road and no cop cars or black Peugeots behind him. He reached down into the passenger-side foot-well for his iPhone. He had people to warn.

10

PARIS

Boris Malevich drained the last of his takeway coffee and scanned the building's doors from across the street. He checked his watch. Forward intelligence, weeks' worth of telephone transcripts and hacking of the reporter's online diary, had placed Renard here today, ready to meet up with a contact in just over an hour. Having watched him enter *Le Figaro* this morning, Malevich was satisfied that those who'd planned this op knew what they were doing. Then, watching the busy Saturday morning start to take shape, he began to have doubts, uncertainties that centred around what those in Moscow couldn't control. With nothing to do but stay here, wait and observe, he worried: What if the reporter had taken another exit from the building instead of the one he was watching? What if he didn't take his car – which Malevich had his other unit covering – to his meeting? What if Renard had left while he was sipping his cold coffee and looking around for cops? What if they'd missed him altogether?

Stupid. This thinking was stupid and this operation was stupid. He should have kept more of the guys here with him. Moscow had sent ten men, and he had just two here to assist him, covering the rear of the news building and watching the reporter's vehicle; a couple of thick-necked guys Moscow had sent to do the heavy lifting work. Eight others had been sent away to Renard's farm near Giverny to clean up a loose end. His case officer had insisted it would take that many men.

But still . . . *eight* men for Lachlan Fox . . . Just to kill another soft target, a reporter like this Renard. They needed eight men to make sure he was dead? And he was left with just two to shadow the French journalist, to potentially move and obtain what had been described to him as 'the most valuable item Russia could ever have'.

Really? That was all?

He looked at his watch again – the farmhouse team should check in at any moment. He had no way of contacting them – they were under strict instruction not to use mobile phones while their mission was underway – but he had thought they would call in their success and meet up with him soon. Until he had ten men here, he would continue to worry. That was justifiable, yes?

Better to have three vehicles following Renard and the document than two. He texted his two men here, requesting an update. One thing put him more at ease. This time, at least, he had *them* to do the killing.

11

HIGH OVER THE MED

The cabin lights went out and the plane was dark, except for the weak daylight filtering through the small oval windows. Hutchinson walked up into the cockpit, all smiles now they'd made it through the turbulence – until he realised the pilots' mood hadn't changed.

'What's up with turning the cabin lights off?' Hutchinson asked, peering out at the heavy cloud around the windows, condensation streaking and snaking along the glass. 'We're coming out of it, yeah? We're – we're good now, yeah?'

The pilots took a while to answer as they were each preoccupied with flight controls. Hutchinson noticed the LCD screens in front were blank.

'All electronics are down,' the pilot said. 'Major failure. GPS, comms, radar, fly-by-wire . . . You name it, if it's electric it isn't working.'

'Why?'

'No idea. We're flying by analogue instruments now.'

'All comms are down?' Hutchinson asked.

'Yep.'

The co-pilot was scanning the radio bands. He shook his head, kept flicking switches, kept calling to towers that should be contactable and muttering expletives.

'What could do that?'

'Serious fucking bug,' the pilot replied. The co-pilot looked across at him. 'Or some kind of interference . . . Though that's unlikely.'

Hutchinson looked back down the cabin at Babich. He didn't look perturbed, like he knew exactly what was going on.

'We should pull in asap,' the pilot said.

'What?'

'We should land,' the pilot replied. 'Asap.'

'Where?'

'Airfield in Corsica is the closest,' the co-pilot said.

Great. Fucking great.

'Can we make it there okay?'

'All mechs are working fine and we've got the fuel,' the pilot said, looking him in the eyes, unable to hide his own alarm. 'I'd feel a lot better if we were on the ground – I've never experienced this kind of system failure outside the sim.'

Fuck. Something was going on. But what other choice was there?

'Head for Corsica,' Hutchinson said.

'Copy that,' the co-pilot said, and he started finalising the course projection.

'And we've got a sat phone back there,' Hutchinson added.

'Worth a try,' the pilot said. 'Bring it up and we'll run through it.'

Hutchinson walked to the back of the cabin to get the gear. He could feel Babich's eyes on him, intent. As if the fucker had never been asleep at all. As if he hadn't a care in the world. Oh, how he'd love to share the load, give the motherfucker something to think about.

'Holy shit!'

The pilot's voice barely preceded the violent jerking of the cabin – Hutchinson just managed to grab hold of a seat as the aircraft levelled off again. He looked up the aisle, Babich was looking back at him.

The Russian smiled.

12

GIVERNY

FRANCE

The winding gravel drive crunched under the low-profile tyres as Fox steered the Golf towards the side of the rustic double-storey farmhouse. All looked quiet, normal, exactly how he'd left it earlier this morning. The white-walled building with its blue timber shutters, orange-clay tiled roof with brick chimneys bookending the ridge was a picture-perfect place in the country. An illusion now though, just another piece of normality that he'd leave behind because of what he did. Everything stemmed from the U-turn he took a few years back, long after he'd renounced this kind of life and moved to an island in the Indian Ocean – a speck of tranquillity that taunted him as he looked at where he was – on the run, again.

His heart was still beating fast from the car chase, but there'd been no sign of the Peugeot since way back at La Defense, forty minutes ago. He'd passed a cop car just as he exited the Normandy highway and he'd sat a little straighter behind the wheel, made sure he was not speeding. He'd checked the rear-view mirror, expecting them to do a U-turn and pursue him, but they kept driving. The sick sensation in his stomach had remained, would until he knew his friends were safe. Part of him wanted to grab his friends and just leave, take the easy route; run. But maybe hiding out here at the farmhouse was the better option? It was remote, a needle in a haystack, just another plot amid the endless farms that dotted the region. Nobody beyond Renard knew they were here.

Renard. Lachlan tried his friend's number again: maybe he'd switched it off on the drive to Dijon? He left a message as he sped up the driveway:

'Renard, it's Lachlan. Listen . . . There was a car following me this morning and it – it didn't feel right so I put my foot down: it chased me. Had a bit of an incident with the cops in the process of escaping Paris, but I lost them all – I think. So keep an eye out, yeah? I'm just pulling into the farmhouse . . . Call me when you can.'

Brujon, Renard's border collie, followed the car. He was a spritely black and white blur, far too much energy, a cunning genius and escape artist extraordinaire. Fox saw Gammaldi at the window in the kitchen – giving him a thumbs-up and huge grin – and he felt some of his tension disappear.

He drove slowly under the stone arch that linked the barn to the house, pulling around the back. The walled courtyard garden was bordered by the vines of the neighbouring farm, separated from them by acres of barley that formed a waist-high sea, swirling in the breeze. He pulled up close to the kitchen door and killed the engine.

About a year ago he'd been chased across Nigeria. And only six months ago he'd been locked away in a Pakistani prison. The last few days he'd been enjoying getting to know Giverny and the surrounding countryside. He'd been planning to visit Monet's studio with Kate, but it looked like any relaxation was over.

Kate . . . He'd brought her to France, thinking it would give them a break from the Babich trial. Not that they were witnesses, but Fox had played a pivotal role in bringing the men into custody and he'd made some powerful enemies in the process. Kate had been dragged into the whole mess too. For six months they'd been protected by the FBI back in the States, but it was driving him stir-crazy – he had to get out, be on the frontline, get a real feel for the story. He'd told Kate where he and Gammaldi were heading.

'Paris?'

'Just a quick trip; a week or so.'

'I'll come.'

'It's safer for you here,' he'd told her, but she'd have none of it. She'd learned of Renard's family house and soon both their bags were packed and his investigative work was fast being redefined as a tourist trip.

'Can't we go to Normandy?' she'd said in bed that night. *'I want to see the landing beaches – don't you? To walk on Omaha Beach where my grandpa landed, to see the skies where your grandfather flew. Can we? We can arrange a side trip from Paris, or from Renard's, rent a little place, lay low in the countryside?'*

They'd spent a few enjoyable nights in the house, talking around the dinner table, sharing stories about the Second World War and memories of family. His grandfather had flown Spitfires in the Battle of Britain, while Kate's grandfather had been in the Canadian Army.

He'd felt free, just the other day, walking the beach with her, almost normal. By the time they returned from Normandy he could see that something in Kate had changed, as if seeing that haunting moment of war's legacy had brought her peace.

And now he was going to shatter that peace.

Alister Gammaldi came out the kitchen door. Fox's best friend since they were teenagers, built like a rugby back-liner: thick-necked with wide, muscular shoulders, his black hair cropped close to his skull, dark crescents under his eyes from hitting the calvados hard the night before. Gammaldi sniffed the air around the car, the smell of hot brakes lingering.

'Broken her in, hey?'

'Hire cars,' Fox said, glancing through the back door and out through a front window. He couldn't see anything, couldn't hear anything. He was sure he'd lost them.

'Fastest cars in the world?' Gammaldi ventured, getting the groceries out of the boot. 'Only cars where you can select reverse from drive while doing two hundred on the freeway?'

'Yeah, something like that,' Fox said. 'You haven't seen or heard anything?'

'No,' he said. 'What is it?'

'Don't know,' Fox replied, checking a sightline through the open door into the kitchen. 'Just a car that followed me; lost them back in Paris in a tangle with some cops. Where's Kate?'

'Still sleeping, I guess.'

Fox got the newspaper out. Babich's face stared up at him.

'You should forget about him,' Gammaldi said, looking at the front page, too. 'Piece of shit's gonna rot in an Italian cell; then, if he makes it out alive, he'll be in a federal pen back in the States or some Siberian Gulag.'

Fox was staring blankly at the newspaper in his hand.

'Maybe we should get out of here . . .' he said. Brujon padded over for a scratch behind the ear. Fox looked across the drive, lost in the history of this place; wars had been fought on this soil for centuries . . . He could imagine the young faces of his grandfather's generation, kids eighteen and nineteen years old, their helmets kicked back on their heads, confident and cocky and victorious, walking under that same arch sixty-five years before, telling the French family living here: *It's okay, those bastards ain't coming back. You're okay now.* He looked forward to the day when he could say the same about Umbra, about Babich, about so many guys who wore uniforms of corporate suits, who ran companies that hid their money in the Clearstreams and Citibanks and in their lawyers' names. There was nothing remotely easy about beating an adversary who walked among you with no outward sign of their sinister purpose; greed and consumerism at the core of all such cash-addicted men. The global financial crisis proved that the time had come for the system to change, for some form of capitalism with a conscience, and surely this group of men – for it was almost exclusively men – were on the fringes of globalisation that, like everything at its most extreme, was killing itself.

'Relax, we're halfway between nowhere and lost,' Gammaldi said, gesturing to the fields that surrounded them. 'We're off the grid here, harder to find than Bin Laden.'

Fox laughed.

'What happened to you going to the air show this weekend?'

'What?' Gammaldi replied. 'You and Kate gonna miss your alone time?'

Fox punched him in the arm.

In the kitchen the worn table was covered in produce, and Gammaldi had already started cooking something in the wood-fired Aga. Prosciutto, cheese, olives and bread were laid out.

'Get the duck?'

'What duck?'

Gammaldi looked alarmed for a second.

'The confit,' he said, 'I asked for confit –'

'Here, fat boy,' Fox said, pulling out a couple of containers of duck slow-cooked in goose fat.

'You really need all that for one dish?'

'Cassoulet, and we'll be eating it for days –'

'You even know how to make that?' Fox asked, putting the milk away in the fridge.

'I was reading some recipes . . . You know, you're meant to leave some of the cassoulet in the pan for the next batch – there's dishes in this country that have been carrying a little part of the same cassoulet along for decades, centuries even.'

'You really know how to sell a dish, Al.'

'I like my food.'

'I'll leave you to it,' Fox looked through the dining area to the front living room and its open windows facing the drive. Silent, no sign of trouble.

'Keep an eye out for any guests, yeah?'

Gammaldi's look showed that he understood something serious was up, but he was his old self, never far away from a laugh.

'I've got Brujon, he'll protect us,' Gammaldi said, giving him a scratch. 'Besides, we've got Big Bertha there to ward off any religious zealots.'

He pointed to a double-barrelled shotgun cradled in a rack above the pantry's doorway.

'Renard probably put that there to keep out evil food spirits like you,' Fox said over his shoulder as he headed up the ancient timber staircase two at a time. He walked the hall to his bedroom – Kate wasn't there. He checked the bathroom, empty. He looked out a little window, over the roof and down the driveway. The hairs on the back of his neck stood up . . .

13

HIGH OVER THE MED

'Uncuff me,' Babich said to the agent opposite, his voice calm and considered, 'and I will make sure you are not harmed.'

'What?' the agent, Brick, looked wide-eyed around the cabin.

Hutchinson listened in – it was the first time Babich had spoken on the trip.

Brick, a specialist heavy hitter from the FBI's Hostage Rescue Team, could easily kill Babich with his hands. He was close to the prisoner's face, directing his anger well. 'What the fuck did you just say?'

Babich lifted his wrists, the chains that ran down to his ankle shackles clanked.

Brick smiled and shook his head, leaned back into his chair and tapped his foot on the Zero Halliburton case that contained the 'rendition assistance medication'.

'You want me to fucking sedate you?' Brick asked. 'That it? Russian fuck?'

Babich's stare was steady and he delivered his line with an even voice: 'Uncuff me. Kill your colleagues, and you'll be spared any pain.'

Brick's anger was back and he shoved Babich hard in the chest and then stood to strike.

'Enough,' Hutchinson said quietly, the satellite phone in one hand, the other on Brick's shoulder to hold him back. For all his bulk and aggression, Brick respected the chain of command and followed Hutchinson's order. Over his shoulder Hutchinson could see that Babich was enjoying getting under their skin. But that's all it was – just a game. Capel took the station opposite Babich, where the no-nonsense law-man resumed reading his book.

The aircraft jerked down five metres, sending both Hutchinson and Brick to the ground. This turbulence was really something else. The jet engines whined as if the Gulfstream were trying to take off.

'Severe turbulence!' the pilot yelled back into the cabin.

No shit.

Again they dipped and in a brief moment while the plane was under control, both agents scrambled into a seat and buckled in tight.

Wham!

The loud banging noise on the top of the fuselage had Hutchinson looking at the ceiling, half expecting baseball-sized hail to start coming through. He looked across to Capel, who stared back at him, wide-eyed.

Wham!

This time the aircraft seemed to rise at the nose, quick – then settle out. Something large had definitely hit the plane from above. Hutchinson craned his neck to look forward into the cockpit.

'Got no tailplane control!' the pilot yelled. 'Hang on back there!'

'Losing hydraulic pressure,' the co-pilot replied. 'Unusual vibration in the rudders.'

Hutchinson looked out the windows, the clouds were grey but wispy and clearing of obvious storm signs. He glanced at Babich, who sat, serene, staring right at him. Big shit-eating grin on his face.

'But why isn't it . . .' the pilot's voice trailed off. 'Oh my God!'

14

GIVERNY

Kate wasn't upstairs. Standing in the lounge room looking out the side windows Fox could smell last night's roast lamb among the wood-fire smoke of the outdoor pizza oven. Wisteria and grapevines hung down from the pergola's exposed timber beams, shading the long trestle table where he and Gammaldi had spent the previous night drinking wine, smoking Romeo y Julieta Short Churchill cigars and playing cards under the ripe red grape bunches. Kate had occasionally joined in the conversation from the open window above, where she'd been having a bath and reading, until eventually she'd called Fox up to the bedroom.

He'd been more than happy to join her then but where was she now? She'd woken with him at dawn, waved him and Renard off into the dark morning . . .

'Kate?' he called.

He found her in a nook behind the staircase – curled up on a cushioned bench-seat by a stained-glass window, her head tilted towards the light. He leaned against the kitchen doorjamb and watched her shift until she finally blinked awake.

'Hey,' Fox said, kissing her head.

'What time is it?'

'About nine o'clock.'

'I tried to stay awake when you left,' she said, looking up, her eyes happier than he'd ever seen them. 'Guess I dozed off.'

'I'll put the kettle on.' He went into the kitchen where Gammaldi was still unpacking the shopping bags.

'How was your first time driving in Paris?' Kate asked, following him into the kitchen, taking some cherries from a small brown paper bag.

'Interesting,' Fox said.

'Crazy drivers?'

'Yeah, something like that.' Fox shook his head, moving around to check the front windows again. All silent out on the driveway. The back of his neck still prickled with sweat, the muscles through his shoulders and back were tense. A good run or swim might help, but he couldn't afford either today.

'What is it?'

'Huh?' Fox said, looking back to Kate. 'Nothing, thought I heard something.'

'Probably Brujon chasing the crows out of the chicken coop.'

'Yeah . . .' Fox said. To leave or not to leave, that was the question. 'Maybe we'll head out for lunch today?'

'I thought we were going to stay in and send Al out.'

'I heard that!' Gammaldi said banging the pots and pans for emphasis before disapearing out the back door.

Fox caught himself staring down the gravel driveway again through the lounge room's lace curtains.

'Lach, what is it?'

'Sorry.' He turned to face her and her expression changed when she saw the look in his eyes.

'What?' She took a step back. 'What's wrong?'

'It's –'

'I've got some egg and bacon calzoni in the pizza oven,' Gammaldi called from outside.

Fox shook his head. 'It's – it's nothing.'

Kate tilted her head to the side, watching Fox closely. Her lips were dark red from the cherries.

'You're afraid?' She moved closer and put a hand on the side of his face, looked up to him and spoke quietly: 'You know no one's going to find us here . . . Or isn't that it? What? Is it me?'

'No,' he smiled at that thought and took her hand in his. 'No way.'

He picked her up and sat her on the kitchen bench and they hugged and kissed; one of those long, wet, five-minute exchanges enjoyed by teenagers.

'Get a room,' Gammaldi joked, standing in the doorway.

Fox and Kate laughed and Gammaldi started to make coffee. Brujon came barrelling in and dropped a tennis ball at their feet.

Gammaldi picked it up and tossed it out the kitchen window – the dog was off like a shot.

'You know,' Gammaldi said, eyeing all the food on the kitchen bench, 'I might not go back to the States next week . . .'

'There's food at home too,' Fox said. 'And a wife and kid.'

'There's nothing like this, though,' Gammaldi said, looking at the basket of fresh produce. He bit the end of a baguette. 'And I'm actually sleeping well. Emma's parents are back home at the farm; they're having a great time without me. Why not hang around here a bit longer?'

'Because we'll make you sick,' Kate said, making Gammaldi laugh.

Fox moved to the door and looked back through the front windows at the view across the driveway – Brujon was out there, ball in mouth, ears pricked and watching something, alert. Fox couldn't see anything sinister out there under the blue Normandy sky, but he knew to be wary: someone was coming.

15

HIGH OVER THE MED

'Losing cabin pressure!' the pilot yelled back to his passengers, through his oxygen mask. 'What the hell was that?'

'Something's hit us!' Hutchinson cried out. He held onto his armrests and looked from the window to the ceiling. 'Something's –'

He didn't know what to make of it. There was a round hole in the ceiling the size of a quarter and the air in the cabin seemed to change into white smoke as it was sucked out with a high-pitched whistling. A few seconds later the smoke had disappeared, the ragged little hole resembling a large-calibre puncture.

They had been descending fast. Hutchinson was being held up high in his seat, his weight against the lap-band seatbelt. He pulled an oxygen mask down and breathed in the rubber-tasting air. He could hear the pilots talking – loud but calm – running through instruments and flight controls.

'Pressure stabilised,' the pilot said.

'I'm getting no response –'

'Descent levelling –'

'That's not me, I'm not getting –'

'Holding at Flight Level 140.'

'No rudder – the rudder's gone!'

Hutchinson unclipped his belt to inspect the hole in the ceiling –

'Keep buckled up! We've got massive failure of the flight controls!' the pilot yelled into the cabin.

A shaft of sparks erupted above Hutchinson – then a loud banging noise.

'There's a larger craft on top of us!'

The two agents jumped from their seats, pulled off their oxygen masks and dived for the case of firearms.

'We're being hijacked!' Hutchinson tried to yell, struggling for breath. He looked out a window. Nothing but cloud – until . . . There, through the wisps of cloud cover he could see white wings far out-spanning those of the Gulfstream's. He looked over at Babich. The Russian was watching the three agents with bemused detachment.

'Capel, take him aft!' Hutchinson yelled, pointing to the prisoner.

The long blade of a sabre saw was cutting a manhole through the top of the thin metal fuselage and plastic cabin lining. Ten seconds and it'd be through.

Hutchinson ran to the cockpit.

'We're on full power and downward flaps and getting no response!' the pilot yelled. 'The thing on top of us is too powerful, too much lift – they're holding us level.'

Hutchinson looked back: Capel had Babich on the ground, while Brick had strapped on a kevlar vest and was positioned near the cut-out.

'Keep your door locked,' Hutchinson told the pilots, and headed back into the cabin.

The sabre saw was turning for the final section. Two seconds . . .

Brick fired off a couple of .45 rounds at where the saw operator would be. There was instant return fire, the FBI agent shredded to pieces by submachine-gun fire.

The sabre saw completed the hole, the piece of fuselage fell to the floor and two grenades dropped down at Hutchinson's feet. Gas began to fill the cabin. He couldn't see, and his lungs began to burn . . . He scrambled for the nearest oxygen mask.

16

GIVERNY

'We've got visitors,' Fox said.

He couldn't see them down the driveway yet, but Brujon was barking like he did when the morning bread and milk delivery was made.

'I can't see anything,' Kate said, also looking down the driveway. 'You sure?'

'I'm sure,' Fox replied, moving to the front room of the house and scanning through all the windows. 'Al, look alive, yeah?'

'What?' Gammaldi paused from making coffee, saw the look on Fox's face and shifted; it was battle stations.

Fox moved from the windows and back into the kitchen. He pulled the shotgun from the rack over the pantry door, opened the breech – an over-under double barrel – and it was empty. He went into the pantry and took a box of ten shells from the top shelf. He loaded up and hid the gun down by his side, the shells on the kitchen bench.

He moved towards the front room, on autopilot, the shotgun by his side ready to shoulder and fire, old instincts kicking in like an animal on the hunt or sensing a predator. Every sound – every breeze – *every thing* carrying information.

He stood still and took it all in. There were big windows along the kitchen wall and the back door was open to the Golf, its keys in his pocket, but the car itself unlocked. The stairs to the bedroom rose from the little nook between the kitchen and front room where he stood.

'Wassup?' Gammaldi asked, peeking through the lace curtains of the front room.

'Not sure . . .' Fox replied as he moved across the room to check the side views. 'Keep the curtains closed.'

Gammaldi looked at him questioningly – then saw how Fox always kept in close cover of the solid stone walls.

'The lace'll stop fragments of glass flying into the room,' Fox explained. He kept scanning sightlines, uncocked and cocked the breech, wishing he had something with more range and rounds than this antique.

Kate stood still against the kitchen door, looking at the gun in Fox's hands, her dark eyes sad.

'What is it?' she asked.

Brujon continued to bark.

'Nothing. Don't worry about it –'

A speck appeared at the end of the long gravel road that fed into the driveway. Fox strained his eyes to see through the growing cloud of dust – a black sedan. A black Peugeot sedan.

'Please, what's going –' Kate started.

'Maybe you should get into the pantry,' Fox interrupted, watching the car approach fast. No one knew they were here. Trees, fields, vineyards and olive groves were the only local witnesses to their seclusion. They hadn't followed him here, so they must have got the address somehow – Renard? Cloud cover moved in, like someone had just dimmed the lights outside. The sound of a jet overhead for the air show.

'You think they've found us?'

Fox looked to his friend. They'd been through the worst kind of situations a dozen times or more, always coming out thanking Lady Luck they were still alive. Gammaldi's arms were tense with anticipation – he picked up the bread knife from the dining table.

'Someone has,' Fox said. 'That's the car from earlier.'

The sedan came to an abrupt stop across the drive, fifty metres out from the house. There'd be no driving out unless he managed to navigate through the rows of trees to the grassed sides. Two figures emerged.

From behind the curtains Fox eyed the new arrivals. Brujon apprached them – and received a pat on the head from the Peugeot's driver, a tall willowy figure dressed in a tight black suit. The passenger, a big guy, popped a cigarette in his mouth, then leaned against the car.

The two of them shared a look, spoke to each other.

Fox passed Gammaldi the shotgun.

'Cover me – I'll stay close to the house.'

Gammaldi nodded, settled the gun into his shoulder as Fox walked outside.

The taller figure turned to face him. A woman.

As they neared each other more detail emerged. She was a very attractive woman, long dark hair, porcelain skin, high cheekbones and bee-stung lips – the kind of face you'd see on the cover of French *Vogue*.

The guy at the car stood still, his jacket open, watching Fox, unflinching.

The woman closed the distance to Fox fast. Early thirties, big black Jackie O sunglasses, the lean body of a runner with a slight curve at the hips. Fox stopped and looked over his shoulder. At the window twenty metres back, Gammaldi's face broke into a wide toothy grin. Fox cracked a smile in relief and turned back to the woman.

Slap! His face stung with the impact. Hard and powerful, like she'd had plenty of practice. He looked back at her, dumbfounded, rubbed his cheek, trying to figure out . . .

'That's for driving like an idiot,' she said. She reached into her jacket.

Fox instinctively grabbed her wrist as it came out with something in her hand, but she shifted her stance in the same instant and flipped him onto his back, pinning him to the ground with a booted foot on his chest.

The wind knocked out of him, Fox traced his eyes up the line of her tight pants to her face. She took off her sunglasses, matched his gaze with striking blue eyes.

'Hey!' Gammaldi walked out of the house, shotgun loose in his hands but the message clear. Brujon remained at the other guy's feet, who now had a black automatic pistol trained on Gammaldi's right eye.

Fox looked back up at the woman as his breath came back. Sky blue almond-shaped eyes framed by long black eyelashes.

In her outstretched hand, pointed at his face, the black item she'd pulled out – an ID wallet.

'It's all right, Al, stand down,' Fox called out. He heard the breech of the shotgun open. Still looking up from the ground,

Fox noticed the hip holster at the front of the woman's pelvis holding a compact service automatic. She lifted her foot off his chest and eased her hold on his wrist. 'She's a cop.'

17

HIGH OVER THE MED

Wind buffeted the manhole in the top of the fuselage as Hutchinson groped around for his dropped pistol in the dark cloud of smoke that was spreading from the grenade canisters. Babich had closed his eyes tight and held a deep breath before the gas reached him. The last thing Hutchinson saw before the smoke engulfed the cabin was Capel dropping his sidearm and making for an oxygen mask . . .

Hutchinson's eyes were burning and his lungs were starting to fade – CS gas? No, he'd met that enough times at Quantico and in the field; this was a taste he was unfamiliar with. He felt someone crash past him – thought he saw the pilot's door open. His Glock was somewhere on the floor, but he couldn't keep his eyes open for more than a second and his fingers felt only empty carpet. Red-hot tears were streaming down his face and his nose was running, but there was no controlling it.

His hands, neck and face felt as though they were on fire, so searingly hot he imagined they were blistering.

The gas seemed to thin just a little – through squinted eyes he could make out what lay beyond the manhole; the interior of another aircraft above. There was nothing he could do. He felt paralysed, his arms and legs useless now, his head dizzy and almost too heavy to keep up. He vomited where he lay across two seats, began choking on it.

A pistol shot rang out. Then the unmistakable gurgling sound as someone's throat was slit. A hot poker of pain, in and out of his thigh, then gone. Warm fluid washed over his leg. Something smashed into him, crushed his chest. It stopped his choking. He fought for air and Babich's eyes, wide and bloodshot behind a gas mask's visor, materialised above him for a second – then he was gone. Those smiling eyes, victorious, knowing. Hutchinson passed out.

18

GIVERNY

'You're a cop?' Gammaldi asked the woman in the driveway.

She flashed her holstered sidearm, the same make of SIG Fox had seen on the uniformed cops earlier that morning.

Gammaldi helped Fox to his feet.

'She's smokin'!' he whispered. 'I thought the French kissed in greeting: Did you hear that slap?'

'Hear it,' Fox replied, rubbing his cheek. 'I was on the –'

'Can we talk, inside?' the female cop asked, making it sound like an order.

'Please.' Fox dusted himself off as they moved indoors. Her partner stayed outside by the Peugeot, scanning the driveway and neighbouring fields.

Gammaldi put the shotgun and box of shells on the sideboard in the dining room.

'Zoe Ledoyen,' she said, her French accent both husky and no bullshit at the same time. 'My partner is Vincent. We are officers with the Direction Centrale du Renseignement Intérieur.'

'What's the "Reneregiment Interwerrier"?' Gammaldi asked, inspecting her ID wallet.

Two years ago Fox had dealt with their forerunner, the Direction de la Surveillance du Territoire of the French National Police, when he'd been working on a story involving a right-wing attempted coup here in France. They were as good as any specialist police agency in the world and they had the peculiar advantage of the French legal system which protected the cops and judiciary over the accused. He was sure that they weren't in the habit of unnecessary house calls.

'The DCRI, Al,' Fox explained, holding Zoe's gaze. 'National Police directorate specialising in counter-intelligence and counter-terrorism – a domestic intelligence agency, kinda like the FBI.'

Zoe nodded, 'A fair comparison.'

He made the introductions and noticed Kate and Zoe measure each other up. They were the same height, up to Fox's shoulders, but their appearances couldn't be more different: Kate, in her summer dress, was relaxed; Zoe, in her Dior suit, was calculating and observing. Kate had bed hair and sleepy eyes, the other woman had a severe black ponytail and clear blue eyes accentuated by black ink and dark eyebrows shaped just so. It looked like he and Kate left one 'stay indoors' situation in the States and here they were probably about to do the same in another country. Whatever this cop said, he'd be leaving with his friends today.

'You're looking for Renard?' Kate asked the cop.

'No,' Zoe smiled. 'I came here to speak with Lachlan.'

'Please, take a seat,' Fox said. The four of them sat at the dining table. Fox checked out their female guest a bit closer. The French cop was probably in her late thirties but could pass for ten years younger.

'So, what do you want?' Kate asked. 'I'm a lawyer and –'

'Yes, I know.' Zoe flicked through a few pages in a small black notepad. 'But you are registered on the bars in New York and District of Columbia, jurisdictions a long way from here.'

The two women shared a look.

Zoe looked at Gammaldi. 'You just made coffee?'

'Yeah,' he said, impressed she'd picked up the scent. 'I'll get you one.'

'*Merci.*'

Zoe ignored Kate and turned her attention to Fox as his friend ran to the kitchen. 'And you are a reporter.'

Fox nodded. He bit his tongue, refrained from asking questions: *Why had she followed him? How had she found them out here? How did she know about them?*

'Specialising in?'

'Hot spots,' Fox said, dusting the remnants of gravel from the driveway off his sleeve. The cop outside, Vincent, was throwing the ball for Brujon, who kept bounding off and bringing it back with the same insane speed. Fox rubbed his face where she had left a red mark – no doubt French women had slapping down to a fine art. Sharp and painful, an exclamation and expletive not to be quickly forgotten.

'Hot spots . . .' Zoe repeated. A small smile when his eyes met hers. She watched him closely. 'Like here?'

'This . . . This is more of a vacation,' Fox replied. He picked at the edge of the antique timber table. He found it really hard to look this woman in the eyes. He knew it was bad to avoid a cop's gaze – but with Kate sitting next to him he felt guilty just looking at her.

Gammaldi came back with the steaming coffee pot, placed it and the milk jug in front of Zoe, turned and got some clean cups from the sideboard.

'You can break that breech again, please,' she said to him. Her tone made him nod and he did as she asked before turning and placing the cups on the table and taking a seat at the other end, chastised.

'So,' Zoe said, pouring herself coffee. 'You are not doing some investigative reporting work here?'

Fox shook his head. He looked at Kate, she smiled back with her eyes. *La belle France.*

'Like I said, we came here for a holiday,' Fox replied. Kate rubbed her leg up against his under the table.

'So you are just tourists?' Zoe asked.

'What do you think we are? Terrorists?' Kate said.

Zoe narrowed her eyes at Kate and then took a sip from her coffee cup. The breeze picked up through the lace-curtained windows and Fox shifted in his seat.

'To tell you the truth, I came for the cheese,' said Gammaldi, holding up a torn piece of baguette with goats' curd on it. 'I think it was Charles de Gaulle who once remarked: *"How could one describe a country which has 365 kinds of cheese?"*. Well, allow me: this is the second greatest country on Earth, no doubt.'

Zoe looked like she didn't quite know how to take him.

Kate laughed beside Fox and it reminded him why he'd go anywhere with her. He pressed his foot against hers. She gave him a look he hadn't seen in a while; unease showing through . . .

As Gammaldi went on about some Paris law concerning the price of baguettes that segued into a soliloquy for his love of all breads, Fox shifted in his seat. What did this Zoe woman want? The way she'd followed him, and was now sitting here . . . He knew she was measuring, analysing, assessing. Perhaps her department's noses were out of joint that the FBI hadn't contacted them? He'd find out, take whatever rap on the knuckles was coming, and then get her on her way. The sooner the better: if *she* knew about them, Babich's network would, too.

'We just needed a change of scenery,' Fox said, interrupting his friend's lament of sourdoughs.

'Somewhere like here,' Zoe gestured around, 'the house of reporter Renard Rochefort?'

'He's a good friend,' Fox replied.

Zoe nodded, glanced at her small black notepad again.

'You must trust him,' she said, absently, more a statement than a question.

Fox didn't know how to reply – it seemed a strange comment – perhaps the FBI had contacted her? Perhaps Hutchinson had asked Zoe's agency to keep an eye on them, despite Fox successfully arguing the point last week that they were safe from reprisals now that Babich was headed to trial. The FBI man knew as well as Fox did that Babich's Umbra network held a grudge like a fatwa; until the person who decreed it renounced the order, you were a marked man. Well, Zoe's agency could get in line.

'And where is Renard now?'

'Working,' Fox said. He checked his watch. 'Driving still, I would imagine.'

'Working on . . . ?'

'A story.'

'His or yours?'

'Like I said,' Fox said, leaning forwards and pouring himself coffee. 'We're here to relax. Surely everyone dreams of lazily feasting on food and wine somewhere in rural France?'

Zoe's eyes narrowed and Fox knew Kate was watching him too. She knew he'd come here for a story, something with Renard that kept them talking late into the night, but neither she nor Gammaldi had bothered asking about it. She'd come to France, *insisted* on coming, and she'd been so happy to get away from the FBI that she'd never bothered to ask why or what for. She probably had her suspicions, but she'd let them slide. Now, from just a quick glance, Fox saw such questioning in her eyes, and he could tell that Zoe had picked up on it, too.

'So, back to Renard. You say he is *still driving*,' she said, looking up from her notes and giving Fox her full attention. 'Do you know where he is headed?'

19

HIGH OVER THE MED

Hutchinson was heading to hell in a handbasket. He could hardly breathe since he'd regained consciousness and his eyes felt like they'd had petrol poured over them. His fingers started to move, then his head, and he could see that the gas had cleared from the cabin. It seemed like a dream. A bad dream, devoid of senses but for the palpable fear of the inevitable.

Sound came back. Howling, deafeningly loud as the aircraft flew with its new manhole cut into the top of the fuselage. He looked out the window, his eyes watery, and saw the sparkling blue-green Mediterranean below. By looking at the horizon he confirmed the unavoidable – he was going down.

'Shit!'

He jumped up out of the seat – and fell flat on his face. He rolled onto his back and examined his right leg; a large patch of deep crimson surrounded a bullet wound through the meat of his thigh. Babich had shot him – he suddenly remembered everything. He sat up in the aisle and leaned against a seat.

Both his agents were down, Babich was nowhere to be seen, and the cockpit door was open. The pilot's head tilted to the right at an awkward angle and the dangling left arm of the co-pilot hung lifelessly between the two men.

Hutchinson pushed the weapons case from the floor, revealing the medical kit below. In a minute he had tied a tourniquet and wrapped a compression bandage around his thigh; there wasn't that much blood, although there was no exit wound. There wasn't much pain yet either. He put a couple of Fentanyl lollipops in his shirt pocket, then dragged himself up to a standing position, light-headed and unsteady. All his muscles ached and he knew then that the gas had been a nerve agent.

Move.

Hutchinson dragged himself to Capel's body, felt for a pulse on the side of his neck; he was gone. Brick's neck was sliced wide open. No time for lingering.

He hobbled forward.

Both pilots were dead. The autopilot was on, but the altitude meter was slowly ticking down – they'd just passed through ten thousand feet. Nine-nine. Nine-eight. If the bleeding didn't kill him, the crash would.

He no longer needed to worry about hypoxia – lack of oxygen – at this low altitude. He just had to worry about time.

'Mayday, Mayday, Mayday,' he said into the co-pilot's headset, dangling by the floor. He flicked through channels – the radio had been shot to shit. 'Mayday, Mayday . . .'

The altitude meter showed he was passing through 9,300 feet.

Emergency evac time.

Back in the cabin, he pulled out clothes from his overnight bag – took off his shirt and Kevlar vest, saw two nine-millimetre rounds had hit his chest – that's why he could hardly breathe before – put on a thermal top, jumper and zip-up jacket. He added a life vest, then slipped on a parachute and buckled it up. He almost tripped over the satellite phone case.

Hurry.

He opened the case and powered up the phone. It had signal – one bar . . . then none . . . then one . . . He typed a text message and sent it through with the GPS read-out on the phone's display screen, selected the 'repeat until sent' option. Sending, trying to send . . . Compared to the DoD sat phones, this thing was a dinosaur . . . Maybe it'd get through, though.

He blew the handle on the emergency door, the stairs sliding out and down into the fast-moving air. The morning sunlight on a brilliant sea. *Probably sharks down there . . . Great.*

He turned away and climbed down the stairs, facing towards the rungs, until his feet reached the last step, closed his eyes, said a prayer, and let go.

20

GIVERNY

Zoe was taking a call on her mobile phone, standing at the open front door, listening to the earpiece. Fox had told her where Renard was headed. It was no big secret, but if he had to guess he would say the cop didn't believe him. When the call came she'd excused herself, and he started to get angry. *Keep it cool, keep it controlled.* If his old CO in the Navy had anything negative to say about him, it would have been that he was impatient when there was a job to be done; something Fox and his unit mates regarded as a positive in most situations. Defusing an underwater mine being one of the few exceptions.

Kate had gone into the kitchen to make a fresh pot of coffee. She was standing at the old timber butcher's block and he admired her curves. She looked so sexy in her summer dress, her hair loosely tied back. Worth fighting for. Fox remembered the night before when they'd made love with the summer breeze coming in the open window, her body fitting with his. She looked across at him – a second of reservation – then she smiled and went out of sight to the stove.

Zoe's voice grew louder, but Fox's high-school French was too crummy to pick up any of her conversation.

He stared absently into his empty cup. All his adult life he'd felt like a foreigner – first with his military postings and then chasing news stories around the globe. Would he ever find a place and time where he felt like he belonged? He'd moved around a lot as a kid as well, for his dad's work, and then the military had been more of the same, until it just became habitual. Six months in one place was enough. Twelve months was a sentence. There was a constant hum in the back of his mind, an awareness that he had to *make* himself feel at home; as a native, you *are* at home, you don't have to contemplate your being quite so much. Kate put the freshly percolated coffee on the table and gave him a look: *What's she doing here?*

Fox's return look implied: *I don't know, but I'll hurry things up.*

'What is *terroir*?' Gammaldi asked, entering the room with a bottle of wine from Renard's pantry. He was peering at the label, thumbing off the dust.

'That is not easy to define,' Zoe said as she returned to the table, looking at Gammaldi as though he were an interesting creature. 'It is a French word, and everyone agrees that it is untranslatable into English.'

'There's disagreement over whether it exists,' Kate interjected. 'A romantic idea to make French wine seem better than it is.'

'It refers to the way that soil, light, topography and microclimate conspire . . . over generations of human stewardship, to endow a wine with its unique soul,' Zoe said to Kate, then looked to Gammaldi. 'How about that? It's a sense of place that you can taste.'

'*Terroir* is a marketing slogan disguised as something poetic,' Kate said. 'A hoax, just another piece of France dressed up to look better than it is.'

'An American should know . . .' Zoe said, 'since they've had precious little luck getting any *terroir* into their own wines.'

'Well!' Gammaldi said, appraising the bottle and leaning back in his chair. 'Whatever it is, I'm gonna drink a shit-load of it tonight.'

Enough was enough, Fox had to get things moving so that they could leave.

'So, Agent Ledoyen,' Fox said.

'Zoe.'

'Zoe. You follow me here. You call off cops chasing me through Paris –'

'It was far too dangerous to continue driving like that,' she said. 'Any other officer would bill you for those damaged police cars.'

Both Al and Kate looked at him – he shrugged.

'Was that phone call about me?'

'No.'

'Renard?'

She nodded.

'He's okay, isn't he?'

'We have someone watching over him.'

Why'd she ask where Renard was if she had someone on him?

'How'd you know where I was this morning?' he asked her.

'Interpol had your name in their system and the car rental agency flagged it.'

Fox thought about it. Interpol? Flagged? She'd been there so soon after he'd rented the car – literally just a couple of minutes – as if he'd been followed on foot since leaving Renard at *Le Figaro*. Maybe those two uniformed cops who'd stopped him . . . However she'd done it, the explanation was bullshit, but he decided to play along.

'Interpol?' Fox repeated. 'I'm on some kind of watch-list or something?'

Zoe sipped her coffee, set it down and measured him up.

'There was an incident two days ago,' she said. 'In Paris.'

'Incident?'

'Murder.'

She watched him closely. He raised his eyebrows and looked down at the table while he thought it through. Murder?

'And . . . ?' he went on eventually. 'Look, Zoe, I'm sorry, I don't follow.'

'It was the Russian Ambassador,' she said. Zoe looked at Fox very closely as she spoke. 'And his wife.'

Fox felt like he'd been hit in the guts.

21

PARIS

Boris Malevich couldn't get the ambassador's wife out of his mind – the look in her eyes as the blood drained from her neck.

Blood, her eyes bulging, brutal, struggling . . . And she didn't even have the diary.

Murderer. He'd live with it forever. But they would only have asked him to do this if the Rodina, his motherland, had been threatened. It wasn't murder when it was for the sake of the country, right? He was a soldier, killing in the line of duty, and they didn't call soldiers murderers, did they? No.

Not most of the time.

His country had come a long way in a short time with all the predictable problems associated with such rapid change. Without doubt there had been hope these past few years, genuine hope, for a prosperous future the like of which he'd never thought possible. When he'd travelled back to his home town the locals seemed at peace, content, happy even. Many of his friends still wanted some pieces of the old USSR to return, those who were angry at the rich men who had profited so much from the transition. But he'd argued there was an aspirational element to living in Russia now that had never really been there before – at least, not for many decades – and in his mind that far outweighed the negatives. There was a price to be paid for such improvements.

His handler had contacted him. *Activated* him, then kept in contact, each time with a new task. It always sounded like he was talking from inside an aircraft. He had been instructed clearly: *get the diary, kill the woman.* The diary would lead to the document: *get the document, whatever the cost.* Then, there would be a flight booked for him at the Charles de Gaulle Airport – under a new name, and the necessary identity papers and tickets would be waiting for him at the Aeroflot desk. The handler didn't say where the flight would take him, and Malevich didn't ask – saying too much over the phone was how the Americans caught you.

In return he'd get a bank account with a million euros in it. He'd have to give up everything he had here in Paris, disappear, but that was okay. A price had to be paid. *And oh, how he'd paid . . .* He could still see her blood when he closed his eyes. *Look at what they make you give . . .*

He looked across the street at the front doors of the *Le Figaro* office. Quiet. Someone coming and going every ten minutes or so. A thin, dark-haired woman exited, walked across the road and unlocked the car in front of him. She walked like a dancer. Reminded him of his sister. He would share a new life with her: they'd use this money and open a little bar, as they'd talked about so many times. Some place warm. It would mean freedom for her, away from the husband she'd married to get out of Russia, and a chance to set up a long, happy life, remember childhood fun and make new memories. The woman in the car in front signalled and drove out into the street, leaving behind a cloud of blue diesel smoke.

He'd finish this job and start a new life. He rubbed his eyes and tried not to think of the woman's dead face. Her neck. Her eyes.

His phone rang – the guys covering the back of the building.

'Yes?'

'He just got into a taxi –'

'Where?' Malevich started the car, scanned the street.

'Out back, following him now, about to drive behind you. Ten seconds.'

He ended the call, put the car in gear and followed the cab and the Citroën van as they flashed past.

22

GIVERNY

'We saw that on the news,' Kate said.

'No,' Fox said. 'We saw the report that the *ambassador* was killed there. They didn't mention his wife, and to my knowledge neither has the print press since.'

Zoe nodded, still watching him. *Yes*, Fox thought, *you know I've been following the killing. So what?* He remembered back to the footage of the ambassador being laid out on a stretcher. Surely, if Renard knew something about the wife's death, he would have said something?

'Are you saying they both died in the embassy explosion?'

Zoe shook her head.

'It wasn't from the local wine, I hope,' Gammaldi suggested with a grin that faded after Fox shot him a look.

'Forgive him,' Fox said. 'He was dropped on his head as a baby.'

'I'll go take your partner some food,' Gammaldi said. Zoe nodded and he looked relieved, as though the teacher had let him out of detention.

'The ambassador's wife,' Zoe said, turning to Fox, 'was found dead in their residence the same night as the explosion.'

She continued watching Fox's face carefully.

'How did she die?' Fox asked, knowing any reaction might make him look guilty. He felt sweat running down his back.

'Violently.'

'Russia is investigating?' he asked.

'Of course,' she replied. 'Through all the usual channels. This is a delicate matter for my government as the Franco–Russia relationship is an important one for us.'

Fox nodded. He was well aware that the two countries had strong economic ties – around thirty billion dollars and change annually between them. Russian exports to France were much like its relationship with the rest of Western Europe: dominated by energy commodities, metals and timber. In turn, Russia was a big market for imported French machinery, chemical products, and food. Recently, they'd been doing military projects together, and not just the small stuff: a ship worth half a billion euros was being considered for purchase by Russia. So there was a military angle, and France's standing as a leading country for diplomacy – well, no country wants a foreign diplomat murdered on their turf, let alone he and his wife in two separate attacks. *Important* was an understatement.

But he knew there was more.

'And there's something else?' he asked, prompting the detective.

Zoe topped up her coffee, stirred it, tapped her teaspoon on the saucer.

'I think the murder was, as you would say,' Zoe said, 'an inside job.'

'What – a domestic case between the husband and wife?'

'No,' she said, picking up some of Gammaldi's brioche with foie gras. 'I believe that the ambassador's wife was killed by a Russian agent.'

'As in an officer, or a sleeper?'

'The latter.'

Fox thought about that – an *agent*, not intelligence *officer*. Someone recruited by a serving member or Russia's own intel services, someone undercover, activated and likely deactivated now the job was done.

'Do you have any details you can share?'

She hesitated, then shook her head.

'So you're chasing a ghost on a hunch?'

'A chase would imply that we knew where he is,' Zoe said. 'But we are getting close, I'm sure.'

'How do you know that?'

'A source.'

'Your source FSB?'

'Something like that.'

Which meant it could be the FSB, Russia's internal intelligence agency, or the SVR, their external agency and CIA equivalent. Probably the SVR, Fox thought. The Sluzhba Vneshney Razvedki had taken over from the old First Chief Directorate of the KGB, and like their predecessor they handled the bulk of the field spooks out in embassies around the globe. That meant they were the ones who ran most agents abroad. Fox didn't press it.

'He was contacted on the day of the attacks,' Zoe said, 'earlier in the day, *activated* that day. You see?'

Fox tried to read her . . .

Zoe stirred her coffee.

'But he's not why you're here,' he said. *She had something connecting Renard, maybe? No, he couldn't be, could he?*

'No. Not specifically.'

'How does this relate to me then?'

Zoe dabbed her mouth with a napkin.

'Lachlan,' she said, tilting her head a little. 'A name was found on the ambassador's computer, several times, and it was last accessed moments before the explosion.'

Fox knew what was coming.

Zoe looked him square in the eyes: 'Your name.'

23

HIGH OVER THE MED

Hearing his name spoken and conversing in Russian was a beautiful thing, something he'd fantasised about for months. But this was no fantasy: this was homecoming.

'Welcome, Roman Babich, welcome,' Colonel Mikhail Lavrov of the SVR gave Babich a jubilant slap on the shoulder. Lavrov was a squat man, with a heavy brow, flat nose and square shoulders that reminded Babich of his grandfather's war photos of fellow tankers from Stalingrad. Lavrov's features were those of an old boxer, earned as a street thug in his youth working in East Germany. The first friendly face Babich had seen in six months. 'You're safe now.'

'Thank you.' Babich took the damp towel and bottle of water offered him by an operative and wiped his face again – his eyes burned, red and watering, and his lungs felt full of smoke. He'd been given an injection to counteract the nerve agent, and he'd felt almost immediate relief.

'My wife?' Babich asked.

'She's safe, hidden in St Petersburg.'

'You've done well,' Babich said. He thought back to the other plane: *A masked figure emerging from the cockpit. He was uncuffed, helped to a chain ladder that led to the ragged hole in the roof. He'd stopped at that agent, Hutchinson, who was writhing in pain from a leg wound and two shots to the chest that incapacitated him despite his bulky vest. Babich took a pistol from the floor and fired a round through the man's leg. He'd bleed out, yet still be alive in the crash. Let the self-righteous American suffer.* He cleared his thoughts.

'Where are we?'

'High over the Mediterranean,' Lavrov replied. 'Headed east.'

Babich looked around the aircraft, an Antonov 148. Its high-wing monoplane design – with the twin jet turbine engines mounted in pods under the wings, well clear of the bottom of the fuselage – made it perfect for the docking procedure they'd just performed.

It was a popular plane with the Russian leadership – he used this model himself for Umbra Corp's Siberian operations – but he could see that this particular plane had been modified by the Russian space team, Roscosmos. It had been customised with a hatch set into the middle of the floor. Lavrov must have sequestered this from his employer, the SVR, who operated such aircraft for mid-air rescues and take-downs. Babich liked what that act represented.

'All or nothing,' Lavrov said.

Babich nodded. Lavrov had risked a lot for him. He would pay him back.

'Relax,' Lavrov said. 'This is a Siberian long-range model – we will make the flight to Shanghai without refuelling.'

'You've done well.'

Babich clapped a hand on his shoulder. Lavrov could be depended on.

'The good days are arriving again, my friend,' Babich said. 'And we will be present to herald in their dawn.'

Lavrov nodded and passed Babich a flask of vodka. He took a couple of sips, closed his eyes and smiled. Like mother's milk. He could have cried; he'd been dreaming about this taste for months. He looked out the window, the sky was clear and bright as they headed east.

'The American aircraft?' Babich asked, although he didn't really care.

'It will fall from the sky soon,' Lavrov said. 'They will waste their time following it, before watching it go down. More time still retrieving the wreckage, sifting through it. It will buy us the hours we need to be out of their reach.'

'Time, time, time . . .' Babich said, smiling. He took another sip. 'They wasted so much of mine, it's only fair that we waste theirs.'

The Americans would watch their aircraft go down and they'd assume he was on it. By the time he went public he'd be untouchable.

'Now,' Babich said, taking another sip of vodka, 'where are we with the operation?'

24

GIVERNY

'So he was looking at some of Lachlan's news items?' Kate offered to Zoe. She sat forward, ready to defend Fox while being apprehensive of the unknowns. 'Some news piece about Roman Babich's arrest?'

Zoe shook her head. 'I do not believe in coincidences.'

She paused, waiting for Fox to fill in the blank.

He shrugged and turned his attention to Gammaldi who sat back down and grabbed a hunk of cheese.

'Wassup?' he asked Fox. He knew Fox was stalling for time and was milking his pain for fun.

'Nothin'. Wassup with you?'

'Nothing like what you've got going on,' Gammaldi said, leaning back in his chair. That was Gammaldi. You'd assume he was constantly thinking about food or football or books about war, but he was always alert, always in the present, taking in the conversation even if he wasn't a part of it.

'I don't know how I can help you,' Fox said to Zoe. 'I've never spoken to the ambassador. I've had nothing to do with him, no contact at all.'

'Okay,' Zoe said. 'We also came across your name in the ambassador's residence –'

'Maybe from another news item?'

'It was found among his wife's papers,' Zoe took a folded page from her notepad and held it out to him.

It was a picture. Katya. The Russian Ambassador's wife. Fox couldn't hide his interest.

'Tell me, Lachlan,' Zoe asked. 'Why were you in contact with her?'

Fox looked at the sheet of paper for a long time. He wondered why Renard hadn't returned his call. He wondered if the Frenchman knew about this.

'She contacted me about a month ago,' Fox finally admitted.

Zoe continued to eat, she didn't appear surprised. Neither did Kate, but he could feel her questions hitting him – silent, full of anger. He turned to talk to her, wanted to tell her how much he loved having her here, that it wasn't just about Umbra and Babich, it was about so much more – it was about getting their life back. But Zoe wasn't done.

'Why did she contact you?'

Fox exhaled, loudly.

'She said she had some information that might help my story and the case against Babich,' he said. 'In return, she wanted help – US government kind of help . . . I got the sense she wanted to defect.'

Zoe's expression changed. 'Come on, Lachlan, you make it sound like the Cold War is still going on.'

He didn't much like her tone. Gammaldi lit up a cigar and gave him a look: *You're the one that brought us into this fire.*

'She wanted money . . . and safety. She felt threatened by what would happen if she spoke out.'

'Spoke out?'

'Yes. Babich has people everywhere.'

'Why would she ask for this kind of help from a *reporter* . . .'

'Maybe she trusts reporters more than she trusts the authorities.'

'I do not buy that.'

'Well, I don't know what to tell you.'

'Try.'

'Some questions don't have answers – especially when it comes to other people's motivation.'

Zoe pulled out a silver lighter and lit a slim cigarette. 'Or maybe you just don't want to share?'

'Maybe she trusted you, Lachlan?' Kate offered. But she made it sound like any trust was misplaced. 'Maybe she'd seen your work on the Babich case and thought you'd be a safe bet. Maybe she knew you too well, that you wouldn't let the story go, no matter how hard it got, so she thought, *Why not? He'll help me, he helps everyone, can't say no –*'.

'Kate . . .'

Zoe sat up, like there was a new target in the room. Maybe she was hoping that this would get a rise out of Fox, that some other truth would be revealed in the domestic exchange. Fox turned to Zoe while Kate seethed.

'I hadn't met with Katya, if that's your next question,' Fox said, bringing Zoe's gaze back to him. 'Nor do I know exactly what it was she had to offer.'

'Some people say Babich, on his way down, will take half the Russian establishment with him,' Zoe said. Her voice became both matter-of-fact and dreamy at the same time, as if she were spelling it out in neon signage. 'And all this because of you, the reporter from Australia . . .'

'I helped bring him in, that's all. I wrote a few stories – like Kate said, Katya must have seen my name in some by-lines and knew I'd be interested.'

'How did you bring Babich in?' Zoe asked, still focused.

'It's kind of a long story,' Gammaldi offered. 'Not *Les Miserables* long . . . more Le Carré long – his recent stuff –'

'I found a kink and I opened it up,' Fox said, ignoring his friend's musings. 'Babich was a former spook and kept all his intelligence officers around him when he went into the business world. He had seasoned personnel and serious capital to burn. He was good at fostering relationships, and smart enough not to bother those in Putin's power circle. Eventually I found a way in.'

Zoe leaned back in her chair. 'So,' she said, 'the real reason you're in France was to meet with Katya?'

'And holiday,' Fox said, looking across at Kate, but she'd gone silent. 'And Al's here because he thought he could single-handedly eat the local economy out of recession.'

Gammaldi smiled through a mouthful of cheese loaded on a long baguette and gave a thumbs-up and a wink. 'Thank me later.'

Zoe blew her smoke towards the open front door, took a sip of water and focused on Fox a little harder. 'Then why the shotgun, why the car chase, the hiding – who from?'

'Bad guys.'

'Babich's guys?'

Fox nodded and felt Kate's uneasiness beside him.

'Anyone know you're here?' Zoe asked.

'Besides you and Inspector Clouseau out there?' Fox replied.

'I followed you, remember?'

'I thought I lost you in La Defense?'

Zoe smiled, stubbed out her cigarette, and ate a slice of fruit. Fox figured maybe the hire car had some kind of LoJack system, like the kind the police used to track stolen cars. He could have driven half-way across Europe and there'd be someone behind a screen somewhere tracking a little dot on a map.

'No one knows we're here aside from my boss and the FBI agent who's in charge of the operation.'

'You don't think you need protection here?'

'We're off the grid, no one could find –'

'I found you.'

'Yeah, well . . .'

'If Babich is as connected as you make out,' Zoe said, 'his people will find you, yes? Then what? He will have you killed?'

'There might be reprisals from those loyal to him,' Fox said, leaning forward, 'but know this: Babich will not be allowed to harm anyone again. His days of giving orders are well and truly over.'

25

MEDITERRANEAN SEA

Hutchinson came to the surface, gasping for air. He'd landed in a mess, the parachute falling over him. He untangled himself from the lines, rolled onto his back and backstroked away. His eyes burned, his leg was numb, and the muscles all through his shoulders felt strange. Closing his eyes, he floated in the water and caught his breath, letting his adrenaline settle. He kept his movements slow, steady, not wanting to appear like the wounded snack that he was. There would be sharks below, waiting. Hungry.

Great.

When he next saw Babich . . . He had some good ideas about what he'd do. The moment would come none too soon. The aircraft was fast disappearing, soon to be just an invisible speck closing on the horizon. His own descent had been silent but for the wind buffeting his face as he free-fell the first few thousand feet. Once his chute was deployed he'd felt a sense of calm to be floating away from the aircraft and all it contained.

He tapped the little plastic emergency radio beacon mounted on his life vest as he floated along, out at sea, alone. It said in small stencilled type that it had a water-activated switch. That it was made in China. That was okay, his chute probably was too. What wasn't? A US-made rescue aircraft, that's what. Flown and crewed by American servicemen. That'd be a sight. He reached into his shirt pocket, a tight squeeze under his life vest. Took out the painkiller lollipop, unwrapped it and savoured it like a fine cigar. He looked up at the sky and waited. If his message got out, there would be search and rescue crews on their way. If it didn't . . . He really didn't want to think about that. Nothing to do but wait for whatever was coming.

26

WASHINGTON, DC

USA

It was just past 3 am when Bill McCorkell arrived at the headquarters of the Department of Homeland Security (DHS). He rubbed the sleep out of his eyes as he sat in a line of about five vehicles awaiting entry at the visitors' gate. He re-read the message Special Agent Valerie Child, Hutchinson's second in command, had forwarded through after she'd woken him from a bad dream. It seemed he'd gone from one nightmare to another. The message was the simple distress signal in the form of a text message, picked up from the sat phone Hutchinson had with him: *B taken in air. SOS going down, all hands KIA – AH.*

Everyone killed except Hutchinson? And Babich taken in the air? It wasn't possible. Sure, the Brits and the US had a few aircraft capable of docking with others in flight for emergency rescue, and maybe the Ruskies had something similar sitting in mothballs from better days . . . But *overwhelming* another aircraft in flight? A Gulfstream with Navy pilots and armed FBI agents aboard?

He showed his ID at the gate and parked his Lexus RX 450h close to the building the Umbra task force had been using as a headquarters for the last few months. Housed in the federal western campus on the sprawling grounds at St Elizabeths Hospital, Anacostia, there was an odd feel to this place. The site, established in 1855 as the Government Hospital for the Insane, was now leased by Homeland Security and staffed by intelligence and security desk drivers; still a hospital of sorts. He walked fast to the building, the clear brisk night a good wake-up.

Valerie had insisted the message had been verified by the National Security Agency (NSA). He'd met her a few times and was more impressed at every turn; she was a smart operator, good under pressure. She wouldn't have got him out of bed for a drill.

He noticed her as soon as he entered the building's security airlock and she looked relieved to see him. He'd served under four presidents as a special assistant for National Security, including three stints as that office's principal adviser. Now, on the other side of fifty-five and with some greener pastures looming on the retirement horizon, he was winding down, taking more of a back seat. The current West Wing team was good, the best he'd seen, and truth be told the last couple of administrations had worn him out; he knew it was time to move on while he was still capable, still useful. He was now counting down the days and working out of a cubby hole in the EEOB next to the White House, clearing his desk of old business, offering advice when sought, being called upon in emergencies. Like now.

'Hutchinson?' was the first thing McCorkell said as he neared earshot.

'Still hunting for him,' replied Valerie.

'Don't DoD life vests have beacons?' he asked as they shook hands.

'They do, but we've got nothing on the grid,' she replied. 'He might not have put one on.'

McCorkell couldn't imagine Hutchinson bailing out of an aeroplane without grabbing a vest. Then again, it would have been a harrowing, quick decision, death all around him; he may not have been thinking straight. No – he'd had the presence of mind to send out the sat phone message. He'd be out there somewhere, a drop in the sea.

'Maybe the transponder is malfunctioning,' McCorkell said, rubbing a hand through what was left of his cropped hair.

'Yeah,' Valerie said. 'They're on it . . . If it pops up, we've got him. SAR crews are closing on the GPS location of where he sent the message; six aircraft and counting. Our guys, NATO, Italian Coast Guard; if they have a plane or a boat and eyes, we're getting them out there. Call it fifteen minutes to station and then they'll set up a search grid.'

'Our aircraft – the Gulfstream?'

'Dead in the air, still following its flight path, but descending.' She looked strained, he could tell she was thinking about the agents on board. 'Navy's got F18s scrambling out of Naples, they'll have a visual any second.'

The F18 pilots would track it now and if it didn't respond, they'd be forced to shoot it down before it entered the skies over the Italian land mass. The hustle of the joint agency and departmental staff proved they weren't capitulating.

'Sorry to call you in the dead of night,' Valerie said, 'but you were first on Hutchinson's "break glass in case of emergency" list.'

'Well, I guess I should earn my spot,' McCorkell said. Already sixteen bleary-eyed agents and staffers milled about the room, many on phones, their voices more animated than their outward appearance. Every few minutes another one would enter the doors, yawning away the last of their sleepiness. FBI, CIA, NSA, DoD; they all had a role to play in a task force that was meant to be in the process of winding down and closing up shop.

'Use the desk next to mine,' Valerie offered. He put his jacket over the chair, saw the picture on the desk – Hutchinson with his wife and kid.

'How can you best use me?' he asked.

'We need someone to quarterback the play here,' Valerie said. 'Make sure the priorities are straight and the workload efficiently spread.'

He read between the lines: *Make sure the multi-agency and military staff play nice.*

'And deal with any overseas brass or station chiefs who slow us down.'

McCorkell nodded, studied the end wall, made up of a movie-theatre-sized LCD screen not dissimilar to the one in the White House's Situation Room. One segment showed a map of the Mediterranean with a small blinking dot. The last known GPS point. Right in the middle of nowhere, empty all around.

The automatic doors hissed open again and a figure with a noticeable limp walked in.

Bob Bowden. CIA department head – he'd made plenty of friends and a few enemies in the intel community when he was one of the more senior CIA officers to speak out against the creation of the Office of the Director of National Intelligence, seeing it and its offshoots as a threat to the standing of his agency. McCorkell didn't mind such redundancies when it came to national security, but at the same time he respected men like

Bowden, who were vocal and steadfast in their belief in their agencies.

'Bill?' Bowden said, making a beeline for McCorkell. 'What are you doing here?'

'Hi Bob.' The guy looked awake, he'd give him that. A life used to sleeping on a knife-edge. Didn't bother with a handshake. 'I'm helping out.'

'Any news on Hutchinson's location?' he asked Valerie.

'No, we'll have eyes over his last known position in ten to fifteen minutes.'

'Good,' Bowden replied. For the last six months he'd been the lead CIA officer on this task force. McCorkell knew he'd relish control of the op. Didn't take a crystal ball to conclude that this CIA man would have handled everything differently from the start; a covert action 'snatch and grab' rendition of Babich to some place where torture was taught in the schoolyard, a dank cell where the Russian would see out his days as he was bled for information. Bowden was convinced Babich's case was an integral part of the Global War on Terror and as such beyond legal issue, especially one handled by some mid-level FBI investigator like Hutchinson. No doubt there were others in this very room who felt the same way.

'We got anything happening out of the normal?'

'Intelligence traffic has picked up among known Babich loyalists in the Russian political and military contacts,' Valerie replied.

'Picked up how? Significantly.'

'Almost tripled.'

'We haven't seen that pattern since his arrest.'

'Yep.'

Bowden was silent. There were two things that struck McCorkell above all else about the guy: he didn't trust *anybody*, and he was a man of action. A veteran from the CIA's Special Activities Group, he was shunted to a desk a couple of years back after years of directing paramilitary teams in Pakistan to capture or kill top leaders of al-Qaeda. These small teams, designed to carry out surgical strikes on High-Value Targets, were phased out with the last administration and largely replaced with armed Predator and Reaper drones as the potent new weapon against the enemy. While CIA officials continued to pursue the program of specialist boots on the ground as an additional lethal option – every military and intelligence commander wanted to have such capacity because one cannot predict opportunities – McCorkell knew that the kind of pointy-end work Bowden had specialised in was coming to an end. A drone flying at ten thousand feet, armed with Hellfires and piloted by operators sitting at screens here in the States had become the more politically and financially acceptable mode of covert action. Bowden was not so much a dinosaur as a practitioner of what was becoming a lost art: the hands-on field spook.

'You work on finding Hutch, I'll take Babich,' Bowden said to Valerie, then looked at Bill, before he limped over to his team.

'What didn't you tell him?' McCorkell asked Valerie. She looked at him.

'So,' Bowden said, turning all his energy on his CIA crew down the far end of the room. 'Where's this son-of-a-bitch Roman Babich?'

Valerie said quietly to McCorkell, 'Well, the dog's off his leash. How long do you think it'll take them to find Babich?'

McCorkell was wondering not so much where Babich *was*, but what he'd be doing.

'Not soon enough,' McCorkell said. 'But you didn't answer my question.'

'One of the intelligence files,' Valerie replied. 'He'll find it soon enough, but I want to find Hutchinson before he freaks and takes our operators away from the SAR effort.'

'What was the file?'

Valerie handed him a print-out: NSA call sheet, a phone intercept of a conversation between two parties. Neither named beyond their code-word covers, which meant maybe the NSA knew their IDs or maybe they didn't.

'How'd we get the intercept?' McCorkell asked.

'Echelon hit it a few months back, keywords lighting up that it was Umbra and Babich-related. Been tracking the caller's voice pattern ever since, but he uses an encrypted cell –'

'So we're not getting every call?'

'Maybe twenty per cent.'

McCorkell nodded. He knew that the NSA had made good inroads into Russia's scrambling equipment since acquiring their last-generation encrypted satellite phone from a dead FSB officer in the South Ossetia War of 2008. Clearly their new set-up had improvements. The location of the caller was, 'In transit, Ukraine, unknown cell number,' and the receiver was in Moscow with what was designated as a known landline number. He scanned over all the restricted handling information:

TOP SECRET – SCI UMBRA TASK FORCE.
Translated from Russian by #4016 at NSA FM.
INIT: Subject RED.

RECIP: Subject MOSCOW BRAVO.
R: 'Get ready to move.'
MB: (Surprised) 'When?'
R: 'Now. Twelve hours –'
MB: (Louder) 'That is too soon!'
R: 'It is what it is. Be prepared for the fallout. You need to move before they do.'
PAUSE, TEN SECONDS.
MB. 'We will be ready.'
Call ENDS.

McCorkell looked up from the transcript in his hands. 'Twelve hours?'

'I know. If they were referring to the break-out of Babich, it happened earlier,' Valerie said. 'This deadline was for around noon our time, which means . . .'

'That maybe they weren't referring to that . . .' McCorkell said.

'Yeah, could be anything,' Valerie agreed. 'One thing I know: counter-terrorism intel operators like Bowden get pretty twitchy when they intercept words like *fallout.*'

An agent beckoned Valerie over to talk on the phone.

McCorkell sat down in the chair at his – Hutchinson's – desk. The intercept was too vague to draw conclusions. What would Babich do now he was free? What kind of orders would roll off his tongue first? Revenge on those who'd brought him in? People like Lachlan Fox. Fox had earned McCorkell's respect several times over – the guy's conviction in following the truth through extreme adversity could never be underestimated. McCorkell would give the man any job, he trusted him implicitly. He'd never doubted Fox's ability to look after himself, but everybody was fallible. It was just a matter of time.

He watched the dots converge. *Could be anything.* Looked at his watch. He pulled out his phone and sent Fox a quick text: *Hutchinson had trouble in transit. Babich loose. Watch back. Call in asap.*

27

GIVERNY

'You live in America?' Zoe asked.

'Don't hold that against me,' Fox replied.

'Those days have passed,' Zoe looked at Kate for a second, then back to Fox. 'We fought in their country to help them achieve independence, they fought here to rid us of Nazis. Let's call it square.'

Gammaldi laughed.

'Having watched the recent eight years with horror,' she said, 'I am of course thrilled about their last election because the potential to go wrong in America is so huge and now, at last, is someone genuinely impressive, someone who can help heal that great wound in American life and so the rest of the world.'

'You think?' Kate asked.

'Yes,' Zoe replied. 'And you got yourselves and therefore the rest of us in terrible fiscal trouble, now we all have to work harder to get out of it.'

'Well,' Kate said, 'I guess that's the disadvantage of being the world's leading economy.'

'I am a believer that this is still an American world, that you will still hold the mantle, as it were,' Zoe said. 'You are down, but you're not done yet. It will take time and sacrifice, but you handle both well; yours is such a young country.'

'And France is going where, politically?' Kate asked, one eyebrow arched. 'Western Europe seems little more than an open-air museum to me. Nothing wrong with that, but it's all about the past, there's no direction for a future; certainly nothing like where you've come from a couple of hundred years ago.'

'You're probably right,' Zoe said, looking at her mobile-phone screen. 'When our president was elected in 2007 on a right-wing, pro-American platform of *la rupture*, he promised to break many of the traditions and laws of a calcified Fifth Republic.'

'Expectations ran high,' Fox said.

'True. He appointed a diverse cabinet, including socialists, a number of chic women, and members of minorities . . .' Zoe went back to her closed, guarded self. Then looked to Kate. 'But, you know, it is interesting that you say this is a museum. Perhaps in a couple of hundred years your nation will have a similar history – a playground for tourists marvelling at what once was.'

The women traded a look and Fox tried to end this conversation.

'It seems to me,' he said, 'that America is a wild place, an awesome place and, like Henry James, I very much believe it to be a world in itself rather than a country. As a place it is very difficult to generalise.'

'Hmm, listen to us, fixing the world around this table,' Zoe said. She sipped her coffee and sat more upright, looking directly at Fox. 'Tell me about Renard.'

He knew what she meant: Could Renard have killed the Russian Ambassador and his wife?

'Renard's not that sort of guy.'

'Not what sort?'

'Not a murderer.'

'How long have you known him?' She lit a new cigarette and waved the smoke away.

'Not long,' Fox admitted. 'We met in '09, covering the Summit, then we did some work on the Clearstream scandal together. He's done freelance work for our organisation, GSR, for over seven years, almost two decades at *Le Figaro* –'

'Yes. Where's his wife?'

'Dijon, I think,' Fox said. It was true.

'Yeah, I remember,' Gammaldi said, 'because of the mustard. She took the kids to visit their grandparents.'

Fox shifted in his seat.

Zoe took a folded piece of paper from an inside pocket of her coat. Passed it to him.

'Call log from Renard's phone,' she said. 'The day he called you.'

Fox scanned it, a list of numbers. Two stood out – his GSR office number, and then a mobile number that was repeated several times. Those calls were made about twenty minutes before the one to him, and once again a few minutes afterwards. Duration was always less than a minute.

'I have seen the transcripts of the calls,' Zoe said. 'He was talking with Katya.'

The wheels of Fox's mind were turning. The call sheet didn't match his version of events. Katya had first contacted him, then *he'd* called Renard to bring him in on this. It was on the same day. That call to his office had been transferred to his iPhone – he had been in Connecticut at the time. He'd then spoken to Renard and asked him to assist on this story as his local specialist, his fixer. But now what Zoe was saying, and what this call sheet seemed to prove, was that Renard knew about Katya first.

'Katya contacted him, and then – what, he told her to contact me . . . and then played dumb when I called him?'

Zoe shrugged.

This made no sense . . . Gammaldi and Kate looked at each other and back to Fox, sharing in his concern, but they were even more in the dark than he was.

'You've read the transcript of this conversation I had with Renard?'

'Yes,' Zoe said. 'He was – how did you say this . . . Playing dumb?'

'He organised to have me come here?'

'That is a possibility,' she said. 'We will know soon enough – I have agents watching him.'

'In Dijon?' Gammaldi asked.

'No,' Zoe said. 'He is in Paris, still at his office.'

Fox couldn't put it all together. Why would Renard invite him out here to the Normandy countryside then go off and work behind his back? Could he have killed Katya?

'You need to realise he was using you.'

'Why don't we just call Renard and clear this up?' Gammaldi offered.

'Because, my food-loving Australian friend,' Zoe smiled and picked up a fig with some cheese on it, 'that's not how police work goes. Let me tell you what we are going to do.'

Before she could say more, her phone rang again. She looked at the screen, as if weighing up whether to answer or not, then stood and took the call. She headed out the front door for privacy.

Gammaldi shrugged and pulled the cork from a bottle of red.

'What?' he said, pouring himself a glass. 'It's like midnight tomorrow back in Australia.'

Fox went to the kitchen to get his iPhone.

He'd heard it bleeping and as he picked it up realised it was Kate's . . . She'd been on it a lot these past few months – friends back in the Netherlands, he supposed, and her estranged parents back in Manhattan who were making up for lost time and misplaced grief. She had a missed call, overseas area code . . . *China?*

Kate came into the kitchen. She wrapped her arms around his waist and hugged his back. He put the phone down. He turned – could tell she saw frustration and fear in him – and leaned in to kiss her.

'You slept well last night,' she said, running a hand through his short mess of hair. Her own hair had gone back to its natural auburn and she had put it up in a short ponytail. Dark eyes, a couple of years younger than Fox. When he'd first met her she'd reminded him of actress Eva Green, but she looked different now: freckles peeked through her tan, she wore no make-up except some eyeliner and lip gloss . . . He thought about that first meeting in St Petersburg. Their train ride from Russia to Lithuania. It had been dark then, when they'd first kissed and come together. *'Don't leave me alone again,'* she'd said, moving towards Fox, wrapping her arms around him. She put her head hard against his chest and held him tight, as if he might disappear . . .

'I won't,' he'd assured her. It was so easy to lose time with her.

'Here I was thinking maybe we could go for a drive today,' she said. 'Just me and you, take a late lunch somewhere; Rouen, maybe? Drink wine and watch the sunset, make love on the bank of a river and sleep in the summer night . . . Guess that's gone to shit.'

Fox looked at the wall. Felt Kate's heart beating against his chest. Her phone bleeped again – it was buried among the produce on the bench. He put a hand to her face, guided her lips up to his and kissed her. He wanted to stay with her and lay in the shade of a tree out back, listen to music and never move or change a thing. He remembered a night he'd spent with her on a house boat on the East River, looking back at Manhattan, when he'd woken from a nightmare and she'd comforted him, saved him from thoughts that had chased him for years. He knew she could read all that now, in his eyes – that and so much more.

'You don't always have to be the one to make everything right,' she whispered to him.

'I know.'

'I don't want you to investigate anything, I mean. Let it go –'

'It's not that simple,' Fox said. A small lie, and the dots weren't connected yet so it was almost the truth. It was simple, sure. Leave it be. Walk away. But he'd never been able to do that. He wanted the running and hiding to stop as much as she did. He had to work to make that happen.

Hard work.

'Look,' he said, 'I'll go with Zoe to Paris, suss out Renard, get all this cleared up, and then we'll just chill, yeah? No more reporting work, I'll leave it be. Stay in the middle of nowhere until the money runs out, then I'll get a job.'

'A farm job . . .'

'Ha! Sure, a farm job.'

'Do you really think you could do that? Walk away from this life?'

'I'd sure like to try.' He looked pleadingly into her eyes, hoping for understanding.

'But there's just this one last job . . .'

'Yeah,' he said, moving to the sink.

Kate smiled, rested against him. 'Okay.'

He smiled back. Upbeat. But it was an act. She may have seen through it, but really she didn't know the half of it.

His eyes were everywhere. Scanning. Sightlines. The directions of the birds outside. Listening. The sounds coming in the open back door and kitchen windows. Brujon ran out from the side courtyard and stood by the car; the dog's posture alert, listening. He turned towards the driveway, still, ears pricked, then sped off to bark at some visitor out of sight.

This was it. That last job. It was happening now. This was the end.

28

HIGH OVER EUROPE

'We had to put an end to him,' Lavrov said, as Babich chewed a thick slice of Italian sausage on black bread. 'Our ambassador in Paris? He was selling you out.'

'What?' Babich responded. This was news. He'd owned that man for over a decade. Still, owning something meant it had a price. Anything with a price was for sale. It was a game he'd never really lost, adhering to Pablo Escobar's silver or lead – 'take the money or face the bullets' – school of thought.

'He made a deal with Moscow –'

'When?'

'After you were taken in.'

'How long after?'

'Three months.'

'When the papers said I was going to trial?'

'Likely, yes.'

'At least he waited. How did you deal with him?'

'With finality. Paris police are sifting through dust, they'll be chasing ghosts for months.'

Babich nodded. He watched as Lavrov's men played cards in the aft section of the cabin. Nothing to worry about, the ability to switch off like that, switch on when called upon, a simple existence. He'd never felt like that.

'He only knew of the diary?' Babich asked, dipping the crust of his bread in some vodka. It had been a long time since he'd had such a decent meal. The closest he'd had to this in the United States was a hot-dog and a non-alcoholic beer while in detention in one of the FBI's cramped windowless prisons. So short-sighted, those law-men. So reactionary.

'The diary, and an idea of what it led to, that was all.'

'So he thought he'd go out and get a better offer from our so-called government . . .' Babich ate some more sausage. Looked out the window at the bright day. Probably nearing Turkey now. No, they'd probably fly over Syria, the Caspian, Iran, then skirt around Pakistan. Lavrov's pilots would know the safest route outside American spheres of military influence.

'He was a foolish traitor.' A simple statement. The way Lavrov said it and the way he shook his head made Babich think he would have liked to have ended the ambasssador with his own hands.

Babich shook his head. 'No. He respected money more than anything. Simple as that.'

'His wife was leaving him, too,' Lavrov said. 'Either way, the whereabouts of the secret protocol was going to go direct to Moscow, or to the Americans via the wife. We had to move as we did.'

'You did well.'

Lavrov smiled. Babich asked him, 'Where are they now?'

'Who?'

'Not who. The diary and –' Babich stopped himself. He could see the answer written on his man's face.

Lavrov stammered. He said, 'They are – we'll get them.'

Babich's grip on his glass tightened. 'You don't have them?'

'We had to move.'

'And where, my dear friend . . .' Babich began, leaning in close, 'where is the document, this secret protocol?'

Lavrov looked uneasy.

'We are gaining possession of the diary at any moment –'

Babich clenched his fists.

'There was no choice!' Lavrov said.

'You couldn't get what we needed at the same time?'

'It – it was our only choice given the time frame,' Lavrov reasoned.

Babich put his drink down on the floor. The cabin was sparse, decked out for paramilitary operatives. Lavrov had five men on board, one shot through the hand, but resting it.

'If people look closely into *their* business,' Babich said, 'they might then find out about *our* business, see?'

'By then – it will be too late – we will have made our move.' Lavrov could see his boss was not impressed. 'We have just hours, not days, to see our success, comrade. Hours . . .'

Babich reminded himself of all Lavrov had done. He was no fool, to be fair, and he wouldn't have acted on a whim. His hand had been forced. Okay, sure; it was forced and he acted, but to come away empty-handed? And they had only hours to go. *Hours!*

'Where is it?'

'Paris.'

They *knew* it was in Paris? Big place, small document, hidden by a Russian diplomat over a century ago. Until Babich saw it with his own eyes, he did not *know* anything. He winced and felt at his heart.

'And the timing . . . Hours to go,' Babich said. 'You are killing me, Mikhail, killing me.'

He closed his eyes and let himself smile. He was a free man and he would soon be the leader of his country. Why not believe optimistically like his friend here? Was it a weakness to be so? Was it being ignorant to the realities?

'It will all work out,' Lavrov said. 'It was perfect having you moved to Italy and tried there first.'

'You orchestrated that?'

'It was nothing,' Lavrov said. 'Money in the right hands . . .'

Babich laughed. Why bother infiltrating the Americans to get info on his movements when the Italian security and judicial services were so easily bought? He could imagine the elaborate moves taken to confuse anyone trying to second-guess his flight plan from the US. If you wanted the right people to like you in Italy, you just had to spend a little money and they would quickly value your qualities. They knew it came from a dubious place, sure, but they were used to that. It was so simple. A painless place to operate. Money trumped all, you could buy anything. He missed the place.

'I do have one good piece of news,' Lavrov said. 'That bastard reporter, who helped put you –'

'Lachlan Fox?' Babich picked up his glass from the floor, tore off another piece of bread.

Lavrov nodded. 'He will be dead soon.'

Babich stopped. Put down his food and drink. Wiped his hands on a napkin.

'Roman?'

Babich looked up into his eyes. He imagined the look was enough, but he'd explain it all the same: 'Mikhail, I *wanted* Lachlan Fox to be there – at the end – to help us with this,' Babich said. 'I expected it. I have thought about it for months . . .'

Lavrov's face was flushed. His neck bore splotches of purple and crimson, his cheeks were ruddy and his capillaries flared. *Good. Feel it. Even the best men are fools.*

'Contact your people,' Babich said, his tone leaving no doubt. 'Call them off.'

Lavrov looked him in the eyes, shook his head.

Babich's appetite was gone. There at the end, that's where he wanted Fox, there at the end.

'It's too late to call them off,' Lavrov explained. 'It's order and forget, and these guys never fail. Fox will be dead in moments, if he's not already.'

29

WASHINGTON, DC

'Come on, answer already ...' McCorkell said. He couldn't shake Lachlan Fox from his mind. He could already be dead. Or captive. He pressed redial and watched the image on the big screen tracking the SAR crews to Hutchinson's last known position. Tapped his fingers on the desk. 'Come on ...'

Fox's mobile phone rang through to voicemail again so he tried a New York number. It was answered on the third ring.

'Yeah?' Despite the hour the voice on the phone sounded wide awake.

'Tas, it's Bill,' McCorkell said to his old college friend and Fox's boss, Tas Wallace.

'Do you know where Fox is? I can't reach him on his cell.'

'He's on leave, has been since the last Babich stories,' Wallace said. His voice changed – his concern for his reporting staff was paternal, especially so for his never-say-die duo, Fox and Gammaldi. 'What's up?'

'I can't really say, but I think you'll get the gist,' McCorkell said. 'We had an incident moving our prisoner.'

'He's out?'

'Yep.'

'Jesus . . .'

'Tell me about it. I think Fox might be in danger, maybe not, but as no one seems to know where he's got to . . .'

'France,' Wallace said. 'Or so he told me. A farmhouse in the middle of nowhere. With Kate and Al. That's all I know.'

'You think he's safe?'

'Fox is canny, by far the most capable operator we've got to send into a hot zone,' Wallace said. 'He's used to looking after himself . . . Hell, you know that as well as anyone.'

It was true, McCorkell knew that. But just what Fox would do if cornered and something happened to Kate . . . *again*. About a year back, Fox practically tore Nigeria in two, driven by revenge and anger and his stubborn drive to uncover the truth no matter what the cost. Jesus. The man couldn't go on like this forever; even the best's luck ran out, eventually. Those who survived into old age knew when to walk away.

'Tas, if you can get hold of him, tell him what's happened, to keep his head down until we get someone to him,' McCorkell said. 'We need to get him back Stateside and under FBI protection asap. If not for me or himself, for Kate.'

'Got it,' Wallace replied. 'You sound tired.'

'Haven't had a good sleep in thirty years, Tas,' McCorkell said with the smallest of smiles. It was still dark outside the windows, the sunrise not even a glow. 'Why can't we be back at Oxford, in the prime of our lives and chasing girls in bars?'

'I don't know if it was ever like that, but yeah, bring back the good old days,' Wallace replied with a chuckle before turning serious. 'I'll get onto Fox and keep you posted.'

He hung up. McCorkell could hear Bowden down the other end of the office – like a court-side coach going nuts at his guys during time-out – demanding to know what more could be done to get Babich back; not sold by the agents' feedback that they were putting everything out there to get him.

'We find him under a rock or he pops up on the grid. Either way, when we've got him, we take him heavy!'

Bowden's staff knew their jobs, and they knew how to dig a little deeper to hustle for their boss.

McCorkell watched the screen, the designated SAR units nearing Hutchinson's dot. They were converging, coming at him from several directions. Just like the unknown forces headed to a farmhouse somewhere in the French countryside.

30

GIVERNY

'Just us,' Kate said, following Fox to the sink and kissing him again. He reluctantly let her go and filled a water jug.

He picked up his phone as he followed her into the front room and noticed it was vibrating –

'Tas?'

'Lachlan,' his boss said. 'Bill McCorkell has been trying to contact you. Babich is out there, on the loose.'

'What!' Fox said. 'When?'

'Just now, the last hour or so.'

'Oh shit . . .' The others in the front room stopped talking and looked at him. His shoulders and arms tensed. Everything seemed to go quiet – his world on the head of a pin. 'Hutchinson?'

'That's all I know,' Wallace said. 'Look, get to the nearest police station and I'll arrange a security team to pick you up.'

'No,' Fox said. 'We'll stay on the move and lay low. I'll check in on the hour. Just keep me posted on the search.'

'I will, but let me send –'

'We're better off on our own.'

'You need police protection.'

'I can handle it,' Fox said, looking into the front room. 'Matter of fact, there's a couple of French cops here right now. We'll head into Paris. I'll call you once I'm there and I've spoken to Bill, okay?'

There was silence for a moment.

'Keep your head down,' Wallace said.

The line went dead.

'What was that?' Kate asked, getting to her feet. They all turned to Fox expectantly. Vincent was leaning through the window. He was a sharp-looking cop the right side of middle-age. He had been joking around with Gammaldi, but was now fully alert.

'Tas – my boss at GSR – giving us a heads-up,' Fox explained.

'About what?' Kate asked. She was worried, but Fox didn't fully register it.

Zoe said something to Vincent in French. There was a strange sound in the distance Fox couldn't place. Brujon barked, then silence.

Fox spoke, but he was listening more than speaking: 'Babich. We're in danger . . .'

That sound again, a hollow clap. Familiar.

'Al,' Fox said, moving fast and pushing Kate down and towards his friend. 'Get Kate to the car, drive to the nearest police station. We'll stall them here and meet you there.'

Zoe was on her feet and speaking to her colleague. Gammaldi was moving Kate towards the kitchen. She looked back at Fox wide-eyed.

'They're coming,' Fox said to Kate, 'I'm sorry.'

Those words. She knew. She kept low, Gammaldi bustling her out of the front room.

'There's no one out here,' Vincent said in stilted English. He scanned around, his sidearm drawn. 'I can see down the driveway. All clear. No one.'

The sound again and this time Fox identified it. A low-velocity round fired from a silenced weapon.

'Lachlan?' Zoe called.

Fox didn't answer, he was reaching over to the sideboard, gathering the shotgun, filling his pockets with shells.

'Get down!' Fox yelled. 'Do it – now – down!'

Zoe started drawing from her hip holster.

Something flew across the room – Fox looked across to see Vincent at the side window, turning, shaking where he stood. Blood splattered the room. The Frenchman looked down at the dark crimson gushing from his chest and collapsed across the windowsill.

'Down!' Fox yelled again. Gammaldi had Kate hunkered down on the tiled floor of the kitchen, Fox knelt and shouldered the shotgun, still in the front room. He could hear Brujon barking madly outside. Zoe was already braced to the side of the front door, firing quick shots outside. Fox tried to pinpoint where Brujon's barking was coming from.

Rat-a-tat-tat!

The front doors and windows were shredded by submachine-gun fire, the lace curtains catching most of the flying glass.

Zoe closed her eyes for a second, then opened them with new resolve. Nodded to Fox. She peered around the doorjamb.

'I can't see anything . . .'

Brujon still barking. The submachine-gun fire halted. A couple of silenced rounds hit the wall above Fox's head.

'Can we get to your car?' Fox asked. Through the open front door he could see the boot of the Peugeot where it was parked across the driveway.

Zoe nodded.

'I'll move up and cover you,' Fox said.

Zoe looked around the door and ducked back – bullets sprayed through the doorway, a stream of nine-millimetre steel on full auto turned the masonry to dust . . . Then a new sound: *KLAPBOOM!*

A fragmentation grenade went off against the front wall of the house. Shards of metal and glass flew through the doorway and windows. Fox glanced back as Kate screamed – she was okay, just spooked. Gammaldi kept her close to the floor, behind the solid butcher's block. Bullets whistled past, tearing into the kitchen's back wall; the escape route out the back door cut off.

Fox turned to Zoe and squinted through the dust of the blast.

Not two seconds after the grenade going off there was a far larger explosion – the Peugeot, hit by a rocket-propelled grenade. Fox was knocked back by the concussion wave. Debris and fire swirled around him before his world turned black.

31

WASHINGTON, DC

McCorkell was pacing behind the FBI desks. The SAR aircraft would be flying over Hutchinson's last known GPS coordinates any moment now. Fox had been warned. Now he was waiting for news. Useless.

Bowden was still chewing out his team in the far corner of the room, demanding updates and explanations. The hands of his NSA and CIA agents were a blur over their keyboards, most multi-tasking by talking on phones at the same time. Around the world agents were being activated, sources were being milked, payments were being made. The dragnet was fanning out around the globe; wherever they found Babich, assets would be nearby, ready to play.

'Sorry, what?' McCorkell asked, realising Valerie had been talking to him. Her team was hushed. The prisoner transfer had been organised by them and they were feeling the heat; finding their man Hutchinson alive was the best they could hope for.

'Babich,' she repeated. 'It's how he's survived so long.'

'How?'

'He took out insurance. Something up his sleeve. Something big.'

'I'm gonna need more,' McCorkell said.

'He's not going somewhere to hide,' she said, looking into middle-distance as she searched for threads that would make sense. 'He's going somewhere to gloat, not to clear his name. And – and he's not going to wait around. I mean, for what? Someone to take him in? To kill him? He knows the score. He'll act fast.'

'Where's he got to turn? Can't be Russia or Italy, those havens are dead to him.'

'He's gotta have something somewhere.'

'No one will stand for it,' McCorkell said, playing devil's advocate. 'No one will listen to him.'

'It has to be an offer that the world can't refuse. Gotta be . . . Gotta be big.'

'He'll never be heard.'

'He'll use the press . . .' Valerie said, lost in her ideas. 'Something that will threaten to pull apart our world. Not financial markets, but public sentiment for our political systems – he wants instability; we've seen him exploit that so often . . .'

'Why?' He liked her thinking. Could have used her back in the day at the White House. He looked at the SAR's 'time to station' reading on the screen. Measured in seconds now.

'To make change, to force it. He'll emerge with – no, *as* the solution.'

Time . . .

'Solution?' McCorkell repeated. 'You're too far ahead, go back. So, where's the audience? Where's his lifeline?'

'Somewhere we can't extradite him from.'

'Where could he possibly get that kind of coverage and audience, where we can't touch him?'

Valerie looked at him, shook her head, then stopped.

'That deadline? That time clock in the NSA intercept?' McCorkell said. 'What's happening this weekend? What's happening where there's an audience, where we can't extradite from?'

Valerie's face lit up. She looked as if she would burst out of her skin.

'China,' she said. 'He's going to China.'

32

GIVERNY

Fox, recovered from the aftershock of the explosion, looked across at Zoe who was reloading in a cloud of dust. He crouched and blasted two shots out the front window. Submachine-gun fire raked the front of the farmhouse in reply. More rounds were finding their way inside, powdering the plaster-lined masonry behind him. The attackers were closing in.

'Al!' Fox yelled in the direction of the kitchen. 'Take Kate and head out the back – get to the car!'

'I'll stay –'

'We're all going!' Fox shouted, shielding his face from flying debris as he reloaded the gun. At least four shooters out there. Nearing. No way did he and Zoe have the firepower to repel the assault. They'd delay them a couple of minutes at most. 'I'll stay and draw their fire – go!'

He got up on one knee, fired a barrel through the side window and one out the front door.

'Zoe!'

Zoe clocked what Fox wanted to do, nodded, and they tipped over the heavy table and pushed it up against the door. Two inches of century-old hardwood was immediately peppered with bullets, but it would buy them some time.

'Moving!' Gammaldi called from the kitchen.

'Keep low!' Fox hissed as he and Zoe crawled in towards them.

Fox paused behind the foot of the stairs. Reloaded two more shells from his shirt pocket, crawled to the side window facing the pizza oven – saw two figures running in, ten metres away – got up on one knee: *blam, blam!*

Winged one. Fox stuck close to the wall, broke open the breech and ejected the spent shells as the other attacker sprayed the window, plaster and debris coating him again. Fox closed the loaded gun, launched around the kitchen table to Zoe, seeing Gammaldi and Kate cowering down by the back door, ready to make for the car. Fox signalled, *Five seconds!* and kept moving, scanning. Crashing sounds coming from the front of the house. He passed the stairs and ducked into the alcove seat, pushed the small stained-glass window open, slid the barrel out: *blam, blam!*

The attacker, one leg through the kitchen window, flew through the air as both blasts hit him. The man he'd wounded before was crawling away, slowly, out of the action.

Fox backed around, headed for the kitchen.

PHFT!-PHFT!-PHFT!-PHFT!-PHFT!-PHFT! – silenced automatic-weapons' fire raked into the front room as Fox took cover at the bottom of the staircase. Back against the masonry he could feel the rounds hitting the wall. He watched as Zoe led his friends out the back door to the car, then he reloaded in a brief silence and heard the metallic *katang!* and rattle of a grenade that had been tossed into the front room.

He crouched down, hands over his ears, eyes closed, mouth slightly open against the concussion.

KLAPBANG!

A loud and bright detonation, but no debris. A flash-bang grenade.

KLAPBANG!

Another one in the front room. His ears rang as he ran up the stairs. There'd be guys entering the house under the cover of the grenades' impact, submachine guns blazing. They'd clear the house in twenty seconds, half that if they were good.

He ran to the upstairs bedroom that faced the back, shut the door behind him, pulled the dresser over – it wasn't that heavy, but would give him precious seconds to evacuate – opened the double window and looked down into the rear courtyard.

Zoe was crouched behind the engine block of the Golf – Kate and Gammaldi must be inside the car. She glanced up at him.

'Keys!' she said.

Shit.

'In the kitchen,' he mouthed out the window. 'On the bench!'

Zoe nodded, disappeared into the house. Gammaldi peered out from the open sun roof.

'Al, I'm coming down!'

A window shattered and a guy leaned out the other bedroom's window, his submachine gun tracking towards the car.

Fox let off one shot; the guy's exposed hands and face exploded in red and his gun fell to the ground.

'Al!' Fox yelled out. 'Catch!'

Fox emptied the shotgun and held it out; his friend was already out of the car, waiting below the window – caught it like he was carrying a load of wood. Fox tossed down two shells and saw Zoe emerge, keys in hand.

He was about to climb up on the windowsill when the door behind him rattled against the dresser, a weapon appearing – he ran to it, slamming into the dresser hard, crushing the attacker's gun arm against the doorjamb. The guy fired on full auto for a couple of seconds as Fox grabbed an overturned vase and smashed it across the exposed wrist. There was a grunt and splash of blood and the submachine gun fell to the floor.

The man smashed his way into the room as Fox grabbed the gun. Fox gave the intruder a smile before pointing the gun at him: *Click*. Out of bullets.

The man grinned – he was huge, built like a Coke machine – and pulled out a combat knife.

Fox backed away as the blade slashed through the air. He threw the gun – it bounced off the man's head. He hauled a chair across the room and the assassin smashed it to the ground.

Fox ducked as the knife arced through the air where he had just been. He parried around, back to the door that was hanging ragged from its smashed frame. A glance out, the hall was empty. The man charged and Fox moved quickly, parrying the attack so that the guy slammed into the door as Fox rode his momentum into it from behind. He landed two good blows into the assassin's kidneys, while tearing a knife-size splinter of wood from the shattered doorjamb. It wasn't a knife, but it'd do.

Now they were both armed.

The guy grunted through his pain, grinned, wiped his bloody lip on the back of his hand and took a pace towards Fox, each of them ready to pounce.

The attacker moved first, launching with the knife in his right hand, the momentum of his bulk following fast behind it. Fox shifted, grabbed the guy's wrist as the blade glanced his forearm and he let himself keep falling hard to the right, his other hand coming around and slamming the wooden shard down into the man's neck. They crashed to the floor, two hundred-plus kilos landing on the guy's outstretched knife arm causing a terrific snapping sound.

Blood spouted from the assassin's neck wound and he clung to it with his good hand. A loud, high-pitched scream.

The assassin's eyes were wild, blood was pouring from him, arm bent – both bones torn clean through his forearm – his hand vibrating to its own frequency of pain.

'How many?' Fox asked, twisting the wooden spike, feeling the sinewy neck muscle of his opponent tearing. 'How many were sent?'

'Eight . . . Four to the house . . .' he said in heavily accented English between heaving breaths. 'Two cars . . . Down the road . . .'

'What's your mission?'

Fox moved the shard of timber.

'Kill you all.'

Fox had heard enough. He stood, climbed up on the windowsill, hung down and jumped, taking the landing in a reverse roll off the back of his heels.

Zoe was waiting, pistol in hand, tossed him the keys, while Gammaldi climbed into the back seat with Kate. Fox and Zoe jumped in and spun the car around towards the gate.

Ahead, a dark blue Audi four-wheel drive was tearing up the approach to the house. They were only five hundred metres away, but they'd have to navigate the burning wreckage of the Peugeot. Fox slammed on the brakes.

'What are you doing?' Kate yelled out.

Fox opened his door – 'Brujon!'

The border collie leaped up on his lap and Fox scooted him into the back towards Gammaldi and Kate.

Zoe looked across at Fox, but didn't say anything.

He turned the wheel, headed away from the drive to the dirt track that led to the neighbours' place, and gunned it.

33

WASHINGTON, DC

Valerie sat across the desk from McCorkell, but her eyes kept tracking to the communications techs, waiting for news of Hutchinson.

'What did Bowden say?' she asked.

'About China?' McCorkell replied, settling back into his chair. She nodded.

'Grunted, said he'd look into it.'

'Doesn't he see –'

'Don't worry about him. I'm going to contact State and get them to alert some Chinese authorities we got on-side,' McCorkell said, picking up the landline phone and cradling the handset between his shoulder and chin as he dialled a number. As the line began to ring he asked Valerie, 'How many people knew about this op to move Babich?'

'Only Hutchinson knew which aircraft and flight plan he was taking – he chose it at the airport.'

'We've got two aircraft on-station and working up a search grid,' a DoD tech said loudly. 'Real-time images are feeding in.'

McCorkell and Valerie jumped up and watched the LCD screen over his shoulder – brilliant sea in every direction, the morning summer sunshine picking up the water like a million little pieces of glass.

'Talk about a needle in a haystack,' Valerie said. 'Navy will have a surface vessel in the area in two hours. Doesn't sound like much of a Plan B, does it?'

McCorkell shook his head, then spoke rapid-fire to a colleague on the China desk at the State Department and hung up seconds later. He moved closer to the main screen, where Valerie and several of her FBI colleagues stood, watching, waiting.

'We got radio traffic from the scene,' the Air Force officer said, returning to his headset mic, 'Repeat last NAVSO. Which bird? Copy that.'

He tapped away at his keyboard and a new image was brought up on the screen. They watched as the picture zoomed in on a speck in the ocean.

'Is that – ?'

'Parachute,' McCorkell said. That was good. The image changed again, focusing in on another spot in the ocean that was revealed to be . . . a man, wearing a life vest, floating on his back, waving.

'We've got him!' Valerie said. She jumped up and yelled to the room, 'We've got visual on Hutchinson – he seems okay!'

The room erupted in whoops and high-fives and a couple of hugs were shared among the FBI staff. In the CIA corner Bowden didn't skip a beat, focused hard on one thing: hunting Babich.

'Beacon on his vest is activated but the signal was weak, PC3 out of Naples did this visual fly-over and – as you can see – he waved to 'em,' the tech said. 'Navy has an SH-60 headed there now, five minutes out.'

McCorkell was beaming – one piece of the puzzle had been found. Three more remained: Fox, Babich, and a deadline to something.

34

GIVERNY TO PARIS

Fox drove hard along the dirt track to the neighbouring farm – the Golf almost launching into the air as they mounted a grassed ledge and careened back onto the gravel driveway. They had maybe six hundred metres' lead on the pursuing car. Five-fifty. The Audi was gaining fast, a blur of motion in his rear-view mirror as he kept the accelerator flat to the floor.

'Al, how many cars back there?' Fox asked. The guy at the house had said *two*.

'Just the one,' Gammaldi replied, peering over the back seat.

Fox slid the Golf through the tight sweeping bend before the road that led onto the highway. There was another hostile vehicle waiting somewhere.

'Hang on!' Fox said, braking hard at the final turn and then flooring the gas through it, power-sliding onto the smooth bitumen. The engine buzzed up through the gears, the Audi gaining on them with every second. At the very least there was a six-cylinder turbo diesel powering that thing – he hoped that was it.

'They're five hundred metres back,' Zoe said.

'I know!'

'Take the highway to Paris?'

'I think so, we're too out-gunned to stop and leave the car.'
Fox saw her pulling her BlackBerry from her belt.

'I hope there's help close by,' she said, putting it to her ear.

Tang tang tang!

The Audi gunner fired at them, the rounds hitting the hatch
door of the Golf and shattering Gammaldi's side window.

'Shit!' Gammaldi got down, pushing Kate into the foot-well.

They were closing fast on the town of Giverny. There was
a truck up ahead – the Audi four hundred metres behind and
gaining on them.

'This'll be tight!' Fox yelled. 'Hang on!'

He swerved around the truck, but the Audi was caught for a
moment in the intersection as they skirted the town. Five seconds
and their pursuer was back in the chase again, now some eight
hundred metres back.

'There's an armed unit near Vernon. We'll meet up at the
highway,' Zoe said, ending her call.

'We'll need more than a couple of cops –'

Fox slammed on the brakes as a car veered in front of them,
which he overtook on the inside and then headed out of town.
Behind, the Audi was nearing them, fast.

'There's no way –' Fox began as his foot stayed flat to the
floor and the engine red-lined and whined its way up through
its seven gears. 'There's no way we can outrun them!'

35

WASHINGTON, DC

'Hutchinson is in a SAR chopper,' Valerie said. 'Gunshot to the leg, but he'll be fine.'

'The others?'

'They . . . they're all dead,' she said, her voice flat. 'The aircraft is still en route to Rome. Navy and Italian Air Force are working on options.'

'Okay,' McCorkell said, looking towards Bowden's team. A pair of new arrivals had joined him – Air Force non-commanders, setting up gear in a hastily cleared piece of bench-space. 'Let's hope that Hutch will be back on deck any moment.'

'He wanted to check in on things – the medic had to threaten to knock him out to stop him demanding a radio.'

'Least we know he'd be good to go,' McCorkell said.

'We need to move on now, to Babich.'

'Abso-fucking-lutely. You take your team and work on all known references between Babich, Umbra Corp and China; government, businesses and underground.'

'On it.'

'I'm gonna plough through Babich's background, see what we've missed, and I'll keep on State's butt.'

Valerie nodded and went over to her fellow FBI agents to brief them into teams.

McCorkell plugged his laptop into the secure LAN and watched some video files of Babich's 'interrogation' – his softening up over the first couple of months of detention, where they just got him to talk about whatever he wanted – usually either the current political machinations in Russia, the good old days that he missed, or some of his achievements in the seventies and eighties working for the KGB. There, Babich had made a name for himself writing papers on how Reagan's presidency so successfully hindered the Soviet Union's economy. He explained how the US held up Russia's ability to sell natural gas to Europe while actively working to keep gas prices low, starving the Soviet Union of foreign capital and accelerating its fall by encouraging it to over-extend its economic base through the arms race. Babich had sworn he'd not let that happen again, and saw economic and business success as the tool with which to beat the West: fight the capitalists at their own game within a regulatory system that was far easier to 'navigate'.

After watching a few mpegs, McCorkell realised the difficulty of his task: finding the needle in a haystack *before* it struck. Locating Babich's wild card would be like connecting all the dots pre-9/11 and being in a position to prevent the hijackings – an impossibility . . . He went back to the files, opened up the transcripts. They were indexed, a kind of CliffsNotes version of six months' worth of discussions Babich had had with members of the FBI and Justice Department.

Skim-reading, McCorkell discovered that Babich had a love–hate relationship with Gorbachev. By the late eighties, when Gorbachev ushered in his programs of *glasnost* – political openness – and *perestroika* – political and economic restructuring – the Soviet economy was already suffering from both hidden inflation and supply shortages. This was aggravated by an increasingly open black market that undermined the official economy, and so many of Gorbachev's *cheka* pals were in on it – the corruption was endemic. This was when Babich first started to make money on the side, selling oil syphoned off from surplus state military reserves, importing old Western vehicles and selling them for incredible profits. After three years he'd made close to two million US dollars, a decent fortune for that place and time. His continued work for the KGB through to its transformation into the FSB in 1991 kept him safe, connected and valued. So, by the time his country fell apart, he had the start-up capital, contacts and security to be among the most successful of the emerging oligarchs.

McCorkell looked over to the FBI team; they were young – late twenties and early thirties – driven and adept, a testament to the good work his country could do when it wanted to. Almost impossible to imagine them going down the path that so many of their counterparts in Russia had gone down in the politics vacuum . . .

He skipped a few paras until the collapse of the Soviet Union in 1991 when Boris Yeltsin seized power. Babich's first 'legitimate' business was formed then, a few years after Gorbachev had enacted the Law on Cooperatives, allowing for the first time in the communist country *private* ownership of businesses in the services, manufacturing and foreign-trade sectors. Late 1991 Babich started making his big moves – he'd quietly been buying up oil rights in a syndicate, profiting hugely from the Gulf War price shocks, and by the end of that year he was a billionaire.

McCorkell could see that with the emergence of Babich's Umbra corporation and feeding the state money to keep the ministers happy, Babich himself was free to do more on his own, out in the open. He kept his trusted former security comrades with him and . . . McCorkell knew the rest, knew it well. That's when the file got really detailed: drawers full of intel, terabytes of data linked to agencies around the globe, surveillance photos and audio and visual intelligence, much of it collected by the Russian security services. But Babich had kept the right people happy, never interfering with Russian politics or offending those in power, unlike so many other oligarchs.

But he was never quiet.

Glasnost . . . It kept running through McCorkell's mind. *Glasnost* . . . It resulted in greater freedom of speech. *Glasnost* . . . openness . . . the people . . .

McCorkell sat up, typed in some search terms, looked at the date of Babich's last government employment: 1992.

The last two years of his KGB/FSB employment were blank. Before that, he'd been assigned to a special project reporting directly to the president, and then he'd retired with a full pension – the monetary compensation he graciously turned down, citing the tough economic times the state was going through . . .

McCorkell clicked through the links on Intellipedia to hunt references to Babich's last assignment. Nothing but a vague lead into a higher clearance CIA file, code-word protected. *No wonder it wasn't included in these notes.* He typed in his level one Yankee White clearance, itself good enough to access anything the President was cleared to know about. Thirty seconds later he received a call and coded into the crypto desk at Langley. Moments later the file was remote-opened. It was small, just a few lines. Babich's last reported task before those missing two years was an assignment to the *Special Alexander Nikolaevich Yakovlev Project.*

The only details were that it was . . . *a specific order from Gorbachev to find a state document. Success unknown.* Strange . . .

36

GIVERNY TO PARIS

Fox turned a hard right – the tyres squealed in protest as he hammered the Golf through the outskirts of town, dog-legged through a small street that took them behind the main avenue, glimpses of the Audi in between buildings.

'Hang on!' he said, as they flashed through an intersection, Fox pulling a handbrake turn and heading up the ramp to the highway.

'Duck!' Gammaldi yelled.

The window next to Fox's head exploded as two shots ripped through the roof and tore a jagged wound through the top of the windscreen. It was cracked like a spider's web, but didn't smash.

Zoe banged at her window control, held in place. She smashed the glass with the butt of her pistol and bashed out the safety glass. They were doing a hundred and forty as Fox merged onto the highway while Zoe manoeuvred her torso out the open window like some kind of ballerina.

The Audi raced along the emergency lane, sticking hard along the shoulder through a bend in the road and gaining fast. Zoe was taking aim.

'Zoe – back in!'

She ducked into the cabin as Fox crossed in front of a Smart car stopped at the hard shoulder, its driver standing on the grassed embankment. The Audi followed hard on their tail, didn't veer or slow as it punched into the stopped car, sending it airborne and into the back corner of the Golf. Fox tried to control his car as it slid, brakes locking and unlocking as the electronics fought to compensate, while metal and glass rained down behind them, the remnants of the demolished Smart car. He took the pressure off the accelerator, turned the steering wheel so the tyres pointed into the spin and powered out of it – pedal to the metal. They were going flat-out to rebuild speed.

The Audi regained momentum and had closed the gap. The gunner leaned out and fired, but he'd aimed too low, the submachine-gun rounds chewing up bitumen near the Golf's tyres. Fox turned just enough to get away from the stream of lead that was tearing up the highway in their wake.

Still the Audi kept charging forward, cutting across lanes and slamming into the back of the Golf. Fox fought to straighten as Zoe leaned through the seats and aimed her pistol out the back window.

'Cover your ears!' she yelled. Kate and Gammaldi were already hunkered down as low as they could get in the foot-well as Zoe blasted off ten rounds in four seconds into the grille and bonnet of their pursuer. She ejected the SIG's clip and slapped in another. The Audi fell back a few metres as some of her next fifteen rounds blasted through the windscreen on the driver's side; an eruption as the glass was painted with blood. The Audi moved sharply, speeding across the lanes, its engine steaming and rubber screeching, the high-speed turn making the tyres bite into the road and forcing the vehicle to roll and bounce in mid-air twice, before bounding along the road in a shower of debris and smoke, finally sliding onto its roof and into an adjacent wheat field.

Over his shoulder Fox saw the mayhem, a cloud of dust and then an explosion from the field. Brujon, who had been cowering on the back seat, brought his head up and Fox smiled at him.

The others in the car were quiet, still. Zoe looked at the empty SIG pistol in her hand like she was seeing it for the first time. Maybe that was the first time she'd taken a life with it, all that muscle memory-training taking over. She started to shake.

Fox kept the speed climbing. One-fifty. One-sixty. The wind howled through the glassless windows and cracked windscreen.

'Is anyone hurt?'

'No,' Gammaldi said, sitting up again. 'We're good.'

The fireball of the Audi grew smaller in the background, smoking, steaming; the chaos of the traffic slowing to inspect, but Fox kept driving. Away. Towards Paris. As fast as he could, but even at this speed it was a good half hour.

Then, in the rear-view mirror . . . A ghost? *Oh shit.*

'Get down!' Fox yelled, as he swerved, bullets ripping the back of a campervan that they were flashing past.

Fox weaved fast through the other vehicles on the highway. In the rear-view mirror, an identical Audi was in hot pursuit, a heavily armed guy hanging out the passenger-side window. Predator and prey. Closing fast.

37

WASHINGTON, DC

'Thanks,' McCorkell said, as an FBI tech helped him access some archived files. He wasn't a total Luddite – he managed to keep up with the best of them, but sometimes computers and he . . . He opened the file and waited a moment for it to decrypt.

Top Secret-SCI-CI

Special Alexander Nikolaevich Yakovlev Project.

PROJECT DESCRIPTION: Since the Great Patriotic War (WWII) it had been the official policy of the Soviet Union to deny the existence of the secret protocol to the Soviet–German Pact, for fear of local political fallout –

Soviet–German Pact? McCorkell scrolled down to read the description . . . *the pact is known as the Molotov–Ribbentrop Pact.*

Okay. That was the Nazi–Russia pact of World War II where they signed some kind of non-aggression agreement. There was a secret protocol attached to the treaty, revealed by the Germans, but denied by the Russians. They were good at that, masters of misinformation or simply withholding it from public view. He knew of the non-aggression pact, but in no more detail than anyone who knew World War II history and he remembered reading about these secret protocols in the media coverage at the time they came out in the press. When was it . . . 1992? Yes, he confirmed, as he scrolled further down the document, the story broke in 1992 . . . Same year Babich got out. This report was compiled by a former Moscow CIA desk at Langley, dated 1993. He read on:

It was only after the Baltic Way demonstrations of 23 August 1989, when over two million people created a human chain on the 50th anniversary of the signing of the pact, that the Russian policy of denial changed. At the behest of Mikhail Gorbachev, Alexander Nikolaevich Yakovlev, the 'godfather of glasnost', headed a commission investigating the existence of such a protocol . . . It was on that search team that Babich spent his last official working years. In December 1989, the commission concluded that the secret protocol had existed and revealed its findings to the Soviet Congress of People's Deputies . . . In 1992, the document itself was finally declassified, after the dissolution of the Soviet Union.

So . . . Babich had been tasked to trawl the state's most secret archives to find this protocol.

Then Babich left government service, using his money and smarts to pick up as many of the old security operators and political guys as he could.

Babich had found it, Yakovlev had confirmed its existence to Yeltsin, and it became public in 1992. Babich left the office two years after this job. He'd disappeared off the CIA's grid for those last couple of years:

Roman Babich, whereabouts currently unknown (21 March 1992).

So this job corresponded with the blank space in his personnel file, and then he'd quit. That document would never have come to light if it were not for *glasnost*. But what was Babich doing in all that time, between '89 and '92?

Glasnost . . . McCorkell could almost taste that he was closing in on something, but what? And what would it look like? He probably wouldn't know until after the fact . . . Jesus. He got up, went to the drinks cart to make a cup of tea. Rummaged through the tea bags in the jar that hardly anyone else dipped into – they all preferred to be jacked up on coffee – looking for his Irish Breakfast . . . There. No, it was a peppermint, similar green label. *Glasnost* . . . openness . . . Babich had opened the most secret archives his state had ever known, looking for something. He dug around . . . Searching . . . Stopped. Looked at the similar green tag on the tea.

What if Babich had been looking for this secret protocol, and found something else? He was deep in Stalin's secret archives for months . . . maybe years. McCorkell looked over at the teams – they were looking for Babich. Babich was looking for something once and he *had* found something; something that he'd never fully played, but it had been hot enough to protect him all this time.

38

GIVERNY TO PARIS

'Time for some fancy driving!' Gammaldi said, ducking down again with Kate as another stream of rounds ricocheted off the road outside his window.

Fox checked the rear-view mirror – the Audi was coming, faster and much better armed than the four of them in the Golf.

'Where are your cop buddies?' Fox asked Zoe.

'Five minutes!' she replied, checking her phone.

He pushed the car with everything its little engine had, holding each gear change to the last moment as his foot was planted to the floor.

'They're closing fast!' Zoe said.

'I know!' Fox replied, zipping in and out of the overtaking lane, then out onto the emergency lane and around other vehicles.

'Faster!'

'We're in top gear!' Fox said, seeing the speedometer needle was about to pass one-ninety . . . moving slowly towards its two-twenty max. Why hadn't he sprung for an Audi S8 back at the car rental? That'd solve some problems now. Behind, the massive Audi was within a hundred and fifty metres; the gunner opened up again with a spray of submachine-gun bullets that fell to the left as Fox tweaked the steering wheel to the right.

'Get off the highway!' Zoe shouted.

Loud impacts rang inside the Golf as incoming rounds shredded the rear hatch – it wrenched clean off the car and clattered in their wake.

'Give me the shotgun!' Zoe said. Gammaldi passed it through, barely able to get it into the front seat because of the long barrel. Zoe leaned out her window, her knees on the seat and her arms braced on the window frame.

'Wait till he's closer!' Fox said, using the emergency lane to bypass a traffic jam.

Zoe pulled herself back in, still facing the rear.

'You say when and I'll tap the brakes – let them get close before you fire!'

She nodded.

Fox veered back onto the highway, slalomed through the traffic, racing towards an on-ramp – a stream of cars merging.

'Hold on!' Fox just made it through by splitting the two lanes.

The Audi tried to squeeze after him – skidding – sparks flew as the Audi ground along the side of a truck, forcing the passenger gunner back in – but they monstered onwards, closing the gap to a hundred metres.

'Hang on!' Fox said, weaving through some congestion, a van swerving off into the emergency lane and locking up its brakes in a cloud of smoke . . .

The Audi was leaving a trail of totalled cars behind them. *Fuck it.* Fox hit a few cars too, light taps into corner bumpers, making his pursuer navigate the mess. He may have been able to shed the cops earlier, but not these guys, not on the open road. This car, they had to fight. It was eighty metres behind, the passenger gunner getting back out to fire.

Zoe leaned out the window, braced herself with her butt against the dash.

'Brake now!' Zoe said, aiming the shotgun straight back.

Fox touched the brakes and the car slowed fast – he saw the Audi's nose dip as the driver reacted and braked; Fox hit the accelerator when it was twenty metres behind.

Zoe unleashed both barrels. The Audi's gunner fired at the same time, but shot wide as he was clipped with pellets. Their windscreen looked like it had been sandblasted, and the driver lost control, spinning to a stop in a cloud of smoke. Fox kept on the gas, wanting to put distance between them while he could.

39

WASHINGTON, DC

'What have we got?' McCorkell asked, falling into step next to Bowden as they arrived at the DoD op team. Members from each service were working consoles and manning phones.

'We've got an unknown aircraft,' an Air Force operator explained. 'Present location fits, it could have been at Hutchinson's mid-air hijack.'

'What is it?' Bowden asked.

'Flight plan from this aircraft,' she replied, pointing to her screen, 'was set as a flight from Sardinia to Kazakhstan. Currently entering Black Sea airspace, Turkish Air Force transport was just talking with it, and they were close enough for a visual.'

'And?'

'Flight was logged as Aeroflot, looks legit on radar and paper, but it has no livery –'

Bowden asked, 'Could it be Russian Intel?'

'We've been through dozens of contacts that have checked out and this is our only remaining suspect aircraft on that flight path sir.'

'Keep on it,' Bowden said. He turned to his CIA team: 'Activate assets in Kazakhstan, ready to get to wherever they touch down – over the border with Russia too, he may be landing in Russia. He touches down, I want human eyes on him. Observe and report. Get to it.'

His staff jumped on their new tasks.

McCorkell watched the designated aircraft blinking its way across the Black Sea towards Kazakhstan. China bordered that country to the south-east – maybe this was going to be a refuelling stop, or maybe they were just flying over friendly airspace.

'Bowden,' McCorkell said. The CIA man looked up from some NSA Echelon transcripts. 'This flight path? Valerie's hunch about China? We gotta talk . . .'

40

ROAD TO PARIS

'Faster!' Gammaldi said, peering over the top of the back seats.

'I know!' Fox replied.

No time to lose. The Audi was back on his tail, unshakable. Fox threaded through the cars in front. The Golf was running hot, but slowing to save the radiator wasn't on the cards.

Behind, the gunner had kicked out the shattered windscreen and was taking some pot shots at them, the long muzzle flash ominous.

Several rounds ripped through the roof and tore through Fox's headrest.

Zoe opened the breech of the shotgun, its barrel out the window.

'No more shells,' Gammaldi called, crouched down flat against the back seat, Kate quiet beneath him in the foot-well.

Nothing about this car chase was fun. Fox knew from operating in Iraq and Afghanistan that a vehicle provided little ballistics cover; it gave you the option to bug out of trouble or use the car itself as a heavy offensive mass. They had no advantage against the Audi, certainly not on open road. He had to do something drastic. Now.

They were nearing the outskirts of Paris and the traffic was building. The pursuers were gaining – two hundred metres back. Still no sign of Zoe's back-up cops.

'How many rounds you got in your pistol?' Fox asked, then took the emergency lane as the shooter took a sweeping shot at their back wheels.

'Full clip: fifteen,' Zoe replied.

'Swap you,' he said. 'Take the wheel.'

'What?'

He drifted back into the lane and weaved between a couple of buses.

'Here, slide over, now!'

She slid across, sitting in his lap, before he let the seat back a little and moved into her seat, taking the SIG. Zoe struggled to keep their vehicle ahead of the more powerful Audi, which tried to spin them out by hitting their bumper. The gap widened as they manoeuvred through a group of a dozen antique cars.

Fox said, 'When they're close again, hit the brakes like I did before, but harder.'

'What?' she asked, expertly moving the car through the traffic as though she were a seamstress threading the eye of a needle.

'When I say, hit the brakes – hard this time, let them close right in.' The Audi was a hundred and twenty metres back, one ten, one hundred. Matching their weave through the other vehicles on the road. Fox faced backwards, crouched in the seat, one hand tight on the pistol and the other on the lip of the open sun-roof.

'Wait for it . . .' he yelled over his shoulder. The hatch door of the Golf was long gone and what remained were sharp pieces of jagged metal, hanging from the hinges – he wanted to avoid those.

'Three seconds!' he yelled, then crouched, ready to jump up and out.

The Audi closed, the gunner lined up, taking aim out of the windscreen, the wind buffeting him as his car moved at high speed –

Fox let off two rounds; one pinged off the Audi passenger's side pillar, sending the gunner for cover. Fox readied himself.

'Now!'

The Audi was twenty metres back. In a second, it was less than five and just before they hit, Fox moved.

Up and out, he leaped onto the Audi's bonnet.

He hit hard, his pistol clattering into the Audi's interior, its driver back on his accelerator, giving just enough change in momentum to slide Fox towards the open windscreen. The gunner aimed –

Fox grabbed the foregrip of the passenger's MP5 submachine gun as the driver swerved left and right to shake him. Neither he nor the gunner were letting go. Over his shoulder he could see the road ahead – swerving, the Golf now corralling its pursuer.

Zoe braked long and hard, forcing the Audi to slow as well – they were moving as one in a cloud of smoke and dust from protesting tyres and brakes.

Fox hauled himself into the passenger compartment, holding the MP5 across with his right hand and lunging with his left for the gunner's throat. He caught the guy's throat, pushed off the dash with his feet, felt the windpipe crush under his own ninety-kilogram frame, and the submachine gun went off. The full-auto nine-millimetre rounds sheared both the driver's arms off above the wrist, the interior of the vehicle erupting in a mist of blood and gore.

Fox sunk into the front seats between the men, back to the windscreen, his left elbow jabbed hard against the gunner's temple knocking him out, while his right hand grabbed the steering wheel and he pulled his legs down into the cabin and planted his foot on top of the driver's, squeezing on the brakes. Wind whipped in through where the windscreen had been. After five long seconds, the Audi was stationary on the hard shoulder. Both assassins had passed out, the driver convulsing and losing blood fast. The bonnet of the car was pocked with bullet holes, the radiator hissed and steamed. The Golf had stopped, ten metres ahead; both Gammaldi and Kate were gazing apprehensively over the back seat. Fox looked around, checked the guys' pockets, nothing. He climbed through to the back seats, picked up Zoe's pistol, exited through the rear passenger's side door, walked back to the Golf and climbed into the empty passenger seat.

He was covered with blood, his chest ached from where he'd dragged himself across the remnants of broken windscreen and his heart was still racing. He knew that in a few minutes he'd come down, be in a flat funk as his adrenaline wore out. He looked up from the pistol in his bloodied hands.

Zoe stared at him, wide-eyed.

'Drive,' he said to her, his throat dry. 'Just drive.'

PART TWO

41

HIGH OVER EUROPE

Babich looked out his side window. The sky was overcast. They were flying forwards in time, heading east as fast as the aircraft would take them. If their flight was identified he didn't like his chances in the air; the US could reach you anywhere. The Russians, too, in this part of the world. He had no doubt that any number of nations would shoot him out of the sky, given the order from either the US or Russia. Not Kazakhstan, though. Money in the right hands, again, paid dividends. Two Kazakhstani jet fighters, MiG-29s, provided an escort through their airspace. Once over China, they'd appear on radar like any civilian Aeroflot flight en route to Shanghai. Lavrov had planned the mission well.

'Your man in Paris,' Babich turned to Lavrov. 'He's clean?'

'Yes, I recruited him personally,' Lavrov said. 'He is a deep undercover agent, never been used.'

'Do we own him?'

'No. Russia does.'

'He's for the country?'

Lavrov nodded.

'He's doing this for Russia . . .' Babich broke into a grin. 'That's priceless.'

'He thinks that this is the assignment he's been waiting for his whole life.' Lavrov smiled. 'He will do a fine job.'

Babich watched the MiGs out the window. He'd soon command many of them. And bombers. Attack helicopters. Naval vessels. Tanks. Ballistic missiles. That kind of power, even the idea of it, even the deterrence factor, was unbelievable in scope. For too long his country had sat idle. For too long they had watched the world prosper in a system he knew how to work. Russia deserved better.

'I am a cynical old man,' Babich said after a while. 'If I trust anyone, it is most often those who value money, because I know I can pay them the most. This man of yours – a patriot? That could get complicated . . .'

'He can't be bought,' Lavrov said firmly. 'But he works for me and he respects that.'

'Everyone has a price.'

Lavrov crossed his arms.

'That Lachlan Fox, he could never be bought.'

'True . . .' Babich said, remembering a discussion he'd had with Fox six months ago. He'd put everything on the table and it had indeed seemed that the reporter could not be bought. 'But he was a unique case, and I'd read him wrong.'

'Wrong?'

'I've had time to reflect,' Babich said. He held up his hand and shook his finger, 'I figured his price.'

Lavrov smiled, nodded.

'Well, this man, my agent, cannot be pressured into doing your bidding or anyone else's – he thinks he's doing this for

Russia, his Rodina, and it's best we leave it at that,' he continued. 'Do not get me wrong, we are paying him well, but that's to disappear at the end of this.'

The more Lavrov spoke, the uneasier Babich felt. Less certain. He had no time for that.

'He has already killed for us,' Lavrov said. 'He will see it through. He's working with some of our best special operatives.'

'Keep a tight leash on him,' Babich gazed at the MiG jet out the window, thin vapour trails coming from its wing tips. 'But I want insurance, in case he backs out.'

'There's no way he'd –'

'Just in case.'

Lavrov knew not to argue.

'He must have someone he values,' Babich said. 'Wife. Family. Whoever. Pick them up. Hold them until it is done.'

Lavrov nodded. Babich put a hand on his shoulder, looked his trusted man in the eye.

Babich said, 'We go tonight, and it will be great. We go with what we have, from your man, or we can't go at all. It will be tight, but it is what it is.'

'It is a great thing we are doing.' Lavrov looked at his young men, government men like him, who were backing a new leader in Babich. 'It all changes tonight, doesn't it, old friend?'

'Call in to Shanghai and Moscow,' Babich said. 'Make sure everyone is where we need them to be.'

Babich poured them both a measure of vodka. They raised their glasses.

'Tomorrow, a new dawn for everyone. Tomorrow, we arrive.'

42

PARIS

'Here we are,' Zoe said, parking the beaten-up Golf outside a large, austere building.

A squad of armed paramilitary police out the front looked at the smashed-up car with interest. Zoe went over and showed her ID, and they turned their attention elsewhere, scanning for threats. Zoe was giving orders to one and he relayed the info into his radio. She went back to the car.

'Lachlan, will you come with me?' she asked. 'Alister and Kate, there is a café on the corner of Rue de Saint-Simon, just there, see? A DCRI colleague of mine will meet you there soon.'

'But how –'

Zoe cut Gammaldi off, 'He will know you.'

Gammaldi and Kate shared a look, but knew it was useless arguing. Fox looked as though he'd been run over with a lawnmower – he'd torn off his sleeves to bandage his forearm and the front of his shirt was ripped from where he'd crawled into the Audi.

'They will be fine,' Zoe said to him as they watched them walk away, Brujon following.

She led Fox to the building's entrance, 'The Russian Ambassador's residence,' she explained.

Like much of the rest of this neighbourhood of the seventh *arrondissement*, it screamed expensive. A tiny cobbled street, lined with four- to six-storey residences that abutted the pavement.

'You can see why we were so interested in you this morning,' Zoe pointed at the address plaque on the wall: 79 Rue de Grenelle.

It took a while before it clicked in Fox's brain. He'd parked on Rue de Grenelle this morning by the market, not far from here.

'We thought you must have seen us follow you along Saint Germain, and assumed that was why you turned off early, to backtrack here on foot,' Zoe explained, watching Fox. 'We had plain-clothes officers on foot, following you as you shopped.'

'Really?' Fox tried to recall the faces, but there were far too many.

'I noticed your car,' he said, thinking back to earlier this morning. 'When you followed my dog-legged route to the market street.'

She smiled.

'You see, at that time I thought for sure you were looking for this place,' Zoe said. 'And instead you were just shopping for food.'

'Well, you've met Al,' Fox said, walking in step with her to the entrance. 'He would have "cassouleted" me if I'd come back empty-handed!'

They reached the doors, and the six paramilitary men waved them through. They were decked out in black Nomex overalls, Kevlar plating, knee pads and helmets, pistols in thigh holsters and chunky SIG SG 552 Commando assault rifles slung across their chests. The kind of paramilitary cops Fox could have used back at the farmhouse. As he passed them they eyed him carefully.

'The *gendarmerie*?' Fox asked, standing next to Zoe in the cobblestoned courtyard.

'No,' Zoe replied. 'Recherche Assistance Intervention Dissuasion, or RAID, a SWAT-type unit of the National Police. Our primary anti-terrorism unit. So they are like my, how would you say, cousins?'

'Wouldn't want to pick a fight over the Christmas table with those cousins,' Fox said. He watched them shut the heavy timber door behind them so that he and Zoe were enclosed in the high-walled space. 'Is this Russian sovereign territory?'

'No,' Zoe replied. 'Marquis de Touresol sold the villa to the Russian government in 1864. The Russian Embassy *was* situated here till the October Revolution. When the new Soviet Embassy building was finished in 1977, this became solely the residence of the ambassador.'

Fox noticed several security cameras attached to the building and walls. He pointed, asked, 'Do you have the – ?'

'No,' Zoe said, pre-empting any question about security footage. 'They took it all, we are working in the courts to get it back but it will take a while – too long.'

Fox nodded. If this murder was the work of one of their own, he couldn't imagine the Russian authorities ever giving up the footage; if forced, they'd probably hand over doctored tapes of the night before.

'Were there guards on the gate the night of the murder?'

'Yes.'

'And they let the killer through?'

She stopped, looked at him, questioning.

'I mean – this place is a fortress,' Fox said. 'The glass in the windows at the front, out on the street, it could stop a mortar shell.'

'Yes,' she said, leading them towards the front door. 'They let him through and he entered through here.'

Fox glanced at the lock as he walked in. A recent addition, it was a big brass mechanism, anti-tamper steel sleeve . . .

'He had a key,' Zoe said. Her look gave nothing away. Perhaps she had no more information.

'As you said, an inside job,' Fox agreed.

'Our killer entered the front door,' Zoe continued, walking to an open-plan living area. She pointed to a sofa in front of a big LCD screen. 'Katya was sitting there with the television on. She did not notice him until he was attacking her. It was quick, but messy.'

There was some crime-scene gear still set up in the lounge room – lights, measuring tapes and marks, notes on small plastic cards.

'I found a note in her diary about meeting with you next week,' Zoe said. The throwaway comment snapped Fox out of staring at the blood-stained carpet.

'Yeah . . . Wednesday, I think; my iPhone is back at Renard's farmhouse.'

Zoe nodded, detached. 'This is where she was killed. Bled out quickly, they say.'

'Knife?'

'He killed her with glass from the table,' Zoe said, motioning to a broken coffee table. She mimed a slice to the side of her neck. 'Dead quickly, like I said.'

'That's a brutal way to murder someone,' Fox said. 'Stupid and amateurish. Almost like it was unplanned, improvised . . . Or something went wrong.'

She looked at him with a little more respect.

'Come, follow me.'

He watched the sway of her hips as she walked up the stairs, tried not to notice. It was a pleasant distraction, though. He held the banister with his left hand and winced with the pain of a deep cut along his forearm.

'We'll patch that wound up in a few minutes,' Zoe said. She stood at the top of the stairs, a magnificent tapestry behind her. She pointed. 'There, the second door.'

They entered a small room with a single window that looked back over the courtyard. It contained an ancient timber desk furnished with a new Aeron chair and an iMac. There was an in-tray filled with papers, a vase of blood-red poppies, and an open diary. The air was stuffy.

'Her study?'

'Yes,' Zoe said. 'And, yes, Wednesday is when you were to meet her: 11 am, with Renard, at the Louvre.'

'Okay.'

'And then it was crossed out, and a new date and time set.'

'Oh?' Fox said. That was news to him.

'We found an email to Renard cancelling the meeting, and mentioning she was giving the information to a friend, for safe-keeping, until she was sure of things.'

'Who's her friend?'

'Raymond Durand. Her lover, a local architect. He did the designs for this building's renovations,' Zoe said. 'She'd been seeing him for some months.'

Fox was about to speak when he stopped himself. Looked around the room and back to Zoe.

'Is it okay to talk in here?' he asked. 'I mean . . .'

He pointed to his ear, and signalled around the room.

'Yes, we swept it for bugs, found at least one in every room,' she said. 'They're gone now, but I'll get to that in a minute.'

Fox was having a hard time catching up.

'Later that day, Katya sent a parcel to Durand at Hotel Martinez in Cannes,' Zoe said. 'Concierge there says that he received the package, about the size of a hardback novel, and delivered it personally to Durand.'

'And that's the information she wanted to hand to me?'

'Yes.'

'And it's in Cannes?'

'It arrived yesterday, but has already moved.'

Fox shook his head. He not only felt tired and beaten up, he felt out of the loop. There was more to this than was being lost in translation. There was *clearly* more to this than a macabre tour for his sole benefit. *What the hell did Zoe want from him?*

'Durand checked out of his hotel and travelled back to Paris this morning,' Zoe continued.

'So he's here – he's here in Paris right now?'

'Yes,' she said, watching Fox closely.

'Well, can we go see him?'

'He's meeting with your friend Renard as we speak.'

Fox took a step back. His mind was reeling. *Renard was now meeting with this guy? Without him? To deliver the information that Katya had contacted Fox about? What the hell was going on? And why was Zoe playing with him . . . Was he a suspect?*

'But . . .'

'Don't worry, we have Renard under close surveillance,' she said. 'But it takes me back to the bugs, and why I wanted to bring you here.'

43

NAPLES

ITALY

The ceiling was bright. Hutchinson blinked his eyes, his vision blurry, light-headed . . . The room started to spin.

A face appeared over him, short brown hair flecked with red, friendly eyes behind thick-rimmed glasses.

'Hello.'

She didn't answer as she checked his IV connection and then his vitals. He could feel her down at his legs, prodding and adjusting, but couldn't see her. He tried to lift his head, but it felt too heavy.

'Hello?'

'Hi,' the nurse said, popping back into his field of vision. 'How are you feeling?'

Her accent was American, a fellow Bostonian, in fact.

'Numb,' Hutchinson replied. 'My leg . . . A little sore in the leg.'

'Good.'

'Good?'

'Pain's good,' she replied. 'Apparently you self-administered some Fentanyl lollipops.'

He remembered floating in the water. Being winched up to a grey Seahawk helicopter.

'Where am I?'

'Naples, Sixth Fleet Headquarters,' she answered, efficiently prodding him. 'You're in the base hospital.'

'Right,' he said. 'How long have I been here?'

'Less than an hour. You passed out in the helicopter after they rescued you from the sea,' she replied. 'We cleaned out and dressed your leg wound . . . You don't remember?'

He tried to play back the memory. He remembered the flight. Watching the Gulfstream's altitude meter winding down. Jumping out of the aircraft. Free-falling through the air. Parachuting into the sea, bobbing there . . . How long had he been in the water?

She was watching him, concerned. 'You know your name?'

'Bourne?' he said.

She laughed.

He remembered Capel and Brick and the two pilots. He remembered Babich.

'Look, I need to make a phone call.'

'Doctor will be here in a minute, and I'll bring you a phone then,' she replied. She beamed a smile at him. 'If you need anything, just say so, I'll be sitting right here.'

'I need a phone.'

44

PARIS

'Some of the bugs we found in the building were ours,' Zoe said. 'Some were American, some Russian. There were three in the bedroom – even the Russians put one in there.'

'Maybe it was part of the ambassador's performance review . . .'

Zoe showed the slightest of smiles.

Fox asked, 'So you have audio of the killer?'

'Yes,' Zoe replied. 'This was recorded by our bug, and we assume by the Americans as well.'

Fox guessed the American feed went to the CIA station at their embassy. He wondered how many Russian speakers they still had on the payroll. Enough, surely?

'Have they said anything about it?'

'Why would they?' Zoe asked. 'This is a murder on French soil, an internal policing matter for us to handle. If it stretches across borders, it's an Interpol issue, nothing more.'

He adjusted his makeshift bandages, tried to speed things along: 'Can I hear it?'

'Like I said, it's why you're here.' Zoe put a digital recorder on the desk. 'Translated for our Interpol colleagues.'

She pressed play. Fox heard the sounds of a struggle, a muffled scream, indecipherable murmuring, then some shouting and apparently the shattering of glass. Then the incident played again with the sound levels changed: voices were isolated and an English translator spoke over the conversation:

KATYA: Who are you – what are you doing here?
UNKNOWN MALE: You know what I want.
KATYA: You have to leave, my – my husband will be here any –
UNKNOWN MALE: Don't be stupid – You just saw him leave the embassy.
KATYA: Is he . . .
UNKNOWN MALE: Dead? Yes.
Silence for a few beats and then a quiet sobbing.
KATYA: It wasn't meant to be like this. Please, don't hurt me.
UNKNOWN MALE: Give me the diary and you will not be hurt.
Pause.
UNKNOWN MALE: Where is the diary?

Zoe pressed 'stop'. Fox knew there was more, as the shattering glass of what had been the coffee table downstairs – the very murder weapon – had yet to play in the translated version of the conversation.

'And?'

'Do you know anything of a diary?' Zoe asked, watching him closely. She was no further than a pace from him, and although not much more than half his weight and a few inches shorter, she had the advantage. Fox didn't like games. Especially those played by police.

He shook his head. Pointed to the table, to a leather-bound ledger. 'A diary like that?'

'This is Katya's diary,' Zoe said, opening it to the marker on the current week. Fox wondered why they hadn't taken it for evidence, but then he remembered the cops at the door – this was as secure a crime scene as there could be. 'They are talking about a diplomat's diary – Eduard de Stoeckl – found in this room, in the panelling, during the renovations.'

Fox took it in, memorised the name, knew it was pivotal: enough to kill for, something about – or important to – Roman Babich.

'I've never heard of him,' Fox said, matter-of-factly.

'Did Katya mention a diary?'

'No.'

'But she wanted to give you something?'

'All she said was that she had information that would implicate Babich . . .' Fox said. 'No, wait. She said she had something that Babich *valued very highly* – something that her husband wanted to sell to him. She was scared of what might happen when her husband found out she was going to give it to us.'

'She told you that on the phone?'

'Yes, it was a brief conversation, and as far as I knew I'd put Renard in touch with her to arrange a time to meet and discuss it further.'

'She told you just that and you flew out here, from the safety of the FBI protection, to chase a lead against the very man who wants you dead.'

'I didn't say my actions made any sense,' Fox said, a little smirk playing on his face. 'Look, Zoe, I've been doing this a while now. I've seen some shit. You've read my file. I've done my time in special forces and Naval intelligence. I know how the world works. Katya contacted me; she was spooked and anxious, and I believed her. And guess what, she was right to be spooked by this. Only I guess she underestimated Babich's reach.'

Zoe's eyes never left his, and something seemed to resolve itself in her look.

Fox asked, 'Who's this Stoeckl guy?'

'A Russian diplomat,' Zoe said. 'Posted for some time to the US. He died in Paris in 1892.'

'Bit before my time.' Fox motioned to the digital recorder.

Zoe pressed play.

UNKNOWN MALE: Where is the diary? Stoeckl's diary?
Long pause.
KATYA: I don't have it.
Pause.
UNKNOWN MALE: Where is it?
Silence.
UNKNOWN MALE, YELLING: Where is it?

Fox could hear struggling, and the sound of the coffee table shattering.

KATYA: Please, no!
UNKNOWN MALE: Tell me where the diary is.

The sound of crying. Real sobs, defeated. Another struggle.

KATYA: My husband . . . He had to deliver it to Shanghai . . . by midnight, Saturday.

Fox instinctively checked his watch.

UNKNOWN MALE: I know you had it. You sent it in the post. Where is it? Who did you send it to?

Sounds of a struggle, broken glass moving.

KATYA: Please, no . . . Please . . .

Sobbing.

KATYA: A reporter – I sent it to a reporter! Fox, it's with Lachlan Fox. He's in Paris now.

Pause.

UNKNOWN MALE: You are sure? Fox? Not your friend . . . a Mr Durand?

There was the sound of another struggle, more breaking glass and then a gurgling sound for about five seconds, then silence.

UNKNOWN MALE: I'm so sorry . . .

Zoe switched the audio device off.

Fox studied her. Okay, he could see why she was interested.

'Zoe, I don't have –'

'I know,' she said and pocketed the recorder. 'She didn't send it to you. It's what she sent Durand – to Cannes.'

Fox followed her out of the study. At the end of the hall by the stairs they paused at a window and stood, both thinking, while Fox re-wrapped his aching hand.

Sunlight streamed in from double-door windows that looked out to a grassed area, filled with brightly painted totems. They were tall cylindrical figure drawings with smiling face outlines and flowers. *Maybe they were meant to symbolise missiles rising out of silos, reborn as art, taken over by the people. Maybe they were symbols of male power. Maybe they were just pretty.*

'A Paul Flickinger installation,' Zoe said, standing close to him. She smelled of citrus and lavender, the faintest perfume. 'French artist, his works are displayed throughout the residence and in the garden.'

'Hats off to the Russian Federation for showing some taste,' Fox said.

Zoe looked at him with what he read as respect. *Maybe the revelations of hers were over. Maybe that's all she had about this case and it went no further and they'd be on their way and he could get his friends to safety and he'd leave her to have words with Renard.*

Zoe asked him, 'What are you thinking about?'

'I'm wondering what's so special about this diary.'

'That's what I want to know too.'

'And you think that's all that they were killed for?' Fox asked. 'The murder here, the attack at the embassy?'

'The assassin tore apart the ambassador's safe at the embassy, we know that much,' she replied. 'And he did the same here.'

'And this Durand guy?'

'He was the one who found the diary when they were renovating. It was hidden in the wall of Katya's study.'

Fox looked at her, making the connection: 'Stoeckl had used the room in the past.'

'Yes,' Zoe replied. 'Durand couldn't read Russian so he handed it to her, about six months ago, and then she gave it to her husband . . .'

Her phone bleeped.

'My guy is here.'

Outside the compound, Gammaldi and Kate were leaning against a Peugeot hatchback, holding take-away coffees.

Zoe took the keys from her plain-clothed colleague and motioned him to the Golf. He directed a few words her way; Fox caught 'Vincent' among them and remembered that Zoe had lost a friend just before, a colleague to both these cops before him. He looked away.

'Your friends can go with my colleague,' Zoe said.

'No way,' Gammaldi said. He stepped forwards like he was ready for a fist fight.

'Uh uh,' Kate said. She looked at Fox, resolute. 'We're sticking together.'

Brujon looked up at him, trusting.

'We can't leave him either,' Gammaldi said.

Fox shrugged to Zoe and she gave a little, 'Meh,' in resignation. 'But the dog goes with my colleague, no arguments.'

Zoe hopped into the Peugeot's driver's seat while the rest of them piled in.

'Where to?' Fox asked.

Zoe gunned the engine and took off with a wheel-spin.

'We need to talk to Durand and find out why he was meeting with your friend Renard. We need to see that diary . . .'

45

HIGH OVER KAZAKHSTAN

'I have a majority ready to move in the Duma,' Babich said, thinking about those in his country's House of Reps who he could rely on. Men who had been waiting for their chance to lead for a long time, many of the current government who were fed up with being overlooked by their leadership. So he'd have to give away many ministerial positions, sometimes to unqualified men; so what? A small price to pay for loyalty. But. The fact that the Russian Ambassador in Paris had been ready to betray him . . . He'd need to make some phone calls when they reached Shanghai. Not many, but some, to those weaker ones, those who needed to be told first-hand how and when to step in line, to be called to action. The rest were smart enough to seize the oportunity. He just wished he could see the look on Putin's face when it all went down. That would be . . . priceless.

Lavrov was looking at the list of political names they'd triple-checked, his smile fading. 'Some . . .' he said. 'Some are sceptical that you can do this.'

'Who?'

'Some. Not the list here . . . Outside the Duma.'

'Military?'

'No, those we need will follow . . . It is . . . The current government have been entrenched for so long now . . . So many of the business leaders are their guys . . . You know how it works.'

'But that was always the way, yes?'

Lavrov nodded.

'It was always the impossible long shot, for me or anyone,' Babich said, a reassuring pat on his man's knee. 'That is why we need this secret protocol, this treaty amendment, before we move. It is our weapon for us to show our people a new economic way forward, a new era – a change to how things have been done.'

Lavrov nodded, forced a smile, looked a little sick.

Babich was sitting up, his eyes alert. 'We, as a country, have to move on, evolve, you see?'

'*I* see, *I* understand that . . .' Lavrov said. There was something else.

'But . . . ?'

'I am not sure that *they*, the *people*, will.'

Ah, the people . . .

'They will come around, they will see sense,' Babich assured him. 'Lavrov, you and I did nothing when the current regime came to power. We did *nothing* to stop them in 1999 . . . Now we get to right that wrong. The people *want* change. They *yearn* for the prosperity of which they've had only a taste.'

Lavrov nodded, but didn't look convinced. Time to tell him.

Babich leaned forward. 'What do you know about the secret protocol of which I speak?'

'Too little,' Lavrov said. He stammered in realisation that he was about to be entrusted with everything.

'You remember the secret protocol of our Great Patriotic War?' Babich said. 'The Nazi pact?'

'The one you uncovered in the archives?'

'Yes.'

'But . . . that is old,' Lavrov said. 'That was made public, long ago . . .'

'Well, my friend, what if I told you that in my search, when I had unfettered access to our nation's most secret diplomatic archives, I found something else . . .'

Lavrov's eyes brightened at the turn the conversation was taking.

'Yes, quite something indeed,' Babich said. He settled back and looked out at the view as the plane headed further east. Every mile travelled he felt safer. He was closer to home now, closer to his destiny. He looked back to Lavrov. 'What do you know about the history of Alaska?'

46

PARIS

Fox sat in the back of the vehicle, next to Kate, who had just bandaged his forearm.

'It might need stitches,' she said. She stuffed piles of bloodied gauze into a plastic bag and was cleaning up a few scrapes on his hands.

'It'll be all right,' Fox reassured, watching her work. Here they were, in the fire again because of his choices. *But we don't all choose, do we? Not the little things, not the variables, the reactions of others.* Her eyes never looked up to meet his, they just kept steady on the task at hand. Whatever cleared this business up with Renard and Zoe and whatever the hell this diary meant, he'd do it. He'd do it for Kate. He'd do it to set them free.

'Ouch,' he said, as she pulled out a piece of windscreen glass from his left palm. She helped him into a fresh shirt, courtesy of the cop who'd provided the car.

'Great, I look like a Bolo,' he said, stretching out the snug black Lacoste polo.

'I was going to say an Abercrombie and Fitch model,' Gammaldi said over his shoulder from the front.

They hung on to their seats as Zoe cornered hard and powered up through the gears. Several cars tooted their horns as she wove through the traffic. It was an unmarked car and she didn't bother with a police light on the roof. *She was French – she probably drove like this when she was off duty, too.*

Kate's phone rang, its screen illuminated between them. She answered it and handed it to Fox.

'It's Andrew Hutchinson,' she said, her hand over the microphone. 'And when you were sightseeing back there, McCorkell left a bunch of messages for you to call him back asap.'

'Thanks . . .' Fox said. 'Andy?'

•

Hutchinson sat up, the phone tight to his ear. He told Fox about the mid-air incident on the Gulfstream, then he listened as Fox relayed the story about the morning's attack. He scratched at his leg, bandaged tight and elevated. The FBI Legal Attaché from Rome had arrived five minutes ago and set up a video conference so he was linked back to the Umbra task force in DC. A Navy representative was posted to act as a doorman when required as the conversations would contain some classified information. He was itching to get back out there, to drag that fucker Babich in, dead or alive.

'You're sure it was a clean-up squad?' Hutchinson asked as Fox finished.

'They weren't delivering the mail.'

'And they were Russian?'

'Yep.' Fox said. 'Seriously, you think it was a garden-variety home invasion? It was an eight-man special forces squad. The guy I questioned confirmed that they were there to *kill* us, Andy.'

Hutchinson looked at the computer screen, saw that McCorkell and Valerie were listening in intently.

'They were definitely from one of their Spetsnaz teams,' Fox said. 'I recognised the training, but whether they are still on the payroll . . . Nah, I doubt it. They were slow. A little soft. Anyway, my new cop friend organised a chopper assault back at the house. They'll get more answers.'

'If they're still there.'

'I can't imagine any of them having gone far in a hurry.' Fox paused on the line. His voice changed, lower register, quieter. 'Any word on your prisoner's whereabouts?'

'We might have a lead but it's still a bit sketchy. Bill and Valerie are working on confirmation.' Hutchinson saw them nod. Much as he wanted to be there in that room directing the play, he wanted even more to be in the field. Mobile, ready to strike wherever the son of a bitch showed up. *Well, mobile as one could be with this leg . . .*

Fox asked, 'Bill, need anything else from me?'

McCorkell looked to Valerie, and then turned back to the camera to Hutchinson and shook his head.

'Nup, just wanted to make sure you're safe,' Hutchinson said. 'Keep your head down, ya' hear?'

•

After Fox disconnected he handed the phone back to Kate. She seemed uninterested, just scrolled through her messages. Fox was about to say something, when –

'We're here,' Zoe said, as they pulled up abruptly outside a new-looking building. A giant glass pyramid, a good fifty storeys high. They all got out of the car. A valet took the keys, Zoe showed her ID and told him to keep it close.

'Le Project Triangle,' Zoe said as they entered the lobby. 'The first skyscraper to be approved since Paris lifted a thirty-one-year ban on high-rise construction in the city centre.'

'Swiss architects Jacques Herzog and Pierre de Meuron,' Fox said.

Zoe looked at him, didn't say anything.

'He likes to show off,' Gammaldi said. 'A jack of all trades, he's been called. An endless vessel of useless knowledge.'

'They designed Beijing's bird's nest Olympic stadium, too,' Fox said. Here, they'd come up with a building just as startling: an impressive glass and steel pyramid, looking from its side profile like a shark fin. 'I'm amazed Paris has started to change her skyline.'

'Progress,' Zoe said, nodding to a guy who got into the lift with them – another plain-clothed cop, Fox thought, obviously one who'd been trailing Durand. 'I assume that city planners think this is the way forward, to give our country some kind of future, some edge on the rest of Western Europe – given that some see it as a museum.'

Kate looked to Fox, he shook his head: *Don't bite.*

'This looks more like something you'd find in Vegas,' Kate said, as the lift pinged and the doors opened to a party.

'Exhibition opening,' Zoe's man said. They shuffled through the throng, met with another guy, who leaned in and whispered something to Zoe.

She turned to Fox. 'Our man, Durand, is outside on the deck, black shirt.'

Fox saw maybe fifty guys in black shirts.

'You two stay here,' she said, moving off with Fox in tow.

'Of course,' Gammaldi said, his mood shifting as he caught a waiter passing with hors d'oeuvres.

'The man there; he is our architect,' Zoe said quietly to Fox, pointing out a thin guy in his mid-forties standing next to an even thinner woman. Both dressed in black, in a sea of dark colours, coiffed hair and tall drinks. They stood on an expansive deck that looked out across the roofs of Paris towards the Eiffel Tower. Fox bumped into Zoe as she stopped by the wide open doorspace. They waited a while in the architect's eye-line, and when he finally looked over, Zoe flashed her suit jacket to reveal the holstered SIG.

Durand got the message and excused himself from his group. He approached them quickly.

'Please,' he said, with a covert motion back to his wife. 'Not here. Not in front of her.'

47

PARIS

Four blocks away, Boris Malevich was following Renard on foot. He could count maybe four plain-clothed police between him and his guy. He felt nauseous. His two guys were on the other side of the road. *Maybe if Renard got onto the Metro they could make a move, close in on the cops . . .* It would be risky, but he didn't need to check his watch to know that such risks would have to be taken.

At least things were happening fast now. After nearly two hours waiting outside the *Le Figaro* office, then following Renard to the big modern building where he'd met up with the architect . . . Malevich had to be careful; the architect had seen his face before. The day was heating up. The air was still and he felt suffocated. He loosened his collar. Walked faster.

What if he didn't get a chance soon? His deadline was nearing . . . and it was so close now, his target, just a block ahead of him.

One of his guys had seen Durand hand the diary over at the pyramid building. Renard had put it in his satchel and Boris wanted to move in then, but the cops were there, watching. *They must have worked out there was a connection between these guys and the ambassador's death . . . Fuck it.* He didn't have time to figure it out, he just had to get the job done.

One of the cops looked over his shoulder and Malevich crossed the road, swapping places with one of his own men. *Where were his back-up guys from Giverny?* With another eight men they could take these cops and . . . *Fuck it!* He wrung his hands together, sweat coating his back. He took some deep breaths, felt his heart palpitating, and thought back to Katya, her sticky hot blood on his hands . . .

His phone rang.

'Where are you at?' The voice was scrambled to avoid detection on voice-recognition software, but he knew it was his handler.

'Paris,' Malevich replied, running across the street to make it before the traffic lights changed.

'I mean, do you have it?'

'Almost,' Malevich said. 'Can you call some cops off a target for me?'

Malevich gave him a brief description of the cops following Renard, and the street address.

'I will take care of it. Just get what I need.'

'Of course.'

'I need it tonight, it must be tonight.'

'You'll have it tonight,' Malevich replied, nodding to his guy ahead of him and switching places again. 'Where do I meet you?'

'You are booked on an Air France flight at de Gaulle, leaves at two-thirty today.'

Malevich paused. *That quick?*

He said, 'That's not much time.'

'It is what it is – you knew you had until lunchtime today.'

Malevich waited for more; a destination, but none was forthcoming.

'But where am I meeting you?' he asked.

'Where the aircraft takes you.'

'Please . . .' He'd known Lavrov for so long. They'd not spoken in almost ten years, sure, but he trusted this man – and couldn't he see that he was dedicated to this, all the way? That he was doing everything he was asked by the state, everything that was expected?

'Please?'

'I can't tell you exactly. Just a country, yes?'

Then Malevich got it. The Americans, maybe others, might hear their phone call.

'China,' Lavrov said. 'You're flying to China.'

Malevich almost stopped in the street, but kept walking. The ambassador had been scheduled to go to Shanghai tonight. *What the hell was going on?*

'You're in China?'

'You'll be met at the airport when you touch down, it's all arranged.'

'I'll get there on time,' Malevich said, his pace slowing to a stop as they all waited to cross roads, still a block apart. He looked away when a cop turned towards him. Felt like throwing up. 'Just make sure you're there personally, and transfer what we've agreed.'

'Of course,' Lavrov replied. 'I will contact you again in an hour.'

48

PARIS

Once they were far enough away from Durand's wife, Zoe introduced herself properly. It didn't put the guy at ease.

Zoe said to him, in English: 'You are aware that Katya was murdered?'

Durand looked sick. He leaned against a nearby bar and signalled for a drink.

He replied in French, 'I . . . I was told . . .'

Fox looked to Zoe. She translated, then asked Durand to talk in English.

Fox asked, 'Did Renard mention it? Did he tell you?'

Durand looked him up and down. 'Who are you?'

'I'm a reporter –'

'I can't have anything in the press!' Durand's face flushed. He grabbed the bourbon the barman put down for him.

'Relax,' Zoe said. 'He's helping with my investigation.'

Durand gulped down half of his drink. 'Who killed her?'

'We are working on that,' Zoe said. 'Tell us about the diary.'

'I didn't know what it was,' he said, continuing in English. 'It was an old hand-written journal, in Russian, and our builders found it during the renovation when – it doesn't matter, does it? We found it in the wall. Hidden, unmoved for decades, I'd say.'

'And you gave it straight to Katya?'

'Sure,' he looked into his drink. Took another sip. 'There was – you'd be surprised what we find, hidden in walls and under floorboards or ceilings, squirrelled away during one of the wars . . . The Nazis were particularly fond of looting buildings for valuables. They even stayed there in that building during the war, but evidently never found it.'

'Did you make copies?'

He looked at Zoe, puzzled.

'Copy the diary? Why would I?' he replied. 'Like I said, it was in Russian. I took it to Kat, we had a drink and we got along. She asked me out for coffee later that week, it turned into lunch, a long lunch . . .'

'So you started an affair then?' Zoe asked, shifting in close to him, her voice comforting. Fox saw something in Zoe he hadn't noticed earlier: she was an artist at gaining trust, at being persuasive, at coaxing out information. As someone who'd interviewed hundreds of people over the years, Fox was impressed.

Durand nodded, shot a look across the room to his wife on the deck. She had her back to them, laughing with friends.

'Had she read the diary?'

'Some of it, yes,' he replied.

He held Zoe's gaze for a moment. Sipped his drink, knew they were expecting more of an explanation. 'It referenced some kind of document hidden in Paris . . . That was its main importance, it seems – the rest was personal entries of the diplomat.'

'What document?' Fox asked.

'Does it matter now?' Durand replied, anger in his wet eyes. 'Katya's husband was convinced that, if used properly, it would bring billions of dollars to Russia, hundreds of billions or more.'

Fox and Zoe looked at one another.

'I know; sounds crazy, right?' Durand went on, finishing his drink. 'But that is what her husband said and he was a man who went by the book, you understand? He would not . . . He would not have lied about a benefit to Russia. He was convinced. Made plans.'

'What was he going to do with it?' asked Fox.

'He was going to sell it.'

'Who to?'

'Some wealthy Russian guy, I don't know . . . Badovich?' Durand looked strained, trying to remember. 'That tycoon, oligarch or whatever.'

'Babich?' Fox prompted. 'Roman Babich?'

'Yeah, that guy who was arrested. Katya didn't know him, but her husband did, and he was sure it would be worth millions to the guy,' Durand looked outside, searching for his thoughts. 'But when he was arrested, Katya said her husband had organised secret meetings with the Russian government.'

'To hand it over?'

'I guess. If he couldn't share in its worth he at least wanted to be a hero or something, but he was wary of who he trusted in there – he thought they'd not see the – the potential, I guess . . .'

'When was he going to hand it over?'

Durand checked his watch. 'About now.'

'What?'

'He was meeting Putin's guys in Shanghai – at the G20 Summit.' Durand looked thoughtful. 'We were going to leave before then. Katya . . . She had this idea that we could sell it all to the Americans, the diary and the document.'

'And this *document*,' Fox began, 'did you learn anything about what this document said?'

Durand looked into his empty glass at the melting ice and nodded.

Fox and Zoe shared a look, stood straighter, moved closer.

'Not much,' Durand said, 'but it was deeds or something – a treaty? No, a *protocol*, it was called a protocol. This Russian diplomat had it signed and hidden, some kind of personal insurance. It was about Russian America –'

49

WASHINGTON, DC

'So you're really convinced that Babich is headed to China?' Bowden asked. 'But you've still got no proof?'

'Yep,' McCorkell said. Bowden looked from him to his task-force personnel. 'None of these guys have come to that conclusion, you know that? But hey, that's why you're the man, right? So I can take all my guys here off their search, tell them to call off their assets in the field . . .'

'We need to get some assets in China, just in case,' McCorkell said, not about to engage in a pissing contest. 'Hedge this bet.'

'I don't gamble.'

'It's the G20.'

'You know how many security services are in Shanghai for that? Babich showing his face? Sorry, I don't buy it.'

McCorkell didn't know what else to tell him.

'Know this, Bill: we will find him, and soon,' Bowden said. 'Damned if this is gonna turn into a Bin Laden, where he's hiding in the fucking hills because he slipped through a torn net. If we can't take Babich in easy and quick, we're taking the shot.'

'Whaddya mean?' McCorkell asked.

'He's a terrorist. He's attacked American soil – directed those guys who tried to storm the White House a year back –'

'I was there.'

'Course you were, you're *the man*,' Bowden said. 'Just saying, is all. This fucker's a Tier One Personality and the protocols on how we deal with them are clear.'

'We're doing this through the courts, that's always been the object –'

'We get the shot, we're taking him down.' Bowden had that 'no bullshit' look, couldn't be swayed. 'Got a few Navy and FBI widows from this morning who would fucking pull the trigger themselves, given the chance. So, even if he *is* headed to China, where we can't extradite or operate with overt forces, it won't matter any way. Wherever, whenever, he's gone. You know that.'

McCorkell knew that. He'd suspected it was Bowden's intent and now it had been confirmed. The G20 Summit being underway meant all the heads of state were there already – and so it was possible that some political manoeuvres could be brought to the table that would force China to hand Babich over, should he enter the country . . . But that was a long shot at best. Fact was, Umbra's corporations did plenty of business in China, equivalent to a mid-sized country, and particularly in the vital energy and resource sector that drove the behemoth economy.

Still . . . Taking a shot . . .

'Can you get word along to your guys in Shanghai?' McCorkell asked.

Bowden looked at him, his eyes weighing up the request. He knew that McCorkell guessed he had a direct line not only to the Director of the CIA, but also to the president.

'I'll look into it,' Bowden said, going back to his work.

McCorkell headed back towards his own desk. He was well aware of the CIA's High Value Target protocols, which specified the names of terrorist leaders the agency was authorised to assassinate if capture was impractical and civilian casualties could be kept to an acceptable number. He also knew about the Agency's SOG units which executed clandestine missions in countries that denied access to US military special operations forces, like Pakistan and Iran. Just recently, McCorkell had learned of a new initiative that consisted of teams of Special Activities Division paramilitary officers, organised to execute targeted assassinations against al-Qaeda operatives around the world in any country. For senior intelligence officers, it was an attempt to avoid the civilian casualties that could occur during Predator and Reaper drone strikes using Hellfire missiles. What would be Bowden's directive if he found his man in Shanghai – an air strike from the seventh fleet? A team of door-kickers shooting it out with Babich's security? Either way would be messy, and China was a country they couldn't afford to mess with right now.

McCorkell sat at his desk amid the FBI team. Their demeanour had changed; they were invigorated, less tense, more chatty.

Bowden's voice provided a constant thrum of orders and requests for updates from across the room, and his legacy and mission were constantly at the back of McCorkell's mind. The intel officer had been brave enough to point out some flaws or deficiencies in his own agency. From a 2010 career high, when he had been appointed to head a task force that uncovered failings in the CIA by asking some painful questions about its own performance: How could a would-be suicide bomber have flown to Detroit despite a strong warning to a CIA station that he might be a terrorist? How could a Jordanian double agent have penetrated a CIA base in Afghanistan and killed seven agency employees? Talking to veteran counter-terrorism officers, Bowden reported a common theme that united those two disastrous lapses: the CIA had adopted bureaucratic procedures that, while intended to avoid mistakes, actually heightened the risks. The two cases were very different, yet both illustrated what can happen when intelligence managers are eager for results to take to their political superiors and not worried enough about risks. The consequence was a breakdown in tradecraft that proved to have fatal consequences. The post-9/11 intelligence reorganisation that was supposed to improve efficiency had made the bureaucracy problem worse. Bowden's conclusion: the Americans have a system that is overwhelmed. He was feted for this reasoning. He'd become a specialist intelligence star who was in the fold and tough enough to criticise it. He was a man of action in an army of men equipped with explanations.

McCorkell was worried. The danger here? An action man at the helm of a very delicate operation with a lot of unknowns.

He knew Bowden had talked with the CIA Director, who was almost certainly now speaking with the other agency and department heads about exactly who was holding the reins of power in the Umbra Task Force. Doubtlessly, Bowden would be confirmed as king, and he'd be given the green light to do whatever it took to extract a proportional response against Babich and Umbra. Whatever it took to make the problem go away, so they could get back to the real war of fighting al-Qaeda.

'Valerie,' he said, and she swivelled her chair around to face him. 'We gotta talk to Andy.'

50

PARIS

'Russian America?'

'Alaska,' Durand said. He signalled for another drink. 'The diary belonged to the diplomat who sold Alaska to the United States.'

'I don't understand . . . Sold it?' Zoe said, looking to Fox.

'Russia used to own what's now called Alaska,' Fox said. He thought back to the conversation he'd had with Zoe in the ambassador's residence.

'Who's this Stoeckl guy?'

'A Russian diplomat. Posted for some time to the US. He died in Paris in 1892.'

'Sold it to the US in the late 1860s. Known as Seward's Folly . . .' He turned to Durand. 'So Stoeckl was the diplomat who handled the sale on Russia's behalf?'

Durand shrugged.

Fox asked him, 'What did this protocol say?'

'I have no idea,' Durand said. 'But the ambassador was going to sell it for a lot of money . . . Well, not now . . .'

His eyes welled with tears.

'Katya was leaving him. I had booked tickets to London . . . She'd given me her passport to hold onto –' he pulled it out of his inside jacket pocket and put it on the bar, useless now. 'Please, my wife doesn't know anything, I want to leave it that way. It's over now.'

'Did Katya ever speak of being in danger?'

'No, not like what happened, but she knew that she was followed sometimes, by her husband's embassy guys or maybe French or American agents.' His eyes grew a little more alert, as if he'd made some sort of connection. 'Last week, a man approached me; he spoke fluent French, but perhaps he was Russian. I pushed him away but he knew *everything*. About me, about her, my family, even the diary. I thought he must have worked for her husband, but then he said if we got the diary for him, he'd pay us a hundred thousand euros and put us in touch with someone else to help us move and set up new identities – he gave us an option, an out; it was perfect.'

'Too perfect,' Zoe said. It all came together. *That* guy, or someone connected to him, had killed Katya. He'd pushed him away. Maybe he could have saved her. Zoe quickly sent a text.

'We need to know everything you can remember about this man,' she said. The plain-clothed cop from the lift hovered close by. 'When we go you will tell my colleague everything.'

Durand nodded. His hand was tight around his fresh drink.

'And then what – Katya found out the diary was worth something?' Fox probed.

'Katya . . . Recently she mentioned that we should take the diary from her husband and use it as insurance,' Durand said. He looked angry. 'She sent it to me in the mail. She added a note to give it to Renard, should anything happen to her. She was scared. She didn't tell me that, but by sending it to me, she knew . . .'

'Did she say why the diary was so valuable?' Fox asked. Durand looked around. He drained his double shot on the rocks, set the tumbler down hard. He looked up at Fox, and it was a look Fox had seen plenty of times before: he wanted revenge.

'What about this treaty?' Zoe prodded further. Durand looked to her. 'Was Katya afraid that they'd kill to mask the existence of it?'

'No, no you don't understand,' he said. 'The diary? It points to the place where this treaty amendment – this secret protocol – is hidden.'

Zoe turned to Fox, 'We need to meet Renard – now.'

51

NAPLES

Hutchinson pulled on a T-shirt and pants as quickly as he could. He'd just got off the phone with Fox. First McCorkell and Valerie had told him Babich was going to China, and when he heard that the dead Russian ambassador was due to go to Shanghai – *tonight* – he was sold. He answered his new BlackBerry as he was helped into a pair of Nikes by the Naples FBI Legat, a genial man from Denver who was nearing retirement and seeing out his days in this posting from the Bureau.

'Yep?'

'Andrew, it's Bowden. What are you doing?'

'I'm going to Shanghai.'

'No, you're not.' Bowden's voice was somewhere between authoritative and condescending. 'I'm shutting this down. It's no longer a legal issue, it's a covert action.'

'You're not doing shit!' Hutchinson stood, but had to sit back down again. He still felt a little shaky. 'I've got this –'

'Not even a couple of hours ago Babich's guys killed a French cop in broad daylight, tore up a whole goddamned highway –'

'So what?' Hutchinson responded, sitting on the edge of the bed. 'You're going to throw away a couple of years' damn hard work built on over a decade of multi-agency tracking of this son of a bitch?'

'He killed DoD guys on that Gulfstream too.'

'You think I don't know that?'

'We don't have the luxury of time,' Bowden said. 'We lose him now he goes to the mattresses and we miss our chance; he's another ghost for our country to hunt by sending tens of thousands of boots on the ground into some speck of shit country no one can find on a map.'

'Your point?'

Bowden was silent long enough to hear him exhale loudly.

'There's a French cop in on this,' he said. 'With your buddy Lachlan Fox.'

'What are you saying?'

'This shit is getting far too complicated,' Bowden's voice was resolute. 'It ain't about prosecution in court anymore, it ain't about containment or corralling Babich into a legal net somewhere.'

'You *can't* call this off –'

'I'm issuing extraordinary rendition protocols.'

'It's not yours – you don't have the authority!'

'This became my show when you dropped the ball,' Bowden said. 'And you know what? I was right: it never should have been an FBI operation.'

'It's a multi-agency operation.'

'Bullshit,' Bowden said. 'There are no multi-agency operations. Everything has a command. I'm it. It's my operation.'

The phone connection ended.

The Legat remained silent by the open doorway.

Hutchinson was shaking . . . Rage coursing through his veins. Bowden was a calculating guy – he wouldn't have made the move without clearance from up high. Hutchinson was out of the game. His BlackBerry chimed, a text message from McCorkell:

We're here, buddy, we'll keep you in the loop and ahead of the curve.

The base Air Wing Commander stepped through the doorway – he'd been listening. He was tall, a newly minted Commander, a 'mustang' – a guy who'd entered through the enlisted ranks and gone on to become an officer – with aviator's wings, about ten years older than Hutchinson and in much better shape. He, like the rest of those here, were treating Hutchinson like one of their own. Many had shaken his hand, wishing him the luck he'd need to bring the guy in who'd just killed a couple of their mates.

'Reminds me of my old CO,' the commander said. Smiled to the Legat, who nodded. 'He was a real son of a bitch, too.'

'Yeah,' Hutchinson said, looking down at his leg, knowing that even if he was near Babich, he was too slow to really be in the fight.

The Navy commander had a glint in his eyes as he stepped forward and extended his hand. 'Call me Jinks,' he said. 'And anywhere you need to go, son, *anywhere*, I'll make sure you get there. Fast.'

Hutchinson grinned.

'Thanks.'

52

PARIS

Malevich watched as the scene unfolded, fast. The four plain-clothed police moved in: they stopped Renard on the Pont de la Concorde. The reporter was startled, as if he was being robbed, and didn't seem to relax much when they showed him their ID. One of them passed him a mobile phone and he put it to his ear.

Time was running out. He had to make a move, and make it in minutes. If Lavrov couldn't get these cops off the scene . . . It would get messy.

•

Fox listened as Zoe spoke rapid-fire into her phone for thirty seconds, while navigating the Peugeot through the Parisian streets with a heavy foot. She disconnected, holstered her BlackBerry and blared the car's horn to speed through an intersection.

'Renard is near the Louvre,' she said. 'We will meet him there in five minutes.'

'Yeah, I caught that,' Fox said from the passenger seat, holding on to the dashboard.

'Can we backtrack a sec?' Gammaldi asked from the back. 'You were saying Russia *owned* Alaska?'

'Yep,' Fox replied.

'Bullshit.'

The car jumped as they mounted a kerb to get around a traffic jam.

'They sold it to the US after the Civil War,' Fox said. 'Kate?'

'It's true, Al. 1867,' Kate said, checking her iPhone. 'For just over seven million. You can even see the treaty, signed by Seward and this Eduard de Stoeckl guy, online. Look here.'

She passed the iPhone to Gammaldi, who squinted at its tiny screen.

'Why'd they sell it to the Americans?'

'To stop the British expanding further into North America.'

'For seven million?'

'About two cents an acre,' Kate clarified.

'Bargain.'

'Yeah, only it wasn't seen as so wise back then,' Kate said. 'It was pretty much just a fur colony, and a lot of the natural stocks had been depleted. They called it Seward's Folly, and the House of Reps did their best to stop the purchase by holding out over a year on the payment.'

'And there's some document hidden in a wall somewhere,' Gammaldi began, 'that will – what? – that will renege that sale?'

'Not exactly sure what it says,' Fox said, 'but the two diplomats signed *something* to cover their arses, and they had it kept safe. What it was exactly, and if it's still there . . .'

'Could it be a copy of the treaty?' Gammaldi asked.

'It can't simply be a copy of it,' Kate said. 'That's in the public domain, and it's been long ratified; it's law. If it's an amendment though, a clause . . . But I just can't imagine anything that could impact it this long after the fact.'

'Durand referred to it as a . . .' Fox turned to Zoe. 'What did he call it?'

'Protocol,' Zoe answered.

'That sounds like the right terminology for an amendment,' Kate said.

'Well, I'll tell you one thing,' Gammaldi said, watching Paris flash by his window. 'I think Sarah Palin would have something to say about it. Seriously, she'd be pissed, and I wouldn't want to annoy her – if you can kill a moose, you can kill a Russian.'

Fox almost laughed. 'Well, Babich believes it's enough to kill for, so I guess he's gonna take his chances.'

'And now it's hidden here in Paris?'

'That's what Durand said,' Fox replied. 'We gotta get the diary first, and I have to speak to Renard.'

'What if this protocol has already been found?' Gammaldi asked.

Fox didn't have an answer for that.

53

WASHINGTON, DC

Several freeze-frames showing news footage of a car chase through Paris were magnified on the computer screens in front of Bowden, along with the CIA's files on Lachlan Fox.

'That was your boy Lachlan Fox this morning,' Bowden said to McCorkell.

'Aren't we looking for Babich?' McCorkell asked, standing next to the CIA man. Bowden seemed out of place in a suit; he would be more at ease in fatigues and turban with a rifle, hunting al-Qaeda in the mountains.

Images changed to shots from traffic cameras on a highway. Some grainy images of Fox climbing out of a wrecked SUV.

'Lachlan Fox, again.'

'He gets around,' McCorkell said.

'Well – if he's after this –' Bowden checked the print-out of the NSA intercept transcript in his hands, 'this *document*, can you make sure he gets it into our hands?'

McCorkell smiled. 'Fox is a tough son of a bitch. He's his own guy.'

Bowden tried to stare him down. McCorkell took a bite of the apple he'd been eating.

'What about doing it for the country?'

'No.'

'No? What, doesn't he like America?'

'He loves America.'

'So what is it?'

'He's not really someone to be ordered around,' McCorkell said. 'Never quite stuck with him.'

'Yeah, I read his military jacket. I'm just saying, he's over there, in France, doing something related to our case and destroying all sorts of shit in the process . . .' Bowden could see he wasn't getting anywhere. 'You know, I'm not Hutchinson.'

'I noticed.'

'I mean, I enforce *policy*, not the law. There are other ways we can do this –'

'Follow him with HUMINT, satellites, put him on a tight leash?'

'Drag him in, put him through the ringer.'

'You can't pressure him,' McCorkell said, taking another bite. 'He's got morals that would make good men cower. He's probably achieved more in the last few years than your entire AQ workforce combined.'

A few people nearby sniggered – until they realised McCorkell was serious.

'You're not going to help us get him onside?'

'He's onside.'

'You know what I mean.'

McCorkell finished off the apple.

'You going to get some assets into China?'

'I got plenty in China,' Bowden replied. 'You talk to your boy or I'll get someone who can.'

'I'll talk to him, sure.' McCorkell binned his apple core in Bowden's trash can with a three-pointer. 'But there's no betting on this guy doing what you want – he'll do what's right.'

'*We're* what's right.'

54

THE LOUVRE

PARIS

Zoe had pulled a hard left, double-parked and was already heading toward the Louvre's forecourt.

'Okay, you two need –' Fox did a double-take. 'Al, where's Kate?'

Gammaldi gestured behind the car, where Kate was ending a call on her iPhone. The day was hot and bright as they waited on the kerb.

'I'm sorry,' she said, catching Fox's gaze, 'I've been trying to tell you –'

'Come on!' Zoe said, running back to Fox. She didn't even look at Gammaldi or Kate as the breeze whipped in off the Seine.

'Let me guess,' Gammaldi said, 'us kids have to wait in the car?'

Zoe looked annoyed. 'I told you both to stay with my colleague earlier,' she said.

'Look, we know Renard,' Kate said, getting frustrated. 'It's not like –'

'I want to ask him some questions,' Zoe said. 'Better you are not there for the moment.'

'She's right, guys,' Fox said. 'We'll be quick.'

Kate gave up, shook her head a little.

'It's cool; Kate and I will go find an ice-cream,' Gammaldi said, putting his arm around her shoulders and leading her away. 'They wouldn't appreciate one anyway. Did you hear there's a McDonald's here, serves beer . . .'

Fox watched them go and then followed Zoe across the crowded courtyard.

'Your friends are annoying,' she said.

'They've been through a lot today.'

Zoe glanced at him hard. *Yeah, so had she.*

'We all have,' he said, trying to catch up. 'How'd you get Renard to the meeting?'

'I can be persuasive,' she said, texting on her phone.

Something wasn't right. She'd had men watching Renard all this time. Why not just take him in to a police station somewhere? Was she waiting for him to get this diary from the architect? Fine, but why hadn't she taken him in earlier? Why wait until –

'You're using him,' Fox said, as he caught up.

'Sorry?'

'Renard – I've been trying to figure out why, if this is all so vital, you didn't just get him this morning,' he said. 'Instead, you've let him do all the work while we've been picking up crumbs and chasing –'

'Lachlan,' she stopped near the glass pyramid that served as the entrance to the Louvre. 'As fascinating as this diary sounds, this Alaska whatever; that is not my game. I am after a man, a *murderer*. Vincent was, too.'

'And you're using Renard to flush him out!' Fox said. 'Look, I'm sorry about Vincent, I really am, but maybe you don't realise what's at stake here. Umbra is far bigger than any murderer!'

Zoe was scanning the crowd in the courtyard, thousands of faces, mostly tourists shielded behind cameras.

'You know this guy will *kill* for this diary, but you are willing to dangle Renard out there to catch your man.'

'Yes.'

'And you don't care what Roman Babich, a fugitive much bigger than any single murderer, is after?'

'I work for the National Police, Lachlan,' Zoe said, moving on. 'And I have a job to do.'

•

Boris Malevich had watched as the four cops escorted Renard to the Musée du Louvre – and then left him there, alone, in the wide open terrain of the court. He saw a van pick the police up and take them away. It seemed Lavrov's contact there had finally come through.

Malevich waited for the signal from his men that they were in place on the other side – he couldn't risk Renard fleeing now. When they were ready he would leave his cover, walk straight across the court and take the diary. His job was nearly over.

•

Zoe walked briskly through the crowd towards a statue of Louis XIV.

'You've got some agents around here?' Fox asked.

'Officers,' she replied, scanning the crowd from behind her sunglasses. 'Four of them.'

Fox couldn't make them out, but then he hadn't been able to this morning either. Maybe they were using the cover of English tourists, plenty of them about, even a group of Americans here wearing *Crack the Code* T-shirts.

They reached the equestrian statue of the Sun King. Renard appeared from behind its base, leather satchel slung over one shoulder.

'Lachlan?' he said, visibly taken aback, as if caught in the act. 'What are you doing – ?'

'He's with me,' Zoe said, showing her ID. He looked back up to Fox, like a deer in headlights.

'Renard . . .' Fox said. 'Why'd you lie to me?'

Fox could see Renard trying to work it all out.

'Katya. Durand. The diary . . .' Fox helped him out. 'You drove me into town this morning and said *nothing*.'

'I'm sorry, Lachlan,' Renard said. 'I – I should have been honest.'

Fox shook his head, looked around. Nothing but milling tourists and herding tour groups.

'Just tell me: what's this about?' Fox asked, taking a step towards him. 'Who are you working for?'

Now Renard looked confused. 'You know who I work for.'

'Umbra?'

The Frenchman cracked a smile.

'Lachlan,' Renard laughed. 'You think I am with them?'

•

Malevich strode out towards Renard, hand on the grip of the pistol concealed beneath his jacket –

A man and woman approached the journalist.

He stopped mid-stride and paused. Tourists shuffled around him. Watching, the two arrivals were talking to Renard – they knew each other. He saw the woman show an ID of some sort. *More cops!*

He searched the faces around him, signalled to each of his guys to hold off.

He headed quickly for cover behind one of the smaller glass pyramids. *What the hell?*

Change of plans. They would triangulate and go in hard, his point man a few paces ahead of him while his other guy stayed closer to the street, keeping them covered if any uniformed cops got involved.

•

'So, what – you leave me out because you're chasing a scoop?' Fox asked after Renard had explained why he'd gone it alone – he wanted a *headline*? 'Come on . . .'

'I didn't know, I just thought this had fallen in my lap as something big –'

'Tell me who you have been in contact with,' Zoe cut in, scanning the crowd again.

'What do you mean?'

'How did you know to meet Durand?'

'Katya told me about him; should something happen to her, she asked me to get word to him,' Renard replied. He was looking down at his feet as he spoke. 'I told him about her murder, he said that she'd sent him the diary.'

He looked up. 'We arranged to meet.'

'How did you know about Katya's murder?'

'A friend in the police,' he replied.

Zoe looked like she was going to ask about it, but she bit her lip then looked around the crowd in the forecourt.

'Renard, they tried to kill us,' Fox said.

'What?'

'This morning, when I got back to the farm. They attacked us at your house.'

'Who?' Renard looked confused and genuinely concerned. 'Guys from Umbra?'

Fox nodded.

'Look, Lachlan, that's your heat, not mine, I've never had anything to do –'

'Have you noticed someone following you?' Zoe asked. Fox felt her stance change, more alert.

'Not until your guys approached me,' Renard said. 'And I didn't notice them until they had me surrounded.'

Fox looked around instinctively, he still couldn't pick Zoe's agents out of the crowd.

'Has anyone else contacted you about this, anyone at all?' Zoe asked.

'No. Like who?'

'Durand was approached by a man offering money for the diary, a week ago.'

'He didn't mention that to me,' Renard replied.

'Do you know what this is about?' Fox asked him. 'These murders and attacks on the Russian Ambassador and his wife?'

'You made the Umbra connections out of Katya's information,' Renard said. 'She had something valuable to them – this diary. I mean, a diplomat's diary from over a century ago . . . How is that worth murdering for?'

Fox answered, 'That's what I want to know.'

'Durand told me it has something to do with an amendment to a treaty –'

'Between the United States and Russia, we got that,' Fox said. Someone nearby laughed loudly and spooked him – just some young travellers clowning around. He turned to Zoe – surely she could see that Durand wasn't implicated in this? Surely she could see it was far too risky to be in this crowd with unknown assailants after this diary. 'Can we get out of here now?'

A tour group of about forty people was approaching.

'Come,' Zoe said to both men. 'Keep walking; stay with the group around the pyramid and then go back towards the car.'

They walked at the edge of the group, the breeze picking up and cooling them with water vapour from the fountains.

Zoe made a call, eyes everywhere on the crowd as she walked close to Fox.

Fox asked Renard, 'So where's the diary?'

The Frenchman patted the leather satchel around his shoulder, a beaten-up lucky charm that had seen about as many conflict zones as Fox.

'It states the location of this document?'

'Apparently, yes.'

'Where?' Fox asked.

'Here, in Paris,' Renard replied. 'It's in Russian, but Katya translated it into French and inserted a loose page into the diary – for Durand, I assume.'

He tapped what appeared to be a notebook in the pocket of his linen jacket, a folded piece of paper overhanging.

'It was hidden in the Elysée Palace.'

They stopped walking. Zoe looked to Fox, back to Renard.

'Do you think it's still there?' Fox asked.

'Well, the building hasn't gone anywhere, and it is mostly unchanged,' Renard said. 'In fact, its last renovation was 1867.'

'Same year as the Alaska Purchase treaty was signed,' Fox said.

'And,' Renard added, 'they even used some of the same building contractors who worked on the Russian Ambassador's residence – I Googled it earlier.'

Fox's demeanour lifted. 'It does sound promising . . .'

'More than promising, my friend,' Renard said with a twinkle in his eye. 'It's still there, at the palace, I know it.'

'I think Babich's guys know it's still around too – and are willing to kill for it,' Fox said.

'This will be a massive scoop!' Renard looked starry-eyed. 'This will make my career.'

'Keep moving,' Zoe said as they caught up behind the tour group. 'Are you two serious? You want to go get this document?'

'Why not?' Fox replied. 'Why not beat them to it?'

'The Elysée Palace is a big place,' Zoe said. 'And it is not like we can tear down the walls looking for it.'

'Neither can Umbra,' Fox said.

'The room it is in has only ever undergone minor cosmetic renovations,' Renard said.

'Room?' Zoe questioned. 'It – the diary gives a specific spot?'

'Of course,' Renard said. He pulled out the hand-written page. 'It's in the Presidential Study.'

55

WASHINGTON, DC

'You all know our man: Roman Babich. We need to bring him back at all costs.' Bowden turned to his left. 'Special Agent Valerie Child is gonna bring us up to speed. It may rattle something loose that we can use, and I want to hear some dialogue as a result. Valerie?'

Valerie stood up front, a few pictures of Babich on the big screens behind her, along with images of several overseas section chiefs who were on a live feed on the video-con briefing.

McCorkell made himself another cup of tea, rubbed the sleep from his eyes, and tuned in from his seat at the back.

'Roman Babich. Sixty years old. Best known for his role as a Russian oligarch, media tycoon and prominent leader of privatisation during the presidency of Boris Yeltsin in the nineties. He's a close friend of the Yeltsin family and was seen as a member of their inner circle.

'Babich made his fortune by capturing state assets at knockdown prices during Russia's rush towards privatisation. His personal fortune at the time of his arrest was 12.4 billion US dollars, and his Umbra Corp umbrella company has been valued at about twenty times that.

'His power base is the loyalty and connections of his senior staff – all ex-spooks.'

She clicked through some digital slides to show Babich as he'd been when he'd left his final government position.

'He had almost five million US dollars to his name when the USSR collapsed. Four years later, he had bought and sold companies as diverse as Aeroflot and Russia's leading television station, ORT. His large stake in an oil and gas company, Sibneft, was bought out after a couple of years and with those profits he started his own oil and gas company, UOil. He made billions from the Sibneft deal alone and founded Umbra Corp. That's when our CIA started its dedicated Umbra task force. We've been looking into him with little joy. While most other oligarchs were driven out of Russia by Putin's government, who saw their power and influence as a threat, Babich kept out of politics and remained squarely in the business of making money. Three of his former business partners from the early days have since been murdered.'

Their familiar faces flashed up on the screens. McCorkell knew the agency had a hand in one of those killings, as Babich had been a double agent for them then, about to sell back to Russia's Federal Security Service, of which he'd also been a senior player.

'Babich was far less flashy than the other mega-wealthy Russians and that also helped him survive. No Dr Zhivago coats for him. His business MO is low-key, comparatively, which he learned from the mistakes of others. Under Yeltsin, the oligarchs were the shadow government. When Putin moved in, the *Siloviki* took over.'

'They're regarded as a direct counterpart to the Umbra network,' Bowden added. 'Same kind of concept, different league of guys, different power base entirely.'

A couple of slides of the two known family trees went up. A 'who's who' of the Russian political, business and intelligence services, split roughly in half, as if to highlight two big opposing power bases.

'That's a fair call,' Valerie said. 'The *Siloviki* are the ex-spooks currently in power, and then there're those who for various reasons are opposed to them, residing in the Umbra block.'

She clicked the slideshow forward, revealing Umbra's organisational chart of legitimate companies.

'This is circa mid-nineteen-nineties; it's more streamlined now with Sibneft oil company – shareholder in the country's main television channel ORT, which he turned into a propaganda vehicle for Boris Yeltsin in the run-up to the 1996 presidential election.'

She paused, motioned to the CIA Station Chief in Moscow.

'If you look closely at Babich's political rivals, and even moderates who are within his own block,' the Moscow SC said. 'He's got so much on so many . . . There'd be hundreds in Russia who want him dead, like seriously dead. And that's grown since his arrest.'

'Mark, we're working on that,' Bowden said. 'How about since his break-out?'

'There's been plenty of chatter from the Umbra block,' the Moscow SC replied. 'Our computers here are working overtime downloading all the chatter going on out there. Word's out, they know he's on the loose. Matter of time before it hits the press here.'

'Then we've got a whole new problem to deal with,' Bowden said.

'Putin moved to regain control of the ORT television station and to curb the influence of the oligarchs, who were extremely unpopular with the Russian public,' Valerie said. 'Seems Babich entered some kind of truce, selling out of all the former state-owned companies that he'd bought up cheap, but keeping those he founded from scratch – under Umbra.'

'Which means he's got enormous popular support back here, I can tell you,' the Moscow SC said. 'But the government had declared war on him. Just last month, a Moscow court found Babich guilty in absentia of massive embezzlement – related to a decade-old charge he settled on the quiet, way back when. He was sentenced this morning – to eight years in jail and ordered to repay 180 million dollars that the court said he had stolen from the state airline, Aeroflot, in the initial privatisation purchase.'

McCorkell sat a little more upright. That kind of thing certainly was a statement from the Russian government – the sentencing was meant to come after another few months of trial. It was as if they were moving fast to discredit the man who was out there in the great unknown, some kind of phoenix rising.

'It gets better,' Valerie said. 'Two hours ago, they brought charges against him for involvement in the murders of several leading critics of Putin's regime, including ex-spook Litvinenko and journalist Politkovskaya.'

'Timing on that's too coincidental . . .' the Moscow SC said.

'They know about the hijacking,' Bowden said. 'They know he's out and on the run. And what – they know he's gonna make a play?'

'It's a major shift in how they've been treating him,' Valerie said. 'Now they're attacking him from their political base.'

'How so?'

'In 1999 Babich supported Putin's appointment to the Prime Minister's position as a result of a secret agreement, where Putin promised his loyalty to Yeltsin and his closest circle, including Babich, guaranteeing them indemnity. Just before the March 2000 elections, Babich unleashed a propaganda blitz that obliterated the opposition. At least two candidates who were widely felt to have a reasonable chance of winning over Putin – the Mayor of Moscow, Yuri Luzhkov, and the former Premier Yevgeny Primakov – were swiftly eliminated through an elaborate smear campaign. Babich has been untouchable ever since.'

'Until now.'

'Until now,' she said. 'Now, we see the Russians want him to stay behind bars as much as us – they've helped the Italian prosecution and now they're ramping things up at home in an attempt to make it impossible for him to return.'

The Moscow SC said: 'I can speak to my channels in Russian intel, tell them to start sharing –'

'No,' Bowden took centre-stage. 'We don't know if word will get through to Umbra – they're fucking everywhere, we know that, plenty of them serving in the FSB. Level Five Extraordinary Rendition protocols have been ordered. That comes from the White House. They want this problem to go away.'

McCorkell knew what that meant, and most of the others here would, too: the White House was doing what the government in Moscow was now begging them to do. Politically it was a no-brainer: getting Babich for them would be ridding them of a threat to their power base and they'd reciprocate in kind, with something diplomatic; put pressure on North Korea or Iran, maybe even a peace-keeping force somewhere. The facts were, if Babich were to enter Russia, he just might take his final role of the dice: a tip at power. Not a guy anyone needed in the president's chair of the world's second largest military force.

'Make no mistake: the Russian government wants him – perhaps even more than us,' Bowden said. 'They're scared of what he's told us in detention these past few months, and they're even more scared now that he's out there. The race is on, and I intend to win.'

56

THE LOUVRE

PARIS

Zoe still had her phone to her ear and was listening.

Fox noticed her stance change – she was tense as hell, her hand up and lingering at her concealed hip holster. He scanned the crowd behind Renard.

'My guys got pulled off,' she said, reaching for Renard. 'We have to leave, now!'

•

As Boris Malevich approached Renard from behind he fingered the compact nine-millimetre Glock in his pocket. He'd had it at the ambassador's residence, but he hadn't used it. He'd never fired a gun at a person in his life. Had never wanted to. But he'd already killed now, hadn't he? He'd felt Katya's blood over his knuckles. It could only get easier. Guns made it easier.

From ten metres out the tall man in front of Renard turned around. He looked familiar – and suddenly Malevich knew why he still hadn't heard from the eight-man team he'd sent to Giverny.

The tall man was Lachlan Fox.

Through the summer weekend crowd, he saw Fox, Renard and the woman start to move away – fast.

Malevich drew his Glock.

•

'Come!' Zoe said, and they jostled through the crowded courtyard.

Fox saw a couple of *gendarmes*, MP5s slung across their chests, chatting to some girls. The cops looked up as the running trio headed their way.

Next to Fox, Renard was spooked, clutching his satchel tightly to his body.

'Come on!'

A gunshot echoed around the courtyard, sending pigeons into the air and tourists to the ground. Fox knew it was a nine-millimetre pistol, up close. Renard faltered beside him. A second shot rang out – Fox hit the ground. He pulled Renard down hard, beside one of the smaller glass pyramids.

The Frenchman was bleeding heavily, coughing. Fox pushed Renard's hands to the wound on his chest.

'Hold it tight!' he yelled to him.

A bullet hit the thick glass wall near Fox's head and he ducked lower, turned – the attacker was moving in, less than ten metres away – Fox locked eyes with him.

People were screaming and fleeing in all directions. Zoe bumped into Fox, fired towards the shooter; one shot winged him and the other nailed him square in the chest.

More pistol-fire in quick succession. Fox looked across the forecourt – the two *gendarmes* were on the ground; one still, the other writhing.

'*Mitrailleuse, mitrailleuse!*' Zoe shouted to Fox. 'The machine gun!'

Fox was already running towards the fallen cops. He picked up the dead *gendarme*'s weapon, scanned the crowd – the other *gendarme* pointed his gun up at him –

Fox was a sitting duck. Before he could say anything –

Blam!

The *gendarme* dropped the gun, blood streaming from his arm – Fox looked up. Zoe. She lowered her gun and screamed into her BlackBerry for an ambulance, while Fox kicked the guy's firearm clear.

Someone pointed at him and yelled in English: 'He's got a gun! He's got a gun!'

And he did – Fox crouched and aimed the dead *gendarme*'s MP5 to his right – swinging it around as he searched for the shooter he'd heard – there.

FtFtFt! FtFtFt!

The recoil against Fox's shoulder was light. Two three-round bursts tore into a burly guy who was drawing an aim at Zoe. As Fox ran over to her, he swept the scene down the gun's sight – it was like a magic wand scattering the crowd. He couldn't see any more targets, but he was sure there was at least one.

Two uniformed officers were running up the road – pistols drawn and radios going berserk – Zoe yelled at them and flashed her badge, pointed to the crowd – she'd seen someone.

Fox crouched next to Renard – he didn't have long, but he managed to lift a finger and pointed to the crowd. The back of a man running – Renard's old leather satchel swinging – the two officers in hard pursuit as he vanished into the fleeing crowd.

Renard nodded as he clutched tight to the bleeding wound in his chest.

Two gunshots rang out in quick succession, then a third.

Fox ducked, but the shooting was over.

A hundred metres away, the evacuating crowd near the road had scattered in panic once again. In the space where they'd been lay the two uniformed officers. The man with Renard's satchel had gone.

57

NAPLES

'You like to fly fast jets, son?' The commander walked with a spring in his step.

Hutchinson grinned as he was wheeled out to the aircraft, the wheelchair and the flight suit not exactly how he remembered Mav in *Top Gun*. Next to the row of muscular F-18 Super Hornets lined up along the runway's taxi lane was a sleek F-35C Joint Strike Fighter. The two seater F-35, a Navy variant with arrester hook, looked like a peek into the future alongside the F-18s. Hutchinson was manhandled up into the cockpit by a couple of well-muscled ground-crew. It was a snug fit, they slapped a helmet on him and the commander signalled he was ready to go.

'Ladies and gentlemen,' the pilot said, climbing into the cockpit. 'We're gonna fly balls-out non-stop to meet up with the Seventh Fleet in the sea of China.'

'Non-stop?' Hutchinson asked.

'We'll slow for a few minutes for in-flight refuelling over Turkey.'

The canopy hissed shut around them.

'How long to Shanghai?'

'Nine thousand clicks . . . The way I fly, call it wheels-down in about seven hours,' he replied.

Hutchinson checked his watch. He'd be in Shanghai tonight, local time.

'Good to go?' the commander sensed his nerves.

'Let's do this,' Hutchinson said, fighting down the bile in his throat.

They taxied to the take-off strip, and before Hutchinson could ask what the commander had meant by '*Meet up with the Seventh Fleet in the sea of China*', he was pressed hard back into his seat and they were climbing fast into the sky, Joint Force Command Naples becoming a speck on the ground beneath them.

58

THE LOUVRE

PARIS

Fox scanned the scene – the man had vanished. The two attackers close to them – dead. Four cops were down, and he knew at least one of them was dead, too. Someone was screaming, someone else was shouting in French. A father was still, covering his child on the ground under him. A couple of teenage girls were huddled against the building, crying. Most other people were frozen in shock or running from the scene.

Zoe administered first aid to the *gendarme* she'd shot and used his radio to direct the ambulances, which Fox could hear approaching.

Renard was fading – he'd been hit twice in the chest – his mouth was foaming with the bright red blood of a punctured lung. Death from the blood loss was imminent.

Fox lowered the MP5 and applied pressure to the entry and exit wounds. Zoe returned and helped, blood on her shaking hands. Fox glanced to her and shook his head. She got it.

'I'm . . . sorry . . .' Renard said. His breaths were short and sharp, husky.

'Don't be sorry,' Fox said, taking Renard's hand. 'Hang in there.'

'I got my . . . adventure . . . Hey?'

'Yeah, buddy, some adventure,' Fox said. His mind was flashing with all the other men he'd seen like this, ghosts he thought he'd learned to deal with. He blinked hard and tried to push the memories away.

'He took the diary,' Renard said, heavy where he lay on the ground.

'Did you see him?' Zoe asked. 'Did you know him?'

Renard's eyes looked blank . . .

'You don't . . . need . . . diary . . .'

The notebook in his hand, the folded piece of transcript; they fell to the paving.

Fox checked Renard's pulse, nothing. There was blood everywhere and the breeze had died. He looked across the now near-empty forecourt. Gammaldi and Kate were walking towards them.

Zoe took Renard's press card, the notebook, his ID: everything.

'Come,' she said, as the first ambulance tore towards them. 'We have to leave.'

59

WASHINGTON, DC

'Bill?' Valerie called, quietly.

McCorkell looked up from his laptop – she waved him over.

'It's Paris.' Her voice was low as he came to stand beside her, looking over her shoulder. 'They want to know if Langley has an asset operating on their turf.' She pointed to an image on her flat-screen, a blurry still from a CCTV camera, but the figure was unmistakable: Lachlan Fox.

'This from the car chase?'

'No. It's new, and it's big. Paris office just sent through footage of a shoot-out in the forecourt of the Louvre.'

'Fox okay?'

'Appears so, but it doesn't look good . . .' Valerie motioned towards Bowden and his CIA team. 'It won't take them long to jump to conclusions.'

McCorkell glanced over and could see Bowden's change in stance as images of Fox in Paris began filling the screens at the CIA end of the room. They'd start connecting dots that they shouldn't – Fox, his connection to Umbra, his appearance in Paris, his continued antics this morning . . .

'Can you get through to him?' McCorkell asked Valerie.

'His cell phone is on but it's not on him – it's stationary, in the Giverny region.'

'Must have left it behind. How about Kate's?'

'Hers is off; she last used it about fifteen minutes ago at the Louvre.'

'Might have run out of battery?'

'Or she may have switched it off,' Valerie said, but her look implied there was something else bothering her.

'And?' McCorkell probed. 'What is it?'

'I had them bring up her call sheet. She rang a cell phone in Shanghai.'

'What?'

'She rang a staffer with the EU delegation to the Summit,' Valerie replied. 'Dutch national; she's made calls to him sporadically over the last six months, and several in the last couple of hours. I'm sending you his file.'

'You have a transcript of her last call?'

She shook her head. 'We've had no reason to monitor her calls like that.'

McCorkell's head was spinning. Now *he* was connecting dots that a moment ago he would have thought outlandish.

'Keep trying to reach Fox,' he said.

Valerie nodded and went back to her work. McCorkell headed towards the end of the room.

Bowden was pacing in front of the main screens and muttering commands to the CIA and DoD staff. McCorkell knew he'd been waiting for an opportunity to run the show exactly how he wanted. Well, now he had an excuse to pull out all the stops. *Good luck trying to pre-empt whatever was happening next.*

They were running through footage from the Louvre surveillance camera, scanning for Fox's arrival.

Bowden was watching, a hawk hovering over prey: 'Go – keep going – go . . . Wait – stop – you went past it!'

The CIA tech working multiple terminals brought an image up on the big screen.

'Make it tighter.'

He punched it up.

'There,' Bowden said, 'the woman he's with; I want an ID. Keep moving.'

McCorkell stared at the screen as another image was brought up and the screen split up into smaller panels showing a montage of Fox's movements. Fox in attack mode, grabbing the fallen cop's MP5, handling it with ease. Another screen, another angle, the prone French cop, pistol up, aimed at Fox and – blam – a woman came into frame; she'd fired in the cop's direction. Fox hadn't missed a beat – he'd tracked left, fired a couple of bursts off-screen – another angle showed a guy going down, all Fox's rounds hitting his torso.

The French cop – on the ground, winged but alive, squirming, out of action.

Fox running to a guy on the ground who was bleeding out fast. The woman came back into frame. Another angle showed the final actions with better clarity. Fox and the armed woman hung around the dying man for about a minute then left.

'There it is – that shot!' Bowden made the tech stop the frame and clear it up: Fox taking something from the dead body.

'What did he take off him?'

The tech zoomed, crisped up the image. A small square object, too blurred and pixellated to know exactly.

'A book, maybe?' a CIA tech suggested.

Bowden turned to face McCorkell. Slight vindication there. He pointed to the freeze-frame of Fox with the shouldered MP5.

'That look like the action of a fucking *reporter* to you?' Bowden asked with a grin. 'He's in this up to his neck.'

60

PARIS

'You shot a cop,' Fox said as the Peugeot zigzagged through the traffic.

'You're welcome,' Zoe replied.

They were headed for Zoe's apartment. Gammaldi and Kate reminded silent in the back.

'He will be fine – get a medal, even,' Zoe said, her eyes darting about the road as she drove. 'What? We had no time to stop and explain, right? He would have shot *you*.'

'Yeah, I know . . .' Fox said, figuring she was articulating it as much for her own sake as his. He watched the street flash by. He could feel how uncomfortable his friends were in the back seat. 'Thank you, Zoe.'

She'd taken her sunglasses off and he could see the strain in her eyes, and what might have been tears. He knew he couldn't press her about why her plain-clothed officers had been called off before the attack.

No one spoke for the next few minutes.

Fox flicked through Renard's notebook. It was full of research notes on Babich – a combination of his above- and below-board dealings with French businesses.

One word caught Fox's eye. *Arktika* – it had been circled several times and there was a whole section of pages covering it. The first mention was of a 2007 Russian expedition composed of *'six explorers employing MIR submersibles that descended to the seabed below the North Pole . . .'*. Fox remembered news footage of that, from when they'd planted the flag of Russia and taken water and soil samples for analysis. *'. . . continuing a mission to provide additional evidence related to the Russian claim for the mineral riches of the Arctic Sea Floor'*.

Fox couldn't read more than half the French in there, but understood enough to paint the picture. He kept looking through the notes.

'The expedition aimed to establish that a section of seabed passing through the pole, known as the Lomonosov Ridge, was an extension of Russia's landmass. Several countries are trying to extend their rights over sections of the Arctic Ocean floor. Both Norway and Denmark are carrying out surveys . . .'

Fox looked out the window. Zoe was driving sedately now, as if winding down. He zoned out, too, for all of ten seconds, until he remembered Vladimir Putin making a speech on a nuclear icebreaker, urging greater efforts to secure Russia's 'strategic, economic, scientific and defence interests' in the Arctic. It was a throwaway news piece that no one seemed to care about, even those in the few countries that had territorial stakes in the region . . . *Did the Alaska treaty's secret protocol affect the Arctic?* There was no direct answer in Renard's notebook, but there was one significant page: the transcript that Katya had made and inserted into the diary. Just a few lines in French beside a universal diagram, obviously copied from Stoeckl's own work. By the time Zoe pulled up outside her apartment, Fox knew exactly where in the Presidential Study the document was hidden. How to get it was another matter . . .

61

PARIS

Malevich washed his hands, then his face with cold water. The person who looked back at him in the bathroom mirror was a stranger. A week ago he'd been a teacher at the Sorbonne, living a life that he enjoyed. Now it was over. Now he had a new life.

He'd just taken two lives. Cops, no less. His hands had hardly shaken. He hadn't vomited. *Was it getting easier?*

No.

There was no time to think about it, that would come later. He would keep forging ahead or all this would be for nothing. He checked his watch. There had been some speed bumps, but he was on schedule. He assumed he wouldn't be hearing from any of the eight-man team he'd sent to Giverny, seeing as Lachlan Fox was alive. He could have taken a shot at him in the Louvre's courtyard but the reporter's bag had been more important. The outcome of the mission. The time . . .

The diary of Eduard de Stoeckl was heavy in his hands – a chronicle of major achievements, political musings and notes, most of them mundane. He put it on the sink, then took a piss.

There was one part that he'd read carefully after he'd skimmed through the whole diary. A four-page entry covering the Alaska sale. Stoeckl spoke warmly of his friend, Secretary of State William H Seward, and explained how they'd agreed on the deal. There were details about how they'd pressed the case to the Tsar, how they'd argued that the sale of Russian America to the United States would be beneficial strategically, both for the immediate and in the long term for both countries. It would allow the Russian government to concentrate its resources on Eastern Siberia, the caucuses, and at the same time strike a long-term blow to England by giving them a more powerful foe in the Americas. By doing so, the two diplomats reasoned, Russia would avoid any future conflict with the United States. Instead, it would help to solidify a friendship between the nations. It was win-win.

Stoeckl then cited political pressure, from the American politicians and perhaps even President Johnson, not to go through with the $7.2 million deal. The Americans dragged their feet: their Senate ratified the treaty in April of 1867 . . . The money, however, was delayed by more than a year due to opposition in the House of Representatives. The Tsar wanted action, he wanted answers: he wanted the money paid up or to end the sale – maybe even to sell it to the British. Secretly, Stoeckl and Seward made a deal, *insurance* for the Russian diplomat should things drag on. They drafted and signed a document and hid it in Paris where Stoeckl saw out his days.

A secret protocol.

It was created simply as insurance. Should Stoeckl be dragged before the Tsar, he would be able to show this document, at any time in the future, and have it enacted. Smart. A good Russian manoeuvre. It was a deal sweetener, a 'just in case'; there was no doubt about that. In Stoeckl's time it would have been beneficial for the Russian Empire in terms of commerce and trade. Today . . . Today it was *priceless*.

Malevich stood before the mirror and his hands started to shake. He banged them down onto the stainless steel sink, again and again and again until they were numb. He could do this next part, he reminded himself. With any luck, he would not have to harm anyone. This was a static thing, simple: he'd go in, get the document, get out as quickly as possible, and leave this city. Forever.

He buttoned up his overalls and walked out of the bathroom. He was in an old motorbike repair shop, a windowless brick warehouse lit by greasy old neon tubes. Two men from St Petersburg were making some final touches to the van that they'd used earlier in the week for the attack on the embassy. They were dressed as gas company workers, like Malevich.

They signalled, *five minutes*.

What a morning . . .

The time ticked over to 11 am.

Right on cue his mobile phone rang.

62

PARIS

Fox took off his watch, ran the cold water on full strength in the basin and rinsed the blood off his hands. They were at Zoe's place, a small one-bedroom apartment in the second *arrondissement*, just a few minutes from the Louvre and the Elysée Palace. She had shown them in and then headed for her balcony, shutting the glass doors behind her as she talked on her phone.

Fox soaped up a washcloth, pulled off his shirt and cleaned up. He had Renard's blood splattered all over – his neck, his face, his forearms . . . His wrist was caked with blood, mostly his own from this morning. He washed it all off, rinsed his face and hair, and dried off with a towel.

The door opened and Kate came in with some medical gear from Zoe.

'Here,' she said. She sat on the edge of the bath while he stood in front of her, and she applied antiseptic to his stomach, which was badly grazed from dragging himself over the Audi's broken windscreen. *The second car chase of the morning or, technically, was it the third?* 'This is disgusting – it looks like shingles' ugly cousin.'

Fox laughed.

'It feels like it – ah, fuck!'

Kate held up a piece of windscreen glass she'd pulled from his side, about the size of a shirt button. She applied a piece of adhesive gauze over the oozing hole.

'Here.' Gammaldi entered, passing him a bottle of beer and a few paracetamol.

'Thanks, mate.' Fox gulped them down with half the beer. 'You guys are like my personal medics.'

'You need at least two,' Gammaldi said. 'Maybe more, the way your day is turning out.'

Kate wasn't impressed. 'Want me to dress the graze?'

'I think I'll let it breathe,' Fox said, inspecting the cleaned-up wound. 'Thanks.'

Kate shrugged and left the room before he could touch or kiss her.

'Is she okay?'

'She's all right,' Gammaldi replied. 'I think she's just confused. You should talk to her.'

'Yeah,' Fox followed him out of the bathroom, watching Kate check her iPhone, which was charging in Zoe's iPod dock. 'Soon. Just hold her together while I get this done, yeah?'

'Hey, what else am I gonna do?'

Fox drained his beer, gave the empty to his mate, and clapped him on the shoulder.

Zoe came in from the balcony and moved fast, loading her SIG's mags from a box of nine-millimetre bullets, which were stashed in an antique music box on her coffee table.

'Imbeciles . . .' she said, holstering her pistol. She tucked her dishevelled hair behind her ear and looked as fresh as she did just a few hours and a whole lot of grief ago. 'The security chief at the palace does not think this is serious – because it is not al-Qaeda or some Algerian vendetta outfit. Told me to file a report via my captain on Monday.'

'Can't you get your superiors to get things moving?' Gammaldi asked. 'Call in the cavalry . . .'

She shook her head. 'No. They are somehow compromised.'

'Zoe's guys at the Louvre today were called off, ordered away from the scene,' Fox explained. Zoe nodded in agreement.

'Jesus . . .' Gammaldi bit his lip, looked to Kate.

'If they kill like that in broad daylight,' Zoe said, 'then they will not worry about killing us in some deserted hall of the palace.'

'You miss him at the palace, you'll never get another chan –' Fox stopped, cut himself off; it was clear he and Zoe were on the same wavelength. 'You *want* to go to the palace?'

'Two minutes,' she said, heading to the bathroom.

Before he could answer, Kate touched his arm. 'Can I talk to you for a second?' asked Fox, leaing her onto the balcony. She closed the doors behind them.

It was hot and he was feeling the effects of the post-adrenaline rush with the beer chaser.

'Can't you stop this now?' Kate asked. Her eyes were both sad and angry.

'Kate . . .' he tried to pull her into a hug, but she put a hand out to stop him.

'Renard is dead, Lachlan. Dead! They've already tried to kill us!'

Fox looked down to the honking traffic scooting by below, the people in the streets, the life of the ordinary. *There was something soothing about the safety of that kind of life, sure.*

'I can't leave this now,' he said, '*especially* since Renard . . .'

'What, so his death can *mean* something?'

'Please Kate, I don't expect you to understand but you have to –'

'I don't have to do anything!' Kate said. 'Neither do you, don't you see that? We can walk away, right now. You're going to get yourself *killed*, and I don't want to bear that! I *can't* bear that!'

Fox felt sick. His stomach was churning and it was all because he cared about her. He wanted this to end and he wanted it to mean something at the same time. He wanted to do what was right . . . what was right for the bigger picture, not just for now, in this moment.

'I have to do this,' Fox said. 'I'm sorry.'

Zoe rapped her knuckles on the glass door, signalled it was time to go.

'I don't deserve this,' Kate said. Her eyes searched his for some final sign he'd give it up for her, but there was none. She went inside, straight through to the open front door where Gammaldi was waiting.

'No one deserves this . . .' Fox said to himself, quietly.

63

WASHINGTON, DC

The Umbra task force was abuzz for the wrong reasons and there was little McCorkell could do to change the mood. All the main video screens were showing images from the Louvre forecourt. Blood was in the water and these sharks, who'd been hunting since 3 am, wanted an easy feed. Fox's face – frozen at a dozen angles, gave them that taste. The CIA techs were working on the images, bringing them in closer, clearer – the body on the ground, the woman with Fox – over and over Fox took a small object off the body and exited in a hurry.

'Find out who the woman is before Bowden does,' McCorkell instructed Valerie. She nodded and began looking for a good angle to send through to the databases in Paris. It was an illegal link-in, but it was a grey area – security services used other nations' CCTV footage in emergency terrorist-attack type situations all the time. *Hell, CNN would probably be playing it by now.*

McCorkell looked at the main screen down the CIA end – a still frame of Fox looking directly at the camera.

It pulled back to reveal another shooter who had taken a satchel from the fallen man, now identified as a reporter for *Le*

Figaro. There was no image of this shooter's face, the one that had got away, shooting two cops dead as he fled the scene.

McCorkell looked at the screens nearby – FBI analysts were scrutinising each of the two fallen shooters and the dead reporter from different angles. All up there had been six people involved, as far as they could tell: three on each opposing force – not counting the four uniformed police who became involved. Two of them were dead, one was critical and another stable but with two gunshot wounds. *A right fucking mess . . .*

'One dead shooter is Russian military intelligence,' an FBI tech called out. McCorkell went over to the guy's screen. 'GRU black ops, known to have operated in Chechnya 2004 to '07, where he'd been running Russian-sanctioned death squads.'

'Who's his friend?'

'There's no clear facial shot, probably have to wait for the French police to tag him.'

'How about the shooter who got away – the one who took the bag?'

'Same story,' the tech said, 'although Paris police are on the scene and they're pulling in bystanders' footage; that may bring up something.'

'Right,' McCorkell said, imagining how many of the tourists in that area had cameras – hundreds, thousands even – someone must have something. Hell, it was probably already on YouTube or their travel blog by now.

They had the guy with the satchel from at least twenty angles – twenty different camera locations – and not one usable face shot. Instead, everything was centred on Fox and his mad scramble outside the Louvre.

Bowden was pacing around, looking from one screen to another, conferring with aides in hushed tones, making battle plans with his Paris Station Chief who, justifiably, was going apeshit.

McCorkell had to find something to shift the focus from Fox onto the unknown shooter who took the satchel.

'What do they have on the streets?' he asked. 'The surrounding area? They must have something.'

'We're working on that . . .'

McCorkell rubbed at the tension in his temples as Valerie approached him.

'What?'

'Bowden,' she said. 'He's coming over for a show and tell.'

'That'll solve everyone's problems.'

'Sir . . .' another FBI tech said, his voice urgent. He'd found something.

McCorkell turned to him.

'It's someone's uploaded footage,' the tech said. 'You can just make out . . .'

'Enhance it,' McCorkell leaned over the guy's shoulder. A clear image filled the screen. And there he was. The shooter with the satchel, running out of the Louvre forecourt, fast. It was a decent enough profile, although still no good front-on facial.

'That's our guy,' Valerie said. 'That's our guy.'

64

ELYSÉE PALACE

PARIS

Fox stood behind Zoe, waiting for the security checkpoint at the Elysée Palace to clear them. In his mind it played out like one of those scenes in *Hot Fuzz* or *Shaun of the Dead*: all in quick-cut flashes of everything going swell, back home in time for a cold beer and a spot of telly. Kate and Gammaldi were in the car a block away, ready to roll in at a moment's notice. Fox would go with Zoe and get the document, and while she would stay and lie in wait for the murderer to show, the rest of them would head straight to the airport for the first flight back to the US. *Sipping beers over the Atlantic in no time.* Gammaldi, to his credit – and Fox knew he owed him yet again – was doing his best to keep Kate from heading back without him.

Fox watched down the street as a van-load of hard-hat workers did their thing by the palace's wall, a few guys around an open manhole on the pavement running tubing into the ground. Zoe had clocked them too. She approached the armed palace guards – in ceremonial garb, standing next to a guard shelter the size of a phone booth – and motioned to the workers. The guard explained they were undertaking precautionary work on the gas main following the Russian Embassy explosion.

At the front of the queue Zoe showed her ID to the uniformed cop manning the gate and explained she was looking after a reporter, Fox. Fox wore Renard's *Le Figaro* press pass on a lanyard, backwards so that *PRESS* was visible, rather than Renard's name and photo.

Zoe turned the card over, her fingers obscuring the photo, stated Renard's name and *Le Figaro* – and they were waved through to the waiting area.

•

Boris Malevich had been all smiles as the palace guards accepted their credentials and his guys busied themselves around the gas main on Rue du Faubourg Saint-Honoré. Not a few minutes later, he saw that face again: Lachlan Fox.

He watched him disappear into the palace with the female cop. *Shit!* He pulled his BlackBerry out with shaky hands; it was still a long time until his next scheduled check-in. Lavrov couldn't help him this time. *Shit.*

'Hurry up,' he told one of the guys. At least they knew what they were doing – they'd carried out the Russian Embassy job without any problems. He leaned into the van, opened up a compartment under the hoses and revealed a flat case that matched the bottom of the van. He opened it up – gas masks and a full assortment of the finest Fabrique Nationale de Herstal gear: P90 assault rifles, FN Five-seveN pistols and a forty-millimetre grenade launcher. He hesitated just a moment then took a pistol – weightier than the compact Glock he'd ditched back at the warehouse – chambered a round, checked the safety and trigger mechanisms, put it to the side, ready but concealed, and closed the hidden tray. The other two would no doubt take the heavier gear. 'How long until you'll be ready?'

'Five minutes,' the guy replied.

Malevich looked back towards the palace entrance. Security was not as tight as normal, because the president was in Shanghai for the G20 Summit. A couple of uniformed armed guards wandered in and out every now and then, looking up and down the street. He glanced back to his two guys, working on the pipes, attaching C4 charges underneath the gas lines. They'd need to hurry up . . .

•

Zoe and Fox had a chaperone. Poor guy had the trifecta: short, bald and fat. Dressed in some kind of official garb, he looked like he'd been showing tourists around since the last war. Zoe was doing a great job flirting, and Fox was confident the man would soon do anything she asked. They headed up some stairs to the first floor, finding the opulent palace surprisingly empty – Fox knew it wasn't just a residence for the President, it was his office, as well as that of the First Lady, and plenty of their staff. Then again, it was Saturday and the boss was away, and they may adhere to the thirty-five-hour work-week or whatever it was the French did these days.

The man was stopping here and there to provide details about the palace in English, for Fox's benefit. They didn't need to bother with any subterfuge for Baldy's sake, and once he learned that Fox was Australian rather than American, he treated the reporter like a true compatriot.

Fox stood next to him and Zoe as they paused to admire the English-style gardens at the rear of the palace – they stretched out towards the Champs Elysées. They continued on the tour, Baldy setting a surprisingly quick pace: he walked fast and talked slow, like a hobbit on crack.

'This building was once the home of the mistress of King Louis XV,' he said, the twinkle in his eye directed towards Zoe. 'A different time, then, no? I fear we have lost much romance, as a people . . .'

'Oh, I don't know. It's now home to an Italian-born former model and a five-foot tall, twice-divorced politician of Hungarian descent,' Fox said under his breath, just audible enough for Zoe to shoot him a look. 'Le Président Bling-Bling or something, don't they call him?'

'I am sorry, sir?' Baldy said, stopping and turning around. 'I am a little hard of hearing.' He didn't seem annoyed, but he wasn't smiling. Then again, the French didn't exactly give away their smiles for free.

'Just saying what lovely carpets there are here,' Fox said, smiling. 'And how they match the drapes.'

'Yes, you will find the attention to detail here quite extraordinary,' he said, as Zoe linked her arm through his and led him down the corridor. 'The architect was Armand-Claude Mollet, the design brief was for an *hôtel particulier*, fronted by an entrance court and backed by a garden. Finished and decorated by 1722 . . .'

•

Malevich was about to ask for an update on where the guys were with rigging the C4 charges and detonators on the gas main, when one of the guards approached, both hands on the submachine gun strapped across his Kevlar body armour.

'How much longer?' the guard asked one of the square-jawed grunts working over the open manhole.

'Not long,' Malevich replied, confident his French was as good as the next Parisian. 'Fifteen minutes or so.'

The guard looked amused. He took his hand off his gun's forward-grip and reached into his pocket. 'You sound like the guys who come to fix the plumbing at my apartment. I bet fifteen minutes really means three or four days for you too, hey?'

Malevich smiled, trying to appear sincere.

'Not when we are working for the boss,' he replied, pointing his thumb at the palace wall that abutted the pavement a few metres from them.

The guard smiled, brought out his hand and a pack of smokes, shook one loose and took it out with his lips.

'I would light that back at your post,' Malevich said, gesturing to the hole in the ground and mimicking an explosion with both hands.

The guard grunted and headed back towards the gate.

As soon as he was gone, Malevich's men went back to their real work fixing the charges. Malevich leaned against the van and took a few deep breaths – he felt like he'd run a marathon.

•

'. . . and though it has undergone many modifications since, it remains a fine example of the French classical style,' Baldy said, showing Fox and Zoe a reception hall. Fox motioned for Zoe to hurry the guy along and she gave an almost imperceptible, *I'm trying.*

'During the French Revolution and the Napoleonic Wars, the building receded in importance, becoming a furniture warehouse, then a print factory, then a dance hall. Russian Cossacks camped at the Elysée when they occupied Paris in 1814, or so they say – I am not entirely convinced, but it's something –'

'How about 1867?' Fox asked, hoping to skip a few decades.

The man looked at him, interest in his eyes.

'That's quite a specific date,' he said, staring off at a tapestry on the wall. 'Let me see . . . 1853 saw the coup d'état that ended the Second Republic, Napoleon III charged the architect Joseph-Eugène Lacroix with renovations, and while he lived in the Tuileries Palace, he kept the Elysée as a discreet place to meet his mistresses, moving, some say, between the two palaces through a secret underground passage.'

He gave Fox a wink about the mistress arrangement and Fox smiled and acted impressed.

'In regards to 1867, that is when Lacroix completed his work,' he explained, waving his hand towards the cornice moulding and detailed panel inlays in the walls. 'It was completed in time for the Universal Exposition of that year, and foreign sovereigns – including Tsar Alexander II, the Sultan Abdul-Aziz of Turkey and Emperor Franz-Josef of Austria – were received here. The essential look of l'Elysée has remained the same, and from about then on, during the French Third Republic, she became the official presidential residence.'

'So it has been unchanged since?'

'Oh, I wouldn't say unchanged,' he answered, 'but mainly just cosmetic alterations and repairs, a few modern upgrades. Hard to improve on perfection, you see?'

'And what about the president's study?' Zoe asked, her hand on the man's arm. 'Could we please see that?'

'He – he has a couple,' the man replied, and Fox's heart skipped a beat. *A couple?*

'The original one from 1867?' Zoe pressed. 'The one in all the state photos. The gilded salon, I think it is called?'

'Yes, that is still used, especially for receptions, but it's not really somewhere we show visitors, unless you have an appointment with –'

'Monsieur, surely a quick look . . .' Zoe said, her voice low, speaking close to his good ear. 'After all, our President is abroad.'

He gazed at her face for a moment and then seemed to melt under her charm.

'Yes, this way,' he said, leading them down the hall. Fox's smile was as big as the Cheshire Cat's.

•

Malevich's guys gave him the thumbs-up and headed back to the van.

'We back this van fifty metres down the road, away from the gate,' the bigger one said, revealing a little plastic box with a button, much like a garage door opener. 'Hit this, it will blow this wall and the path here, ten metres at least; nothing left but a big opening.'

'Okay,' Malevich said. He thought back to their little red Renault van parked around the corner, masquerading as a fire-response medical unit. 'What about the guards up ahead?'

'As soon as that idiot goes back inside, we move,' the big guy replied. 'We reverse, we detonate, and I keep hitting the entrance with the CS grenades while you two go in through the palace's new door and get what you need.'

'Good, get ready.'

•

'L'Elysée certainly is beautiful,' Fox said as they reached a biometric security checkpoint. It was a glass wall that split the hallway, a piece of ultra-tech kit amid the baroque.

'She is my mistress,' Baldy said, guiding his open palm onto the mirrored scanning surface, a thin line of green light passing beneath his hand making the heavy bulletproof glass doors hiss open.

Fox followed Zoe into a large, ornate sitting room filled with elegant Second Empire furniture. Everything he'd seen was so grand, every room so impressive, that he'd have believed any one of them could have served as the President's ceremonial study. Through the tall windows to his left was the sun-drenched garden, a boxwood maze framed by blooming wisteria, gravel paths winding to a parade-ground-sized courtyard.

'This is the salon,' Baldy announced, opening double doors by the windowed wall and leading them into yet another luxurious room. This one had a small desk, several armchairs, a sofa and sitting chairs, and more large windows overlooking the ceremonial gardens.

'Beautiful,' Fox said.

'Isn't it?' Baldy replied, pleased with himself. He stood by the door, watching them intently as they moved to the first window to admire the view. 'The *Salon Dora*, it is called, the Gilded Salon.'

'Faint,' Fox whispered into Zoe's ear.

'What?' she replied out of the side of her mouth, turning to smile at Baldy, who gave a little wave back.

Fox crossed his arms, brushed up slightly against Zoe and pinched her arm.

'Ouch –'

She moved her hand to rub her arm and Fox put her in a wrist-lock and dropped her to the floor, her face covered – eyes, mouth, everything – with his other hand.

'She's fainted!' Fox said loudly, so that Baldy could hear and Zoe got the idea. He felt her go limp and he released the pressure.

'*Sacrebleu!*' Baldy exclaimed, his pudgy little hands up to his face as he looked down at her.

Zoe made a good job of appearing to come to, slowly, groggily.

'The cushion,' Fox said, pointing to the closest armchair, and the Frenchman went over and retrieved a small cushion from it.

'She's diabetic,' Fox said, and heard Zoe do a little choke that may have been to cover a laugh. 'She needs some sugar – maybe a Coke?'

Baldy looked at Fox blankly.

'Coca-Cola? Chocolate? Sugar?' Fox said, miming drinking and eating.

'Aha!' Baldy held up a hand as it sank in. 'I run, quick minutes, you wait.'

And he was off. Fox helped Zoe to her feet and shut the study door, sliding the heavy brass bolt across.

65

WASHINGTON, DC

'This is how Lachlan Fox operates.' McCorkell pointed at the screen image of Fox looking down the MP5's sight at the deceased gunman they had identified.

'This?' Bowden asked, flicking through the images: Fox scanning the crowd with the MP5.

'This?' Fox on the highway, climbing up the bonnet of the Audi SUV.

'This?' Fox hammering the Golf hatchback through the streest of Paris, smashed cop cars in his wake.

McCorkell had had enough. '*This* is what he does; he gets the job done where your guys can't.'

'And what is this job, exactly, hmm?' Bowden prodded. 'You call shooting it out with the cops in the middle of fucking Paris *getting the job done?*'

McCorkell could tell that several of the CIA staff were trying to pretend they weren't listening in on the exchange.

'Yeah, you're right,' McCorkell said. 'I forgot the CIA had the monopoly on that kind of action.'

Bowden's eyes narrowed. 'I was a sanctioned intelligence officer, doing my job for this country,' he said slowly, emphatically. He pointed at the main screen. 'This Fox guy, a *reporter*?'

'Just give him his space – make contact with him, sure, but leave him –'

'Who the hell's he doing this for? Hmm? Or aren't you thinking about that? Are you too close to him to see?'

'I'm saying, Bob, don't read this wrong until you know the full story. Don't jump to conclusions that have no base in reality.'

'Bill, there's no way I'm having this fuck run all over Europe. Not like this. I'm bringing him in. You and Valerie have him turn himself in at the embassy, explain himself, go for it, but I'm not waiting for more shit like this to go down.'

Bowden nodded to his second in command and the junior officer picked up the phone.

'There's something you should know about him,' McCorkell said. Bowden turned back to face him. 'He's always a couple of steps ahead of the curve. He's working on angles and leads you haven't even anticipated yet.'

Bowden almost laughed.

'If you're smart,' McCorkell said, 'you'll just get out of the way and let him do what he's doing.'

'Interesting,' Bowden said, talking through his teeth. 'Here's something you probably don't know about him: he's a dead man walking.'

McCorkell shook his head.

'Babich, French cops, unknown Russian gunmen with Chechen War pedigrees – his number's up on this one.'

'Let him be.'

'Additional target,' Bowden announced to the room, 'Lachlan Fox. I'm designating him a Tier One Personality and issuing full rendition protocols: I want him in a room, or, if he puts up a fight, I want him in a bag – and I want it done today.'

66

ELYSÉE PALACE

PARIS

'We have to be quick.' Zoe ran to the double doors at the other end of the study and locked them as well.

'Yeah . . .' Fox looked about the room. It was roughly ten by ten metres, one wall was a series of windows and glass double doors that looked over the enclosed courtyard, with three massive arched mirrors on the opposite wall. A desk in front of a fireplace, hanging tapestries and decorative architectural details picked out with gold-leaf gilding. A flat-screen TV on a stand by the desk was the only obvious twenty-first century mod con. The furniture, carpets and crystal chandelier were almost lost among the built-in decorations. Behind the elegant red-leather-topped desk was a simple sixties' wicker chair with its back to the fireplace. There were three seats opposite, and to the other side of the room beneath a huge tapestry was a sofa and chairs arranged around a coffee table – for more relaxed meetings.

'Something's not right . . .'

'What is it?' Zoe asked.

'Give me the sketch.'

Fox studied the diagram Katya had transcribed – a crude pen drawing, not to scale and with no measurements. Fox faced the wall with the three mirrors. The drawing indicated large doors and a tapestry instead. *What now?*

'Well, let's hope that's all they changed . . .' Fox said, moving for the fireplace.

The diagram indicated that the document was in a low recess in the wall, near to the door, to the right of a fireplace and beside windows. Fox stood next to the desk and surveyed the entry points to the room. There was only the one fireplace, double doors either side, the ones to the right were near the windows.

'So it should be here,' he said, squatting down.

He moved a small bookshelf, lower than waist height, and a little side table with a lamp. A twenty-five centimetre figurine of a nineteenth-century French legionnaire fell to the floor with a crack and its head rolled away.

Zoe stared at Fox.

'Sorry.'

Fox inspected the decorated panel behind, knocking on it, pulling at it, testing its solidity.

'Is it behind there?' Zoe asked.

There was no discernible difference, it all sounded fairly solid.

'Only one way to find out,' Fox said. He grabbed a letter opener from the desk, positioned its tip over the target section of wall with one hand, his other palm over the top to reinforce it and –

Smash.

'Fuck!'

'What?'

'Nearly went through my hand,' Fox said, noting that he'd hardly dinted the wall. He tried a couple of angles around the gilt timber edging, but was getting nowhere beyond chipping away at the paint.

He walked over to the sofa and lifted a silver Statue of Liberty from the coffee table – it was about half a metre tall and heavy as hell. Then he noticed a couple of swords also on the table – silver, ornate, ancient things; heavy and sharp enough to use in combat.

'Only in France . . .' he said, carrying one of the swords over to the panel. He inserted the tip of the blade into the woodwork, wriggled it so that it went deeper in between the timber cladding and the wall to which it was affixed, deeper still, until he had leverage. He pushed the blade, moving it back and forth a few times, slowly prying the sheet of timber panelling away from the wall . . . The sound of nails creaking, protesting . . . Plaster and paint dust fell, the wood giving way a centimetre, two, three –

POP!

67

WASHINGTON, DC

Valerie and McCorkell watched the latest footage: Fox leaving a car, two others staying behind, a woman walking down the street with Fox. Not fifteen minutes old.

'Who the hell is that?' McCorkell leaned in closer. 'Can you zoom that image for me?' he asked the nearest FBI tech.

The tech tapped away.

'No, that corner there, enhance it.' McCorkell watched the picture of Fox and the woman enlarge. 'Okay, now the one with the woman in the Louvre forecourt, when she has the pistol.'

The tech nodded. It took him all of five seconds to get a frame where she drew the pistol from a quick-release hip holster.

'It's a SIG.'

'And she's got it in her holster now,' McCorkell said, looking back to the image of her on the street with Fox. 'Or she did have fifteen minutes ago, anyway.'

'She's a cop,' the tech said, making the connection. 'We're looking for a French cop.'

McCorkell nodded. The tech's hands blurred with speed over his keyboard, doing God-knew-what to access the French police database.

'Let's get a map up,' McCorkell said, not missing a beat. 'A grid map on Paris. Everywhere Fox's been, everywhere he's gonna go, I want to see it marked up. Get every camera and eyewitness and carrier pigeon's testimony; I want it marked up.'

'Bill?'

McCorkell looked across to Valerie – she held a hand over her phone's mouthpiece: 'That car chase Fox was involved in early this morning, it was called off by a cop who's since gone AWOL.'

'Let me guess,' McCorkell said, looking at the tech's screen that had the woman's details up and there was no mistaking her ID photo, 'officer Zoe Ledoyen of the National Police?'

'Yep,' Valerie said. 'Her command can't contact her.'

'She was the cop who was sent out to him this morning?'

'Fox said he had a cop at Renard's house, and what – you just assumed it had to be a guy?' Valerie replied with a grin. 'And there's more: that car chase this morning? Result was Fox put two cops in the hospital, wrote off three police cars and a couple of million euros' worth of collateral damage. Paris cops have just ID'd him and put out an APB.'

Silence. Like the floor just fell away. Bowden would lap this up, with the French police doing his work for him to boot.

McCorkell looked at the image of Fox. *What the fuck is he doing?*

'Maybe it's to do with Babich's break-out,' Valerie said, now standing next to him.

'What? How?'

'Maybe this is an elaborate wild goose chase, designed by Umbra to keep Fox in play, keeping us busy looking elsewhere, while Babich does something else?'

'Tying up our resources,' McCorkell said, looking back over at Bowden, who had certainly taken that, hook, line and sinker. 'Maybe . . . But Fox is too smart to be sucked in. We've just got to make sure our guys are the first ones there.'

Bowden caught his gaze and there was a moment between them. The CIA man was steely-eyed, determined to clean things up: he might not have Babich in his sights right now, but by God he had the world's most capable military and intelligence at his fingertips and he was closing in on the scent of another prey.

Another tech held up her hand.

She said, 'Kate just turned her cell phone back on.'

'Where?'

'Literally around the corner from where that image of Fox was taken just before,' she replied. 'Stationary. She's currently on it, we don't have real-time voice data but we can get that if we ask our NSA buddies over there.'

'Wait,' he said. 'Keep it quiet. Let her talk, get the transcript of the call, and then punch through as soon as she's finished so I can talk to her.'

McCorkell looked at the map of Paris, seeing nothing but uncontrollable space and scenarios ahead. *What the hell was Fox trying to get out of this . . .*

68

ELYSÉE PALACE

PARIS

The nails popped out and the panel swung open on concealed hinges. Inside was a dark void. Fox put his head in.

'Anything?'

Inside was a little nook, but he couldn't see anything. He felt around. Nothing but timber framing.

'There's nothing in here . . .'

'Are you sure?' Zoe asked. He made room for her to crouch down next to him and she put her hand in the nook, feeling around. She looked annoyed and disappointed.

He took an antique gold lighter off the desk and put it in the opening.

Zoe put a hand on his forearm.

'Careful.'

He nodded. He wasn't going to start burning down national palaces. *Then again, the way this day was going . . .*

He lit the lighter, looked around inside, the orange glow flickering –

There, tucked in the hollow of a vertical timber stud to the left was a rolled-up, dusty leather cylinder the length of a piece of A4 paper. They'd found it.

•

'Let's move.' Malevich turned to the smaller guy and tapped a small schematic of the palace's first floor to reiterate his point: 'We go in, you follow me to this study, and you just watch my back and get us out in one piece.'

'Okay. This is good, very nice.'

'A couple of minutes,' Malevich said. 'Right?'

The shorter guy smiled, revealing gold teeth.

'Don't forget,' Malevich addressed the other guy, 'The emergency response crews will come from the same direction as where you've parked the van.'

'Good. I've packed it with enough incendiary to burn a hole to China – set it off when we need it, not before.'

The big guy showed the mobile phone he'd use to trigger the detonation.

'Kaboom! Ha!' The guy with the gold teeth laughed.

Great, Malevich thought, as he climbed into the back of the van, loosening his overalls to reveal the hidden fireman's uniform underneath, *I'm heading into this with a maniac.*

•

Fox placed the leather cylinder on the table and undid the binding.

A single sheet of paper inside. US Secretary of State letterhead. About a dozen lines of text, two sprawling signatures, the names of the American and Russian diplomats. This was the secret protocol to the Alaska Purchase.

'The dates are correct,' Zoe said.

'Give me your BlackBerry.'

Zoe handed it over and he took a couple of photos before he put the sheet of paper back into the cylinder.

'We should go,' Fox said.

'You take your friends back to New York, I will wait at the guard station here, with the –'

Noise at the door. One of the door handles rattled.

'Quickly!' Zoe whispered.

Now there was a banging at the door.

Fox popped the panel back – it looked okay, although it was slightly ajar at close inspection – and Zoe shifted the little bookcase and side table back in front while he stashed the sabre in an umbrella stand that was next to the desk.

'What should we do?' Fox asked, tucking the cylinder into the back pocket of his pants.

Zoe undid her top few buttons, messed up her hair –

The banging on the door grew louder, the handle rattling hard, a muffled voice –

She kissed Fox, long and wet, her tongue in his mouth as she pressed him up against the door.

She took a step back and Fox caught his breath. He noticed that her bright poppy red lipstick was smeared around her lips; no doubt it would be even more obvious around his . . .

She opened the door, Fox straightened his shirt. Baldy was standing there with a can of Coke in hand, flushed with stress. Zoe made a show of doing up her shirt buttons and Baldy's annoyance changed into the slightest smile. Then Fox walked out, appearing embarrassed as he made a show of doing up his fly.

Baldy nodded as if he understood, smiled like they'd made his day. Zoe took the Coke, and the three of them went down the corridor.

Fox adjusted the cylinder as he walked, he couldn't help but check out Zoe's sway as they passed through the glass security wall.

'You did good back there,' he whispered as he stepped into stride next to her.

'Not bad yourself.'

'Stanislavski method of acting,' Fox said. 'I'm always in the moment, yet never quite lost in it.'

She smiled, about to say something –

Baldy pulled over and held out an arm to signal they should take some side stairs down to the –

BOOM!

69

WASHINGTON, DC

The CIA desk was a hive of activity. McCorkell hung around the periphery, listening, watching.

'Fox!' A tech called out and Bowden looked up from the transcript he was reading. 'Sir, we've got a new visual in Paris.'

Bowden moved quickly to the tech's side.

'Where?'

'Elysée Palace has security footage of his entry. Twelve minutes old.'

'Elysée Palace? The French President's home?'

McCorkell looked back to the FBI corner – Valerie had heard, she was repeating the info to her team.

'He signed in as a French reporter from *Le Figaro*, a Renard Rochefort.'

Renard? McCorkell thought back – he knew the name . . . He looked around . . . The TV screen in the corner.

'Isn't that the reporter who was just killed at the Louvre?'

Yes, McCorkell thought. Jesus. The cop had taken the guy's ID from his body. Fox had just used it. This was going to feed the sharks up this end of the room.

'He sign in with anyone?' Bowden asked.

'Officer Zoe Ledoyen signed in at the same time.'

The tech brought up an image of an attractive woman McCorkell already knew plenty about.

'Well, that's not Kate Matthews,' Bowden said, looking at the image closely. 'Who is it? Bill, can you shed any light?'

'Wish I could,' McCorkell replied. Wouldn't take them long to realise that she'd changed outfit since the Louvre just before, that it was one and the same woman.

Bowden looked across at the grainy image close-up from the Louvre –

'Elysée's security log has her down as a senior officer in the National Police . . . Here's her file; it's legit, she's a cop.'

Bowden read it over the tech's shoulder.

'Jesus. What are they doing in there?'

McCorkell said, 'It's the same woman from the Louvre.'

Bowden compared the two images and nodded back to Bill. McCorkell hoped her being a cop would end all this rubbish and Bowden could go back to waiting for intel on Babich to emerge.

'Want me to call the palace security?' a CIA analyst asked.

McCorkell could almost hear Bowden's cogs turning.

'Not yet,' he replied. 'Get her superior on the line. I want to find out what she's working on. Move our assets to the area, I don't want to lose them when they leave.'

70

ELYSÉE PALACE

PARIS

Fox slipped in and out of consciousness.

In his mind, all he saw was Kate in a slideshow of memories. *Wearing a striking dress in an ornate ballroom. Dancing. Him smashing in a door and seeing a big guy on top of her. Blood and death and then they were on a train heading out of Russia, Kate in front of him taking his hand and – was this happening? She took his hand – moving it down her body – staring at him the whole time – both of them silent. His hand – her skin – overwhelming . . . Pulling her towards him – kissing – she's on top of him, naked, moving slowly, crying into his eyes.*

He opened his eyes, felt pain, heard nothing, blacked out again.

Manhattan . . . Kate's there. She's come to see him. He feels relieved, but then . . . there's someone else in her life . . . He sees her again; a different view of Manhattan. It's raining and he's cradling her in his arms and she's dead, dead . . . dead . . .

Fox opened his eyes. Zoe's face was close above his, as if she'd just given him mouth-to-mouth.

His head was pounding. No, it's another explosion . . . Or someone at the door. Zoe's lips are moving, but he can't hear.

Then, sound. Piercing, monotonous. A fire alarm –

'Lachlan!'

'Yeah,' he groaned, and Zoe smiled with relief. She helped him to his feet.

Baldy was on his hands and knees, coughing, but okay. The room was full of smoke. A beam had come down from the ceiling. Fox's head was spinning.

'Come!' Zoe said, taking his hand. She ran, pulling him along with her. In her other hand, she held the cylinder.

'Left!' she yelled, and they ran down a corridor, a couple of office workers running past them holding clothing to their faces to shield them from the smoke.

'It's tear gas!' Fox said.

'Keep going!' Zoe said, pulling him on. They rounded a corner. Up ahead were empty offices on either side of a carpeted hallway – a big hole was blown in the side of the wall. Through the smoke and gas Fox could see down to ground level and into the street as half the hallway they were standing in had already fallen through to the floor below. Tear gas poured into the hole as two figures appeared like ghosts . . .

71

WASHINGTON, DC

McCorkell studied the image on the screen in front of him. Zoe Ledoyen. Her police ID photo. 'She's thirty-seven,' Valerie said beside him. 'Born in Nice. Mother was an actor. She died in ninety-five. We don't have the father, left when she was a kid. Two sisters, we're trying to track them down.'

An agent manning a phone, covered the mouthpiece: 'Got one in Madrid, works as a teacher, married local with two kids.'

McCorkell took it all in; he was going to work this angle and get to Fox first: two FBI agents from the embassy in Paris were en route to the palace now. *Screw Bowden.*

'Personnel file on the screen, here.'

McCorkell read through it – political science background at university, masters degree in modern history, worked in human resources for a political party and then joined the French National Police as a researcher. Worked her way up through their banking fraud department, then shifted into their counter-intelligence branch. Brought down a few major intel networks – on paper, Zoe seemed damned good at her job.

'Kate still on her phone?'

The agent responsible didn't need to check. 'Yes.'

'Keep on it,' he said. 'Get through as soon as she's off.'

McCorkell leaned forward, spoke quietly to Valerie: 'Get Zoe's cell phone, email, BlackBerry, everything. I wanna know when she makes a call and I wanna be able to hear it.'

She nodded.

He walked back over to Bowden's area. He too was discussing Zoe.

'No political affiliations?'

'None that are noteworthy,' the CIA analyst reported.

'What's the relevance?' McCorkell asked.

Bowden shrugged, a *wanna know, is all* that wasn't going to fly.

'You think this is tied to the Russian Embassy thing? To Umbra?'

Bowden's glasses were low on his nose. He pocketed them in his shirt and motioned McCorkell over to the corner near the urns of coffee, out of earshot.

'Bill, Babich has been sprung, four are dead – seven now, if we include the cops and the French reporter.' Bowden motioned to the photo of Renard. 'And near his body, we've got a French cop shooting another cop –'

'That looked like self-defence.'

'And we've got your amateur spook, this Lachlan fucking Fox,' the rise in volume of Bowden's voice caused several sets of fingers to stop tapping away at their keyboards, 'running around Paris – and now he's in their presidential palace! I mean, for Christ's sake, that all?'

'He's with a cop –'

'Who may just be a double agent, have you thought of that?'

McCorkell's expression said that he had. All this was far too coincidental to *not* be tied up with Babich and Umbra, but proving which side they were on was going to be tough. He knew Fox would be thinking the same and wouldn't let it go . . . but to take Kate over there, into the dragon's den, where Umbra people were now kicking around . . . And this cop, Zoe, *had* shot another cop . . .

'If it's a cover, it's a great one,' McCorkell conceded, looking at the image of the beautiful French police officer. 'We're going to have to explore that possibility.'

Bowden said, 'We're exploring *every* possibility –'

A CIA analyst called out: 'We've got an explosion at the Elysée Palace!'

72

ELYSÉE PALACE

PARIS

Fox pulled Zoe into an office and ducked down as two black-clad paramilitary cops ran along the corridor.

They'd stopped outside the office. Fox could see their boots, then heard them talk on their radios.

Zoe shook her head, signalled it was okay. She had her SIG pistol in one hand and the cylinder in the other.

The two cops ran back the way they'd come, Fox heard them shouting at someone and the noise of a spray of automatic gunfire rang out, then silence.

Fox and Zoe ran through a connecting office until they came to an open door. The gas outside had dissipated enough to see down the hall. The two cops were visible, on the ground, motionless. Two guys were standing there in firemen's uniforms, one of whom had a submachine gun pointed down at the cops.

Fox pulled Zoe up close under the frosted glass wall of the corridor.

One of the firemen moved into the doorway and Fox looked up into a mouth of gold teeth.

Fox was on him fast, twisting his gun wrist and giving him an uppercut that sent the just-fired P90 out of his grip. The guy fell back against the wall, dazed. Fox turned and glanced over to Zoe – she'd just sent the second guy sprawling backwards.

Fox turned back and saw Gold Teeth pulling up an FN pistol to fire. Fox was still turning – all his weight moving in a single fluid attack – a sweeping kick that spilled the pistol and slammed the guy back into the frosted glass wall. The safety-glass shattered with the impact, the man caught the metal-frame doorjamb on the way down and was already re-balanced, snatching the P90 and bringing it up to fire –

Fox grabbed its foregrip as a full auto blast tore into the ceiling above him creating a plaster-dust storm until the gun clicked empty –

Fox pulled the firearm away and tossed it, landing a good punch in his attacker's sternum – the guy winded, but still fighting back, both hands swinging at Fox . . . Kill or be killed. Fox's attacker pulled a knife – Zoe screamed and Fox looked over to see she had been knocked to the ground, kicking up at her attacker. Standing above her was the guy from the Louvre. The one who'd taken Renard's satchel.

Gold Teeth lunged – Fox parried, shifted and pulled the guy into a wall – he hit hard, head first. Fox brought down his heel onto the back of the man's leg – *SNAP!* – the leg bone shattered and the guy was on his knees trying to fight back, but Fox turned him face-down with a wrist and shoulder lock and landed three jackhammer elbows into his back – *crack-crack-crack*. Gold Teeth pushed himself and picked up his knife, but Fox slammed his head against the doorjamb – blood spraying from his nose – sending him out cold – and Zoe –

Zoe was writhing on the ground – gasping for air –

Fox bounded towards her as she struggled to reach her SIG pistol on the floor. Her attacker had his booted foot pressed down on her throat as he reloaded his pistol –

Fox crash-tackled the guy over a desk. He started to rise up to punch him – but he saw figures approaching down the corridor. Six RAID guys, heavily armed.

Machine-gun fire tore down the corridor, shattering the glass partitions around them as Fox rolled one way, the guy the other, towards Zoe. The guy grabbed Zoe's pistol – so fucking fast – and he had it right up against her forehead – right on the edge of pulling the trigger – *he is, he's gonna shoot her* –

'Don't do it!' Fox yelled.

The glass wall shattered next to Fox.

'Where is it?' the guy screamed at Fox. 'The document, where is it?'

The RAID guards fired another volley at them, tearing up the walls they were shielded behind.

'There,' Fox said, motioning under the window where the document had rolled against the wall.

Another burst of fire, some shouts from up the hallway –

The attacker shot off four quick rounds around the wall, grabbed the cylinder that was just within arm's reach, took a gas grenade off his uniform and tossed it down at the RAID team.

'Don't follow me!' he yelled, sprinting off, bullets tearing up the hall in his wake. He shot across the opening, past Fox, down the corridor, towards the hole in the wall.

73

WASHINGTON, DC

'. . . If not, I'll call you back in fifteen minutes,' McCorkell said, ending the phone call to Kate and turning to Valerie. 'Fox and this cop, Zoe, are in the palace retrieving a document. Babich's guys have been after it all morning.'

'They've got it?'

'Not yet,' McCorkell said. He looked over at Bowden's guys, conferring around a map of Paris, setting up blocks for when Fox emerged from the palace. There was commotion up the other end of the room. Already dozens of local response vehicles were headed to the scene of the explosion and getting a CIA grab team to covertly pull Fox out was going to be hard. A small break.

'Fox is going to have to start doing things quietly,' Valerie said.

'He does,' McCorkell said. 'It's the guys pitted against him – he's only as loud as the forces he goes up against.'

'Let's hope this is the end of it,' Valerie said. 'What are our options for getting him to safety?'

'I don't want them out in the open yet, not with Bowden's order out there on the streets,' McCorkell said. He had no doubt that if Fox made a beeline for the embassy now, one of about forty assets in the Paris area would be ready, waiting for the 'kill shot' should he not come in quietly. 'And the cop – I told Kate to be wary of her.'

'What's her take?'

'Not much beyond a personal dislike. Kate's pissed at Fox too.'

'You read her latest phone transcript?'

'Not yet,' Bill said, looking at the fresh print-out on his desk of her last phone call to the number in China. 'Is it –'

'Seems a legit personal call. Wouldn't want to be Fox, though.'

'We just gotta hope he gets out and keeps his head down long enough to use this cop, Zoe. She'd know the area well – if they could slip out . . .'

'Through the Almighty's net,' Valerie mocked and smiled at the thought. 'Bowden will go berserk.'

'He does what he does,' McCorkell replied, smiling as well. He knew that if you couldn't keep your sense of humour in this kind of work, it'd kill you.

An FBI agent approached the desk and leaned in close. He was all smiles too.

'It's Babich,' he said. 'That deadline? I think I now know what it is – and it's definitely in Shanghai.'

74

ELYSÉE PALACE

PARIS

'Move!' Fox yelled at Zoe as gunshots raked the corridor.

He picked up the FN Five-seveN, fired the full clip into the floor towards the RAID team to keep them at bay and received a few full-auto assault rifle bursts in reply.

'And call Al in!' he yelled, as they moved back through the offices in a crouched run, pulling Zoe along by the hand while she dialled.

Their route opened up to a conference room. Fox jammed a chair under the door handles leading in and ran to the windows along one wall. Ten metres below was the courtyard – a sheer drop and crawling with cops.

'We've got to use the hole in the outer wall, the same way that guy did,' Zoe said, her BlackBerry still to her ear.

Fox nodded and they headed back out to the corridor. The RAID team would be in the offices, stalking them. The opening was up ahead, on the opposite side to the central courtyard. The hallway floor here was a ragged mess. Fox hugged the wall, peered around the opening, looked down to street level –

The floor's edge gave way and Fox was dangling six metres above the rubble below – one hand clutching the corner of a joist. Zoe helped him up and back onto the first floor. He caught his breath. There were gunshots on the street, a van visible down the end of the road – that gas worker's van, cops shooting at it – *KLAPBOOM!*

The vehicle erupted in a bright flash of light. The force flattened Fox and Zoe, blasted through the glass of all the hallway windows, flames licking into the building.

'Come on,' Fox said, coughing, crawling around the hole in the floor and getting to his feet.

They raced around the corner to the palace's western wing. He tucked the pistol into the back of his trousers.

'Tell Al to pick us up here!' he yelled as he opened a double-doored window inwards. The avenue outside was quiet, tree-lined.

'Avenue de Marigny!' Zoe said into her phone. 'We are coming from a window, on the first floor!'

She hung up, nodded that she was ready.

There was a little wrought-iron handrail on the window. Fox climbed over it –

The drop to the street was a good five metres – to his left was one of those phone-booth-like guard shelters.

'Zoe.'

She looked over to where he motioned with a tilt of his head. 'Think you can make that?'

She nodded. He lowered his legs down, found purchase on the ground floor's top window ledge. The palace façade was made of large stone blocks with at least a couple of centimetres of paint-work in between – a good grip for fingers, lousy for squeezing the toes of Fox's size thirteens in. Fox had never been good at rock-climbing exercises – he tended to lean back too much – but he kept close to the wall now, inching across to his left, his feet leaving the reassuring ledge of the window below and his fingers having to do all the work of holding his weight. He swung across and dropped onto the roof of the little guard shelter then jumped down another three metres, rolling onto the bitumen pavement.

Zoe moved out the window like a cat, fast and agile, as though she had no weight and was all strength. He watched her cross the ledge in a line that wasn't there for him, climb down the stonework like it was a ladder, and land on top of the guard shelter to the side.

She jumped down into his arms. He held her for a second more than he had to and she smiled at him.

In a screech of brakes, Al stopped the car in front of them. Kate was stony-faced in the front as they climbed into the back seat.

'Drive!' Zoe said. 'Back the way you came!'

75

GARE DU NORD

PARIS

Malevich emerged from the bathroom in his civilian clothes. He wove through the crowded arrival hall to the RER trains. He checked his bag on the escalator, making sure that the zip was fully done up, the precious cargo safe and sound. He slung the bag over his shoulder and fished his vibrating mobile phone out of his pocket.

'Yes?'

'You sound surprised. The hour is up, time for your call.'

'Time flies.'

'Do you have it?' Lavrov asked. He sounded like he was speaking from inside a tin can.

'Yes.'

'You are a hero to your country! Anything you want –'

'We'll get to that,' Malevich replied, boarding the train. 'I know what it is you're after now. I can only imagine what it must be worth, although how you intend to use it, to enforce its legality . . . I don't want to try to comprehend. In the meantime, I have a request . . .'

He could tell that he'd caught Lavrov off-guard. It was fine for *him* – he was off the grid, far away from this frontline. Malevich was the one they'd be after. He was the one who had been through all this . . .

'Like I said,' Lavrov began, 'you will be –'

'This was much more dangerous than anything I'd been prepared for,' Malevich said, finding a clear space to sit for the twenty-minute journey to the airport.

'Boris, you will be well compensated.'

'I know,' he said. 'I also know that the Americans would like to get their hands on this. I can only imagine the lengths they will go to to stop this from –'

'Listen, do you have it on you now?'

Malevich paused, looked around, despite himself.

'Yes.'

'Good. Good. You have done very well, you can have any role in my –'

'I don't want a job.'

A pause.

'I just want to be left alone. I do this and that's it, I've done my job.'

'Of course, that's easy,' Lavrov replied.

'It's not that easy. They will track me down. They will have footage of me, and they will hunt me. My whole life has changed.' Malevich looked around the carriage. 'There's more.'

'Yes?'

'That reporter, the one you organised a separate team to fix; he is still alive. He was at the palace.'

'You are sure?'

'Yes.'

'Do not worry about him – he can't do anything now. In fact, it's better this way.'

Malevich couldn't comprehend that either, but he let it slide. To be safe for the future he'd need more than the meagre state compensation he was getting. He'd need money to fund his and his sister's existence, way off the grid somewhere, hidden from reprisals or silencing missions. He'd heard too many stories of men like him who'd done work for the state and never made it back. They owed him. Big.

'Hello?'

'I'm here,' Malevich said. 'Change of plan. I want five million euros sent to my account.'

There was silence for a beat and then laughter over the phone.

'You're a good boy – my kind of Russian, a ruthless capitalist,' Lavrov said, still laughing. 'When you land, check your bank balance. Safe travels.'

Malevich didn't know what to make of it. *Such a quick capitulation? No haggling?* Before he could say anything else, the call was ended. Always no more than a minute.

Maybe he should have asked for more? He put the bag down between his feet – the document was worth untold billions and power and prosperity for Russia. All that, right there, on the floor of this train. He tried his sister again; still her phone was switched off. He left another message for her to call him back. It had been a long morning, but he was almost there. He closed his eyes hoping the train would rock him into a calm state of being. Useless. He kept seeing blood. His heart would not slow. He imagined cops waiting for him at the airport. He imagined the prison in Siberia or wherever the motherland now sent its unwanted, where he'd perhaps end up for being greedy over the phone to Lavrov just now.

The passenger next to him was reading the *International Herald Tribune*. The front page: a picture of Roman Babich. Bastards like him were everything that was wrong with his country today.

76

PARIS

'Yeah, I know, we need to get out of here *today* . . .' Gammaldi said, as he drove under Zoe's directions.

Fox had Kate's iPhone: 'You've got no idea of the net falling around you in Paris,' McCorkell was saying on the other end. 'The Agency operations leader here is convinced you're part of this Umbra conspiracy – he's been watching footage of you tearing up Paris all morning.'

'Hasn't he seen this other guy?' Fox asked. 'The one at the Louvre and at the palace?'

'We've got nothing but a few bad shots from the Louvre,' McCorkell replied. 'You or your cop friend know who he is?'

'No,' Fox said. 'But we think he was the one who murdered the Russian Ambassador's wife earlier this week.'

'And the MO on the explosion at the Elysée Palace looks the same as the one used on the Russian Embassy.'

'Exactly,' Fox said.

'Listen, Lachlan, you need to lay low, disappear, don't try and head for any mass transport hub – every cop in France is after you. Interpol, Europol, everyone.'

'Too bad they're not looking for the bastard who just took the secret protocol.'

'We're all working on that, believe me. Where're you headed?'

'As far away from here as we can get – take a breather and get a flight outta here –'

'You don't understand. Every airport will have your details.'

'We've got one possibility that might work . . .'

'Where?'

'I can't say . . . It'll tip them off.'

'You think they're listening?'

'I know they are,' Fox said. 'Umbra, the French, hell – probably NSA for all I know. That document come through yet?'

'Hang on.' Fox could hear McCorkell checking his email. 'Not yet.'

'Look, if you could just buy us a little . . .'

Fox trailed off. He'd been thinking if they could just make it to a small airport out of town, they could charter something, but . . .

'How much time you need?' McCorkell asked. 'Lach?'

They were flashing across the Seine on Pont de la Concorde and Fox had caught a glimpse of a billboard on the side of a bus.

'It's okay, Bill,' Fox said. 'I think a solution has just presented itself.'

77

SHANGHAI

Jacob was onto his third pre-dinner drink. The Summit leaders would be having their own reception, then dinner. He was hanging out with the worker bees. Campari and soda, twist of orange, seemed the drink du jour. The view was pleasant, the company about as good as he could have hoped. Talk was simple, low-key, non-political. Tonight was about fun.

'When did you get in?' the pretty reporter for Reuters asked. She'd approached him at the bar fifteen minutes ago, but he'd already forgotten her name and didn't have the heart to ask it again.

'Twelve days ago,' Jacob van Rijn replied. 'I was with an advance team from the EU.'

'Oh, you're with a delegation?'

'Don't expect any scoops from me; I've had one too many of these.'

He held up his empty glass.

'Usually that's when the scoops start flowing,' she replied, but let him off the hook. 'It's fine, I'm not working tonight.'

304 • JAMES PHELAN

'Good,' he replied. He signalled to the barman for another round – she was drinking vodka tonic, he remembered that.

'Excuse me,' she said, and touched his arm before heading off to the bathroom. He watched her walk away, and then watched as his drink was being mixed.

He'd avoided the hotel bar in the Park Hyatt up till now, despite the spectacular view over Shanghai. He and the others had found some wonderful little places in and around the Bund and the older districts of Shanghai that evoked a different time and place. This, despite being so high above the city, was just another hotel bar.

Now that the summit was underway, and the world leaders and their entourages were here – the US President had over three hundred staff and security guards housed in the hotel next door, not to mention a small naval armada out at sea in case a quick helicopter evac was necessary – the security made it too hard to leave. They were hotel-marooned.

It meant no more nights out in the Bund. No more nights out with Helena, an attractive woman from the Danish contingent who had something of a name among the male staffers. He'd constantly reminded himself that given her role as the EC President's right hand, an affair with her was too dangerous for his career. Still, they'd come close on a night out, returning to the hotel at 3 am, drinking through Jacob's mini-bar and singing karaoke until the sun rose, ending with a kiss that led them into bed, but ten minutes later he'd prised himself away from her while they still had their underwear on. The next morning, over a greasy breakfast across the river, he'd learned that his reservations had been well-placed: his friend from the Dutch consulate told him that Helena was a spy with Denmark's foreign intelligence agency. When Jacob had seen her at lunch today, laughing at a window seat with yet *another* guy from the Russian delegation, the world had made so much more sense.

The drinks arrived as the reporter came back. He realised she'd left her purse on her chair the whole time – he could have used the opportunity to take a peek at her ID and learn her name. As she sat back down she nudged the purse, revealing her press card: Felecia.

'Cheers,' she said, holding out her glass to meet his. 'So, shall we order dinner or go out?'

'Out?' he said. 'I don't know, Felecia . . . With all the security . . .'

'True,' she replied. 'We could just get room service?'

78

PARIS

They had ditched the unmarked police car and joined the tourists ambling along the banks of the Seine. The tourists were seemingly oblivious to danger, the earlier shooting in the nearby Louvre not spooking them enough to change their holiday plans.

'So slow and dumb a getaway, no one will look here,' Gammaldi said, seating himself at the prow of a tourist barge.

'We had to get off the roads,' Fox said. 'And mate, it's a similar pace to your driving, anyway.'

Gammaldi pulled a face.

'This barge follows a canal to Parc de la Villette,' Zoe said. 'I have friends living near there.'

Kate stared at the river as they passed along it.

'Canal Saint-Martin is a piece of Paris that locals like to keep secret . . .' the tour guide began over the barge's PA.

They passed under the Pont Royal, a beautiful stone bridge with five arches. Fox was thinking back to that billboard he'd seen not five minutes ago. He ran through the map of Paris burned into his memory. They'd be heading the right way, but it would be a tough sell to the others . . .

Fox sat next to Kate, but she wouldn't look at him.

'We're seeing Paris,' Fox said, trying to lighten the moment.

She turned to face him now, but her eyes were angry.

'I know . . . This isn't anything like how you wanted to see it,' he said. 'I'm sorry.'

They watched the view as their barge turned past Notre Dame Cathedral.

'Can you even imagine being here as a tourist?' Kate asked, quietly. 'Could you do that, ever?'

Fox wanted to say yes, he wanted to believe it himself, but he knew whatever he said right now would only lead to a fight. He remained silent and put his arm around her.

They navigated around the Ile Saint Louis, where Gammaldi stood to take in the sight, and the barge continued on, below the Place de la Bastille.

The tunnel was dark with only the occasional beam of light glistening on the water, while vines snaked down from the concrete above. Another world. So quiet, but for the dull thrum of the barge's motor.

Kate's iPhone rang. She passed it to Fox. McCorkell's number.

Fox asked, 'You get the image of the document?'

'We have to get it back,' McCorkell said.

'Good luck with that,' Fox said, almost laughing. 'He's probably halfway to –'

'You read it?'

'Not in detail –'

'It gives Russia the Arctic waters that currently belong to the US.'

'How can that – ?'

'I've got some experts headed here now to confirm it, but it doesn't look good. We're talking economic and security concerns that are almost incomprehensible.'

Fox's eyes had adjusted to the darkness and he could see his three companions were all listening in close.

'Babich has popped up, just spotted in Shanghai,' McCorkell said. 'Hutchinson is headed there as we speak.'

'So that's it – the document is headed for China?' Fox replied. An opening above allowed a shaft of bright sunlight to cut through the darkness and he could see the look of fear and anger on Kate's face. *When would he let this go?* he imagined she was asking. *When it ended.*

Shanghai. So far away. He couldn't look Kate in the eye. He told McCorkell about the flights the Russian Ambassador had booked to Shanghai as well.

'With the G20 we've got all the major world leaders and media there this weekend,' McCorkell said. 'Babich has the biggest audience he could hope for.'

'Would they stand for it?' Fox asked. 'Couldn't they – ?'

'We can't extradite from China, neither can Italy,' McCorkell said. 'And the Russians won't if he has leverage back there, which we know he has.'

'What kind of – ?'

'There's all sorts of stuff brewing, no clear picture yet.'

'Can someone there stop him?' Fox asked. 'Surely you've got guys you can use in Shanghai?'

'There's no easy or obvious options,' McCorkell said, letting it hang a moment. 'The odds on us getting a bead on him are slight, and the implications of a sanctioned snatch and grab or assassination . . .'

'Yeah, I got it.' Fox thought about it.

'Why don't we make Russia believe that the US *want* Babich to succeed in this?' Fox asked. 'How about we make them think we are behind this whole thing – and we're letting him go, so he can run to a safe place and start bitching to the media to air all his dirty little secrets.'

He could tell that McCorkell was thinking about it.

'They'd buy it, easy,' Fox said. 'If you sell it right. If you say that Babich had been a CIA guy all along, or at the very least that he'd rolled and made a deal after we caught him. That he's out now pushing for a regime change in his own country.'

'That's probably not far from the truth.'

'I've been working against this guy for a long time.'

'Yeah, I know . . .' McCorkell said. 'You want to force them to take care of it for us?'

'It might help put a rocket under them,' Fox said. 'Worst case, it could buy us some time as Babich scrambles to set the record straight with them. Get him moving. He might make a mistake we could exploit.'

There was a long pause.

'One thing we don't have is time,' McCorkell said eventually. 'We've got teams working up a heap of options here. Let me kick this around my end a bit more; you get somewhere and lay low.'

'Got it, talk soon.' Fox ended the call and handed the iPhone back to Kate. She looked like she wanted to throw it in the water. The Canal Saint-Martin opened up to the sky again. It was a glorious bright day, but Fox couldn't rest just yet.

Gammaldi said to Fox, 'Are you thinking what I'm thinking?'

'Pie and a beer?'

'Please . . . *Pizza*. And a beer.'

'I have to go to Shanghai,' Fox said.

'See, I knew you were thinking that! I knew it!' Kate almost hissed.

Fox explained, 'Babich was spotted there –'

'And that's our problem – because?' Kate looked sick.

'That guy from the palace is headed there right now. It's where the document was going the whole time, only it was going to go to another recipient.'

'The Russian government,' Zoe said. 'Only now it has a different courier, it is going to Babich.'

Fox nodded.

'I will go, too,' Zoe said. 'Catching this man is the only thing that will save me from . . . Well, probably from jail, now.'

The morning's actions had finally sunk in for Zoe. Fox had no doubt that if she ended today empty-handed, she'd be hung out to dry.

'Hutchinson is in transit to Shanghai as well,' Fox said. 'I'll get there and help any way I can. You guys can stay here if you want, but I have to see this through to the end.'

Kate was staring at the buildings overlooking the canal. Little cafés dotted here and there. Busy normal life.

'Shanghai, hey?' Gammaldi asked. 'As in Shanghai, China?'

'Yeah, Al, Shanghai's in China,' Fox said. 'It'll be an adventure, like that time we went to Venice.'

'I got my arse kicked in Venice.'

'You made it through, though, right?'

'Minus a tooth.'

'You got plenty in that big gob of yours,' Fox replied.

Kate wasn't amused.

'You really are going to go?' she asked Fox.

'I have to.'

'You have a lifetime of bad decisions to make,' Gammaldi said. 'May I suggest we don't make this one? Sit it out from here, no more car chases and breaking into palaces?'

Fox shook his head. 'I gotta stop him, Al.'

'You can't just go back to Manhattan and blog about this one?' Gammaldi pressed, for Kate's benefit, Fox guessed. 'Make up what happens next?'

'Who do I work for, *The New York Times*?' Fox replied. Kate wasn't laughing or even smiling, she just kept staring at the happy people as the barge drifted past them.

'How would you get there?' Gammaldi asked.

'De Gaulle,' Zoe interjected. 'It's about twenty-five kilometres from here.'

'Here we are coming up to the cruise's end,' the guide announced. *'This is Parc de la Villette, the abattoir that once supplied all the meat for Paris, but now is transformed into a modern family park. Enjoy the rest of your day.'*

Fox thought back to that billboard he'd seen earlier. Advertising the Paris Air Show.

'Wasn't there a closer airport?' he asked, looking at Zoe, and then Gammaldi.

'Well, there's Le Bourget,' Zoe said. 'It's only about ten kilometres from here.'

'It's the air show this weekend,' Gammaldi reminded them. 'It'll be closed to commercial traffic.'

Fox looked at Gammaldi, a glint in his eyes.

'What?' Gammaldi asked.

'No way,' Kate said, reading Fox's mind. 'You can't do that.'

'What?' Gammaldi repeated. 'What can't we do?'

79

CHARLES DE GAULLE AIRPORT

PARIS

Malevich checked into his Air France flight and pocketed the ticket. He walked over to an information counter nearby.

'Terminal three?'

The attendant was on the phone and pointed in the direction.

He took the shuttle to the terminal, and five minutes later he was at the counter for a charter airline he'd called during the train ride from Paris. Ten minutes after that, he was walking towards his aircraft with the flight crew.

Seventy thousand euros. Most of what remained of the operational budget he'd planned to keep for posterity. He didn't like the expense but he was sure he'd done the right thing. Too many people had already been killed for the diary, this document, and he was beginning to think he was a throwaway asset. He was wary of Lavrov now – he'd agreed to the five million too quickly. Wouldn't he need to check that through Moscow? And, the more he thought about it, the more he knew there would be others willing to kill for the document he had in his bag.

Imagine what the Americans would do if they knew I held the title, all future claims, of their waters off Alaska . . .

But he had to see this through, for himself and, more importantly, for his sister. She was the only family he had left, and her life was far harder than his.

His parents had both been killed in a random attack when he was a boy. Some thugs had entered their house to rob them. It was the transition time, the Soviet system had folded and with it most people's worlds. His father had fought and they'd shot him. His mother too. She'd died in his arms. The day after their funeral he'd gone to the FSB office in Moscow, determined to help stop that kind of violence. They turned him away – they had too many staff already. A call came a week later telling him that a man would like to meet him to discuss a job: that man, Lavrov, had offered him so much and all he had to do in return was be ready one day in the future for a job that would probably never come. And to prove his credibility, the man had those thugs tracked down and killed in an arrest that 'went bad'. In a way, Malevich had had blood on his hands since then. He'd been sent to Paris as a state-funded student, chose to study science and then veterinary medicine, and had worked the past ten years there, almost forgetting that the rug of normalcy could be pulled out from under his feet with a simple phone call or message.

He thought about the document in his possession. What it said . . . So much space . . . *Priceless, surely?* He himself could hardly believe it – all those rumours about Russia only 'leasing' Alaska to the Americans – *well, that was wrong, wasn't it*? He laughed. This was the next best thing to getting all that land back, surely. He read the science periodicals, knew the kind of resource wealth there was in the Arctic, untapped.

'Thank you,' he said as the air hostess offered him a drink while they waited for take-off. Champagne. *Why not celebrate a little?* He settled into the plush seat of the Bombardier Global 5000 executive jet.

He'd be a hero to his country, Lavrov had said. Malevich was sceptical of that too – such power, such a coup, would surely be claimed by Lavrov. *How well did he really know the man?* He'd bought Malevich's trust many years ago. Bought it. What had he done, *personally*, for Malevich to truly trust him? Compared to what he'd done for the state this week, what had Lavrov *really* done for him . . .

80

PARIS AIR SHOW

LE BOURGET AIRPORT

'Great, this might take a while . . .' Gammaldi said, as the car they'd borrowed from Zoe's friends slowed to a halt behind a long line of others trying to get into the air show.

'Hang on,' Zoe said, in a tone that was going to take no arguments. She drove on the grass verge next to the traffic.

'Okay!' Gammaldi responded from the passenger seat, Zoe driving as fast as she dared off the bitumen. Several cars honked horns at them, either in support or protest.

At the chain-link fence a pissed-off security guard held up his hand.

Zoe waved her ID out the window like it was an emergency.

'All right!' Gammaldi said as they were waved in.

Kate had been quiet next to Fox for the entire journey. She hadn't said anything about China and he didn't press the issue, he just assumed she'd come. When they parked, she got out of the car without a word. He walked beside her as they headed towards the aircraft manufacturers' marquees, but still she didn't talk or look at him. It might take a bit to mend, but he figured he had the time once this was over. He'd do this tonight, and then reassess his options. This Umbra stuff had started as a story of corruption, developed into a way for him to get to the bottom of what had happened to a dead friend, and then turned into a nightmare from which he couldn't wake. Babich was at the heart of it all. If he could just get the guy back into custody, or maybe even have the Russians take care of him . . . then he could sleep soundly at night. He hoped.

'Al, what'll get us to Shanghai fast?' Fox asked.

'The F-22,' Gammaldi said without hesitation. 'Mean machine.'

'Al . . .' Fox pushed. 'How about something that can seat us all?'

'Concorde?'

'Jesus, Al, what was that aircraft you wanted to see here? The one you wanted GSR to lease?'

Gammaldi's eyes lit up. This was it – this was Gammaldi Day.

•

The trio followed Gammaldi, his aviator's nose leading the way. They passed through a marquee and Fox grabbed a laptop and its bag of cables from an unattended table.

Gammaldi looked back at him, an eyebrow raised.

'What?' Fox said, slinging the bag over his shoulder. 'You're about to steal a multi-million dollar aeroplane and I can't take a computer?'

'I'm *borrowing* the plane,' Gammaldi said. 'And if it's good we'll be leasing one back at work – but is that poor guy ever going to get his computer back?'

Fox looked over his shoulder at the stall from where he'd taken it.

'He was from Halliburton,' Fox said. 'I think they can write off the loss.'

Gammaldi's face broke into a smile. 'Our taxes bought that thing anyway.'

•

'There's our ride,' Gammaldi said.

Fox looked over at the supersonic business jet, a joint project of SAI and the Lockheed Martin Skunk Works designed to travel at speeds around Mach 2, twice the speed of sound.

'Steal a state-of-the-art private jet,' Kate began, 'fly to Shanghai, get there before the protocol does, stop Babich getting it and save the planet. Is that your plan?'

'That sounds about right,' Gammaldi said. 'Although maybe we should formulate a Plan B just in case.'

'Plan B?' Fox questioned. 'This is an ingenious plan. It's a Swiss fuckin' watch. Foolproof.'

'It's insane!' Kate said, still refusing to look at him.

'How will we fly it?' Zoe asked.

Fox borrowed Kate's iPhone and approached the two pilots who were fielding questions from several air show attendees. He introduced himself.

'We're about to head back to the States,' one of them said. He was wearing a US Air Force uniform with a captain's rank. 'Just fully loaded her up with gas. Give you a lift back if you want?' he said and smiled jokingly.

Fox handed over the phone, McCorkell was on the other end. The pilot spoke to him with a wary tone, then seemed to snap to attention, said a lot of *yes sirs* and *no sirs*, and handed the phone back.

Ten minutes later, the four of them followed the Air Force crew and climbed the stairs of the world's fastest private jet.

81

SHANGHAI

Babich landed in Shanghai and was met in a private hangar by Colonel Zang, a mid-level officer in the Ministry of State Security, who ran the Shanghai Bureau. That meant he ran Shanghai. Babich didn't like him but he trusted that the man respected money and power more than any political ideology. The air was hot and humid, thick with pollution. They rode in a convoy of blacked-out Chinese knock-off Humvees. They were loud and uncomfortable and the fake leather stuck to his back as the air conditioning struggled to do its job.

Zang's personal security guys looked otherworldly: ceramic armour covered most of their body, faces clad in ninja wraparound masks made from Kevlar and carbon-fibre material, their eyes watching him behind anti-flash tactical goggles. They carried black, compact QCW-05 personal defence weapons with subsonic rounds, and long screw-in silencers. These guys meant business and they didn't want to be identified doing it. *He wanted some.*

Zang sat next to him, Lavrov in the car behind. The Chinese colonel had updated him on the Summit, how all the world leaders had arrived, including the Russian president. Babich said nothing. He was content to ride in silence.

Putin. Babich had worked hard to forge loyalties and respect in the Soviet party system, but he knew now he'd been too soft. He hadn't realised how ruthless things would become. Soon after Putin was appointed Prime Minister there was a series of bomb attacks on apartment buildings, killing three hundred civilians and putting the rest of Russia into panic. Putin blamed the bombings on Chechen terrorists and waged a scorched-earth war against the tiny state. Many thousands were abducted and killed, many thousands maimed or raped. Putin grew from a little known former intelligence officer into a national hero and shortly after assumed complete control with the presidency. It was a brilliantly orchestrated scheme by the secret police to bring one of their own to absolute power. Babich had not spoken out about it.

Until now.

Everyone in Russia involved in the attacks would be held to account. The very men who wanted power, those who benefited from it, would pay. Those who dared go against the new government's line, journalists, politicians, government workers and activists alike, wound up dead; those left, fell silent. Litvinenko was a case in point. The West knew who was responsible, too. Yet here he was, running from American and Western European justice for lesser crimes; and there the current administration was, ruling and acting like the dictatorship they were.

No. No more. Not while Babich lived. He would outplay those in power at their own game. And he'd show the world how he could do it by the law, and in the process put any dirty laundry of his own onto the outgoing government officials and blame them for everything. He had a *gift* for his people, for the world. He would assume power via silver, not lead. There would be no police roadblocks looking for Chechen terrorists that didn't exist, no state-run vigilante groups cleaning up whoever they wanted, no limp excuses for the state to crack down on political opponents. The recent war with Chechnya had been the final straw for Babich. To wage a false war against a people who were being armed by Russian military and security forces on the take – that was *treason*. One thing Babich wasn't, and never would be, was a traitor to his country. He'd built his emprire on the one thing he truly valued and respected: *his people*. He owned them and they did well by that. They stood by him, and worked with him to make Umbra Corp the business it was today . . . And now, with this document, he would lead them. It would be so brilliant and so total . . . He would be their leader, their saviour. And all he'd need to do was reveal the truth.

•

Word quickly got around Shanghai that Babich was in town. He wasn't worried. One of Moscow's delegates for the Summit came to his Park Hyatt suite. That spoke volumes – the President did not come, nor even his finance minister: they sent a bureaucrat. He sat on the armchair opposite Babich, drinking a glass of Cristal champagne, acting like he had every ace in the deck.

Babich put a list of names on the table. It was a typed list; neat, professional.

The delegate picked it up. 'What's this?' He studied the list for a moment. 'It lists many of the members of both houses of parliament.'

'They have until 7 am tomorrow, Moscow time, to announce they are leaving office,' Babich said. 'Or they will be removed by force.'

The guy looked incredulous.

'Who will remove them, you?'

'No,' Babich said. 'They will be removed by those who have the most to gain from their removal. They will be removed by those who have not had a voice for too long now. They will be removed by those who it is claimed voted for them. They will be removed by *the Russian people* and *that*, my friend, is the only reason that you are leaving this room alive tonight. Go and tell your bosses what I have said, and be quick – you have a lot of people to contact.'

PART THREE

82

HIGH OVER CHINA

The two-engine gull-wing aircraft tore through the sky towards Shanghai at an altitude of sixty thousand feet and a cruising speed of around Mach 2. The sonic boom had sounded like a muffled backfire, and Gammaldi explained it was much quieter than earlier supersonic aircraft, about a hundredth that of the Concorde. Inside, it was a decadent ride. Gammaldi had fallen asleep half an hour in, the excitement too much to bear, and Zoe had lasted an hour and two drinks.

Kate sat opposite Fox. There were ten seats in the aircraft, as plush and comfortable as any business-class recliner could be. For the first hour Kate had been stonily silent, watching France and then Europe disappear below. After a couple of drinks, somewhere between the Middle East and Central Asia, she'd started to speak, recounting the events that had led her into the FBI's witness protection scheme, what it had been like to know nobody, be nobody. She shed quite a few tears, and allowed Fox to hold her hands.

'This will all end tonight,' he said.

Kate gave him a look – like there was more weight to what she had been saying than he could comprehend.

'The running, the threat of Umbra, Babich . . . everything, it all ends tonight,' he said. 'Before all this . . . Well, before you came *back* into the picture, I'd wake up some mornings and it would take me a minute to remember who I was, you know? Where I was going, what I was meant to be doing . . .'

'So what, you're scared you'll lose your way if this ends?'

Fox didn't know. There was something that he couldn't quite explain, couldn't quite grasp.

'It's like I don't know who I am anymore. I just work . . . Every day, I just get up and work and I never stop, nothing changes.'

Kate looked out the window at the dark sky. She turned back to him, met his eyes, then squeezed his hand.

'I shouldn't have come,' she said. 'I should never have gone to France, and I shouldn't be here now –'

'It's too late to worry about that,' Fox replied. 'I couldn't have left you there alone.'

'You could have stayed with me.'

'I've gotta do this, Kate.'

'Why?' she asked. 'This isn't your fight.'

'They need me,' Fox said. 'I've gotta do this – I've gotta do it for us, to end this . . . All the shit that happened this morning? The running and the hiding – don't you want that to end?'

She looked down at her bare feet on the plush leather armchair she was curled up on.

'I guess I got used to it,' she said. 'I learned to block it out.'

'Well it's all I think about.'

'I suppose I don't think about it like you,' she said. She looked him in the eye. 'It felt like I always had options.'

83

SHANGHAI

'And how many of your countrymen died because of communism?' a staffer from the US delegation asked, his glass of bourbon spilling over its edge. 'In your country, in just the last century, all those purges and repression, how many – a hundred million?'

'You think I'm ignorant of that?' the Russian staffer opposite replied. 'You think I *like* that part of my history?'

Jacob knew the dinner and subsequent drinks at the hotel bar had gone on too long. Inebriated politics going on at every level. He looked across at Felecia, who rolled her eyes as a guy from the Japanese delegation whispered in close to her ear. She signalled to her watch and Jacob nodded, excused himself to his colleagues and left the table.

He waited at the bar, made small talk with a colleague from the European Commission, a married guy who had a young local girl at his side. The guy was drunk, celebrating the end of his working week, but was wondering out loud what work had really been done.

Tell me about it . . .

Jacob's main role was to draft initiatives that defined new environmental legislation and to ensure that such measures, when agreed to by the EC, were actually put into practice in the member states. It was about protecting, preserving and improving the environment for present and future generations, and promoting sustainable development. This guy, one of a dozen EC staff at the Summit, had a background in banking and was spearheading what had turned out to be – through a last-minute hijacking of priorities – this Summit's key agenda: reform and improvement of the financial sector and international financial institutions. This was still an economic Summit first and foremost, no matter how the environment affected such things. The quick buck ruled.

'I'll catch you back in Brussels,' Jacob said, leaving the guy and his Made-in-China doll at the bar. The scene was repeated throughout the room – staffers letting their hair down, plenty of local girls on hand to provide service with a smile who would no doubt work the men for information that the Chinese government could find useful. Seemed no one here found his area of work useful; not that he wanted that kind of female attention right now. Convincing the delegates, that was what was frustrating. His task of pushing to maintain and improve the quality of life through a high level of protection of natural resources, effective risk assessment and management and the timely implementation of community legislation . . . The repsonse was always the same: 'How much does it cost?' Fostering resource-efficiency in production, leading world's best practice consumption minimisation and waste-disposal measures, integrating environmental concerns into national policy areas, promoting growth that takes account of the economic, social and environmental needs of both citizens and future generations . . . Addressing the global challenges facing the world, notably combating climate change and the international conservation of biodiversity was deemed 'too costly'.

At the lift lobby, Felecia tapped him on the shoulder.

She asked, 'Were you talking to yourself just now?'

He laughed. 'Around here, I'm my best audience. Hell, I'm about my *only* audience.'

'Where are you going?' she asked. 'There's a party on the observation deck.'

'Sorry, it's been a long day,' Jacob replied, 'a long week.'

'Come on, one more drink, a quiet one,' she said. 'I've got duty-free Glenlivet – shame to waste it . . .'

One drink.

'Okay . . .' he said, and laughed as the lift pinged. They walked to her room in silence, that anxious walk where they knew what was likely to happen and the thought of how they'd first come together was the most exciting aspect of it. Jacob tried to clear his mind, reminded himself he should be staying sober.

•

'Ice?'

'Thanks.' He walked over to the window. It looked down across the pretty lights of the river that ran through the historic area of the Bund, the old International Zone under the unequal treaties – this would have been such an impressive city then, a microcosm of what could become of the future China. This city had degraded in importance since the Second World War and through the second half of the twentieth century under communism, re-emerging as this schizophrenic mega-city in recent times, heavy on the bling. There was always more identity in the past, while the future seemed . . . such hard work. 'Your view is better than mine.'

'I need *some* perks with this job,' Felecia replied, passing him his drink.

They clinked glasses, he looked from her wanting eyes to the glow of the the Huangpu River.

Jacob said, 'Good Scotch.'

'Only ever as good as the company.'

'Ha.'

'Can you help me stay awake?' she asked. She held up her BlackBerry. 'They've just called a press conference on the observation deck for 1 am.'

'Why so late?'

'Some special briefing designed to meet press deadlines in the west,' she said. 'Another perk of this job.'

'I'll bring you an espresso at midnight.' He sipped his drink and watched the view.

'Who is she?' Felecia asked.

After a moment he looked at her. Her eyes were understanding, yet it was easy to surrender to her gaze.

'She's someone special, who I haven't seen for a while now, but I hope to,' he replied. 'An American woman – unlike anyone I've met before.'

'Americans . . .'

'I know, who would have thought it? I met her in Amsterdam,' Jacob replied, sipping his Scotch. 'Then she – about six months ago, she moved back to the States and I haven't seen her since.'

'And you are still holding out hope of being with her?' Felecia's head was tilted to the side. He smiled, put a hand to the side of her face.

'I am,' he said. Felecia smiled back. They watched the view together and sipped their drinks. 'We talk all the time.'

'All talk and no play?'

Jacob smiled. 'Yes. She's just been going through a . . . a personal crisis, self-searching or something.'

'Well,' she said, her hand finding his. 'If you ever get sick of waiting . . .'

He squeezed her hand and let it go.

'What's her name? No, wait, I don't want to know.' Felecia put a finger to his lips to stop him from speaking, kissed him, briefly. Her eyes were like sparkling city lights looking up at him. 'I'm happy just to remember your kiss.'

He put the empty glass on the table and made for the door.

'Goodnight, Jacob.'

84

HIGH OVER CHINA

Fox lifted Kate up onto the basin. She wrapped her bare legs around his waist. As he kissed her, she pulled up his shirt and he stood back a little to pull her underwear off. She held his head down, her hands tight with fistfuls of hair, caressing and forcing until she pulled him up. He stood. She undid his pants, they fell to the floor. She pulled him in hard, their tongues exploring as they moved.

She held onto his arms, her fingers tight. Her open mouth on his ear, nibbling and sucking.

She was different, he thought, as they changed positions and he saw her face in the mirror. She was hungrier, faster, present. Maybe it was the day they'd had. He didn't want it to end.

85

WASHINGTON, DC

'Is it valid?' McCorkell asked.

Her name was Reagan, she was a lawyer, a specialist in international treaties, sequestered from the State Department. She took her time scrutinising the photograph of the protocol on the big screen before she confirmed the worst with a nod.

'Where'd this come from?'

'Buried in a wall,' McCorkell said. She looked at him like he'd just said he'd found life on Mars. 'Seriously, a goddamned wall. Not twelve hours ago this was pulled from inside a wall cavity in a room at the Elysée Palace.'

'As in France?'

'Yep.'

'I'd need to study it first-hand with specialist archivists from the Smithsonian and Library of Congress, but from what I can see here – the signatures, the wording – it looks legit.'

Bowden looked a little shell-shocked by the news.

'Yeah, that's what we thought,' McCorkell said. 'So where would our copy be?'

Bowden interjected: 'Copy?'

'Wouldn't we have a copy of this?' McCorkell asked. 'From Secretary of State Seward?'

Reagan replied, 'Have you tried looking in walls?'

'Maybe we never had one, maybe it's buried somewhere in Seward's papers,' Valerie said, studying the image. 'Or maybe he did put it in a wall, who knows.'

'Area 51?' Reagan said.

'Right,' McCorkell smiled.

Bowden was steaming, trying to catch up fast. 'If we have a copy of this I want it found.'

'We've got researchers going through national archives and Seward's papers right now,' Valerie said.

McCorkell asked, 'How could we never have heard of this?'

'We have and we haven't,' Reagan replied. 'There was a transatlantic cable dispute involving Seward in March 1867 when the Russian Minister to the US sent an encrypted 1,833-word cable to St Petersburg. The cable was transmitted through the newly organised State Department telegraph office at a cost of about ten grand – a lot of cheddar for back then. The cable contained the basic treaty conditions for the purchase of Russian America for seven million dollars and was sent, according to the Russian Minister, at the request of Seward, who he asserted would pay for it. The charges for the cable were then transferred to the American account – for the State Department to pick up the tab, which by then had tripled. Anyway, I'm rambling. Where was I?'

Bill looked to Valerie.

'A Russian cable . . .'

'Yeah. It was intercepted – the telegraph company . . . A few years later, we broke the Russian code and it was translated. It mentioned a protocol had been drawn up should the need arise to impose pressure on the Americans to pay up.'

'So . . .'

'So, yeah, this protocol is looking more and more legit. Seward and Stoeckl were close friends, they obviously knew how to keep a secret,' Reagan said. 'From what you've told me and what I know about the treaty itself, I'd say that this protocol was made to appease the Tsar should Stoeckl have to appear before him and explain why the Americans were not paying for Alaska.'

'Because the Senate wouldn't agree to the purchase?' Valerie asked.

'House of Reps held up payment,' Reagan said. 'The date on your image of the protocol puts it about six months into that stalemate.'

'It eventually took them a year or so to pony up with the cash,' McCorkell said. 'Russians were getting cold feet . . . Might have pulled out and sold it to the French or English.'

'Or worse, kept it,' Reagan said. 'Would have made the Cold War a little different.'

Bowden asked, 'And you're telling us – you think this would be legal today?'

'I'd say so. You rescind on this . . .'

'Yeah, all of a sudden every treaty we've signed falls to shit,' McCorkell said, looking at Bowden closely. 'Makes this worth killing for, wouldn't you say?'

'Hell,' Reagan said. 'We turn our back on this, maybe the French would come back and say, "Hang on, you know how we sold you about half your country in the Louisiana Purchase, that agreement ain't worth shit anymore."'

'I know a few people in DoD who'd love to see the French try and take it back,' McCorkell said.

Bowden asked, 'Why didn't the Congress know about this protocol at the time?'

'Didn't have to go before them, because it didn't involve any additional payment,' Reagan explained. 'It was a state *agreement*, no money changed hands.'

'An agreement between a couple of friends . . .' Bowden said, the cogs turning with this new complication.

'Jesus . . .' Valerie said. 'Makes you wonder what else we don't know about.'

'What about Seward?' Bowden asked. 'Could we argue Seward was not of sound mind?'

'Right,' Valerie said, thinking it through. 'Lewis Powell, the associate of John Wilkes Booth, attempted to assassinate Seward, the same night Abraham Lincoln was shot.'

'He was badly injured,' McCorkell added, remembering.

'That won't fly,' Reagan said, resolute. 'He was sound, smart, a good operator, hell of a guy.'

'Just a thought,' Bowden said. 'So where's it leave us?'

'Under international law,' Reagan said, 'no country currently owns the North Pole or the region of the Arctic Ocean surrounding it.'

'That might change, too.'

'The five surrounding Arctic states – us, Russia, Canada, Norway and Denmark – are limited to a two-hundred-nautical-mile economic zone around our coasts, and we each administer corresponding regions to the pole. Think of it as a giant pie chart.'

'And what – this means that our two-hundred-mile sea limit will disappear?'

'That and more,' she said. 'Upon ratification of the United Nations Convention on the Law of the Sea, each country had a ten-year period to make claims to extend its two-hundred-nautical-mile zone. Russia ratified in 1997 –'

'Matches with their *Arktika* date in 2007,' Valerie said.

'Coincidence, huh? They went and planted their flag down there on the seabed, on their claimed limit of the continental shelf.'

Bowden asked, 'When did we ratify?'

'We haven't,' Reagan replied. 'The United States has signed, but not yet ratified the treaty.'

'Where's it at now?'

'Does it matter? That won't stop this thing.' She looked exasperated. 'Look, as it stands the status of the Arctic Sea region is in dispute. While Canada, Denmark, Russia and Norway all regard parts of the Arctic seas as "national waters" or "internal waters", the United States and most European Union countries officially regard the whole region as "international waters".'

'So Russia has been claiming a larger slice extending as far as the North Pole,' Bowden said, 'laying stake to future oil and gas finds on the seabed because Moscow believes the Arctic seabed and Siberia are linked by one continental shelf –'

'And now they will own our sector, too,' McCorkell finished for him. Bowden nodded.

'The Ilulissat Declaration was announced in May 2008 by the five Arctic circumpolar nations during the Arctic Ocean Conference in Greenland,' Reagan said. 'One of the chief goals written into the declaration was blockage of any "new comprehensive international legal regime to govern the Arctic Ocean". An additional pledge for the "orderly settlement of any possible overlapping claims" was expected.'

'So . . .' Bowden prompted.

'If this protocol is presented, Alaska will be surrounded by Russian-controlled water,' Reagan said. 'They'll be in the driving seat – we'll no longer have a voice at the table in talks about the Arctic region. And you can forget a nuclear warning window for them, and any kind of missile shield – I mean, they'll now be in *rifle* range. Got any friends in Alaska? Tell them it's time to sell up.'

'Yeah, we got that,' McCorkell said. 'Not to mention we lose hundreds of billions of dollars in future oil and gas revenues.'

'Minerals too,' Valerie said. 'And the unfathomable cost to the Arctic wildlife and global climate change should they decide to make the Arctic seabed an industrial zone.'

'And transit routes, if they want to play tough,' Reagan said, the full consequences setting in. 'Our best hope is to get this protocol – before the Russians take it to the UN or the Hague or some place.'

'Yeah, we're working on that, Reagan. Thanks for your time,' McCorkell said. 'We'll be in touch.'

86

HIGH OVER CHINA

'We touch down in Shanghai in thirty minutes,' the pilot announced over the cabin speakers. *'Easing out of super-cruise, hope you enjoyed your travel at Mach 2.'*

Next to Fox, Kate's skin was glowing.

Gammaldi stretched out in his chair, yawned himself awake. Zoe had been up for the last few minutes, drinking a juice and working on her BlackBerry.

'My boss, the Interior Minister, has given me an ultimatum,' she said, looking up from her email. 'Deliver the goods or . . . you and I, Lachlan, are . . . What is the English way to explain it . . .'

'Fucked,' Fox said. 'When in doubt, stick with the French.'

Zoe almost laughed.

'We'll get your guy,' Fox said.

'Yeah.' Gammaldi stood up, stretched and shook his arms and legs. 'Meantime, us kids will be someplace else, no doubt. Don't know about you, Kate, but an all-you-can-eat Chinese buffet would hit the spot.'

Fox pulled out the laptop and hooked it up; in a couple of minutes they had Skyped McCorkell.

'So the protocol points out what would happen if the payments were dragged out even further,' Fox said after hearing the latest. 'Reparations and fines. So what, the US paid up, right?'

'We've had someone from the State Department just run us through it,' McCorkell replied. 'There's one point that's still relevant today.'

'What?' Fox asked.

'The sea boundary thing, reverting back to the antiquated three-mile limits.'

'It states just how –' Fox cut himself off. 'Jesus . . . the *wording*.'

'I know,' McCorkell replied. 'It states that if presented, this protocol is binding for *perpetuity* – there's no time clause on it, no time constraint.'

'And this was made up between two men as a "just in case" wild card . . .' Fox said.

'If they present this, it would be accepted as international law and Russia would own all the water in the Arctic that we currently claim as sovereign to the US.'

Gammaldi added, 'No more Exclusive Economic Zone . . .'

'It all links in to what they've been doing lately,' Fox said. 'Their *Arktika* expeditions, claiming the under-seabed as their own while the world laughed at them, but in a way we were all wondering *what if?*'

'What's this *Arktika* expedition?' Gammaldi asked.

'In 1997 a UN treaty was signed, updating water rights,' McCorkell explained. 'It gave everyone ten years to make any claims. In June 2007, a group of Russian geologists returned from a six-week voyage on a nuclear icebreaker. They had travelled to the Lomonosov Ridge, an underwater shelf in Russia's remote and inhospitable eastern Arctic Ocean, and they claimed a vast expanse of area. We've been contesting it since, but this protocol will negate that argument and then some . . . We'd be handing it to them on a silver platter.'

'So if they get this out, if they can claim all that territory and resource wealth?' Fox asked, looking at the faces around him.

'America will be complicit in whatever the Russians decide to do with it,' Kate said.

'Unless . . .' Fox began.

'Unless what?'

'I don't know – nothing . . .'

'As Al said, no more US exclusive economic zone of two hundred miles from shore,' McCorkell said. 'And sure as hell no continental shelf boundary issues – it's practically theirs now, this says we agreed to it over a century ago.'

'So you're saying current US Arctic waters, under this treaty, would revert back to the old three miles from shore distance?' Gammaldi asked.

'The Russians have claim to all that the US currently stakes as ours,' McCorkell said. 'They'd own the vast majority of the territory, with Canada, Denmark and Norway each with a little slice of pie . . .'

Fox thought about it: Umbra Corp, Babich's 'legitimate' group of businesses had been a major backer of that *Arktika* expedition. But how would this help Babich get to power in his country? That had long been his end-game . . . The current Russian government had decided to go to war against the man – but, maybe, if the population were behind Babich . . . Would *that* be enough? No, it wasn't right – there was something else; had to be.

Gammaldi still couldn't quite get his head around the importance of it.

'They could open up the Arctic for resource extraction,' Fox said. 'Use it all, do what they want – the US could no longer block them in the UN because they would no longer have a stake in that area.'

'But who, Babich's companies? He's going to trial for all kinds of –'

'He's going to *use* this,' Fox said, the threads coming together. 'It's his get-out-of-jail-free card. What if he hands this to the Russian government in exchange for amnesty?'

'Maybe . . .' McCorkell replied. 'Thing is, what would *they* do with it?'

'That's what I was trying to think of before,' Fox said. 'I mean – they could decide *not* to enact this, swap it, put an end to the US missile shield or something. It's the mother of all bargaining chips.'

'Whatever they did, you could bet your ass it would cost us,' McCorkell said.

'If he presents this and it works,' Gammaldi said, almost to himself, 'he'll be popular to Russians, Europe and China, too; whoever wants to buy his resources – hell of a lot of fossil fuel under there.'

'And he's already hugely popular in Russia because of all the work his companies have created, and he's seen as a different breed of oligarch,' Fox said. 'This has all been carefully orchestrated – he's been building himself up for years as a statesman, keeping out of party politics.'

'But how will he leverage power from the current guys in office?' McCorkell asked. 'They're a tight ship, no one else gets a look-in during elections in Russia.'

'You think he'll use this to seize power?' Fox asked, shaking his head. 'That's what doesn't add up. There's gotta be something else.'

'Fasten your belts, beginning our descent,' the pilot said over the PA.

'We gotta sign off,' Fox said.

'Hutchinson will meet you at the hotel,' McCorkell said. 'Good luck.'

They ended the connection.

'I think you're missing something,' Zoe said as they each buckled in. 'Perhaps he would stage a coup, like they did when Yeltsin –'

'He may not need to,' Fox said. 'He may already have the numbers he needs in the houses of government, not to mention the military and intel communities, to transition the government out. If he can somehow drive a wedge in there, get enough to denounce the current regime . . .'

'He's got his own media,' Gammaldi said. 'He's got the money – and now he's got this secret protocol.'

'If this is legal,' Zoe said. 'Maybe it's –'

'It's legal,' Kate said. 'I worked for a legal department in the government –'

'I know your background,' Zoe interjected.

Kate let fly, 'If you renege on a standing international treaty,' she said loudly, 'especially such a massive one like this, your standing in the world, especially as a world leader, is questioned, diminished, and then lost. The US can do nothing if he presents this document to the world. Worst case, Russia could use their military to enforce the treaty terms.'

'Maybe this is the end of the US as a world leader,' Zoe said.

'Or the start of Roman Babich's Russia as one,' Fox concluded.

87

EAST CHINA SEA

'Relax,' Jinks told Hutchinson as they approached the USS *George Washington*. *Yeah right*, Hutchinson thought, looking out below. Not much but a few tiny lights on a dark sea. The *George Washington* was a Nimitz Class aircraft carrier, something that conjured impressive size in his mind. From here it looked like a fucking postage stamp that grew to a Post-it note and was still only the size of a napkin as they made their final approach. *Relax, the flight deck's 4.5 acres of prime runway real estate,* the commander had said, like it was a reassuring fact. Hutchinson closed his eyes for the final ten seconds.

The force of the landing, and then the sudden jerk of the tail hook catching the arrestor cable, pulled a pitiful sound out of him.

'Good job,' Jinks said, maybe to himself.

They came to a stop and the aircraft powered down. Hutchinson reached over his shoulder and the pilot shook his hand.

'Thanks, Commander.'

'Pleasure Andy; that was a sweet flight, if I do say so myself.'

Really? Hutchinson felt like he'd left his eyeballs back over Turkey when they'd refuelled in mid-air and then waved goodbye to the tanker and punched through the sound barrier. He'd be happy if he never rode in another aeroplane as long as he lived.

'Watch your legs, they're gonna feel like jelly,' Jinks said.

He wasn't kidding. It took everything Hutchinson had to hobble down to the USS *George Washington*'s flight deck and stand shakily upright, even with guys helping him.

The two white-shirted crew members took Hutchinson under the arms and virtually carried him over to the island, the aircraft carrier's apartment-block-sized command area. Carriers were old school, Hutchinson thought, but, damn, if they weren't awesome, and they were indispensable to the nation: whenever there was shit brewing abroad, those in Washington would say, '*Where's the nearest carrier?*' The USS *George Washington*'s island number was outlined in red, white and blue lights in honour of her namesake's contributions to America's independence. The white-shirts, both hospital corps men, asked him about his leg wound and offered a wheelchair; he opted for crutches and wanted to get off the flight deck, fast.

A guy in a suit came out of the island structure and introduced himself as an agent from the Shanghai consulate's Legal Attaché office.

'Special Agent Hutchinson, I'm taking you by helo to the *New York*,' he said, one of a growing number of Chinese–Americans on the Bureau's payroll. 'Follow me.'

'What's the *New York*?' Hutchinson asked, making his way across the flight deck towards a Seahawk, its rotor already whirring.

'That there, Sir,' he pointed out to the sea. A big grey Navy ship sat a couple of miles out, angular and square compared to the others around, mostly Arleigh Burke class destroyers.

'We'll touch down on her momentarily,' the Legat said. 'Got our HQ set up real good.'

Hutchinson was helped into the helo. It was spacious and slow compared to his last ride but, all the same, he'd give anything to be on dry land.

88

SHANGHAI

'Landing momentarily,' Gammaldi leaned in closer to Fox across the aisle. 'Seriously, do you think we could stop for some Chinese on the way into town?'

Fox just shook his head and watched the vast blanket of lights that hugged China's coast from his window. He felt a sense of dread, but he pushed it away. This would be over soon. He looked at Kate and thought of the endless possibilities ahead. *What would Hutchinson have in mind for Babich now?* Fox knew what he wanted to do.

The touchdown was quick, Kate squeezed Fox's hand hard as the engines reversed thrust. Five minutes later they were walking down the stairs and standing on the tarmac by the private terminals. It was hot and humid, Fox's back was instantly wet with sweat.

'Shanghai is seven hours ahead of Paris,' Gammaldi said, adjusting his watch. 'It's now 11.35 pm local time – we left Paris at 1.25; makes it a four-hour, ten-minute flight.'

'Why can't you be this smart with useful stuff?' Fox joked.

'I want one of those planes,' Gammaldi said as they walked towards a waiting Chevy Suburban. Two Americans were there, an FBI agent and someone from State, along with a Chinese customs agent to issue them visas. Zoe's took a while longer, but the customs guy seemed eager to get back into the air-conditioning.

'We're taking you to the Park Hyatt, Mr Fox,' the FBI agent said, a short, tough-looking woman in her mid-thirties named Sally McKee. 'In the Shanghai World Financial Center, it's where the G20's taking place.'

'Thanks,' he replied, climbing into the back of the SUV with the others. 'Damn, why can't customs always be that quick?'

Fat drops of rain fell as they left the airport.

'We've had downpours like this the last couple of weeks,' the agent said from the passenger seat. 'The odd early-morning thunderstorm, too. Humid as hell but at least it clears the air pollution.'

Fox nodded, noting how uneasy Kate looked. He put a hand on her knee, smiled at her.

'You okay?'

She nodded. Tense.

Fox asked, 'Is Special Agent Hutchinson meeting us there?'

'I called him as you disembarked,' the agent replied. 'He'll meet y'all at the hotel.'

'How many security personnel have you got here?' Zoe asked.

Agent McKee looked back over her shoulder – giving her the same suspicious look Kate had dished out back at the farmhouse.

'It's cool,' Fox said. 'She's good people.'

'We've got about a dozen FBI agents operating out of the consulate,' the agent replied. 'Closer to your hotel, we've got the security on the delegates – the President and Sec State are in town.'

'So you have plenty,' Fox said, a little relieved.

'Their entourage is about three hundred Secret Service personnel deep, deployed in the hotel next door and a few nearby locations,' she said. 'Add to that another few representatives of the White House Military Office and there's a carrier group close in on the East China Sea.'

'Cool,' Gammaldi said. They watched the lights of the big sprawling city flash by, driving in silence for a couple of minutes. Fox could see his friend was going to say something stupid. 'So, Zoe, you got a boyfriend?'

She cracked a smile.

'I am sorry, Alister,' she said. 'Not with all the condoms in the world would I fuck you.'

'Jesus! I was just asking . . .'

'I am joking, you are a good guy.' Her smile made him blush. 'The answer is no. The men in Paris are the same as anywhere: married, gay, or both.'

'Or they've gone all metrosexual,' Kate said.

'What is *metrosexual*?' Zoe asked.

Fox looked over at Gammaldi, bemused by the first friendly exchange between the two women.

'More waxed and preened than we are,' Kate explained.

'Tell me about it! Dieting even.'

'Didn't know you guys had a monopoly on dieting,' Fox said.

'I think there's plenty you don't know about women,' Gammaldi murmured.

'And what, you know everything there is to know about dieting?'

'Don't try and dodge the issue, buddy,' Gammaldi said, big shit-eating grin on his face. 'Your scant knowledge of women.'

'And what, these two know everything there is to know about men?'

'It is a simpler topic,' Zoe said.

Kate laughed; finally the two women had made some kind of connection.

They joked the rest of the way into town, Kate's good mood only fading after checking her iPhone.

89

WASHINGTON, DC

In Washington they were a half a world away from the action, but it felt like they were in the fire. More military aides had arrived, widening the scope of the intel being mined out of China. McCorkell, with Valerie sitting next to him, had Hutchinson on video con.

'Our friend here still has guys looking for Fox in Paris,' McCorkell said quietly, looking over at Bowden who was now hauling all hands on deck to move to Shanghai, pulling in favours and working up contingencies, which were reactive at best.

'Let him,' Hutchinson replied over the video con. 'Makes me sick to think of how things have been run back there, but I tell you what, I'm glad I'm here right now, so close to the epicentre of where this is all converging – even with this leg and all.'

'You spoken to your director about changing things in here, running the plays from your end for the final stage?'

'Spoke to him and begged like you wouldn't believe. His hands are tied,' Hutchinson replied. 'National Security Council are a hundred per cent for this being a covert intel and military action, so Bowden is their point man.'

'Yeah, heard as much from my end.'

'The fact that the President is over here has only strengthened the NSC's viewpoint – you should see the way the Marines are running around on this boat.'

'I think they call it a ship.'

'Whatever, I'm just glad it doesn't fly,' Hutchinson said. 'We're about to deploy. We're gonna leave this ship and head for Shanghai posthaste, call you from the hotel.'

'We'll be here.'

'Bill, if this doesn't work, I mean, if we can't stop him . . .' Hutchinson said. 'This move of Babich's, all the chatter in Moscow pointing to a power play – it's bold and it's scary as fuck, I'm man enough to admit that. A resurgent Russia? Handing our backyard over to them?'

'Jesus, if this pans out like that, I don't think we'll have to worry about it,' McCorkell said. 'We'll all be working in the mail room on Capitol Hill as reward for our job not-so-well-done.'

'I just wish I knew where the Chinese stood on this,' Hutchinson said.

'The fact that they're letting the guy hang there is symbolic enough,' McCorkell said. 'Their only answer to the State Department is some version of *they're looking into it.*'

'It'll take too long to get anywhere with them, let alone shake some form of Beijing truth from the tree,' Valerie said.

'Yeah, well, tell you what,' McCorkell said, 'Babich has Chinese intel onside.'

'And that's a dangerous thing,' she said; it hung in the air a moment.

'Well, at least they won't know why we're there, we'll just be another part of the US security umbrella around POTUS and Sec State,' Hutchinson replied. 'There are limits on the number of security personnel in the Summit Zone but I've got a few Secret Service boys pulling out for fifteen while we meet up with Fox.'

'Just be careful,' McCorkell said.

'I can lie my way out of anywhere,' Hutchinson said. 'Bet Fox can too.'

'We used to have a joke around the White House,' McCorkell said. 'We're just going to keep on telling the truth until it stops working – and nowhere is truth-telling more important than in intelligence. Intel agencies thrive on secrecy – they don't do so well in democracies.'

'Soviets did all right at that, didn't they?'

'They lost the Cold War because their bureaucracy was bigger than ours, simple as that,' McCorkell replied. 'Nothing 'specially wrong with how their KGB worked, all came down to their bloated bureaucracy and all that entailed – bureaucrats are people that get in the way of things getting done.'

'Sounds like our boss here,' Valerie said.

Hutchinson laughed. 'Don't worry, China's got about a billion of them.'

'Probably,' McCorkell said. 'But till they're a democracy their intel machine is one mean mother; a dangerous, wild animal.'

'Yeah, well . . .' Hutchinson looked off-screen, nodded to someone before looking back at his camera. 'Russia may have lost the Cold War, but they're all in power now, those guys.'

'Damn right. Godspeed, buddy.'

'And don't go too hard with that leg,' Valerie said, 'or you'll be sent to Walter Reed and come out part Terminator.'

'Ha! And Bill?'

'Yeah?'

He paused on the phone line.

'Tell me I'm not crazy,' Hutchinson said. 'You think Fox can do something about this – in place of the CIA or our guys, you think that too, yeah?'

McCorkell looked at Valerie – she appeared as apprehensive as anyone in the room.

'He's as skilled up as any agency paramilitary field officer,' McCorkell said. 'And if you've seen the day he's had so far, you'd realise he's in pretty rare form.'

Valerie nodded, convinced.

'He's the only option that we really have time to deploy – short of you and a couple of guys hanging around hoping to see Babich in the building, taking a shot at him and getting this secret protocol back,' Valerie said. 'Sorry boss, I respect you – hell, I think you would have had some moves once, but right now I'd put the house on Fox.'

'Yeah, me too,' Hutchinson said with a laugh. 'And, believe me, the thought of waiting around for Babich and putting a nine-mil through his frontal lobe is tempting, but I don't care much for Chinese jail.'

'I know it ain't the food – you love that shit,' Valerie said.

'Hey, that'll do,' Hutchinson replied, mock serious, then, 'Bowden still doesn't have faith in Fox?'

'He wanted him in a bag before, hasn't countermanded that yet. Will he come around? Maybe,' McCorkell said. 'Ironic, really. Bowden has the same intelligence-officer curse as Fox: he doesn't trust anybody until it's almost too late.'

90

SHANGHAI

'He will be here soon,' Lavrov said, checking his watch against the time Boris Malevich's Air France flight was due in.

Babich nodded. He didn't like waiting now that things were so near. The thought of soon having the document in his hands . . . Something he'd wanted so long to see . . . He picked at what was left of his burger and fries, tossed the napkin on the plate, and got up from the dining table. Lavrov's three guys were seated by the door, quiet, waiting. He looked into the adjoining room.

In the lounge, Zang had made himself at home. Fair enough, he'd arranged this suite, he was the host. His entourage was made up of a few security guards, two local mistresses, and three political guys. The Chinese politicians were chatting. Zang had the girls on his lap. His guards were playing a dice game and eating sweets. They were not quite the A-Team by US or Russian standards but they were the closest thing to it in these parts and they were all wired by one fact – their guy was about to become king. When Babich came to power in Russia, Zang would be the conduit to the security services in China. Whether he then stayed in the military or went into politics, Babich could care less – he had a powerful ally here who'd served a purpose.

Babich left them to it and went to his bedroom. Checked his watch. The press conference they'd booked was just over an hour away.

Lavrov had set up a digital HD camera and put a seat by the wall. Babich sat down, straightened his tie, while Lavrov closed the door, set the lighting and hit record.

91

SHANGHAI

A few blocks away from the hotel there was a huge crowd of protesters and thousands of police in riot gear.

'This seems out of place in China,' Fox said as they passed through the first security roadblock.

'Shanghai is a little different to other parts,' their State Department driver said. 'Place has long been such a melting pot of international trade, it's got something of a unique style to it – it's like another China.'

'They are peaceful,' Zoe noted, looking back at the masses standing there with placards and glowing paper lanterns.

'Both sides,' the driver said. 'Anywhere else in China, save for maybe Hong Kong, the police and military would have either locked everyone up, run them over with tanks, or scared them home before a decent crowd had even formed.'

Fox felt like the day was picking up tempo yet again: he was closing in on Renard's killer, on Babich . . . *It was all spiralling together* . . .

One of the world's tallest buildings came into view as they turned the corner: the 101-storey Shanghai World Financial

Center. Sparkling new, lit from within, it was a jewel in an impressive cityscape of skyscrapers.

They passed through the final vehicle checkpoint. It was a floodlit, cordoned-off area with dogs sniffing for explosives, guys with mirrors looking under cars for hidden hardware, efficient inspection teams checking credentials. They were waved through, the process efficient enough to impress a Formula One pit crew.

From the hotel's driveway, they followed Agent McKee as they were individually screened through a pair of airport-like checkpoints.

Walking through the foyer, Gammaldi whispered to Fox, 'Lots of hardware . . .'

He scanned the mass of hi-tech cameras and sensors cleverly worked into the lobby's decor. US security people were scattered around, recognisable by their dark business suits and communication earpieces.

Once through, they took the lift up to the seventy-ninth floor. Fox rotated his head, easing the travel cricks from his neck.

'Wonder if this is how the space shuttle launch feels?' Gammaldi pondered, noting the hyper-powered speed with which the lift rose. Thirty seconds later they were entering their room, a single suite, fine for their needs. The agent made a call on her mobile, Kate went to the bathroom, Fox fixed some soft drinks for everyone. When he heard Hutchinson enter, he started to make a joke – until he saw the wheelchair.

'Andy – what?'

Fox knew about the mid-air incident with Babich, but Andy hadn't told him he'd been shot. Hearing about Brick and Capel made Fox's neck flush red with anger. *They were damn good men doing their job . . .*

He listened as Hutchison filled him in and then introduced Zoe. Gammaldi needed no introduction.

'So this agent has the document – the secret protocol,' Hutchinson asked.

'Yep,' Fox replied, finishing his Coke. 'Don't worry, we know what he looks like, but I can't see how he's going to get through all that security.'

'Babich has the local Chinese officials onside,' Hutchinson said. 'They like the idea of having a future Russian President who's their new best friend.'

Kate came from the en suite, iPhone in hand. She seemed glad to see Andy.

'Lach,' Hutchinson said, 'you understand we can't be seen to be in any kind of action here.'

'I know.'

'But if you need the cav, if it comes down to it, I can get them moving from just next door – they're in the Jin Mao Tower's Grand Hyatt.' Hutchinson looked serious. 'Sec State is there with a dozen Secret Service and four Delta operators. There's a bunch more service boys and girls nearby, too. If it's an emergency, they can be over here in five minutes – just don't cry wolf or we'll have an international incident in all the news services.'

'Got it. What about you? Where you at?'

'I'm with the big boys.'

Fox gestured for more info.

'USS *New York*, landing ship, out in the East China Sea just beyond the territorial limit, about seven hundred Marines on board . . . I'll helo back in here, pick you up from the roof if need be.'

'Let's hope it doesn't come to that,' Fox said. 'I'd really enjoy an early night.'

'Yeah,' Hutchinson said, 'I hear you.'

'And this room-service breakfast menu looks sensational,' Gammaldi said, eating a packet of pistachios from the mini-bar and studying the menu.

Hutchinson looked back to Fox.

'We know that the handover is happening in this hotel,' he said. 'And that Babich won't risk leaving until he's made his announcement and made his move. You two know the guy's face from Paris – you've gotta intercept him.'

'He is a murderer, I am here to apprehend him,' Zoe said, making sure both Fox and Hutchinson were clear on her intent. 'I take him, the French security delegation will meet me in the lobby where they will assist me in transferring my prisoner out of the country.'

'Yeah, well, good luck with that,' Hutchinson said. 'Just so you know, pretty much all the staff aides and line workers are staying in this hotel. All the senior diplomats and politicians are in the hotel next door as it's a more secure site.'

She nodded like it was going to be a walk in the park.

Fox asked: 'Russians are over there?'

'Yeah, and the French, Brits – most of the G20 are there.'

'What's stopping the Russian delegation or their embassy sending in a heavy team to track and find Babich?'

'Like us they won't risk anything that overt and, like I said, there's limited security personnel allowed, otherwise we'd have fifty agents from the Secret Service in here with you. Chinese military have this building *locked down*. They figure nothing will go down, the foreign security personnel are here more to keep each country's staffers out of trouble when they get drunk. Bet your ass on one thing though –'

'What's that?'

'Wherever Babich is in this hotel, he ain't staying in a room facing the other building – Russian operators would have God knows what ready to rock if they knew what room or floor he was staying on. He's somewhere in here, but the Chinese security are keeping him tight . . . The Russian Embassy across the river is going nuts, NSA intercepts are working triple-time to keep up with all the chatter – seems Moscow is going to send them all to Siberia if they don't make sure Babich is in a casket before sunrise.'

'They know about this secret protocol?'

'If they don't they will soon enough.'

'Unless we stop him.'

'You got it, Lach. Anyway,' said Hutchinson, 'I'll be on the *New York*, got helos and Ospreys ready for emergency evac – if you need it, just holler.'

He gave Fox two sets of comms gear – little radio boxes that clipped onto a belt with concealed earpieces and mics.

Hutchinson showed him a switch: 'Encrypted line. Press it down to do your talking, we're on the set frequency.'

'Got it.'

'I gotta leave,' Hutchinson explained, checking his watch. 'I gotta go so a couple of MI6 guys can come back in and look after . . . whoever. Already late. Good luck.'

'I'll see you on the other side of this.'

'Sounds good,' Hutchinson said, turning his chair and heading for the door. 'The document is priority.'

'I can do that.' Fox walked him to the door.

'Whatever it takes,' Hutchinson said. He handed him a pistol – a Heckler & Koch .45 SOCOM.

Fox held it and the spare mag. A nice, familiar weight.

'On the plane,' Hutchinson said quietly, his eyes serious. 'when Babich and his guys killed everyone else – Capel, Brick, the Navy pilots – I heard them slit Capel's throat. Then the motherfucker personally put one in my leg and two in my chest.'

He pointed at the pistol.

'Lach, you always wanted more justice than the law could provide,' he said. 'Tonight you'll have your chance.'

He wheeled away. Fox felt the weight of the loaded gun in his hand.

92

WASHINGTON, DC

Everyone in the room, including McCorkell, had come to a standstill. The deadline ticked to zero. Every face was turned to the main screen.

Bowden was holding court, 'NSA intercepted this video file – it was being sent over the net from Shanghai to Moscow. From Babich, starring Babich. Twelve minutes long, recipient is a senior Umbra Corp figure – head of their media operations. Message sent with the video orders its dissemination to international media outlets, to air after a live announcement he's gonna make in an hour from now.'

Bowden pressed play.

Babich was seated against a blank background. He was dressed in a conservative suit and tie, he'd had a haircut, and he looked like any other plutocratic statesman.

He introduced himself and spent several minutes talking about how the charges against him were trumped up because he was successful in business. He cited several other proven 'wrongly accused' cases, and he questioned the legality of his arrest. Nothing unusual there. Then –

'I have proof that members of the current Russian government and certain elements of the state security apparatus were behind the 1999 apartment bombings that rocked our nation. I have given these men the chance to come clean on their own accord, or I will present such proof against them in a meeting with the international press. I will name names. Those who framed me because I am successful will be shown to the world as the men they really are. I do not want to live in exile, like so many of my friends have done in London and elsewhere when threatened with similar false charges as have been laid against me. I want to return to my motherland and I want to make a difference for her people. I want to get rid of the criminals. I want to make it a nation to be proud of again.

'The primary purpose of government is to protect the citizens and provide those services which would not be provided by business or those which are considered universally "good", such as healthcare, education, police and the military. We need to work on that. I have the answers – not all of them, but enough to make a difference and enough to start a dialogue with the people.'

He paused.

'Make no mistake: you cannot root out the problem of corruption through imprisonment alone – but you must sling the corrupt into jail anyway. You must be forceful. You must be thorough and vigilant.

'The law is for one and all – for ruling and opposition parties . . . Freedom means responsibility. I hope everyone understands that. Thank you.'

The video ended.

'Jesus . . .' McCorkell said. 'This son of a bitch doesn't want to trade this secret protocol with the Russians for a free pass back home. He wants to use it to trade with *us*.'

'What are you taking about?' Bowden asked.

'He's going to drop this truth bomb into the parliament, bring it down and get power,' McCorkell said. 'He doesn't need this secret protocol for that, he's had that wildcard – this *proof* – all along.'

McCorkell had a blank stare as he ran through the many possibilities.

Valerie got it, repeated: 'He's going to . . .'

'Like we'll have . . .'

'He's going to trade this secret protocol to us . . .'

'Like we'll have a choice!' Bowden said. He was getting it now. 'He can trade it for – well, what *couldn't* he trade it for, really?'

'Missile shield and military concessions, economic compensation . . .' Valerie said. 'How could our leaders turn it down? No matter what he wants, how could they turn it down? They won't. They can't.'

McCorkell looked at the freeze-frame of Babich. He thought back to something Fox had said just before on the phone, how the secret protocol was Babich's get-out-of-jail-free card. He had a nervous weight of dread in his gut – Fox was going to get played.

93

SHANGHAI

Andrew Hutchinson had left them with Agent McKee, and she presented some printed invites and wristbands to the evening's after-dinner cocktail party.

Kate was seated on the sofa nursing a drink and looking out at the fairy lights of the Bund. Fox imagined she was thinking of Paris or Amsterdam. He had a flashback to the ball in St Petersburg, at St Catherine's Palace, where they'd first met.

'The dinner is on the ninety-third floor with two hundred and fifty guests, it will have wound up at midnight, but there'll still be stragglers,' agent McKee said, checking her watch. 'Then there's drinks on the observation deck, for which you need the wristbands. It'll be pretty packed so it'll be hard to spot anyone in the crowd.'

Fox examined the wristbands, which had coded security chips. A secure place in a secure building in a secure zone. Perfect for a handover.

'I'll stay based in here with the firepower,' McKee said to Fox. She opened a case that contained a SIG SG 553 assault rifle, equipped with EOTech holographic sight and a Brügger & Thomet suppressor. It was known for being as reliable and well engineered as a Swiss watch, with a similar operating system to the indestructible AK-47. She took it out, loaded a translucent polymer magazine stracked full of rounds.

'What's in here . . . ?' Gammaldi asked, opening a hold-all. Half a dozen Kevlar vests. 'That was a bit anticlimactic. I thought there'd be a bazooka or something so we could take the building, Cajun-style.'

'You should all put one on,' McKee said, pointing at the vests. 'There's changes of clothes in the wardrobe too, so you fit in to the crowd. Hutchinson guessed your sizes and I ordered them through the concierge, so don't blame me if they're wrong.'

'Yeah, let's get cleaned up first,' Fox said. 'Ready in ten.'

'Hey, you should go check out the toilet,' Gammaldi said. 'Opens its lid as you approach.'

'How'd I ever live without that?' Fox replied, checking over his SOCOM pistol. 'Isn't this the place where they put a Porsche into the lift?'

'Yeah,' Agent McKee said. 'Shanghai Auto Show, Porsche wanted to showboat a little. So what do they do? Send a Porsche Panamera to the ninety-fourth floor of the Shanghai World Financial Center. In a lift – a Porsche!'

'Cool,' Gammaldi said, coming out of the kitchenette with the full room-service menu. 'Room service good?'

'Best in Shanghai.'

'Excellent.'

Fox opened the suite's door, double-checked the sightlines and exits in the hallways and fire escapes, noting how they correlated to the schematics he'd downloaded on the flight.

He went into the bedroom, looked at the black suit and shirt hanging in the wardrobe – seemed about his size. He headed into the en suite and started undressing, filling the basin with warm water –

Zoe entered. She seemed oblivious to him, half-closed the door, looked at the scars on his torso. She started to undress.

'Sorry,' he said. 'I'll let you take a shower.'

'You can join me,' she said. Not waiting for a reply she took off her pants, then removed her shirt, transformed from cop to Victoria's Secret model. 'You have seen some wars,' she said, looking closely at the map of scars on his body.

Fox wearing just his pants; Zoe in her underwear, revealing a smoking hot body, leaner than Kate, but still with curves . . .

She moved in and kissed him, lightly, then licked her lips.

Fox smiled, left the room and closed the door behind him. Out in the lounge, Kate was on her phone, animated. She ended the call when she saw his reflection in the window. She looked like she'd been crying.

Gammaldi was playing *Call of Duty* on an Xbox. Agent McKee was sitting at the table with the assault rifle in front of her.

There was a knock at the door. Fox went to answer it, but McKee was there first, her hand on her holstered pistol as she checked the peephole. She opened the door, spoke through the chain, then let a man in.

Tall guy, late thirties, handsome, friendly, nervous.

'Who's this?' Fox asked. He heard shuffling behind him – Kate had come into the entryway. The guy looked over Fox's shoulder; there was something in that look.

'My name is Jacob,' he held out a hand, his accent was European; Dutch maybe. 'Jacob van Rijn. You must be Lachlan Fox?'

'Yeah . . .'

He looked a little troubled and let his hand fall to his side. His gaze moved from Fox back to Kate.

'I am – how do I say this . . . I am Kate's fiancé.'

94

SHANGHAI

The President of the European Commission sat opposite Babich in the penthouse suite. They had met several times before, and the man had even stayed a weekend in Babich's villa at Lake Como. He didn't own the guy – he thought he'd have another couple of years to cultivate this relationship – but he had influence over him. The fact that he came here at all showed him that.

'So, instead of a primitive economy based on raw materials, we shall create a smart economy,' Babich said. 'Instead of an archaic society, in which leaders think and decide for everybody, Russia shall become one of intelligent, free and responsible people.'

'Look, Roman . . .' the EC President began, staring into his drink, searching for words. He was Danish, but his accent was almost American. 'I'd help if I could, but my hands are tied on this – I mean, the way people think of you at the moment . . . *I can't be seen* with you, let alone speak out and support you.'

Babich explained his arrest as a Russian-sponsored witch-hunt, all because he'd dared to speak out about the government and they knew he would be running for the presidency at the next election. It was a half-truth, but the EC President trusted him enough to buy it. The man nodded and smiled; he was impressed with Babich, and he could see that the Chinese were also behind him. He sat there and listened, wary at first, but soon put at ease as Babich welcomed him like the kingmaker he was.

'You're sure you can ascend to power?' the EC President asked. 'You have the numbers in the Russian parliament?'

'As sure as I know how to breathe,' Babich replied.

'They want to silence me because I am a successful businessman, the future of Russia, a symbol of what can be achieved. They are stuck in the Soviet past and do not like that,' Babich said. 'Sure, like President Vladimir Putin, I am a former employee of a KGB Directorate. But unlike so many who have gone on to head the state companies – for enormous personal gain – I have made myself. I have made myself and they have robbed the state. As long as that continues, Russia will be a problem, for itself and the world. I know that and you do too, yes?'

'Yes, Roman, you know that,' the Dane replied. 'The Soviet Union may have collapsed, governments may have changed, but the people have not.'

'Exactly,' Babich said. 'Tomorrow morning the world will wake and see those in power in my home country for who they really are. I will show the world the evidence I have of FSB involvement in the bombing of the Russian apartment buildings.'

That piqued his guest's full attention – the man had worked as a legal investigator once, Babich had met him when he was working on a European Union inquiry into the bombings and their handling. Babich had been helpful, far more so than most, but always on background, and never with anything specific.

'We warned the Russian government some hours ago, and they have so far refused to respond – beyond, again, labelling me a criminal and accusing me of funding the terrorist activities of Chechen rebels,' Babich said, his smile showing that he was well used to such remarks. 'They are scrambling and it will make their case even worse. I have the *evidence* that shows the Russian government bombed its own people –'

'They will say you fabricated it to –'

'I have witnesses, I have confessions,' Babich said, letting it sink in. 'I am going to produce the people who carried out the Novsyelov bombing, the Ryazan *training exercise*, and the documentation and taped conversations of those official orders. And that is just the start!'

Babich laughed, and his guest was jovial, too.

'Roman,' the EC President said, leaning forward. 'If you prove this – that the bombings were carried out by the state – it means the present government of Russia is illegitimate.'

'Precisely. Precisely.'

The Dane poured himself another drink and topped up Babich's.

'Whatever I can do,' he said to Babich, looking him in the eyes. 'However I can help you, I will do it.'

They clinked glasses and drank. Leaned back. Settled.

'You will be a hero, Roman.'

'We will both be heroes,' Babich said.

'More than that. This is big, for Russia and the world. This is world-changing. This is a historical turning point.'

Babich knew he'd picked the right ally in this man. He was hungry for his own place in history. This would be just the powerful rallying voice he needed in Western Europe.

'All free-thinking Russians are ashamed by what their government has been doing,' Babich said, downplaying his role. 'No longer will they, and the rest of the world, be forced to decide whether freedom in Russia should be sacrificed on the altar of gas and oil. No longer. Enough sacrifice. I will force change through the truth, and that will open a new era for all of us.'

'What about the Americans?' the EC President asked. 'If America does not accept your plans? They will still want to put you before a court.'

'My friend,' Babich said, leaning forward. 'What do you know about the history of Alaska?'

95

SHANGHAI

Fox stood in the bedroom, alone. He watched the big city lights, burning bright. Looked out across the luminous Shanghai city, the river directly below, tourist shops and Chinese junks with incandescent globes strung from their masts. Life going about its business.

He sipped a Maker's Mark, tempted to crawl into the bottle right now. He saw Kate's silhouette in the doorway. The ice-cold glass comfortable in his hand. The ground below seemed to be crumbling.

In the reflection of the floor-to-ceiling window Kate looked worn out. Cried out. She closed the door behind her. Stood there.

Silence. Not a word.

His torso was still a mess, with dried blood here and there, the smell of the antiseptic she'd applied. The smell of her. He looked back at the view, drained his glass, and couldn't not look at her reflection. He felt a sense of déjà vu. This place again. He picked his change of clothes out of the wardrobe, moved past her into the bathroom, took his shirt and pants off, started filling the basin with cold water, grabbed a washcloth; his hands shook as he tried to wash them. Next he scrubbed his body hard, the cut across his chest opened up again, fresh blood. He stopped, turned off the tap, closed his eyes and rested his weight against the stone basin, his hands in tight fists.

He felt her behind him, didn't resist as she put her arms under his and encircled his middle. She rested her head gently on his back, a light embrace.

After a minute, he looked up to the mirror. He patted the wound on his chest with a hand towel, rummaged through the FBI agent's medical pack and applied strips of tape across the cut, pulling it closed. A real mess. He sprayed some aerosol bandage on the skin, coated the wound, cauterised it. Kate stayed hooked onto him the whole time, her grip relaxed, silent.

'I've gotta go,' he said.

She released her arms.

He chucked the tape wrappers and bloody tissues in the bin. Went into the bedroom. Put on the new black shirt – it was a little loose, which was fine with him. Black suit pants fitted well.

Kate had followed him.

'Lach –'

'I'm okay with it.'

'We'll talk about it –'

'Yeah, whatever,' he said, pouring another measure of bourbon over the melting ice and feeling it burn the back of his throat on the way down.

There was a long silence.

'You could have told me any time over the past six months.'

She didn't answer.

'Yeah,' he said. He sat on the end of the bed and put his socks and shoes on, grunted through the pain of the chest wound and other niggling aches and twinges. He stood up, went for his jacket hanging over the back of the chair, but she got there first, took it and held it close.

'He's a guy I met when I thought I'd never see you again. I had no one in my life and he's – I couldn't – I was empty and –'

'You don't need to explain it,' Fox said, reaching for his jacket, but she took a step back against the desk, held it out of reach.

He looked away from her eyes, back out towards the view.

'Kate, I . . . I mean, having you back in my life –'

'This doesn't mean I'm not in your life,' she said. 'I was seeing him –'

'You're engaged to him!'

Her turn to look away.

'I was ready to walk away from this life for you! You know? I was starting to think I knew who I was again. Make a new life – with you!'

'It doesn't matter who you were before. It's who you want to be that matters,' she said, facing him. 'We have what we have and we got dealt a pretty shitty hand a while back and we've played it the best we could.'

'Yeah. You done?'

'No,' she said, tears in her eyes. She pushed up against him, her breath hot in his face. 'I had nothing before and . . . now? I don't know, maybe I have more, maybe it's nothing, but . . . I never *wanted* any of this, this running, this hiding. If you get killed chasing this I have to go on without you. How's that fair? You go on your adventures, and one day, maybe today, maybe tomorrow, you don't come back because you don't give a shit for anything but the fucking so-called truth that you're pursuing

– and it'll get you killed! Don't you see? It will kill you – and you don't give a shit about those around you!'

She slammed her fist into his shoulder, again and again.

'And what?' Fox said. 'The chef from the Muppets out there does?'

'He's a lawyer with the European Commission –'

'Wow.'

'Well at least he won't come home in a body bag!' Kate said. 'How's that for "wow"?'

'I've gotta leave.'

'Of course you do . . .' she said, handing him his jacket. 'You always have some place to go, somewhere you've *gotta be*. Well fucking go! Go until you can't go anymore and don't bother coming back.'

'You want me to do that?'

'Yes.'

Fox nodded. He took her hand, her closed fist in his open palms. And they stood there. Two people who knew each other so intimately and yet hardly at all. Fox reached past her head and she softened a little – thought perhaps that he was reaching for her face, an embrace or a kiss – but he took the SOCOM pistol off the chest of drawers and put it into the back of his belt. He left the room.

96

SHANGHAI

Malevich collected a parcel from the bell desk of the Park Hyatt driveway. He opened it – the hotel reservation and a schedule showing interviews with several heads of state in the morning. He showed these to his security checkpoint chaperone, who, having already checked Malevich's name on his press list, was now satisfied he was a bona fide journalist.

Malevich adjusted the bag over his shoulder, walked to the lift lobby, mindful that Russia and China had signed an agreement on intelligence cooperation in 1992. Every second he was here, Lavrov could have him taken in, then lose him in a Chinese cell for eternity. *In and out, back to the waiting aircraft.* He smiled as he thought how Lavrov's guys at the airport would be waiting for him to emerge from an Air France flight he hadn't taken.

He checked his BlackBerry again. Still no messages from his sister. He tried her number again. Again it went straight to messagebank. The lift doors pinged open. Malevich entered, pressed ninety-three.

97

SHANGHAI

'Al,' Fox said as he walked accross the lift lobby of the ninety-seventh floor observation deck, the mic concealed under his shirt, taped to his chest. 'Al, can you hear me, buddy?'

'10–4, chilly-willie,' Gammaldi replied over the earpiece. 'How's the party?'

'We're not quite in yet,' Fox replied, his thumb holding down the talk button on the little radio clipped to his belt. Zoe stood next to him, in a simple black cocktail dress that had been meant for Kate. Just the two of them on this mission; Fox had local communications set up to go through to Gammaldi, and with a flick of the switch he could talk to Hutchinson.

'Man, that guy, Kate's fiancé . . .' Gammaldi said, trailing off.

'Yeah, what?' Fox said as they passed through a security checkpoint that scanned their wristbands.

'All I'm saying is, of all the hotels in all the cities in all the world . . .'

'You said it, mate,' Fox replied. He took a beer from a passing waitress. 'It's loud in here, Al, I'll contact you when I know something. Stay sharp back there.'

'Not how I would have pictured a G20 Summit,' Zoe said.

The scene was wild. It was the closing night of the Summit and staffers and delegates were letting their hair down. The place was so crowded and dark that the dancers looked like one strange beast, thrashing and swaying to the beat. Most were in suits and dresses, some were in nightclub gear. One corner had a few drunk guys with just their pants on, in another were a couple of dozen young Chinese girls in short skirts hanging off the arms of fat, drunk men.

Fox followed Zoe across the room, where they stopped close to the deck with sweeping views over the city. It was dizzying to see the streets below through a glass floor. Fox adjusted the SOCOM pistol tucked in his pants at the small of his back. Zoe took his beer, had a sip. They shared a look.

They were both so tired and wired – they needed each other's A-game right now. They stood in silence, scanned the crowd, until Fox tapped her on the shoulder and they made for the lift lobby.

'We can't see shit in there,' he said. 'What floor was the dinner?'

'Ninety-third.'

'Let's check it out.'

Zoe nodded and they took the lift down.

•

People were still milling about on the ninety-third floor, talking and drinking at the bars set up outside the dining room. Malevich made a call on his new pre-paid mobile phone. Lavrov answered on the second ring.

'You have not transferred the money,' Malevich said, making for the main bar.

'Where are you?'

'Shanghai. With your document.'

'Your flight –'

'Listen to me!' Malevich said. He wanted to ask Lavrov about his sister, but he didn't want to show that he was fearful. *They might not have her . . . better to be silent about it.* 'I will check the money has been transferred in five minutes. If it's in my account, I will call you back and tell you where to meet me.'

'If –'

'If it's not transferred, I will be selling the document to the Americans.'

He hung up and ordered a glass of wine.

98

WASHINGTON, DC

Bowden had been quiet, doing his thing, doing it in secrecy. Plans would be in motion.

He called McCorkell over, nodded to a CIA analyst and played a phone call between McCorkell and Fox.

'*Hutchinson will meet you at the hotel.*' McCorkell heard his voice. '*Good luck.*'

'You wanna elaborate on that?' Bowden asked, smug.

'No.'

'Okay. I've activated all assets in the area, just a matter of time.'

'And when you find them?'

'Then we're in play.'

'We bring them in,' McCorkell said. 'Unharmed.'

'Look at your boy, Fox,' Bowden said, pointing to a tech who brought up an image of the Elysée scene to sit alongside those of the Louvre courtyard and two separate car chases. 'He's in this, too. Who's to say there's a phantom Russian agent with this secret protocol? Who's to say that Fox isn't there, about to hand it to Babich?'

'Babich is the man we want.'

'We're closing on the hunt.'

'Sounds like you know exactly where he is,' McCorkell said.

'No. The hunt *ends* when we know exactly where he is.'

McCorkell had had enough. There was no way he was going to let Fox hang out to dry – the guy was doing work on behalf of all the people in this room. McCorkell had seen the face of the man with the protocol, a blur at best. Fox had seen him first-hand. He was their best shot, period.

'You still won't accept that Fox may have turned?' Bowden asked. 'What if he's playing you? You ever think of that?'

'That's horse shit,' McCorkell said. 'Where would he turn? He wants Umbra finished as much as we do – probably more.'

'He's loose,' Bowden said. 'He's out of control, an unknown. It's very clear to me what needs to happen.'

Silence. The idea dangling for a moment. Then it was over. Resolve in Bowden's eyes.

'I have work to do,' McCorkell said.

Bowden didn't say anything. He turned his attention back to his team; news and intel was flooding in thick and fast, things were coming to a head. McCorkell moved back to the printers, collecting transcripts, within earshot.

'Kate Matthews just popped up on the grid – vocal match on a cell phone, we got a location.'

Bowden looked vindicated. 'Let me guess . . .'

'Shanghai – Pudong,' the NSA tech said. 'At or close to the World Financial Center building, definitely within the secure zone of the Summit.'

'How old?'

'Ten minutes, and her phone's still on – we'll have an exact location momentarily.'

'So, they're on scene,' Bowden said.

'We just got a confirmation from the building's security screening, facial shots of Fox and his party of three, arrival close on twenty minutes ago.'

'And I'm just hearing that now because?'

The tech shook his head.

'Okay,' Bowden said, looking across to the Air Force detachment. 'Activate the air asset, prepare to wait on final target acquisition.'

The techs and agents looked at each other as the DoD men prepared to activate their mission.

'Should we evac the Summit?' Bowden's deputy asked. 'Communicate a high-priority security concern?'

Bowden shook his head – hell no.

'Can't afford the evac, can't afford targets getting lost in the masses.'

His operators seemed to understand, they didn't like the risks, but they'd never felt things go wrong up close in their face.

'Have the air asset ready to rock and roll within range of the building – and keep tabs on all exits, I wanna know every ID of every person in and out of that damned building,' Bowden said. 'Whoever is giving this protocol to Babich, however, wherever, we've gotta intercept that pass – at all costs.'

McCorkell looked at the last image of Fox they had, from the lobby of the Shanghai World Financial Center. *You're it, Fox – for God's sake hurry up and don't give this SOB a chance to do it the hard way . . .*

99

EAST CHINA SEA

Bowden's air asset was a heavily modified C-130H flying high over a black sea, in airspace controlled by the *George Washington*'s carrier strike group. Designated the ATL001, the aircraft's matt black paint scheme rendered the aircraft near-invisible against the night sky. Soaring high, waiting for mission orders, there was no more-advanced covert-action strike weapon on the planet.

The Advanced Tactical Laser aircraft was built for one main purpose: deniable air strikes. The modified Hercules aircraft was fitted with a high-energy chemical laser. The 5.5-tonne weapons system combined chlorine and hydrogen peroxide molecules to release energy, which was used in turn to stimulate iodine into releasing intense infra-red light. It gave the operators the ability to strike night or day with maximum precision from long distances, the ultimate tool of plausible deniability.

The accuracy of this weapon was little short of supernatural – it could destroy a vehicle completely, or just damage the tyres to immobilise it, from thirty kilometres out. It could assassinate a specific individual standing among a group with sniper-like precision. Targeting was no less advanced. A recent showing of power at Kirtland Air Force Base showed a thirty-second engagement in which the beam destroyed over a hundred separate targets while avoiding collateral damage of dummy personnel standing in close proximity. A three-month deployment to the Afghan–Pakistan border had provided kill results equivalent to no less than a dozen Predator drones flying similar hours. The ATL001's effectiveness had proven it to be a future replacement of the ageing Lockheed AC-130 gunship fleet.

The laser itself was a silent, invisible killer. It could bore a hole through a tank or a concrete wall in a quarter of a second. Whatever the target, one thing was constant: the recipient would never know what hit them. There would be no munitions fragments or ballistics residue for investigators to find. At this time, no pathologist would be able to definitively say that a laser was involved – the injury might resemble a lightning strike more than anything else.

The US Air Force flight crew had flown out from Kadena Air Base, Japan, two hours ago and had been doing a circuit out at sea, waiting for a go order. When they received the encrypted command, the pilots vectored towards Shanghai, while the gunners manning the computer suite in the cargo hold began setting up the fire sequence. Though staffed by DoD personnel, the ATL001 was the exclusive property of the CIA for strikes against Tier One Personalities.

For this mission, they had two targets.

100

SHANGHAI

Babich signalled for another drink for the President of the European Commission.

'It's a legally binding treaty that has been in place since 1867,' he finished. 'This secret protocol? It is but an amendment that has no sunset clause?'

'Correct.'

'Forgive me,' the EC President said, 'but this is a major security and economic issue for them – the Americans; they would be handing you the Arctic seas . . . and those resources. If they refuse to comply?'

'They rescind, it is in violation of the treaty – so the original treaty itself is invalid.'

'And they would have to give Alaska back to Russia?'

'You know, no country enters into a treaty unless it has the intention and means to enforce the treaty provisions . . . Put it this way,' Babich said, 'States who commit themselves to obligations under treaties, arrangements or resolutions from the Security Council at the United Nations – should then follow through with those commitments. Violating such a treaty is a crime, whether the United States commits it, or whether it is

Russia or Denmark, enforceable by all sorts of sanctions and force. They can't lay down a rule of negligent conduct against others and not allow it to be invoked against them as well. They have no choice and they know it. We must never forget that the record on which we judge them will be the record on which history will judge us tomorrow. America's standing in the world, as seen by the Americans themselves, is so important – but you know that.'

That drew agreement. Good. Babich didn't want to be honest with *everything*. He told the man what he needed to know.

'So, you see, they will really have no choice,' he continued. 'I come to power in my country, I exploit these resources in the north, and we have a new relationship to make a much better future for our two countries.'

The EC President nodded.

'And you want Denmark's help with this, to sway the votes when it comes time to move on new agreements in the Arctic?'

'We are helping each other,' Babich said. 'You know, I could have taken this to Norway, or to Canada, but I came to you.'

'Well, we have history,' the EC President said, smiling. 'I will speak with my Prime Minister and get back to you as soon as I can.'

The two men stood and shook hands. Helena, the EC President's only witness to the meeting, rose and followed her boss out. Babich watched them leave.

101

WASHINGTON, DC

Bowden was up front, pointing, pacing, chewing his nails. He was passed a phone, listened, covered the mouthpiece and spoke to the Air Force men.

'Get ready for coordinates coming in. You give the go-ahead to the aircraft.'

'Roger boss,' the senior Air Force operator replied.

Valerie motioned McCorkell over to an FBI tech's console. The young guy was the team's computer guru and he'd been flicking through the CIA team's computers all day.

'Bill,' Valerie whispered, 'the CIA know where Babich is.'

'Shanghai.'

'No,' Valerie said. 'I mean where in the *hotel* he is. They have a double agent in there, a woman in the Danish Intelligence, she's shadowing the President of the EC – he just met with Babich.'

'You got the room number?'

'Yes.'

102

SHANGHAI

Boris Malevich hung up his mobile phone. The money was there, and he'd transferred it to his account in Malta. He now had over five million euros. Enough to disappear for life.

He redialled Lavrov's number, told him where to meet, finished his wine and ordered an espresso. He picked up his phone, confirmed with his pilot that he was on schedule and they would be flying to Valleta within the hour.

Then his phone rang. His sister. He almost cried when he heard her voice.

'Alina?' he said. 'Where have you been? Where are you?'

•

'There!' Zoe said into Fox's ear. 'Two o'clock, at the bar, on a mobile phone.'

On the other side of the room, Fox saw a familiar face – no mistaking it, he was the guy from Paris. Through the crowd, Fox couldn't make out if he was carrying the document, but chances were . . .

'What if he doesn't have it on him?' Fox asked her.

She looked at him, then texted on her BlackBerry.

'Then we ask him where it is,' she said, pressing send. 'I've just notified my French colleagues next door – they'll be on their way over.'

'And if he doesn't want to tell you?'

She smiled, her eyes glinted, 'I can be very persuasive. Come.'

Fox scanned the crowd as they started moving. Nothing but middle-aged delegates in little groups.

Zoe started to head for the man.

Fox caught her, his hand wrapped around her slender bare arm.

'Wait,' he said into her ear, motioning the other side of the room. Three men in cheap suits, serious men in the business of violent negotiations, were making a beeline for their guy.

•

Malevich set his coffee cup down on the timber bar. He hung up the call and was still smiling about his sister when Lavrov appeared beside him.

He stood close, invading his personal space. He was smiling, but there was something very off about him, something dangerous. He didn't shake Malevich's hand or hug him in greeting, nothing of the congratulations he'd expected. *Too late*, Malevich thought, *I should not have delivered this in person . . .*

Lavrov asked, 'Where is it?'

Malevich bent down, pulled the leather cylinder from his shoulder bag, handed it over. Lavrov pulled the top off, inspected the document – smiled again, just as dangerous but this time genuine happiness behind it too.

'You know, I had thought this was going to be harder,' Lavrov said. 'When you didn't show at Shanghai Airport – when you took another flight – I thought you'd not show here.'

Malevich nodded, swallowed hard. He put his bag over his shoulder, ready to leave. He never wanted to see or hear from this man again. That was the original deal. Job done. He was out. Money to facilitate that.

'Stay for a drink,' Lavrov said. It wasn't a question. 'Come, we have a suite.'

'I have to go.'

'To Malta?' Lavrov asked, then tilted his head slightly, watching him. 'To your sister?'

Malevich felt sick – he had to go, but he was hemmed into the corner of the bar by these men. He looked across towards the lift lobby – and couldn't believe his eyes.

•

Fox stopped behind the one doing the talking. Russians.

'You must be Babich's friends,' Fox said. His jacket was open and he readied himself for whatever might go down.

The guy turned around. Thick-set, a good fifteen years older than Fox, looked like he could handle himself, but he'd be slow. The other two guys looked twenty per cent bigger and faster. Zoe bumped in close to Fox. The guy from Paris looked shit scared.

'You have that . . . What is it, Zoe?' Fox asked. 'A certain kind of *je ne sais quoi* about you.'

One of the two heavies opened his jacket, revealing a holstered snub-nosed MP5 that with a few quick sweeps could take out thirty or more guests in the room. He shook his head as a warning and Fox put out a hand to stop Zoe from reaching behind for her hip-holstered sidearm – she turned to him, annoyed, but before she could object he took a beer bottle from the bar and launched it at the ceiling –

It smashed out a sprinkler, setting off the fire alarm and a chain reaction of powerful showers.

Bleep . . . Bleep . . . Bleep.

The room moved as one, running for the lift lobby –

The Russian pulled out his MP5 – Fox broke the guy's arm and then his face, brought the MP5 up towards the other, who Zoe had already flipped onto his back and knocked out with her boot. Fox brought up the weapon and sighted the other two as they made a run for the fire stairwell in the corner. He hesitated on the shot – as they disappeared, Fox noticed that the older one had a pistol in the back of their Paris guy.

Fox and Zoe were right on them – through the fire door after them, before any of the evacuating party got through.

The metal doorjamb by Fox's head pinged from a bullet ricochet – Babich's guy, firing up through the metal balustrades.

Fox with his MP5, fired a three-round burst down the stairwell in reply, the sound reverberating in the silence for a second as they headed down – just before a surge of guests flooded from the bars a few levels above. The fire door to the next level was just closing – Zoe leaned over the stairs, looked and listened – the crush of evacuating guests coming behind them.

'They went onto this floor,' she said. They braced either side of the door, readied themselves, burst out. Fox down low on one knee, scanning the guest-room floor, saw their targets rounding a corner down the hall – and they sprinted after them.

They stopped at the corner – Fox peeked around, down low, MP5 leading – nothing. *Shit.* They ran again.

The lift lobby, both guys there –

Took fire, Fox and Zoe ducked back, waited, then he fired blind around the corner.

They had the two guys cowering, hunkered down as Fox kept a barrage of bursts tearing into the wall above them.

He motioned to Zoe to head towards them as he kept up the cover fire –

PING!

Six heavily armed men from the Chinese security force rushed out of the lift. They looked otherworldly, armoured ninjas. They started shooting –

Oh shit . . .

Fox ducked and kept low as bullets ricocheted all around him. Crawling, rolling, he followed Zoe out of the area, firing at the glass doors that separated the lift lobby from the guest rooms, the glass smashed around the Chinese force's heads – Fox and Zoe hurried away, trying to keep from being flanked.

Click.

MP5 out of ammo. He tossed it, pulled his SOCOM pistol, flicked on the radio.

'Al, Hutch, I'm on the ninety-second floor, taking fire from the lift lobby, half a dozen guys!' he called, before firing a few booming rounds from the .45 SOCOM.

The other way down the hall – the two Russian guys with the secret protocol.

'Come on,' Fox said, laying cover fire as they moved out in pursuit, Babich's guy firing back at them. They rounded the corner – straight into the Chinese crew with their guns trained at head height. Fox and Zoe dropped their firearms and raised their hands. The security team rushed towards them. Fox stood still, but it didn't matter – one of them clocked him against the side of his face and he fell to the ground, Zoe too, and in seconds his arms were behind his back then he felt FlexiCuffs zipping closed.

'Okay . . .' Fox said, for the benefit of the microphone. 'You've got us.'

103

EAST CHINA SEA

A command centre had been set up for Hutchinson's operation in one of the USS *New York*'s briefing rooms. Five men in the darkened room, a communications technician working a laptop's keyboard.

'The fire alarm triggered the Chinese security's response measures. All cell and landline phone systems have been cut,' the technician said.

'Fox – what happened to Fox?' Hutchinson asked, alarmed.

'The comms are down.'

'What?'

'His radio is turned off, we've got nothing but the last-known location – bringing it up now.'

Hutchinson watched as a projected image on the wall changed from the Park Hyatt security footage to a rendering of –

'This is the schematic of the building, and tracking dots on Fox and Gammaldi's radio sets show them . . . there.'

Hutchinson looked at the flashing dots on the wire grid blueprint of the Shanghai World Financial Center building.

'Call in the Delta boys next door!' Hutchinson said to the comms tech. 'Get them over there!'

He turned to the captain of the Force Recon Marines.

'Get your grab team and aircraft ready. Soon as we get eyes on the prize, we roll.'

104

SHANGHAI

Outside, the view was amazing. Inside was a different story.

Fox sucked in deep breaths. Blood poured from his nose and a cut eyebrow, spilling sticky and hot across his bare legs. Turned out the Chinese security were Babich's Chinese security. They'd stripped Fox down to his underwear, removed the radio wire taped under his shirt, and bound him to a chair. His anger was barely contained – it was everything he could do not to struggle against the ropes.

Roman Babich leaned forward, a coffee table separating him from Fox and Zoe.

He nodded to the man named Lavrov.

Fox closed his mouth tight. Didn't take his eyes off Babich. Knew what was coming.

Lavrov hit him in the face. He went with it so it would have less chance of breaking his eye-socket.

It didn't work.

The pain behind his right eye was deep. He was on the carpeted floor, the pain resonating, then he felt hands tipping him and his chair back upright.

Immediately, he could feel his eye was swelling. His face felt heavy and he had trouble holding it up. He felt himself blacking out . . .

He was unbound, water was poured over his head. Babich pushed a bucket of ice across the table.

'As usual, you take the gung-ho approach,' Babich said, the cylinder in his hands. He'd already glanced at the secret protocol and then tucked it away again. He shuffled it from side to side, a gleeful child with a brand new toy.

Fox leaned back in the chair, held a wet towel of ice against his face. He counted one thick-necked Russian goon nearby, and could see the Chinese bigwig named Zang hovering up on the mezzanine lounge with six armed guys. The ones who'd brought them to Babich. The Russian guy adjusted a snub-nosed MP5 on a strap over his shoulder as he brought Babich a bottle of vodka from the bar. Babich poured three glasses; Fox gulped his down, coughed through the pain as it bit at his split lip. Zoe didn't touch hers.

'You are resilient. Tenacious.' Babich leaned forward, poured Fox another drink. 'Seems not so long ago we sat across from one another in Italy.'

Fox looked away from Babich, over at the guy they'd been chasing in Paris, who he now knew to be named Malevich. He was sweaty and nervy. Seated by the window, across from Lavrov, who was evidently Babich's right-hand man. Babich noticed Fox's gaze, looked over his shoulder at them and back.

'He did his job well, but you – *you* made me worry,' Babich said, tapping the cylinder. 'Right down to the wire, hey?'

Fox looked across to Zoe, who was listening intently. He could tell she was busting out of her skin to make a move, but they had no weapons, and there was the thick-necked Russian hovering with the submachine gun. Fox wondered if he could toss him out the window before the Chinese super soldiers got a bead on him.

'I'm very glad you showed up,' Babich said, a slight tick in his eye – old scar tissue – as he spoke. 'I wanted you to; it's fitting. Some might call it destiny.'

'There's no way you could have known I'd come here tonight,' Fox said, nursing his drink. He glanced across at Boris again – he seemed tired, beaten even, as if he was also here against his will. 'No way.'

'Maybe I know you better than you know yourself, hmm?' Babich said. 'I knew you'd make it here like I knew you'd make a mess before you came around to see what needed to be done. You have . . . You have that uncanny knack of being at the right place at the right time.'

'That's a different way of putting it.'

'No matter where I go, there you are.' Babich touched the rolled-up document still in his grip, caressed it, shifted it from hand to hand. 'Finally, I will make that fact *work* for me.'

'So what is it?' Fox said, acting nonchalant. He could see Boris's gaze fixed on the armed Russian standing near them. 'I guess you – what – you expect me to die now, in front of you? That it?'

'No, no, no, Lachlan!' Babich said with a big grin as he sat forward on his chair. 'I expect you to *live*!'

•

The last thing Gammaldi had heard was Fox's capitulation, and then the scuffling noises as he'd been disarmed and the radio set had been switched off. Agent McKee stood by the door, assault rifle cradled in her arms, adamant that they stay in the hotel room and 'let the pros handle it'. He suspected that, charged with their safety, she was not going to let any of them leave.

Gammaldi paced up and down.

'You can't stop me leaving, though, right?'

The agent looked to Kate for support.

'Al,' Kate said, leaving Jacob's side and walking to him. 'They have specialists going to Fox now, he'll be okay.'

He looked at her; the worry, the sincerity, the concern in her face that belied her words.

•

Fox was puzzled by Babich's words, intrigued, but was unsure whether to show it. *Why would he want me alive?* Better to test it. He'd noticed that Malevich was nervously playing with his hands and scanning the room like he was about to do something dumb. Fox took a sip of his vodka, stood, walked over to Boris and gave the rest of the glass to him. The Russian looked at Fox, his eyes softened just a little – and he drank half, seemed a little resolved by it. Fox went back to his chair, mindful that Lavrov and the Russian with the submachine gun never took their eyes off him. He took a Foster's from the ice bucket on the bar, opened it, took a long pull. That armed guy by the door was as alert as Fox had been when he'd had his morning coffee all those hours ago in Giverny – and here Fox was, tired as shit, and being watched from the mezzanine by trigger-happy Chinese storm-troopers as well.

'So, Roman, what's the plan?' Fox asked. 'I'm going to somehow clear your good name? Say I was wrong about you all this time, that we all were, that the problem's really in Russia? That it? You want me to explain how your arrest and trial were all some big set-up to make sure you couldn't enter Russian politics?'

Babich leaned back, appraising Fox, then Zoe. He spoke quietly.

'You are going to help me with this, Lachlan Fox,' Babich said. 'And you know why?'

'No, but I'm dying to hear.'

'I worked out your *price*,' Babich said, pleased with himself. 'You are a truth-seeker. You worship at its altar, and I respect that – I respect that because I can *see* it, because I can *use* it. *You* are going to bring this treaty amendment, this protocol, to the light of day – and I will conveniently be in a position to benefit from it.'

'It's never gonna fly, no matter what happens.'

'We will see,' Babich said. 'Worst case, you don't help me? Well, it's a good thing that I have options, isn't it?'

•

Gammaldi paced over to the window. Far down below it was pandemonium outside – people were still pouring out of the building onto the street. Several fire crews had arrived in response to the alarms. The lifts would be out of action now.

He needed to do something.

•

'You know how *long* I've watched state terrorism committed by my government and turned a blind eye?'

'About as long as you've been in that business yourself?' Fox replied, seated opposite. 'You're behind much of that, we both know it. Only difference is you're outside the government. You can try and sell your countrymen this lie, but not me.'

'They're buying it,' Babich said. 'They will have no alternative. As we speak, things are happening in Moscow. You know this is how the last government came to power, through terrorist activities –'

'I know about –'

'You don't know the half of it!' Babich said. 'You know they caught two FSB agents planting sacks of RDX in a residential tower – why would the FSB bomb a Russian apartment block? Well, we know *why*, don't we? The FSB director called it a "training run", because they were caught by local authorities . . . A *training run!* Planting a bomb that didn't go off and then getting caught in a roadblock?'

'And what, you want to bring all these conspirators to justice?' Fox said. 'Then what, fill the power vacuum with your own guys?'

'Don't you see, they never would have let me see a trial,' Babich said. 'Russia won't let me talk, not those in power, because of what I *know* . . . but I'm not afraid. I'm taking them head on.'

•

Gammaldi's earpiece crackled. He adjusted it.

'Al, it's Hutchinson.'

'I read you.'

'We're headed in real soon, hang tight,' he said. 'Delta boys have just entered the building. We have your location and Fox's too, we're tracking the radio sets – make sure you keep it on your person.'

'Got it.'

•

'You say they do this,' Fox said, 'but what do you call what you've been doing? South Ossetia. India. Nigeria. You've been doing the same.'

'Your media never bothered with them because they are a government, they have economic and military clout!' Babich said. 'The West are too addicted to Russia's energy resources to speak out. You're not a fool, Lachlan. You care about this, about getting me – but those men did far worse. They continue to do far worse!'

'Well, I can do something about *you*, Babich,' Fox said.

'You have no idea what I'm capable of,' Babich was red in the face and it flushed down his neck. 'I deserve this moment! Russia deserves this!'

Fox weighed the beer bottle in his hand, wondering if he could take it to Babich's neck before the armed guys got the drop on him.

'Russia and its people deserve freedom, they deserve a democratic system – they swap the current guys for you, it's the same old bullshit,' Fox said. 'You can try and sell this all over the world, but I ain't buying.'

'I could have had you killed months ago,' Babich said. 'I know what drives you: the truth! You *have* to do what's right here, you can't *help* it. You have to let the truth come out!'

Fox's eyes were burning like he'd never felt them before. Something within him, a weight in his conscience, shifted. He had to do Babich in; this was the end of the road.

'Some truths can't ever be heard,' Fox said. He saw the change in Babich's demeanour – the realisation that Fox wouldn't back down. Fox leaned forward a little in his seat, his thighs tense, ready to spring himself up. 'Guess you had me pegged wrong. Tell you one thing, though: this ends here, right now.'

•

'Help me up there,' Hutchinson said. He used a Marine as a crutch, and together they raced out onto the flight deck of the *New York*.

There, waiting for take-off, was a black tilt-rotor aircraft, a Bell-Boeing V-22 Osprey kitted out for covert night operations.

A squad of Force Recon Marines, specialists in black ops that require direct action, was locked and loaded. Tonight they'd fulfil another part of their mission: in-extremis hostage rescue. As Hutchinson was helped to a jump-seat, he noticed a carbon-fibre ramp structure bolted to the inside deck of the aircraft. The marine captain was the last aboard, and he gave the thumbs-up to the loadmaster that they were ready to go.

Once airborne, the nacelles rotated forwards ninety degrees and within fifteen seconds they were racing low across the sea towards Shanghai.

•

The action had happened so fast Fox felt as though he had watched it in a movie, an out-of-body experience; from his seat to Babich's in a second.

Fox held the broken bottle against the Russian's throat, firmly, so it just cut into the skin.

Zoe was right behind him, the protocol cylinder in her hand.

Lavrov was out of his seat – pistol loose in his hand – but didn't dare make a threatening move.

The Russian guard was pressed back against the wall, frightened.

'Put your gun down!' Fox ordered, cutting harder into Babich's neck. The guard complied and Zoe picked up the MP5 as they were backing out.

'The radio,' Fox said to Malevich. The Russian looked at him oddly, then it registered that he'd been given an order that might just save his skin. He ran to the coffee table, picked up the radio and Fox's clothes, then joined them in exiting the room.

The Chinese soldiers on the mezzanine level were spooked, watching intently with guns trained. Colonel Zang looked to Babich for directions but he wasn't talking – Fox increased the pressure on the broken bottle, and used Babich as a shield as they pushed towards the door. Fox heard Zoe opening it.

'Don't try and follow us.'

105

SHANGHAI

'Come on!' he yelled, tossing the broken bottle and pushing Babich ahead of him as they ran through the empty restaurant. Malevich followed behind, shell-shocked, and Zoe held the rear as they took the fire stairs up to the ninety-third floor, where they'd been earlier, in the bar. Fox pulled on his pants and shirt, tying his shoes while his heart raced. Nodding to Zoe as she kept the MP5 pointed at Babich, they set off.

The sprinklers were still going and there was a good few centimetres of water on the ground. Dark but for the emergency lighting. They ran to the other fire stairs in the far corner –

PING!

The lift opened as they passed through the lobby – a dozen firemen about to spill out.

The fire doors they'd just exited burst open – Zang's troops were taking cover positions, firing as –

Fox and Zoe rounded a wall for cover, too. Zoe put the MP5 around the corner and fired blind to hold the troops off. Fox watched in the reflection of a mirror as the firemen made a hasty retreat to the lift. Key operated, the doors closed and they were gone.

Stairs were the only option. They ran through the long expanse of hastily evacuated tables and headed for the kitchen.

Out of the windows was the neighbouring building where the bulk of the G20 delegates and security personnel were crammed, so close to be almost within reach. Fox remembered Hutchinson warning him about the possibility of Russian sniper fire from there directed at Babich.

Bullets tore into the dining room, punching holes through some of the floor-to-ceiling windows to their left as they cleared through the double doors into the kitchen. Fox shoved Babich over to Zoe, took the radio from Malevich, flicked it on and attached it.

'Al, you hear me, buddy?' he asked, urgently, as he dragged a large cutlery trolley across the doors and signalled the others to run through the kitchen. The sprinklers were beginning to stop, but the kitchen tiles were slippery underfoot.

'Lach!'

'Al?' Fox replied, adjusting the volume and scanning the room for anything useful as the others ran to the far end.

'Where you at?'

'Kitchen, ninety-third floor. You?'

'Still in the room.'

Fox looked at the long line of industrial stoves.

'You still playing that Xbox?'

'Fuck you! We're worried sick, I'm coming –'

'Listen: stay there, don't come up – you get the chance to leave, get outta here!' Fox said. He turned around: 'Zoe – little help – cover fire!'

She tossed Babich to the floor and kept her foot on his back, scanning down her sights to the double doors, ready to fire as soon as she saw their pursuers enter.

'They're here!' Zoe yelled, as full-auto gunfire shredded the kitchen doors from the other side. Zoe let off some controlled single shots from the MP5 to cover Fox. He was down on the tiles, under the cover of a kitchen bench as the gunfire blasted into the tiled wall above. A big chef's knife clattered to the floor and he looked at the oven in front of him . . . Looked down the ovens – fifty of them, all big-arse new stainless steel behemoths.

'Buy me time!' Fox crawled down the line of ovens, the razor-sharp knife in hand, cutting the orange gas lines under the stoves. Soon, he could smell the gas filling the room.

'Run!' he yelled, watching Zoe drag Babich up and running for the fire doors where Malevich was hunkered down. 'Come on!'

As Fox ran out he noticed some large compressed gas canisters – back-ups maybe – lined along the wall of the pantry. *Oh shit!*

'Hurry!'

They were through the fire door, headed upstairs.

'Hutchinson, this is Fox!' he said into the radio. He used the open line. 'Ninety-third floor, southeast corner, Babich's guys en masse! They're all there – we have the protocol and Babich! Too many of them!'

•

In Washington, Bowden heard the intercept and nodded to his Air Force operator in contact with the TLA001 flight, who relayed the target coordinates to the aircrew.

'DC, we have that last radio transmission,' the pilot of the Advanced Tactical Laser aircraft said. 'Target acquisition, ninety-third floor, Shanghai World Financial Center, southeast corner.'

'TLA001, confirm you have the target.'

'That's affirmative; we have biometric measurement lock on two separate groups. Make it Group One as our primary targets, currently ascending, in a fire escape; Group Two made up of several unknown targets in their pursuit,' the aircrew replied. 'On station, awaiting next.'

•

Fox and Zoe ran up the stairs and exited on the hundredth floor, which had the highest observation deck. The transparent glass hall was suspended almost five hundred metres above Shanghai. They ran to the middle of the glass walkway and stopped.

'Which way will they come?' Zoe asked.

Fox shook his head. Scanned out to the east sky for Hutchinson's evac. Willed some kind of intervention. Zoe's French security as well as some US Delta troops would be somewhere in the stairwell, ascending fast. Not fast enough. Shanghai was at their feet, the distant glittering lights reminding Fox just how far from safety they were.

•

Bowden asked, 'Clear shot on both?'

'Group Two is a turkey shoot,' the pilot replied. 'Group One we'll make a turn, wait for another pass once they're in the clear. They've got nowhere to turn.'

'Okay. Take the shots,' Babich ordered. 'Both targets at will.'

'Copy that.'

•

Fox and the others saw a brilliant flash, followed a moment later by an ear-shattering –
KLAPBOOM!

Muffled concussion. The four of them hit the floor. The building shook beneath them as they huddled together. A loud cracking noise as the laminated glass floor beneath them began to spider-web.

Babich started crawling away.

'Zoe – stop him!'

She stood then dropped for cover as . . .

Windows along both sides of the walkway shattered in succession like dominoes falling, the twisting pressures of the gas explosion winding its way through the structure. Glass rained down on the building and street below.

Babich steadied himself against the howling wind through the blown-out windows and made for the far lift lobby.

The lift doors buckled and blew out – Babich was knocked back as the building's lights flashed on and off, staying off once the sprinklers came back to life. Malevich was balled up on the floor, covered in broken safety glass, not daring to move.

Water began pooling on the glass floor. Fox inched towards Babich. The glass spiderweb was just holding together, but the water kept coming. Fox looked back at Zoe; the cylinder with the protocol was between them. In that moment they both knew it was about to get worse.

There was a sound of glass breaking, giving way – and then they were all falling . . .

106

EAST CHINA SEA

'Tell them we're close,' the pilot of the Osprey said over the internal radio-sets.

Hutchinson pulled out his short-range radio linked up to Fox and Gammaldi.

'Holy shit!' he heard the pilots call out.

'What?'

'Our target building – it's a fireball –'

Hutchinson stood, grunted through the pain of his leg, held onto the strap above his head for stability and looked out of the cockpit as the fireball flashed into the night sky. Looked like a whole floor had blown out. Smoke plumed up and the lights of the whole neighbourhood flickered off and on, off and on.

'So that's what a laser can do,' the pilot said.

'Must have hit a gas line,' the co-pilot said.

'Who?' asked Hutchinson. 'What laser?'

They told him about the CIA's aircraft, a good twenty clicks behind them.

'Patch me through to them,' Hutchinson ordered. 'Now!'

As he waited for the connection he watched the Shanghai World Financial Center, a giant totem of China's modernity and capitalist ideals, blink its lights in the night sky and then go dark. Like it had just vanished.

107

SHANGHAI

Fox was on his back, looking up at the sky. Slowly, he felt his senses returning. He could hear sparks and he could see that there was a structure above him – the top beams of the Shanghai World Financial Center. In profile, the building resembled a kind of bottle opener – a tall glass-clad tower with a hollowed-out top section between which the glass observation decks were suspended. Or had been. Now, those very structures had given way, and he was flat on his back looking up at the large beam, maybe ten storeys above him, that served as the very top of the tower. He coughed and then the pain hit – his ribs felt like they were on fire, his face and swollen eye numb. He slowly rolled to his side, still coughing.

Malevich was next to him, on his side. Bright arterial blood fountained up from his leg, a piece of twisted metal spiked through it. Zoe was a little further away, getting to her feet.

They're okay, Fox thought. Then bullets sprayed around him.

He turned –

Babich had snatched up the MP5. There was a large pane of sheet glass standing behind him, like his section of the observation deck had fallen largely intact. He didn't even look injured. He took a step closer to Fox.

'Where is it?' he asked.

Fox had already spied the cylinder containing the protocol between him and Malevich. He dragged himself over and picked it up. He noticed Malevich's breaths were short and sharp, in shock from the pain and massive blood loss, his eyes wet and vacant.

'Here,' Fox said, still on the ground, holding the cylinder up for Babich to see. 'And now?'

'Now I'm going to change this,' Babich said.

'Like what you did in Georgia and South Ossetia?' Fox said. 'Nigeria! The attacks in America –'

'And what about America? It doesn't do the same things to protect its interests?'

'Not like this.'

'How many Iraqis, Afghanis, Vietnamese have the Americans killed?'

'Always as collateral –'

'Always?'

Fox was silent.

'For too long there has been this "us and them" mentality,' Babich said. 'It drove international relations in Western bodies –'

'You're talking moral equivalence?' Fox yelled. He was hoping that Zoe, out of view behind him, would have time to do something. 'It's a goddamned political debating term, not something based in the real world.'

'I'm making a change in the real world. Hand me the protocol.'

'The guys who plug that kind of thinking believe their side is – by definition – morally superior, because of *who* they are, not *what* they do,' Fox said. 'They – what – use selective history to cast the situation as a big-picture struggle against an evil force? Well, you know what, you're right. Russia does that. America does that.'

'My Russia is not that evil force, Lachlan, you need to see that. Move on. Well, too late I guess.'

He lifted the MP5, levelled it towards Fox's torso. This range, he would not miss.

'You're saying your state isn't totalitarian?' Fox dared.

'I'm saying, I'm changing things. Saddam had to go, sure – look at what he did to his people – your atrocities in this way become acts of good, not evil; we gave people freedom, it is the price of freedom . . .'

'Now you sound like Dick Cheney.'

'Lachlan, if you think you and your side are morally superior to me and mine, then *you* are unwilling to negotiate on the basis of moral equivalence. Now, hand it over.'

•

Hutchinson's words still rang in Bowden's ears.

'DC: I say again, we are approaching for final shot of Group One, confirm strike is a go.'

The image on the main screen was like something from a sci-fi movie. Four human heat shapes signatured on a roof high above a city. Another shot showed a low-light live video feed, from a long-lens camera.

'ATL001: target standing with the gun,' Bowden said. There was a clear picture of Babich from one of the ATL's onboard cameras, a multi-million dollar piece of lensing equipment that would put the Hubble Space Telescope to shame. 'I say again: your target is with the firearm. Only him. Take the shot.'

•

Zap. Inside of a millisecond. Blinding light against the window behind Babich, quicker than a camera flash. Fox blinked against it; there and gone again. Babich staggered forward. There was a glowing halo of red in the glass behind him – a hole the size of a fist, molten. Fox could feel the heat from fifteen metres away – the ceramic tiles of the roof were a smouldering mess by his side. Something had shot clear through Babich . . .

Babich looked down at Fox, wide-eyed. His mouth was agape. He made a noise and then his head tilted – a dark hole burned right through his chest. He fell to the ground.

108

SHANGHAI

They got the evac call from Hutchinson. Agent McKee went to the suite's main window, shot it twice with her service automatic, blasting two neat holes into the thick glass. Gammaldi threw a chair at it – the chair smashed to pieces. He went over to the bench, took the silenced SIG carbine and set loose half a mag full-auto across the glass. Still it was held by the plastic sheeting laminated between the thick safety-glass panes. He and Jacob picked up the sofa to use as a battering ram.

It blasted right through, the window and furniture falling to the ground way down below. Wind howled into the room.

'We're good to go!' Gammaldi called into the mic.

'Five seconds!' Hutchinson's voice replied.

Within moments the room filled with the sound of a heavy tilt-rotor aircraft and then the V-22 materialised. It was level with them, an ominous blacked-out insect hovering steady outside their hotel room. It rotated one-eighty degrees, and the rear cargo ramp lowered to reveal US Marines either side of a black skybridge that was being extended out towards them.

'No way!' Kate said to Gammaldi and then Jacob. 'I can't!'

She screamed as Jacob picked her up in his arms. A Marine ran over the telescoped bridge, attached a belt to the FBI agent, who fled across first. Jacob and Kate followed and finally Gammaldi, as the metre-wide carbon-fibre structure bucked and moved, hundreds of metres above the streets of Shanghai. Hutchinson was inside the aircraft. Gammaldi ran to him, yelled into his ear as the Osprey moved away from the building.

'Where's Fox?'

Hutchinson replied, 'On the roof!'

109

SHANGHAI

Fox dragged himself to his feet and moved to Malevich. He was alive but not by much.

'Please . . .' Malevich said. 'I – I didn't know.'

'What?' Fox asked. 'Didn't know what?'

'Babich. I thought I was doing this for Russia,' he said. 'I'm . . . a professional.'

'Yeah,' Fox said. He looked across at Babich, motionless on the roof. 'I've met a few of them today. None of them played nice.'

'Please Lachlan, I'm not an officer . . . I'm just an agent – I've been working as a vet in Paris –'

'I'm not going to kill you,' Fox said. Truth was, there was no way this guy would live long enough to receive medical care.

Malevich smiled. He got it. He knew this was the end. For whatever reason, he wanted to be remembered in the right light. He was on his back, panting hard, sweating; in shock. There was bright red blood everywhere.

Fox had seen a femoral artery wound before – a US soldier who'd copped shrapnel from an explosive in a convoy outside Baghdad's Green Zone. Luckily, there'd been a Black Hawk on the next block bugging a squad out of contact with insurgents. That soldier was in surgery within fifteen minutes. He'd lived. Malevich wouldn't.

'Lots of blood, hey.'

Fox nodded. 'Hang in there –'

'It is okay,' Malevich said.

Fox's eyes showed that he knew it, too.

'I can try and slow it,' Fox said, applying pressure higher up in the pelvis area where the artery originated. 'I could try and clamp it – but I can't see it. You'd have to take the pressure off the wound, means you'd bleed out even quicker.'

Malevich shook his head, his face pale and damp. He looked up at Fox.

'No,' Malevich's breaths were shallow and his pulse was low. 'This is it, hey.'

Fox nodded. Matter of fact. *It had been for Renard, too. Fact was, death was something of a leveller, wasn't it? Even the enemy looks the same when reduced to this.*

'See . . . See what they made me do for them,' Malevich said, bringing his hand up to Fox's, shaking. 'I – I never knew it was for that man.'

'Yeah, I know,' Fox said, looking over to Babich, seeing that Zoe was bending over him now. She signalled he didn't quite seem dead, but like Malevich he wouldn't have long.

'Listen, Lachlan . . .' Malevich said. 'I have a sister, Alina. In Valetta, Malta . . . There's money, an account, enough for life . . . Make sure she knows about me.'

What could he say? Might be him in this position one day, pleading for a final showing of empathy.

'I will.'

'Make sure she's okay.'

'I will.' Fox squeezed the Russian's hand. 'I'll check on her, I promise. She'll be fine.'

Malevich smiled, he seemed more peaceful. Fox applied pressure to the wound and immediately felt it lessen, the blood slippery on his hand as it flowed through his fingers.

'Malevich, I can try and buy you time,' Fox said. 'I . . .'

Too late. He was gone. Fox pulled his hand from Malevich and felt his neck – pulse was just there, so faint, almost nothing.

He took his other hand from the wound; the blood still flowed, but it was a trickle now. He plunged his fingers inside, felt around the metal spike . . . No artery . . . He fished up into the thigh, thought maybe he felt something . . . It was too late.

Fox inched back, the red puddle of blood slowing its spread. His senses filled with the familiar smell of copper and the sticky feel of warm blood. He knew the sensation too well; he'd had enough of it.

He stood, wiped his hands on his pants, pulled out Malevich's wallet. There was a picture in there, his sister Fox guessed. He pocketed it. Picked up the protocol, the cylinder flattened and dented, turned around –

Zoe was there, standing above the unconscious form of Babich. Fox looked from her eyes to her hands. She held the MP5 steady, pointed straight at him.

110

SHANGHAI

'Lachlan,' Zoe said. 'I can't just let you hand that to the Americans.'

Fox stopped moving, Zoe had her finger on the trigger, the business end pointed square at his chest. He looked up from the gun – so steady in her hand – to her face, to those eyes he'd spent so much of the day looking into.

'Zoe . . .' he said, thinking about all they'd been through. 'Oh Zoe . . .'

He was beat. Couldn't hide his heartbreak any longer. Everything that had happened today with Kate was coming to the surface now. He'd had enough.

'Please, Lachlan. Give me the cylinder.'

'So you can give it to your politicians to trade it with Russia – for what? Cheaper energy? Military pacts?'

'This is not your game, Lachlan. It's mine. You write your stories, I play the game.'

'Oh, come on Zoe,' he sighed, and his voice held all the pain of the day. Fox remembered when his grandmother had died and his grandfather, who'd served in World War II, hadn't shed a tear. *'Real men don't cry,'* he'd told Fox at her funeral. A few months later, a tree in his grandparents' backyard came down, a big old thing that they'd planted when they'd bought that house and they'd started a family. His grandfather had cried that day. He'd cried all day long and said her name over and over. In a way it had scared Fox from love. Kept him moving, kept him driven towards discovery, to help paint the bigger picture. Now he realised he wanted to be some place he could call home, that it would be better to have a quiet life last a lifetime and not to lose it until an old age.

'It's been a long day . . .' Fox said, deflated. The Chinese security would be along soon, probably kill them both without blinking. Her own French guys might be here soon, too. *All this for nothing . . . All that he'd done.* His radio earpiece crackled.

'Lachlan, do you have any idea of the consequences of what you have there?' Zoe's eyes pleaded. 'I mean, have you really thought about the *possibilities*?'

Fox eyed the gun in her hand, brought his gaze up to meet her eyes.

'I have to take this to my political leaders,' Zoe said. 'They have the right to decide what to do with the treaty protocol.'

'So they can give it over to the Russian leadership for some kind of extra security in their future energy deals?' Fox repeated. 'So that they can share in the plunder of the resources under the Arctic Sea? So you can keep your job?'

'You'd rather the Americans had it? So that it can be buried and –'

'They're a good voice to have in that region – you can't *just* have Russia calling the shots in the Arctic, you need another large country –'

'What, is this an "us and them" thing now?' Zoe shook her head. 'Lachlan, don't make me take it from you. Hand it over.'

Fox edged backwards half a step.

'We're entering a new era of superpowers, Russia is getting stronger,' Zoe said. 'There's a lot of anger about a lot of things. It's not easily resolved. That's what wars are about.'

'Wars are about prejudice and fear. Hit first before you get hit. Believe me, I know. This has global consequences!' Fox rasped. 'The Poles are the last places on Earth we haven't fully destroyed and you want to return this to your guys to hand to Russia? You know what they'll do with it – they'll exploit it all!'

'I'm sorry Lachlan, I really am,' she said, gun pointed up at him. 'But my country's future is much more entwined with Russia's than America's. The US century has come and gone.'

'And you think it's France's turn?'

'No, but it won't be America. Russia, the EU . . . We have to look after ourselves,' she said. 'I have a job to do, a country to serve as I see best . . .'

Suddenly it twigged.

'You knew all along what this document was!' Fox shouted. 'The diary, this protocol, you knew – you used us all!'

'I did what I had to do,' Zoe admitted.

'You lied to me!'

'I told you what you needed to know.'

'You can't do this . . .' He inched further backwards, towards the edge of the building, glanced at the reflection of the neighbouring tower.

'We all have to choose sides some time in our lives. I choose a long life for France. What's your choice?'

Fox looked at the cylinder in his hand. Such a little thing to bring about so much death. But then what it represented wasn't little, was it? If the Russians got it, if they used it to 'smash 'n' grab' undersea resources in the Arctic, who knew what type of long-term consequences there would be?

'You'll have to kill me for this, Zoe,' Fox said, pointing to his heart. He moved his arm out to the side, over the edge, and held the secret protocol there. 'I'm sick of fighting everyone else's war. You want this so bad, kill me. Take the shot.'

She glanced at the cylinder and then back to him. Her gun lowered a little, she walked to him. He reached for her gun and she snapped to attention, but now he had a hand on the gun too. He moved in close to her so that their bodies were touching and he brought his arm with the protocol cylinder down to his side, her gun arm went a little slack and they locked eyes. Like they were seeing each other for the first time.

Fox looked down off the edge, a hundred storeys below them the city was a sea of lights. *If you're afraid to fall, you fall because you are afraid.* He hadn't been afraid to fall for quite a while now . . . Maybe meeting Kate had done that.

'Zoe, my idea of what the world should be is too far removed from the one we live in,' he said. He thought of Kate, of what he thought was right, of a cause for a greater good. *A sacrifice of love and of self – for what?* He had given more of himself than he could have imagined. Everything he'd held so dear had fallen apart. He'd turned into something he was not. He'd moved from antipathy to apathy, to a place where he just couldn't care anymore. He looked Zoe in the eyes – her eyes were searching his.

'Sorry,' he said, and turned and jumped off the building.

111

WASHINGTON, DC

McCorkell was watching the real-time footage on the big main screen.

He could see Fox and Zoe on the roof, talking, close. The French security force was moments away. He'd heard that Delta were trapped just under the blown-out floor – they were making their way across a lower level to another fire exit, but it would probably be too late.

It appeared as though the French cop had the weapon now, pointed at Fox.

And then Fox jumped off the roof . . . The whole room gasped.

Why would he do that?

112

SHANGHAI

Fox flew through the air, arms out ahead, like he was reaching for something.

The V-22 Osprey came up, its rear cargo ramp down, but it was not close enough – nowhere near close enough.

Fox shot past it – flying towards the ground.

And was wrenched from the sky.

He dangled in the air, his arm burning from the strain. He looked up –

Gammaldi, both strong arms had Fox's in a vice-like wrist-lock. He was hanging out the back of the Osprey, the crew safety cable around his waist like an umbilical cord keeping him attached.

Fox couldn't believe it. Below, his legs dangled a hundred storeys above the lights of Shanghai as they evacuated out towards the sea.

He looked up to see Gammaldi's strained face crack into a big cheesy grin – he yelled something over his shoulder, they were hauled up.

Several Marines dragged Gammaldi and Fox back into the cargo area, while another sprayed the M240's fire-tracer rounds like a laser across the roof, sending showers of sparks and everyone on the exposed area ducking for cover. Fox could make out Zoe and a few armed guys – her French security team. *That was close.*

The Osprey ducked down and headed out of the area, fast.

Gammaldi was catching his breath – Fox too, propped back against the cabin wall, where he slid down, bloody and smashed to shit, beat.

A Navy corps man started attending to him.

Kate and her guy were there, shell-shocked, huddled together.

Fox looked back out the closing cargo ramp to the glow of Shanghai. Hutchinson bumped in next to him, clapped a hand on his shoulder. It was over.

Gammaldi smiled from across the cargo hold, still catching his breath. He broke into another grin and shook his head, then yelled over the engines, 'You don't see that shit every day.'

113

WASHINGTON, DC

'We got them!' Hutchinson's voice came over the speaker at Umbra Task Force HQ and the room erupted. McCorkell and Valerie hugged it out. High-fives all around.

'Babich?' Bowden asked.

'Alive, barely. Chinese federal police just arrived at the roof,' Hutchinson replied. 'They've got him in custody and are transferring him to a secret location outside Beijing – if he lives, they're gonna let him rot in a cell there and bleed him for intel about Umbra.'

'That'll do, I guess,' Bowden said. 'How about the treaty?'

'Don't know, have to ask Fox, he's in pretty bad shape,' he answered. 'We're about to touch down on the *New York*, talk in detail soon. Out.'

Everyone whooped and started shutting down their tasks.

McCorkell could see that Bowden looked vindicated – and was reminded that maybe there was room for men like him in rooms like this. He came over, shook McCorkell's hand, and went to the bathroom for the first time that day.

Valerie stood in front of McCorkell as he packed his briefcase. 'What do you think Hutchinson said to him to make him leave Fox alone – from the laser strike?' she asked.

'I can only guess,' McCorkell replied. 'Whatever works, though, right?'

'Yeah . . . What now – back to your cubby-hole at the EEOB?'

He smiled.

'Only got a few days left,' he replied. 'Better not call in sick tomorrow, I guess.'

'Then what are you going to do?' she asked, walking him to the door. He paused, looked back at the room and all the fine men and women who'd come together to do a good job.

'Well, I'm certainly not just gonna sit at home, feeling miserable about being out of the game and reading *Politico* all day,' McCorkell said. He looked around, made sure no one else was in earshot. 'I've got a new thing going at the UN. Putting a team together. You ever get tired of the Bureau, look me up.'

She smiled, proud. 'Thanks.'

He left the room, walked outside. The car park was mostly empty. The sun was bright and hot. He checked his watch – time to quickly go by his office, see what else needed fixing in the world today.

He got in his car and headed towards town. He'd go out of his government job the way he'd gone in, the way he'd always done it – putting in the hard yards and then some. There was a certain symmetry to it, only instead of the knee-deep snow on the ground and dark skies when he'd started with the Cold War in full flight, there was sunshine all around and hope in the White House.

114

EAST CHINA SEA

Fox was glad to be rid of the secret protocol. It had propelled the day to a strange place, ultimately serving not just to set Kate and Jacob free, but Fox, too. He watched the little torn-up pieces float away in the sea.

'You know,' Gammaldi said, 'you could have just done that at the Elysée Palace.'

'What?'

'Destroyed it. Burned it.'

'Okay, well next time, you're in charge.'

'Cool.'

They sat on the edge of the flight deck of the *New York*, the sound of the waves breaking against its mighty hull. They were both silent. The medic who'd patched Fox up brought them a thermos of coffee, and passed over a small bottle of Scotch. It was a moonlit night and Fox felt as awake as he ever had. They sat on the deck, blankets over their shoulders. The liquored-up coffee was good.

The Osprey was being fuelled to take them to Japan, where they'd be flown back to the States. Hutchinson was on his mobile phone, leaning against the bridge structure.

Kate and Jacob sat huddled together, catching up on six months of being apart. Fox watched how they were with each other, thought about how she had been with him, and realised that he'd never truly had her. Their love somehow just always *was* – had always *seemed* – an ephemeral thing, there and gone again.

They locked eyes for a moment – an intense moment that said a lot about how they still felt about each other. *Maybe. Let her walk away.* That much he knew. He had to let her go.

She came over and asked him to walk with her. They stood over at the starboard edge of the large flight deck.

For a while, neither said anything.

'I knew there was something that I couldn't explain,' Fox said. 'The way you've been . . . Ah, hell. What about the flight to Shanghai – during the flight, you knew – you knew then that it was goodbye? That was goodbye for you?'

She didn't answer. Didn't need to. *Maybe she said goodbye back at the farmhouse. Maybe what happened on the flight was just to make sure.*

'I couldn't see it then, but I knew . . . I guess I knew . . .' Fox said, watching the water below. 'What is essential is invisible to the eye, I guess. You can only see true with the heart, so trust it, whatever it says. I respect that.'

She started to cry.

'Lachlan . . .'

'What about – ?' he faced her. 'What about last night? What about the past few months?'

'That was a memory,' she said, between tears. 'That was . . . It was so nice . . . You have to understand.'

'Why couldn't you tell me?'

'I *tried* to tell you.' she said.

They looked over to Jacob, his back to them.

'Well, good luck to him.' Fox said. 'It'll be like me all over again, you'll keep doing this.'

'*This?* This is different . . . This is how I always wanted it to be . . . He's what I've wanted. He's safe.'

'Yeah, I understand.'

'No, you really don't,' Kate said. 'He's there and he's present and I'm in the middle of his picture.'

Fox shook his head, smiled at the phrase.

'You were gone,' Kate said. 'I was gone. I had nothing, then him. See? I needed someone. You really don't have any idea what it was like, do you?' She pointed a finger back towards Shanghai. 'You back there . . . Nothing's changed.'

'Nothing's changed? Kate, you have no fucking idea. You wanna know what losing you the first time did to me?' He looked out at the sea, fists clenched. 'I was a drunk, I was a drug addict . . . In Nigeria . . . I fucking killed *so many* people! I thought you were dead and I thought about joining you – only I had no idea that you were anywhere *but* not on this Earth.'

He'd finally let it out, but it was too late. She opened her arms, he moved away, but she followed him and held him tight. They both had tears in their eyes.

'You don't look at me like you look at him.'

Kate looked back at Jacob. He remained facing the other way. Fox took her hand, she met his eyes and he saw the last glimmer of summer on her eyelashes.

'It doesn't have to end like this.' she said.

Fox smiled, kissed her, soft and quick, a goodbye. A slight tremble in her warm lips. Her cheeks were wet and she squeezed his hand. She smelled so good and felt so right and something in that made him doubt everything – that this was not meant to be, that he'd regret parting ways – but what could he do? She'd moved on, and maybe he could too . . .

'It's not a goodbye forever this time,' he said, his chin rested on her head as they watched the sea slip by.

She didn't acknowledge it. She stayed in close to him, he felt her heart beating against his chest, not sure whose was fastest.

One day, years from now, time would have passed enough that they could be friends. The desire may never leave, but it would get easier, wouldn't it? Didn't it always get easier?

'It's Sunday.'

She looked up at him, sleeved away her tears.

'It's Sunday,' he said. 'That was our favourite day.'

He stroked the back of her neck, pulled her back to him, close.

'With the last breath of my soul, I'll be blessing you,' she whispered. 'Isn't it pretty to think so?'

EPILOGUE

ITALY

Fox was on his iPhone to McCorkell and Hutchinson.

'Umbra is over,' Hutchinson said. 'My FBI team along with the EU police and Interpol are assisting the Russian government to round up all the known suspects – Babich rolled, we managed to get the motherlode of intel out of him.'

Fox listened.

'Where is he?'

'Dead,' McCorkell replied. 'Died yesterday.'

Fox wasn't that displeased.

'Okay,' Fox said. 'Thanks.'

'Thank you – the President really wants you to come into the White House, talk about some jobs – they don't have to be pointy-end work, advisory type –'

'Thanks, Andy. Tell him I'll take a raincheck.'

Silence.

'Okay Lach,' McCorkell said. 'I got a job for you, too. UN, pointy-end, new investigative team I'm –'

'Bill, I'm gonna take a raincheck on that, too.'

'You going back to work for GSR?'

Fox looked out at the view.

'I'm getting pretty tired of searching for truth in a corrupt world,' Fox said. 'Keep it up and what – I'm destined to die a lonely young man . . . I'm not sure. I'll be in touch.'

He ended the call. Turned to his friend.

'What? I've got my own path to choose.'

'Sure. The adventure isn't knowing what's going to happen next,' Gammaldi said, walking around to the bow of the boat. He looked out to sea and waved his arms theatrically: 'It's accepting that all you have is the present moment, right now, and to make the most of that so that every step you take isn't calculated, it's made in the fullness of being present right now. *To the unknown!'*

Fox laughed, threw a tennis ball at Gammaldi who turned in time to catch it. He tossed it high – Brujon leaped onto the marina and caught it on the first bounce, came bounding back.

'Say goodbye to the folks at GSR for me,' Fox said.

'Yeah.'

'And thanks for organising to store all my stuff.'

'Yeah . . . I might set your TV up in my den.'

'Nice,' Fox said, looking back at Ravello. The little seaside town on Italy's Amalfi Coast was probably his favourite spot in the world.

'Where you going?'

'Not sure,' Fox said. 'Might stay here a bit, then set sail. Home, maybe.'

Gammaldi squinted at the bright water sparkling in the sunlight and appraised Fox's yacht.

'Home – Australia home?'

'Yeah. Maybe. Maybe Christmas Island.'

'Should try for the Bahamas, see how that goes.'

'Yeah, maybe. Any island will do.'

'Manhattan is an island, you could sail there,' Gammaldi said. 'I'd come, cash in my flight.'

Fox shook his head.

'I could come with you,' he repeated, serious – perhaps concerned. 'Wherever you want to go.'

'Al –'

'I mean, that's what I do, right? Follow you, always, wherever, whenever –'

'It hasn't been like that –'

'Hasn't it?'

Fox sucked it up.

'Shit, Al, it's never been hard saying goodbye to you before.'

Gammaldi punched Fox hard in the arm.

'Something to remember me by,' he said. 'I always wondered, at what distance does an electrical current in the water no longer pose a danger?'

'What?'

'If I were somehow able to drop a plugged-in toaster into the water at a beach, how far off would a person need to be in order to be safe?'

'The short answer – don't do that.'

'Yeah,' Gammaldi said, disappointed. 'I think there'd be a lot of fall-off in danger with increased distance though, something to do with *dipole faults* – but quantifying that would be hard.'

'Al, you're an idiot, don't let anyone ever tell you any different,' Fox said, climbing onto the marina and helping his mate up. He gave Brujon a scratch on the head and tossed the tennis ball ashore.

'Anyway,' Gammaldi said, staring at the water. 'You should try for Malta first, that's what I'd do.'

'Yeah?' Fox said. *How did Gammaldi always know so much?* 'And what's in Malta? Maltese?'

'Hot *Maltese chicks*. Smoking hot. Stacked. *Badonkadonk*.'

'Too bad you're married,' Fox said and punched his friend's arm. Truth was, he *was* going to Malta – to fulfil a promise he'd made to a dying man. They ambled towards one of the little bars down on the beach.

'I wanna be somewhere building houses,' Gammaldi said. 'I'd like to build something.'

'I've made something of a career of blowing a lot of shit up,' responded Fox.

'Yeah, exactly,' Gammaldi said. 'So, maybe we can go volunteer in some place that's been affected by disaster.'

'Afghanistan?'

'Maybe, maybe not,' Gammaldi said. 'Maybe somewhere in Africa or some speck in the Indian Ocean. I like the idea of making something tangible.'

'Yeah,' Fox said. 'I miss the quiet . . . The quiet inside my head.'

'It ever been like that?'

'Well, no, not really.' They passed a few happy families with picnic baskets returning from a day at sea.

'How about McCorkell's job at the new UN thing?' Gammaldi asked. He put on a mock announcer's voice: 'You'd be like an international man-about-town, the spirit of opposition, a spy without borders or national accountability, kicking arse on a global scale . . .'

Fox smiled and snorted a laugh.

'How long you going for?' Gammaldi asked.

Fox watched the crowd back at the main pier. The afternoon sun was tiring in the sky, could be the end of any day. The voices comforting in the background, a hum of humanity in a beautiful spot, the sound of people having a good time. A life of fewer consequences beckoned.

'If you have another kid before I'm back, sell all my stuff and put it towards his education.'

'Done. And what, I suppose we'll have to call him Lachlan?'

'Kid could do worse,' Fox said, and smiled.

They rolled up to a bar, took a table in the shade, ordered some beers.

'Here's to you going out to find yourself,' Gammaldi said. They clinked bottles. 'This reporting shit wasn't you and you know it. You belong in the arena, not documenting it from the sidelines.'

Fox knew his friend was right. Maybe. What would it be like if he really let go and went in there, in the arena – *that would be interesting, right?*

•

Early the next morning they said goodbye, Gammaldi headed to the airport and Fox prepared to cast off, head south and not look back.

He thought about Kate. She'd once told him, *Living on a boat is my dream . . . Sailing around the world, going from port to port, following the sun.* He couldn't imagine anything better than doing that with her . . . but that would never happen, would it? No. She'd moved on, it wasn't meant to be. It felt right this way. He felt free.

Casting off, Fox let the boat go with the wind. Brujon slept on the aft deck, every now and then his legs twitching as if he were dreaming of chasing rabbits. The water was like a still pond and the breeze was slight. The sun was low and the only movement was the twinkling of the sea and the occasional kestrel. There was nothing on the horizon but possibility. Maybe he'd keep chasing that sun home. Maybe he was tired of chasing, and would just go where the wind took him.

He slung his legs over the starboard side, the only sound the water lapping against the hull. He closed his eyes and felt the rising sun on his face and listened. Silence, the greatest pleasure of all.

Author Q&A

(WARNING: CONTAINS SPOILERS)

So, is this the end of Babich? Kate?

This is the end of Babich. Umbra has been a great foil for Fox for three books now, and I planned for their relationship to span a trilogy. I always wanted a SMERSH-type outfit and I think it's created some nice interlinking stories through the Fox books.

Kate, as far as I know, is gone for good this time. Over the years no other character has provoked as much feedback – really divisive, for and against. I thought the end of their affair was a satisfying way to end a love story that's been spanning a few books – it suits the realism of the series.

Is Fox leaving GSR for good?

I don't know. He'll never say goodbye forever, and I miss the staff from there and would like to bring them back for an adventure someday to learn more about them as individuals, but for at least the next novel Fox will be doing some work outside GSR.

How was writing this book different from the previous four Fox novels?

Each book has been easier to write than the last. Well, it somehow feels easier – they seem to take about three months to research and three months to write. There's quite a large cast of continuing characters to choose from (although we lost a couple in this book), and it's a lot of fun to bring them back in. This book was exciting to write as the narrative of the three parts took place within twenty-four hours. I considered making it within twelve hours, and just keeping Paris as the setting, but my research at the start steered me towards getting Babich to China, so I had to get Fox there, too – and that chewed up some time, though it is mostly off-page with his flight taking place between two parts of the book.

How much planning went into the book, and how do you actually write your books?

I spend several weeks reading and making notes and collating research material, and then I fill about fifty or so pages of notes before I sit down and start typing. I work every day, from the morning until late at night. I don't refer to any notes or research when I write; if I'm unsure of a detail (time zone, street name, et cetera), I'll put a place-mark in the document and keep writing, and when I finish the book I'll fill in those blanks. I don't plan the story beats in detail, but I have a sense of their tone and feel – that is, how I want the reader to feel – and I try to weave a compelling narrative through that as I explore the story. My main writing rule is: write fast, edit slow. I take as long as I can with the editing process, right up to print date, and then that's it; I never look at it again.

Do you think of your novels as being Australian novels?

In so far as my character is concerned it's as much an Australian story as it is a global story – Lachlan Fox is the quintessential man of the world. That said, he certainly sees foreign climes in the same way as me: through Australian eyes. Like any of us, he can feel lonely and he can feel at home, wherever he may be. The key in these novels is that we only see his life through the points closest to the dramatic climaxes, so he may see things how an Australian does, but boy, what he sees and goes through! I've met plenty of readers in Australia who've said they assumed my books were written by an American, but I think that's more to do with the cover design than content. In terms of the narrative, I write about an Aussie character because it's what I know.

So your style isn't American?

I don't think so, but then that's hard to define nowadays. I've certainly been shaped much more by American writing than by our own. It's that American simplicity and inclusivity of their literature that appeals to me. My own literary heroes and models – the people who made me want to write – are mostly American.

The humour in your novels is one of their distinct and most enjoyable characteristics. Is that a conscious decision on your part?

I think we all need to laugh more, and I write the books I want to write; readers will either respond or not respond. I came into this series with a couple of buddy characters, wanting to explore that humour in both fun times and difficult times – that gallows humour that I loved so much in films like *Butch Cassidy and the Sundance Kid*, *Lethal Weapon* and *Die Hard*. My individual jokes and observations, and use of irony in smaller narrative episodes, come through the actual writing rather than as a result of any preparation, and those fun surprises are a big reason for why I write.

What's next for Fox?

How would I know? Oh, right, okay. Well, I'm answering these questions a day after finishing the editing of *Red Ice*, so my mind has set sail with Fox. I love that this is like a reset of his character – sure, the readers and I know a lot about who Fox is and what's he's capable of, but now he's off into the unknown. I figure I'll let him sail alone for a few weeks before I summon him for a new adventure. I *do* know that in the next book we'll meet him in Malta and I know how that meeting will unfold, who the characters are . . . but that's all; the options for the plot are still percolating. I like that we met Fox on an island at the start of *Fox Hunt*; he's being living on the island of Manhattan ever since, and we'll be meeting him on that little speck in the Mediterranean for a re-launch of his life. Anyway, I still need to think about it, read, immerse myself in possibilities, make my notes, and trust that Fox's *What's next?* moment will arrive.

How many Fox books can we expect in this series?

It's still an open-ended endeavour. I like that Fox is not going to be a character who's doing the same old job for perpetuity. I've known him for many years – about four in his world – and in that time (well, since the end of *Fox Hunt*) he's been working as an investigative reporter. I always knew he'd move about work-wise, and I think these novels are more reflective of the real world than most other thrillers out there; how many of us stay in the same job for years on end, after all? Plus, it's very much in Fox's character to be constantly on the move, to never feel at ease, particularly if he's in one place for a long period of time. Anyway, time will tell.

Lastly, you are also now writing another series?

Yes, the *Alone* series started publication in 2010. It has a post-apocalyptic backdrop with a sixteen-year-old main character in Jesse. He's Australian, and the setting is New York City, but that's where the similarities with Fox end. The narrative is first-person so we feel for him a bit more – which I thought was important for that crossover age-group – and helps to completely immerse the reader in that kind of pandemic scenario. At the time of this interview, the first of those books, *Alone: Chasers,* it out and the feedback from Fox fans and new readers has been encouraging. So I have plenty of novels ahead to write!